06/2015

Advance Praise for *The Assassins*

"There are few writers who can set the scene like Lynds can. *The Assassins* has everything a reader could possibly want in a gritty, action-packed story set amid some of the most tortured lands on earth and inhabited by killers who can trust no one, certainly not the other killers beside them. This is Lynds hitting on all cylinders with a thought-provoking tale that will surely stand with the year's best thrillers."
—David Baldacci

"*The Assassins* hooks you on page one, pulls you into the story on page two, and doesn't let you go until the very last paragraph. This is a classic last-man-standing story of deceit and betrayal with enough new twists and turns to keep you up way past your bedtime."
—Nelson DeMille

"*The Assassins* kept me spellbound. It's the ultimate battle of wits! By pitting master assassin against master assassin, Gayle Lynds has delivered a master class in suspense, where plot twists abound and danger is always closer than you think!"
—Lisa Gardner

"*The Assassins* starts as fast as a sniper's bullet and breaks sideways from Baghdad to D.C. with neck-snapping, high-speed twists. Rich with terrific local color, fascinating historical details, and an insider's knowledge of spycraft . . . Gayle Lynds has mastered the international action thriller."
—Robert Crais

"*The Assassins* delivers on everything it promises: devious players, shifting alliances, and no one you should trust."
—Brad Meltzer

"Gayle Lynds again proves herself a master of the thriller in her latest, *The Assassins*. The story weaves real-world politics and ripped-from-the-headlines authenticity to create a roller coaster of action and suspense worthy of Dan Brown at his best. With characters you'll bleed for, I defy you to put this book down once you start."

—James Rollins

"*The Assassins* is a furiously wild ride from Maryland to Marrakesh to Baghdad, with rich, vibrant characters and a surprise twist that will hit you between the eyes. I loved it!"

—Catherine Coulter

"*The Assassins* is another masterwork of international suspense from Gayle Lynds, which starts with a killer premise—six ex–Cold War assassins pitted against one another—and ends with a violent and stunning surprise. Here's a thriller with rich settings, beautifully crafted characters, and a compulsively readable story line, a magnificent novel from a major talent. Outstanding."

—Douglas Preston

"Gayle Lynds knows what a reader wants and she delivers a tantalizing premise, stylish prose, and a plot that literally takes no prisoners. The result? A perfect piece of thrilling entertainment."

—Steve Berry

"This is Cold War thriller writing at its best. Raw, vivid, utterly credible, with palpable tension that never releases its grip."

—Peter James

THE
ASSASSINS

GAYLE LYNDS

ST. MARTIN'S PRESS ✹ NEW YORK

THE ASSASSINS. Copyright © 2015 by Gayle Lynds. All rights reserved. Printed in the United States of America. For information, address St. Martin's Press, 175 Fifth Avenue, New York, NY 10010.

www.stmartins.com

Library of Congress Cataloging-in-Publication Data

Lynds, Gayle.
    The assassins / Gayle Lynds. — First edition.
        pages ; cm
    ISBN 978-0-312-38090-8 (hardcover)
    ISBN 978-1-4668-4738-5 (e-book)
    1. Assassins—Fiction.   I. Title.
    PS3562.Y442A94 2015
    813'.54—dc23

                                    2015012469

St. Martin's Press books may be purchased for educational, business, or promotional use. For information on bulk purchases, please contact the Macmillan Corporate and Premium Sales Department at 1-800-221-7945, extension 5442, or write to specialmarkets@macmillan.com.

First Edition: June 2015

10 9 8 7 6 5 4 3 2 1

For my husband, John C. Sheldon.
His love makes my world beautiful.

ACKNOWLEDGMENTS

I'm one of the luckiest authors in the world. I not only love my work, I'm surrounded by terrific people who aid and abet me along the way. In particular, I'm indebted to those who read and commented on the entire manuscript several times—my editor, Keith Kahla; my literary agent, Lisa Erbach Vance; freelance editor Frances Jalet-Miller; and fellow author and dear friend Melodie Johnson Howe.

Since my previous novel, and following the death of my husband Dennis Lynds, I've been lucky again: I met and fell in love with John C. Sheldon, whom I married a couple of years ago. John's quite a guy—retired prosecutor, defense attorney, and judge—and still writing scholarly articles for law journals. He's also a longtime voracious reader. I had no idea he would turn out to be an invaluable source for brainstorming and editing. Oh, and that he could write fiction. Thus far, we've collaborated on three short stories. As you read *The Assassins*, you won't know the impact he had on page after page, but trust me, it's there.

My family endures as a never-ending source of help and support.

They bring me ideas, answer questions, and are nice to me when it really counts. My deepest gratitude to Julia Stone and Kari Timonen, Paul Stone and Katrina Baum, Deirdre Lynds and Hudson Bunce, Katie Lynds, Emily Sheldon and Trevor Ross, Jim Sheldon and Vandy Say, and Heather and Craig Geikie. And to our wonderful grandchildren, who are growing up much too quickly: Sophia Stone, Finn Timonen, Duncan Geikie, and Ian Geikie.

St. Martin's is my longtime publisher, where books are cherished. Particular gratitude to Hannah Braaten, Melissa Hastings, Paul Hochman, Kelsey Lawrence, Carolyn McBroom, Justin Velella, and the remarkable Sally Richardson.

Others who have generously helped me include Nancy Colahan, Julian Dean, Celine Godin, Tara and Dominique Harbeck, Bethany Hays, Bones Howe, Elizabeth Huebnor, Randi and Doug Kennedy, Sarah Ketcham, Phillip Kowash, Dan Lord, Bill and Carol McDonald, Cathy McDonald, Jason Merry, Melinda Molin, David and Donna Morrell, Monika Mozdzynski, Elaine and George Russell, Kathleen Sharp and Ray Briare, and Pam and Frank Smith.

I hope you enjoy *The Assassins*.

THE SIX

[The assassin] almost never emerged from the turbid underworld of international crime, and he had no consistent belief system. He switched allegiances with ease. Governments actually paid him just to leave their people alone.

—*Time* magazine, September 2, 2002

1

Death was not something the six men talked about. Instead they used phrases like "the job" or "the assignment." They were acquaintances, not friends, just like workers in any industry requiring initiative, independence, and travel.

Each had been at it more than two decades, thriving in a career notorious for high attrition. They were the best. They had never collaborated, until now.

Night gave Baghdad little relief. Electricity was fitful, garbage rotted along the boulevards, and clean running water was a memory. Gunfire crackled across rooftops as looters carried off computers, chairs, and crates of canned goods. Since the invasion, there was no more dictator and no more law.

In earlier, better times, the country was known as Mesopotamia, a rich land where the wheel and writing were invented. It was all documented in the National Museum of Iraq, which contained priceless antiquities dating back a hundred thousand years.

International law forbade anyone to use cultural sites for military purposes, or to attack them. But the museum was strategically located on eleven acres in the heart of Baghdad, protected by a tall security wall, and dotted with towering turrets perfect for snipers. So the Republican Guard took it over, and when the American soldiers invaded, the Guards blasted them with machine guns and AK-47s. The Americans fired back, and they kept coming. Finally the Guards brought out their big guns—rocket-propelled grenades, RPGs—and sent a firestorm down on the foreign troops.

A U.S. tank responded with a single round from its nosebleed 120-mm main gun, taking out the RPG position but leaving a gaping hole in the façade above one of the museum's reconstructed Assyrian gates. Under the laws of war, the Americans were entitled to defend themselves, but they had also seen how easily they could destroy the museum. So the task force commander ordered the tanks to remain in the intersection in front of the museum—Museum Square—but out of range of the Iraqis.

This was the tense situation near midnight on April 10, 2003, when six international assassins made their way individually through Baghdad's backstreets toward the museum. They were in Baghdad because Saddam Hussein owed them money, and when the Americans won the war, his wealth would be confiscated. This was their last chance to get what was theirs.

2

The night air stank of oil fires. Gunfire crackled in the distance. Watchful, the assassins waited in the night shadows at the museum's rear security wall. They were dressed like locals, in loose shirts, Western trousers, and *ghutrahs*—cotton scarves—wrapped around their heads and across the lower parts of their faces. Only their eyes showed. They checked their watches.

At precisely 12:10 A.M. the door in the wall opened, and General Mulh Alwar appeared. A tall blade of a man with refined features, he wore the uniform of the Special Republican Guard, but his shirt was unbuttoned, he was capless, and his eyes were overbright. His Kalashnikov dangled carelessly from one hand.

"Mierda. Ha perdido el juicio!" snapped the Basque. Shit. He's lost it!

The Russian shoved the general back into the compound, and the others rushed after, weapons up, ready for trouble. The last man bolted the door in the security wall.

The general shook off the Russian and stared anxiously around at their scarf-hidden faces. "Show me you are here, Burleigh Morgan. I need to be certain it is you and these are your people."

"You bloody wanker, it's us all right." Morgan unpeeled his *ghutrah*, revealing corrugated skin, a fighter's broken nose, and a neatly trimmed silver mustache. Morgan was the oldest, in his early sixties, but he still had a tough look about him, as if with the crook of a finger he could hollow out the eye of any of them.

The general stood a little straighter and gave a deferential nod. *"Aash min shaafak, Morgan. B-khidimtak."* It's good to see you. At your service.

Although there was no trust in the venal business of international wet work, occasionally there was respect, and Burleigh Morgan was respected. Other top independent assassins would accept a job from him, which was why Saddam Hussein had hired him to put together a team for a series of particularly sensitive international terminations. Besides Morgan, the Basque, and the Russian, there were a former jihadist, a retired Mossad operative, and a peripheral member of the Cosa Nostra. They had executed their assignments perfectly. The problem was, Saddam had never paid the second half of what he owed them.

"Which direction, General?" Morgan prodded.

With a nod, the general trotted off.

Watching their flanks, the contract killers followed, passing weed-infested lawns and gardens. Lights from lanterns and flashlights moved occasionally behind the dark windows of the buildings towering around them.

Off to the right, a side door opened and slammed back against the wall. Two soldiers stripped down to their trousers and combat boots burst out onto a stone patio. Rifles slung over their naked shoulders, each carried an armful of plastic boxes. They spotted the general and the assassins.

The general bellowed at them in Arabic, *"La'a! Qof!"* No! Halt!

But they bolted, their legs pumping, heading off across the grounds toward the northwest gate, the gate farthest from the American tanks.

"Dogs and thieves! Deserters!" The general squeezed off two volleys from his AK-47.

The rounds hit the soldiers in their backs, slamming them to the ground. Blood rose like black tar on their skin. One lay silent and motionless; the other moaned, his feet twitching.

The general ran over to them and scooped up a handful of little gemlike tubes that had fallen out of one of the boxes. He held them up for the assassins to see. "These are cylinder seals. Our ancestors, the ancient Mesopotamians, carved pictures and writing on them and then rolled them across wet clay for their signatures. Just one of these can be sold for fifty thousand American dollars—"

The Basque had had enough. *"Maria José Cristo!"* he exploded. "Who gives a fucking damn!"

Morgan agreed. He stepped in front of the general. A highly respected line officer, the general had just shot his own soldiers in the back because of a bunch of tiny tubes that looked like crusty cigarette holders. The general was probably not barking mad yet, but his priorities were circling the toilet.

Morgan stabbed a finger into the man's chest. "You stupid arsehole, remember why we're here. You're digging your family's graves!" He had tracked down the general's wife and children in Tahiti and sent him chilling photos showing how easily they could be wiped.

The general paled. He was a close friend of Saddam's half brother Barzan al-Tikriti, who had managed part of Saddam's clandestine financial network. If anyone could get to Barzan and Saddam's money, it was the general.

Without a word, the general jogged off. They ran close behind.

Morgan noted hundreds of 7.62-mm shell casings embedded in the weeds and dirt, the bullets used by AK-47s, not by U.S. assault rifles. "How many men do you have here, General, and where are they?"

"About seventy-five, stationed around the compound."

Morgan knew 150 Republican Guards had been onsite at five P.M., so the general had lost half his force. In the distance, a clutch of men wearing only T-shirts and undershorts and carrying cardboard boxes rushed northwest, in the same direction the two soldiers had been heading with the cylinder seals. It looked to Morgan that the general's troops were ditching their uniforms, grabbing antiquities, and deserting.

His face tight with anger, the general slowed and glared after them.

"Forget it." Morgan jammed his bullpup rifle into his side.

With a grunt, the general ran again. The little group pounded past a pile of sandbags toward a long three-story building. The general yanked open the door, and they slipped into a vast exhibit hall. Moonlight shone down from high windows, illuminating shattered glass display cases, fallen shelves, and empty marble pedestals. It had the feel of a graveyard.

Cursing the thieves, the general led them across the room toward an arched entrance. There was no door.

"It looks bloody dark ahead," Morgan said. "Light your torches, lads."

3

Switching on their flashlights, the six assassins and the general raced down the hall past corridors and doors until they reached another large gallery decorated with wall friezes glorifying larger-than-life Mesopotamians slaughtering much smaller foes.

Slowing, the general gestured around. "This is the Assyrian Gallery." Then he turned to a glass case attached to the wall. "And your tablet is here."

The assassins converged. Inside was a brown clay tablet about twenty-four inches square, but instead of Roman or Cyrillic letters, it displayed the wedge-shaped characters of civilization's first form of writing—cuneiform.

The assassin who had once been Mossad focused his flashlight on an engraved sign in Arabic beside the display cabinet. Excited, he said, "This tablet dates back three thousand years and describes our father, Abraham. He came from Ur." The founder of Judaism, Abraham grew up in Ur, an ancient city in what was now Iraq.

The former jihadist gave him a sharp look. "The *Prophet* Abraham, yes." In Islam, Abraham was considered one of the religion's five prophets, along with Muhammad and Jesus.

Impatient, Morgan aborted the never-ending religious quarrel: "The only thing that bloody matters is getting our money."

He pulled out the key he had picked up in an Amsterdam drop box two days before, and the general handed over a second key. Morgan inserted them into the double lock, turned them, and pulled open the glass door. The general stepped forward and pressed what appeared to be a small blemish inside the frame. There was a soft clicking sound, and the entire display swung away, disclosing a recessed safe with two more locks. A safe within a safe.

Again Morgan inserted the keys, turned them, and pulled open the door. Another tablet lay on the floor of the second safe. Everyone leaned forward.

His pulse accelerating, Morgan slung his bullpup across his back and with both hands reached inside and lifted it out. About twenty inches long and eighteen inches wide, it was not clay but limestone, pale, slightly grainy, about two inches thick. The cuneiform script was carved deep and clean. Morgan felt emotion well up in him, not for the beautiful artifact, but for the castle in Yorkshire he planned to splurge on.

"Here's our twelve million dollars, lads." That was the amount Saddam still owed them. The general had guaranteed the tablet was worth at least that much. Morgan tilted it upright for the others to see. "Let's get the hell out of here. I've got a man in London panting to flog it."

Suddenly a thundering crash sounded in the stairwell. The walls seemed to shudder. Voices quarreled loudly above them, then an arm and head in pink granite thudded down the steps.

"More thieves!" The general dashed inside the stairwell and aimed his AK-47 upward. "Come down here, you dogs!"

Before the general could shoot, automatic fire rained down. Rounds exploded through the general's head and shoulders, spraying blood and bone. He dropped to his knees then pitched forward.

"Kill the torches," Morgan snapped. "We're gone."

The limestone tablet clasped close to his chest with one hand, the bull-pup rifle in the other, he ran back through the dark gallery, the others close around. In seconds, bullets followed, slicing past, the noise echoing loudly. A sharp pain burned across his gun arm, telling Morgan he had been hit. He hurtled around the corner, down a corridor, around another corner, and through a door.

They were in another exhibit hall. Breathing heavily, he dropped to his haunches. The others squatted beside him. The gunfire behind them had stopped. They peered through the shadows across the long room to where two Republican Guards appeared in a doorway. One was talking on his radio, repeating to his cohort that intruders had arrived and they must be killed.

Morgan swore silently. All his carefully arranged plans had gone to hell. He could hear the noise of running boots behind them. They were trapped, but he was not done yet. He pointed at the Basque and the Israeli and then indicated the two Guards across the room.

The Basque slid his knife out from under his shirt. It was slender, tapered, and doubled-edged. Keeping low, he padded off past an up-ended display case. At the same time, the Israeli aimed his M14 modified sniper rifle with sound suppressor.

The two Guards seemed to see or hear something. They lifted their weapons, looking for targets.

The Israeli's M14 gave off a single *pffft,* but both Guards staggered and went down.

The assassins rushed across the exhibit hall. One Guard was dead, a black hole in his forehead. The other was dying, stabbed up under his rib cage to his heart.

The group took off, passing through one doorway then another until at last they blasted out into the cool night air. But as they accelerated away from the building, a dozen Guards chased, firing their AK-47s. Orange-colored muzzle flashes flamed into the night.

The assassins lowered their heads and pounded toward the children's museum. Morgan staggered, a pain burning across his scalp. A bullet had grazed his head. Hot blood soaked his *ghutrah.*

The Israeli grunted—a round had pierced his shoulder.

The Basque stumbled—he was hit in the calf.

Finally they made it through a towering arch, past giant statues of Babylonian lions, and around to the lee of the building. They had managed to lose their pursuers, at least for the time being.

"We can't stay here. Let's go," the former Cosa Nostra killer ordered.

Morgan wiped sweat and blood from his face. His head ached like someone had bashed it with an axe. "Yeah? And where to, dipstick?"

"Out there." He gestured with his Walther past a wrought-iron fence to Museum Square, where a platoon of U.S. Abrams tanks was stationed. There was no way the Guard would follow them into all of that weaponry.

Morgan hesitated. Unless they were being employed by a government, and sometimes even then, governments were a professional assassin's enemy. Still, he stared thoughtfully at the American tanks. It was not as if anyone there would know who the assassins were.

"Brilliant," he decided, "if we survive that long."

"I'll carry the tablet, Morgan," the jihadist offered.

"I'm not crippled, you greedy bastard." Morgan glared at him. "Let's go."

With the building as a shield, the assassins hurried past palm trees. The Israeli gripped his shoulder. The Russian held his side. The Basque limped badly. The air erupted with the piercing noise of another fusillade—the Guards had rounded the building and were pursuing.

The jihadist grunted and staggered. Blood appeared on his hip.

The ex-Mafia killer was out front. He shot open the museum gate, and the others rushed for it. That was when Morgan felt pain explode in his back. He had been shot, but it felt as if a bloody lorry had rammed him. The cuneiform tablet slipped from beneath his arm, and he heard it crash onto the paving stones. His legs would not move. He could not feel his hands. He fell hard.

Vaguely he realized his team was down beside him, picking up the pieces. He could hear someone talking to him, swearing at him, saying his name. Were they going to take him or dump him? An assassin could never be too careful with his friends.

4

From Beirut to Paris

Rescued by two of his fellow assassins, Burleigh Morgan was laid up for a month under an assumed name in a private suite at the Clemenceau Hospital in Beirut. He had multiple wounds to his skull, right arm, scapula, lungs, and ribs. As he drifted in and out of pain, his thoughts kept returning to the castle he wanted in Yorkshire. He could see it clearly in his mind, standing on a green hill, its turrets tall and walls formidable. He had planned to use his share of the proceeds from selling the cuneiform tablet to buy it.

When his headaches stopped, Morgan flew to Cairo, to a secret pied-à-terre on an island in the middle of the Nile River. His flat was on the twentieth floor. In the bedroom, he unpacked. Then he went out to the balcony to enjoy the view.

He did not understand loneliness, could not abide complaining, and deep in his scarred soul knew a professional assassin had no business with "beliefs." An assassin needed to be sharp, plan for every detail, and crave the work. African wild dogs were not the largest predators on the savannah, but they were far more successful killers than most.

So when Morgan looked down from his balcony at the teeming streets and sidewalks with people scrambling and sweating, he smiled to himself. He was a wild dog. They were not.

That night he e-mailed the five other assassins:

> The Baghdad item could still be valuable. I have two pieces. Send
> me yours. I'll get them reassembled and appraised.

Morgan's tradecraft was impeccable. His various e-mail addresses ran through private servers from Kuala Lumpur to Mexico City, from the Ural Mountains to Pakistan. Tracing him was as impossible as a top Chinese black hatter could make it.

The next day, he heard from three of the assassins:

> 3:22 A.M.: You're nuts. The general said it was worth millions
> because it was an ancient artifact. Now it's just a pile of rocks.

> 8:03 A.M.: I'll give you my pieces if you wire me $250,000 holding
> money.

> 12:10 P.M.: How do I know if I send you mine, you won't cut me out
> of my full share?

Controlling his temper, Morgan responded that they bloody well knew he could be trusted to give all of them their fair shares. Besides, money was money, and it was worth a shot to see whether they could make a few million quid off what they had.

The next morning, he received two more e-mails:

> 8:43 A.M.: I've got four pieces. I assume I'm going to get twice as
> much for mine as anyone with two pieces.

> 9:12 A.M.: I want my own appraiser.

The bickering continued until Morgan could not take dealing with the arseholes any longer. Besides, what one of them had written was true—the tablet in pieces could be worthless.

From Cairo he flew to Majorca, where he continued to recuperate, and then on to London to an East End safe house. Finally, he resumed wet work.

Years passed. He spent more and more time in Paris. He bought himself a brand-new, sapphire-blue Cobra MkVI gull-wing sports car and hooked up with a lively blonde who lived on the rue des Fossés Saint Bernard. Her name was Beatrice. She was in her fifties, and she was hot. They were an odd-looking couple—he was in his mid-seventies, skinny, and as wrinkled as a gorilla. He was also strangely happy.

In January, Beatrice and he were sitting together in front of her fireplace, enjoying the warm flames and listening to blues music, when he checked his e-mail. One had just arrived from an anonymous sender, addressed to six assassins. As he read the names, a chill crawled up his spine—it was the six of them who had heisted the ancient tablet. The sender knew far too much about them, including past employers. The information was incendiary.

Beatrice was staring at him. "Some bad e-mail has upset you, *cheri*?" She stroked his silver ponytail.

Closing the laptop, he lied: "No, nothing bad at all. I'm tired, old girl. I'll go back to my place and catch up on my sleep. You and I have too much fun, you know." He forced a smile. In truth, he needed to make phone calls. He slid the laptop into his satchel and stood.

Her worried eyes assessed him. "Very well. I understand."

He took her hand and kissed it.

She watched him put on his coat and leave. She had been a famous dancer in Pigalle and missed the excitement of those days, and Morgan was an exciting man. She hurried to the window, where she saw his grand Cobra waiting near the end of the block. Good—he would not have far to walk. His complexion had been gray.

She turned back into her sitting room. It was time for a *café serré*. Opening the door, she started toward her kitchen. But before she had gone six steps, there was a huge roar. Her apartment shook. As the chandelier swung, she ran to the hallway window. Flames licked up through a brown cloud over the spot where the Cobra had been parked. Her throat tightened. She forgot her coat and ran down four flights and out to the curb, where the concierge and neighbors and shopkeepers were gathering in the afternoon cold, staring at the end of the block.

"*Sainte merde,*" someone murmured in shock.

A woman nodded. "*Une bombe énorme!*"

Sirens wailed.

Beatrice ran into the smoke. Tree limbs littered the area like broken toothpicks. Car parts were strewn about, sizzling. A streetlight had snapped in half. With horror, she saw a charred arm on the sidewalk. And there was a giant hole where the car had been, a black hole that spread across the asphalt and took out grass and parking.

Coughing, she wiped tears from her face.

"*Madame, venez avec moi.*" The concierge took her arm and guided her back. "Your gentleman did not suffer, *madame*. I am very sorry. *Venez avec moi.*"

She could feel people's eyes on her. She was shaking from the shock and cold, but the cold was good. It helped to clear her mind. At her building, she turned to gaze back at the smoke, to think about the enormity of the blast that had killed Morgan. It would have been much simpler and cheaper to shoot him. This was not just about murdering some old assassin. Someone powerful had sent a warning.

THE PADRE

Victory is gained not by the number killed, but by the number frightened.

—Basque proverb

5

Washington, D.C.

It was one of those bitterly cold January mornings that cut to the bone. Snow blanketed the city. Icicles sparkled from phone lines. As a frosty wind burned his cheeks, Judd Ryder shouldered his duffel bag and walked away from Union Station, heading east. He was tall, about six feet one, and thirty-four years old. Seldom did anyone find his face memorable—the arched nose, the gray eyes that tended toward detachment, the jaw that could turn stubborn. That was the way he wanted it. He liked being forgettable.

Turning onto Fifth Street, he entered Metro Cleaners and hefted his duffel onto the counter. "I've brought you a month's worth of dirty clothes. Do your worst."

The clerk pulled the duffel to her. "Happy to take care of you. What's your phone number?"

Ryder related it. She looked it up on her computer.

"I've got two shirts and a sports jacket to pick up, too," he told her.

She frowned. "Says here you got them yesterday."

"I was out of the country yesterday." He thought a moment. "I always pay with my Visa. Does your computer show that?"

Tapping the keyboard, she studied the screen. "Nope, it was a cash transaction." She glanced at him apologetically. "If we find your stuff, someone will call you."

Perplexed, he thanked her and pushed outdoors. He had been in Baghdad nearly four weeks and was glad to get back to Washington and even more eager to be home. Digging his hands into his pockets, he hunched his shoulders against the cold and hurried off, turning onto G Street. Most of the sidewalks were shoveled, but the city plows had not reached the street, where the snow was a good twelve inches deep. Buntings of snow covered the branching trees and the tall row houses and the little front lawns with their little wrought-iron fences. The neighborhood sparkled white and clean in the sunlight. He took in the tranquil beauty.

Then a door closed, an unnaturally loud sound in the hush. A man had stepped outside and was hunched over, locking his front door. What the hell! That was Ryder's row house—668 G Street Northeast.

Remaining across the street, Ryder saw the man turn away from the door, head bowed as he buttoned his trench coat. A gust of wind flipped open the coat. The lining was black-and-green tartan—Ryder had a subzero lining in the same tartan fabric sewed into his trench coat. He focused on the man's boots. They were L.L. Bean. Above the tops showed tan shearling linings. Those were his damn boots. His damn trench coat. The man was a frigging burglar. What else had he stolen?

The intruder raised his head to scan around. For the first time his face showed. It was as if Ryder were looking into a mirror—gray eyes, arched nose, square face. The man was about six feet one. Ryder's height. He had wavy chestnut-brown hair. So did Ryder. The bastard even had a good tan, and of course Ryder was tanned from his month in Iraq. This was no ordinary burglar. Ryder had been professionally doubled.

Knotting his hands, Ryder felt a hot tide of fury. He wanted to strangle the bastard. He could do that. God knows he had killed enough in Iraq and Pakistan. He inhaled, exhaled, calming himself. But dead men did not talk. Tugging his knit cap down past his ears, Ryder slapped on sunglasses.

The double peered to the left, checking out a cross-country skier glid-ing toward the intersection of G and Seventh streets, then he scanned past the elementary school on the corner, and paused at Ryder. Ryder kept his expression neutral, his pace unhurried. Finally the double scru-tinized the far end of the street, descended the steps, and ambled to the corner. He stopped at the curb, waiting for the cross-country skier to pass.

The skier wore a black balaclava, exposing only his eyes, nose, and lips. Suddenly extending his stride and arm swing, the skier accelerated through the intersection as if he were a racer crossing the finish line.

The double stepped off the curb. His boots sank into the snow.

The noise of a powerful engine sounded from around the corner.

The double started slogging across the street.

A big white Arctic Cat snowmobile careened around the corner. Wearing a white helmet, goggles, and jumpsuit, the driver expertly guided the Cat as it bore down on the double.

The man stared. Abruptly there was an explosion of snow as the double reversed direction. His feet slipped and his arms flailed as he fell and scrambled back up.

Two women had come out on the steps of the elementary school.

"Watch out!" one yelled, while the other gave a piercing shriek.

The Cat rammed into the double, sending him high in a spine-breaking backward arch. He landed spread-eagled on his back, blood oozing from his nose, mouth, and ears.

The snowmobile skidded from the impact. The driver turned into the skid, bringing the Cat under control. With a glance over his shoulder at the motionless man, he sat down, revved the Cat's engine, and shot away.

"Call 911!" Ryder shouted at the women. In seconds he was at the downed man's side.

The double's eyes were open, staring up at the icy blue sky. His jaw hung slack, lips parted as if he were about to speak.

Ryder felt for the carotid artery. No pulse. Opening the trench coat, he saw the man was wearing the sports coat and one of the shirts Ryder had tried to pick up at the cleaners just minutes before. Ryder found a wallet inside the jacket—one of his old ones. Inside was about one thousand dollars in cash and a District driver's license forged to appear identical to the one Ryder carried. He returned the wallet, cash, and driver's license. Continuing to search, he found a cell phone. He pocketed that.

He stood up. He had to leave before police arrived. The women were motionless on the school's steps, horror in their faces.

"You called 911?" he asked.

"Yes, they're on their way," one told him. "How is he?"

"Unconscious and in bad shape. My sister lives on Seventh." He was lying. The imposter was definitely dead, and Ryder had no brothers or sisters. "She's a doctor. I'll go see if she's home."

As the women nodded, sirens sounded in the distance.

Ryder got back on the sidewalk and ran. At H, he headed west. It was a busy boulevard, running parallel to his street. Traffic rushed past. At last he slowed and took deep breaths. He needed to focus. What had just happened, and what did it mean?

The cross-country skier had been moving at a normal speed until the double approached the corner. Then the skier had accelerated and hurtled through the intersection. As the double had started to cross, the snowmobile engine had roared to life. The way Ryder figured it, the skier had been the lookout and his speeding through the crossway had signaled the hidden snowmobiler that the double was about to enter the deep snow and be vulnerable.

This was the time Ryder usually walked over to the little market on Seventh to buy groceries. When he did, he always crossed that intersection. His lungs tightened. The double had been targeted for murder—or Ryder had been.

6

Ryder wanted to get inside his row house to search for an explanation of why he had been doubled. As the sirens grew closer, he hurried past insurance offices, down a driveway, and south across a parking lot. Ahead was the rear of his house. Opening the gate, he saw no footprints in the snow. No one, the double included, had been back here today.

Ryder plodded across the yard, unlocked his rear door, and opened it. A billow of warm air enveloped him. The only sound was his refrigerator's hum. He was home at last, but this was not the way he had expected to find his sanctuary; it had become someone else's lair. Smelling burned toast, he stepped into the kitchen. His years in the army had changed him from a slovenly youth to a man who prized order. When one lived with the unpredictability of violent death, orderliness was not only efficient, it was as comforting as a finely tuned weapon. So it was with irritation that he surveyed the grease thick on the stove and the dirty dishes piled on the counter.

Scraping snow from his boots, he went into his living room. *The*

Washington Post was strewn across his sofa. He climbed the stairs. In his bedroom, clothes were piled on a chair and scattered around the floor. Ignoring the mess, he went into his closet, pushed aside boxes, and crouched in the corner. Running his hands over the parquet floor, he located four finger holds then lifted out a square of wood, revealing his subcompact semiautomatic Beretta pistol, ammo, sound suppressor, cash, two billfolds containing cover identities and passports, and pocket litter.

Removing his peacoat and sports jacket, he buckled on the canvas shoulder holster. Then he checked his Beretta, loaded it, and balanced it in his hand. A familiar calmness settled over him, and he felt complete. Automatically, he lifted the weapon and aimed. *If you don't kill the memories, the memories will kill you.* He had been military intelligence, MI, then recruited and trained by an MI black unit for special death missions. He was good at it. Worse, he had liked it. That was why he had retired from the army, why there were moments when a dark cloud seemed to envelop him.

He snapped the Beretta into his holster and packed his black backpack with the rest of the things from his hidey-hole. Then he went to the window and peered down between the slats at two police cruisers and an ambulance parked at angles in the intersection, roof beacons rotating. Yellow crime scene tape already outlined the area. The two women who had witnessed the attack were talking to the officers. They would describe the death as, at best, a hit and run, and, at worst, deliberate murder. At some point soon, the officers would come here to his home to investigate.

Quickly he searched his bedroom. The only items of interest were jeans, a flannel shirt, underwear, and shoes that were not his—but with no identifying tags or pocket litter. He methodically inspected the rest of the rooms, finally going back downstairs to the living room and then into the kitchen. The red light on his answering machine was flashing. He hit PLAY.

Tucker Andersen's voice sounded from the machine: "I hope you're bored. Or you've come to your senses and realize you suck at being a civilian. Call me." Tucker was the number two at Catapult, a Langley black unit that specialized in counteroperations.

Not now, Tucker. First I've got to get the hell out of here. Some home-coming. Pulling on his coat, hat, and gloves, he stepped outdoors. The door slammed behind him, locking automatically. His face already felt frozen.

He slogged through the snow. Waiting inside his garage was his faded green 1978 Ford pickup, which was retrofitted with a powerhouse Audi V8 Quattro drive train. He climbed in. Minimal cranking, and the big engine fired.

In seconds Ryder was driving away through the parking lot. He had escaped without having to talk to the police, but he had no clue what the hell the double was all about. Before entering H Street, he scanned. Seeing nothing unusual and no one seeming interested in him, he merged with the traffic.

As he drove off, he remembered the cell phone he had taken from the dead man. Gripping the steering wheel with one hand, he used the other to fish it out of his pocket.

A snow-dusted Chevy van was parked at the curb across H Street and a half block back. It was an older model, indistinguishable from thou-sands of others in the metropolis. The lone occupant sat in the rear at a darkened window, peering out through binoculars. He studied the man in the navy blue peacoat driving away in the green truck. He rec-ognized Judd Ryder.

He grabbed his cell phone and made the call. "You were right. I've picked him up."

7

There were moments when strong coffee was the only answer. Shaking off tension, Ryder drove through Coffee Blast, got his usual three-shot *caffè americano*, and parked off Maryland Avenue. He drank deeply, welcoming the heat and caffeine. Then he inspected the double's cell phone. It was disposable, anonymous, no surprise. The address book had no password protection, but it did not need any—it was empty.

Ryder checked the calls the double had made. And stared. The man had phoned Eva Blake's home number. His chest tightened. He kept her in a special place in his memory, Eva of the long red hair and the cobalt-blue eyes that could pierce him to the soul. He remembered the first time he saw her—running through a cold night rain in London, no umbrella, hair flying, frightened and furious as she tried to escape her murderous husband. There had been something about her defiance, her bravery despite being on the losing end of a bad deal, that had gotten to Ryder. Now she was at the Farm, the CIA's highly secret facility at Camp Peary, where she was learning tradecraft. Maybe she was home on break. He dialed her.

"Hullo," she answered.

Hearing her, he felt a rush of emotions. He had saved her that night in London, and they had grown close. He'd had fantasies they might have a future together. But when the mission they were on finished, she abandoned her earlier life as a museum curator and joined Langley. The problem was, the clandestine life was one he never wanted again. So it was better to keep his distance.

"Hi, Eva."

"Judd!" There was surprise in her voice. "Are you calling from Baghdad?"

"No, I just got back to D.C."

"I thought you weren't coming home until tomorrow." Her voice sounded strained. Probably stress from the Farm's tough training, he decided.

"I finished a day early, so I decided to move my flight ticket," he told her. "And before you ask, yes, it was a productive trip. We'll talk about it later. Right now I have a question. Who phoned you a little after four o'clock yesterday on your land line?"

"I don't think anyone did. Why? What's happened?"

"I've been doubled." He described watching the imposter leave his row house and then the snowmobiler deliberately run him down.

"My God, that's awful. You're sure he's dead?" she asked.

"Yes, and it's too bad. I had serious questions for him. What about his call to you?"

"Hold on." She read him digits. "Is that his number?" When he said it was, she continued, "According to my phone, he called at four-twelve. But I wasn't home, and he didn't leave a message. Maybe he called to enhance his credibility. You know, trying to get in touch with me would help to make him look real. If I'd actually answered, he could've said he dialed the wrong number."

He nodded. "Makes sense." But then he warned: "Maybe not only my double knows about you, his killer might, too. I don't know why the double—or I—got targeted, but his phoning you makes me think you could also be in danger."

"I'll be careful. Drive over here. We can work on this together."

He agreed. As he said good-bye, he remembered Tucker Andersen had called and left a message on his answering machine. It was because of Tucker that he had met Eva. It had all begun six months ago, when Ryder's father was shot and killed. To find his father's killer, he had accepted contract work with Tucker, who had been tracking terrorist financing based on a tip the old man had given him just before he was killed.

He dialed the CIA man.

As soon as he heard Ryder's voice, Tucker demanded, "What took you so long to get back to me?"

He found himself smiling at Tucker's cantankerousness. "I don't work for you anymore, remember?"

"We both know you should. Are you home now?"

"I am. You haven't been up to your old tricks, have you, Tucker?"

"What in hell are you talking about?"

"I've been doubled," Ryder told him. "It's a professional job. Did you order it?"

"If I were going to double you"—Tucker's voice had an edge—"I would've told you."

Ryder nodded to himself. Then he again related the story of the imposter and the snowmobiler. "The double was wearing clothes I'd expected to pick up at my dry cleaner today, and he was carrying duplicates of my ID. He was killed at the time I would've ordinarily walked to the grocery store. He was following my routine."

"Who wants you dead?"

"Let me count the ways." He sighed. "I searched my row house but couldn't find anything about who the double was or why I got chosen. He was carrying a cell. It's disposable, but he called Eva—"

"You've warned her?" Tucker interrupted.

"Sure. He phoned her land line but didn't leave a message. I need a favor. First, there were three other numbers on the cell. Would you get them checked?"

Tucker agreed, and Ryder related the numbers.

"Second," Ryder continued, "I'm hoping the police and medical examiner don't realize the dead guy is my double, at least not right away.

I'd like at least a week to stay under the radar while I try to figure out whose cross-hairs I've landed in."

Once the news was released, the media would home in like heat-seeking missiles. The District medical examiner had in his icebox a cadaver that not only carried the ID of a former member of U.S. Army intelligence, but also had been made to look like him right down to the color of his eyelashes. Photos of Ryder would be plastered on TV and Internet screens around the globe.

"I understand," Tucker told him. "I'll see what I can do."

"Thanks. Your turn. Why did you want to talk to me?"

"Your trip to Iraq. The situation there is deteriorating again. We're worried something new is in the wind, some big operation, maybe devastating to us and the region. I'd like to know what you saw and heard. Whom you met—and trust."

"Sure, but let's have that conversation later. I'm on my way to Eva's place."

"Right." The line went dead.

8

His heavy wool overcoat buttoned up to his chin, Tucker Andersen wove among the pedestrians in Chinatown. It was lunchtime, and the sidewalks teemed with office workers. Tucker sniffed, smelling Mexican, Greek, and Italian food. Like much of life, Chinatown was not what it used to be. A lifelong jogger, he walked lightly. He was five feet ten inches tall, fifty-three years old, and slender. All that was left of his once thick hair was a gray fringe touching the back of his collar, so to ward off the cold, he wore a burgundy beret. Tortoiseshell-rimmed eyeglasses accented his face, a Grand Canyon of lines. His mustache was brown and his beard gray, short, and, as usual, in need of a trim. He looked ordinary and blended easily, and to him that was what "style" was all about.

As he put away his secure handheld, he wondered why Judd Ryder had been doubled. He had plans for Judd, and they did not include early death. Besides, Tucker liked him, and he did not like many people. He had just made a couple of calls on his behalf. Now it was time to refocus on the covert business at hand.

Tucker was tailing the Padre, a bulky man who was decked out in his signature disguise—black brimmed hat set square on his head, long black cashmere overcoat, black wool suit, and white collar. With his benign smile, it was unlikely the uninformed would know that the man who seemed to be a kindly Roman Catholic priest was in fact an infamous international assassin. A half hour earlier, Tucker had been eating lunch at Teaism Café when the Padre had appeared, laid what looked to be a business card on the table, and walked away. It invited Tucker to follow for a meet. No details, just that it would be worth his while.

About twenty feet behind, Tucker trailed the Padre into a wide paseo and then through glass doors into Gallery Place, an indoor shopping complex of several stories. The contract killer stopped at the Regal Cinemas box office, where he bought a matinee ticket for the new George Clooney movie.

As the Padre stepped onto the up escalator, Tucker bought a ticket and followed. Soon he spotted the three-man surveillance team he had summoned from Catapult. One was at the complex's main entry. The second was near the ice cream parlor. And the third was riding the escalator behind Tucker.

Satisfied no one else was surveilling them, Tucker stepped off the escalator. The scent of hot buttered popcorn infused the air, and the Padre was leaving the concession stand with a large bag of it. Unbuttoning his overcoat, Tucker followed him into the theater, where he had taken the aisle seat in the top row. He was already eating popcorn, his black overcoat folded on his lap. No one was within listening distance.

Tucker made an impatient gesture, and the assassin moved his legs. Tucker slid in and sat next to him.

"I like George Clooney." The Padre's voice was a gravelly whisper. "He owned a potbellied pig named Max. The pig weighed three hundred pounds, but he did not eat the pig. Consider that. They lived together in Hollywood for eighteen years." He nodded at the screen, where Clooney was jumping off a building. "I see all of George Clooney's movies. I never miss one." He ate a handful of popcorn. "Still, I do not understand why people live with animals."

On the screen, Clooney was making a getaway in a speeding Jaguar. Lucky Clooney, Tucker thought.

Tucker kept his whisper neutral. "You wanted to talk. I'm here. Talk."

For more than four decades no one was certain whether the Padre was Spanish or Portuguese. Little was certain about him except he was exceptionally talented with knives. Then two years ago, a Spanish mole in ETA, the Basque terrorist group, reported that the Padre's real name was Sabino Zaragosa and he had come up through ETA. No one was sure why he had resigned years ago and gone independent.

"I would like a favor." Watching the movie, the assassin barely moved his lips. "It is not a large favor, and of course I will give something even more valuable in return."

This is my day to be asked for favors, Tucker thought. "What are you offering?"

"You are perhaps aware of the barrel of weapons schoolchildren stumbled upon last week on a Gaza beach?"

"Of course." Palestinian youngsters had been playing on the seashore when they found an oil barrel—sealed, waterproofed, and painted black—sitting alone on the sand. Inside were grenades, automatic rifles, and mortar shells.

"I think you might very much like to know how those big bad armaments came to land in the heart of Hamas territory."

Not only did Tucker want to know, Mossad would, too. "What will it cost me?"

The Padre smiled, his teeth white and large in the flickering darkness. Then his expression turned grim. "Tell me where I can find the Carnivore."

Tucker's eyebrows rose. Interesting. The Carnivore was also an independent assassin. He was known for making wet work look like accidents, suicides, or natural deaths.

"Why do you want him?" Tucker asked.

"It is a matter of competition. We are competitors—and he has lived a long time. It is personal. Nothing to do with anyone or anything else." The Padre thrust a handful of popcorn into his mouth.

"Why come to me?"

"His last job was with you. Do not look so surprised. Messy operations leak like bad surgery. Naturally, since you and he worked on it together, there is a supposition that if you do not know exactly where he is you certainly know how to reach him. Anyone who has dug deeply enough to discover your connection will also think of your two colleagues on the operation. I will say their names so you know how much I have discovered—Judd Ryder and Eva Blake."

Tucker suppressed a grimace. "I have no idea where he is," he said honestly.

"The Carnivore's need to remain hidden is a threat to you, your friends, and your oh-so-secret CIA unit. To protect his security, it is just a matter of time until he scrubs those of you who know."

Tucker wondered whether the Carnivore had been the person behind doubling Judd.

"Is this sudden interest of yours related to Burleigh Morgan's liquidation?" Tucker asked.

Morgan had been in the assassination business longer than either the Padre or the Carnivore. A Brit from the old East End, he was as tough as a two-dollar steak, at least according to Tucker's French sources. Two days before, Morgan had left his girlfriend's apartment in Paris and climbed into his sports car. As he turned on the engine, the seat exploded under him. Body parts landed a block away.

The Padre adjusted his bulk. "Morgan's death was unfortunate. He had been kind enough to give me the information about the barrel on the Gaza beach." He studied Tucker. "You are certain you do not know where the Carnivore lives? Where he is at this very moment? I would truly like the information as we sit here. On the other hand, perhaps you may not care to know more about the barrel of armaments."

Ignoring the implied threat, Tucker decided he owed the Carnivore nothing on the scale of what Mossad would owe him for information about the barrel. "I want your intel about the weapons barrel now," he ordered. "Don't shake your head at me. If what you say checks out, I'll locate the Carnivore for you."

The Padre's eyelids lowered and rose as he considered the offer. "Very well." He described an arms smugglers' haven on Italy's coast where shipments were packed in waterproof barrels, then the shipping route the barrels took across the Mediterranean Sea, and finally the longitude and latitude of a natural convergence of currents where the barrels were off-loaded. The convergence was known as al-Baraha—the Blessed One.

"From this pool of waters the barrels float in to shore," the Padre went on. "If all is timed correctly, they arrive in the bleakest hours of morning on the same beach. You must admit my information is excellent, certainly worth the life of one old assassin like the Carnivore. You agree?"

"If the intel checks out, we have a deal."

"How will I be in touch?" the Padre asked.

"You won't. I'll call you. Give me your cell number."

Grumbling under his breath, the Padre produced an iPhone, checked it, and relayed the number.

"Wait five minutes, then you can leave," Tucker instructed.

The Padre shook his head. "No, I will stay until the end of the movie. I must watch George Clooney kill the bad guys. It is very satisfying."

Tucker padded down the stadium stairs. As soon as he entered the corridor, he saw his team leader was drinking from a water fountain. The officer looked up and nodded. The signal told Tucker his spies were in place to follow the Padre no matter which exit he chose.

Tucker sauntered past her. "He's in the top row. On the aisle."

At the end of the hallway, the spymaster glanced back over his shoulder. His team leader was no longer in sight, and the cinema door was closing quietly.

9

Passing the theater's concession stand, Tucker saw one of the elevators was empty. He hurried and stepped inside. As the door closed, he took out his secure handheld. With it he sent classified e-mail and text messages, accessed classified networks, and made top-secret phone calls. Appearing ordinary, it could be operated like any smartphone with Internet access while either off or in secure mode.

As he rode the elevator down, Tucker put the handheld into secure mode and called Gloria Feit at Catapult. Once a full-time field officer herself, Gloria was now the black unit's office manager and general factotum and occasional covert operative.

"I thought you'd be here an hour ago," she said. "Bridgeman's been asking for you. You've got to come back right away."

Scott Bridgeman was the brand-new chief of Catapult, a by-the-book manager. Or, as Tucker thought of him, uptight as a knitting needle.

He sighed. "I'll be there as soon as I can. Meanwhile, reactivate the search for the Carnivore. We need to find him, and we need to find him quick."

"I'll get right on it."

He ended the connection, and the elevator door opened onto the ground floor. Striding past the greenery, he checked his messages. The first was from Catapult's communications center with an answer for Judd—the three unknown numbers on the double's phone were to disposable cells, untraceable. Figures, Tucker thought. One more sign the people behind Judd's impersonation were pros.

Then Tucker listened to his second message.

"This is Annie. What in hell have you gotten yourself into, Tucker? Call me."

"Annie" was Annie Chernow, a captain in the metropolitan police force. She had been one of his protégées in the clandestine service, until she gave birth to twin sons and decided work close to home was her career path.

He tapped her office number on his keypad. She was not at her desk, but the sergeant patched him through to her cell. When she answered, he could hear clinking metal and a droning voice in the background.

"Are you at the ME's?" he asked, referring to the medical examiner of the District of Columbia.

"Of course I am. You know, Tucker, I can always count on you not to bore me. Pray tell, what do you find so interesting about the corpse we picked up on G Street Northeast?"

"Why? Did he suddenly regain consciousness?"

"Almost. If he had, he might've said his name *isn't* Judson Ryder."

For a rare moment, Tucker was speechless. How did she know?

Her tone grew tough as she continued. "You're correct that his injuries are consistent with being hit by a snowmobile, but after that it gets hinky. The ME found that prosthetic devices had been applied to his face to give him a nose bump, make his cheekbones prominent, and square his chin. According to the ME, the prostheses are some kind of new skinlike silicone that he'd heard rumors about at an international pathologists' convention last year, but he'd never seen—until now. The silicone was coated with colored polymer layers to duplicate the color of the wearer's skin. The ME took a bunch of photos then he peeled off the prostheses, which was no easy thing, and took more photos. What the hell is going on, Tucker?"

"I can't tell you. If I could, I would."

"This is *my* dead body," she reminded him. "*My* investigation."

"I need a full report yesterday," he ordered, "and this can go no further than you, the ME, and the door, at least for now. You don't have to like it, Annie. Just do as I say. National security."

She sniffed. "National security? That old saw?"

He ignored her tone. "Yes, national security, goddammit. And I need to find out who the corpse really is, pronto."

"Oh, I can tell you that, too. There was nothing on his fingerprints, so I ran him through the tristate facial recognition database. Bingo. His name is Jeff Goos. He's a professional actor. Lives in an apartment in Richmond and does theater and TV up and down the coast. Divorced a couple of times. Heavy child support payments. I could go on and on."

That was the thing about Annie, she was damn good. "Christ," Tucker said. "Wait for me. I'm on my way."

10

As soon as Tucker Andersen left the movie theater, Sabino Zaragosa—the Padre—ripped off his white clerical collar and black vest. His man, Ricardo Agote, who had been sitting quietly ten rows below, was soon at his side. In seconds, they traded clothes, and Ricardo settled into the Padre's seat, the black cashmere overcoat folded on his lap, the bag of popcorn in his hands, the black brimmed hat sitting squarely on his head.

Wearing Ricardo's thermal jacket, the Padre trotted down the aisle, took Ricardo's seat, and leaned comfortably back, eyes half closed, observing a thirtyish woman enter the theater. By turning his head slightly, he saw her settle into one of the higher seats from where she could easily keep tabs on the moviegoer she believed to be the Padre. She was one of Tucker Andersen's surveillance spies.

Smiling to himself, the assassin peered at the screen again. George Clooney and his men were creeping toward a cabin where the villains were hiding. The villains were in terrible danger. The Padre knew intimately what that was like, the threat of imminent attack, of annihilation. It made his gut sour, and yet he wanted Clooney and his men to win. In a rare moment of insight he realized that was the conflict that had fueled his life.

The last ten minutes of the movie passed quickly. At the thrilling end, the Padre felt the sweet heat of redemption.

As the credits ran on the screen, Ricardo marched down the aisle, wearing the Padre's black hat and long black overcoat. His white clerical collar shone in the reflected light.

The surveillance spy rose and descended, too, tailing discreetly.

As the audience vanished, the Padre removed a red plaid cloth cap with ear protectors from his jacket pocket. Pulling it on, he Velcroed the strap tightly, producing a roll of flab beneath his chin. Lowering his head, he shuffled downstairs, out the rear door, and into a long gray corridor toward the main lobby.

Ahead were glass exit doors into the parking garage, where some patrons were awaiting rides. Just then the door opened and cold air blew in, carrying the stink of vehicle exhaust. And standing next to the door was what looked like another of Tucker Andersen's spies, wiry build, brown hair, bland features. While apparently texting on his handheld, Tucker's spy was assessing everyone who left the theater.

As the Padre observed all of this, a familiar nerviness swept across his shoulders and down his right arm toward the *navaja*, the knife, in his pocket. He carried it because it was foolish not to carry something, and he had always disliked the bulk of a pistol. He was long past needing to prove his finesse as a knife fighter, and even less interested, so this weapon was a state-of-the-art WASP injector knife—so fast and powerful it could drop the globe's largest land predators.

Still, the last thing the Padre wanted today was a confrontation and the inconvenience of a dead body. He needed to get away undetected. So he joined the line, shambling along as if feeble. When the spy noticed him, the Padre snuffled then casually wiped his nose on the sleeve of his jacket.

For a moment there was no reaction. Then disgust flitted across the spy's face, and his eyes focused down again on his handheld's screen. His fingers tapped the keyboard.

But as the Padre passed, he glanced at the screen, too—and saw his own photo.

As if the spy had been reading the Padre's mind, he lifted his gaze.

In an unexpected moment, each stared directly into the other's eyes.

Without changing his expression, the Padre cursed silently and shuffled out through the door. Knowing he would be followed, he continued shuffling. In the parking garage, he headed down the stairwell. His footsteps sounded like sandpaper on the cement. At the bottom level, he pushed through the door and slipped around the corner, where he would be out of sight. Breathing evenly, he slid out his WASP knife and listened.

As soon as he heard the door open, the Padre ran back around the corner and used his bulk to slam the smaller man against the wall. At the same time he rammed the point of the WASP blade into the spy's gut. He pressed the button on the Neoprene handle, shooting 24 grams of carbon dioxide gas at the blinding speed of 800 pounds per square inch from the handle through a small tube in the blade and out the tip.

And into the man. The spy screamed. Horror shone from his eyes. As he jerked and writhed, the basketball-size cavity of his internal organs was being snap frozen. Soon he slumped, and the Padre lowered his shoulder and pulled him over it. With one hand, the Padre texted for his limo. He had to get rid of the corpse and hope Tucker Andersen would never be able to associate him with the death.

In less than a minute, his chauffeur was backing the black Cadillac limousine up to the Padre. The angle of the vehicle prevented the passenger in the rear seat from seeing what the Padre was doing. The trunk opened silently. As he dumped the corpse inside, the chauffeur appeared. The Padre gave him instructions about its disposal and soon was sliding in next to his wife, inhaling her expensive perfume. He dismissed all thoughts of business.

"*Hola, generalissimo, querido mío.*" Catalina greeted him in Spanish with a smile and a shy kiss on the cheek.

He felt welcomed to the center of his heart. She was small, just nineteen years old, with the wide face and hips of a solid Basque woman. Her beautiful black eyes glowed in admiration for him. Her teeth were small—straight now, due to the excellent orthodontist he had found near their new home in Gstaad. Her fingers were tiny, but her hands were broad and strong. As he watched, she knitted her fingers into his. This was his first marriage. He lifted his arm, and she slid under it.

"It went well?" She was an innocent and knew nothing of his work.

"As well as could be expected," he responded in Basque. As he had grown older he had yearned for his heritage. One satisfaction was to bring their conversation back to their native tongue.

"Did you locate the man you wished to?" she asked curiously in Basque. "I think I heard you call him the Carnivore."

"Do not worry. It is only business, but I have more to do. The limo can drop you off in Bethesda for shopping, or you can stay with me."

She patted his chest. Her diamond-drenched wedding band and engagement ring glittered. "I'll stay with you."

He was rich and gave her all the money she wanted. Still she had chosen not to go shopping. He prized her modesty and common sense. She was like his mother—solid, reliable, and strict. His throat tightened with emotion as he remembered his mother. He had joined ETA when he was only fifteen years old to help force Spain to give the Basques their own nation. But then his mother was killed in the crossfire between his ETA unit and Franco's police. His unit could have saved her but had decided to sacrifice her to make a political statement.

It was then that he had taken the skills ETA had taught him and left. Long ago he had stopped caring about governments and their small issues. They paid him very well to do their dirty work so they could deny their dirty motives. They were no different from ETA.

Catalina sighed and burrowed against him. He smiled and stroked her silky hair. When his iPhone vibrated against his hip, he slid it out. And smiled again. Everything was on schedule.

11

Silver Spring, Maryland

The sky glistened blue, and the air was warming. As snow dripped from eaves and mailboxes, Ryder drove onto Derby Ridge Lane. Homes lined the left side of the curving street, while on the right a snowy forest spread into the distance. He parked in front of Eva's place, a modern row house with white pillars and shutters. As he turned off the engine, his Samsung Galaxy smartphone vibrated.

Tucker's voice was loud and strong: "I've been to the ME's office to check on the corpse of the man who was pretending to be you. The reason he looked like you was prosthetics."

Ryder frowned. "Are you sure?"

"According to the ME, you would've needed a magnifying glass, or you would've had to inspect his face with your fingers. There are minute seams, and the prostheses feel a little stiffer than human flesh." Tucker described the colored polymer layers, the cosmetic paint that blended the edges, and the waterproof biocompatible drying adhesive.

"Jesus. Someone went to a lot of trouble."

"They sure as hell did. Your double's name was Jeff Goos. He was an actor living in Richmond. I have my people digging into his background. Did you know him?"

"Never heard of him. How long do I have until the cops and ME release the information that he isn't me?"

"The ME wanted to go public immediately, but I convinced him to give you your week. I had to hold 'national security' over his head to get it." Tucker changed the subject. "You once told me you didn't know where the Carnivore lived or how to find him. Is that still true?"

"Yes. Why?"

"Have you ever heard of an assassin called the Padre?" Tucker asked.

"A longtime independent. Works mostly in Europe."

"Right. After you and I talked, I had a meeting with him. Turns out he's trying to locate the Carnivore. The closest he's gotten so far is finding out the Carnivore's last job was with you, Eva, and me. Does Eva know where he is or how to get in touch with him?"

"She's never said anything about it one way or the other," Ryder said.

"If she does know, the Carnivore's got to worry she's told you or me."

"You're saying the Carnivore might've been the one who killed my double, thinking it was me."

"Yes. It'd be a threat to his security."

Ryder studied the street. "Do you have photos of them you can send me?" He had never seen the Padre, and he had been in the Carnivore's company twice, but both times the assassin was disguised.

"We have today's surveillance video of the Padre. I'll e-mail it to you. But as for the Carnivore, no. He's known as the man without a face for a reason. We've never had any video, photos, or drawings, at least that we've been able to dig up. His security is notoriously tight. I'll phone if I learn anything. You do the same." Tucker hung up.

Stuffing his Galaxy into his pocket, Ryder slung on his backpack, hurried to Eva's door, and rang the bell. The street was so quiet he could hear the drone of the East-West Highway from over the hill. He punched the doorbell again. Finally, he leaned across the porch rail and peered into the front window. A club chair was overturned, lying on its side. The coffee table was broken in half. The screen on the television set was shattered. Adrenaline shot through him. *What happened to Eva!*

Ripping off his gloves, he pulled off his backpack and dug out his picklocks. In seconds he was inside. He closed the door softly, listening in the silence. He studied the shadowy living room. Besides the broken furniture, there were scuff marks on the hardwood floor and a spray of blood in front of the television. There had been a struggle violent enough to leave blood. Eva could be dead, or she could've been taken away by force. And now he knew the Carnivore had motive.

Controlling his emotions, he ran through the dining room and kitchen. Everything seemed to be where it belonged. Through the rear window he saw Eva's car in her private spot. It was covered by nearly a foot of snow. He ran upstairs, moving quickly into and out of the deserted office and bathroom, peering inside all of the doors. And walked through her bedroom. He inhaled the scent of rose water, her scent. There was no sign of her anywhere.

Spinning on his heel, he ran out, dialing her cell. He pressed his Galaxy against his ear and heard her cell ring into it—but at the same time a phone was ringing somewhere beneath him, on the first floor.

He pounded downstairs into the living room. Following the sound, he stopped at her sofa and dug among the cushions with both hands. At last he felt two items jammed together. One was vibrating and ringing. Pulling both out, he found a brand-new cell phone—hers, since it was responding to his call—and a GPS tracker. Christ, she was clever. He hit his Galaxy's OFF button, and the ringing stopped. She would expect the Carnivore to appropriate her cell, so she had managed to be preemptive, hiding both items in hopes Ryder would come as he had promised. And when he did, he would see the wrecked living room, break in, call her, and follow the ringing to discover the GPS.

He turned on the GPS. With a faint *beep*, the screen came to life, showing a grid of the state of Maryland north of Eva's house. His pulse quickened—a green dot, which meant some kind of vehicle, was heading away on Route 650 at 63 miles per hour. Ryder smiled grimly. Eva left the tracker because she had planted a bug on herself. With the tracker, he could follow her.

Sprinting out the front door and through the cold afternoon light, he jumped behind the wheel of his pickup and sped off.

12

Washington, D.C.

Set in the heart of historic Capitol Hill, the organization known as Catapult operated out of one of the area's century-old Federalist brick houses. The sign above the door announced the Council for Peer Education, apparently just another group that had settled here so it could conveniently lobby the White House and Congress. In truth, Catapult was a CIA black unit charged with taking aggressive covert action to direct or deter negative events around the planet.

Arriving at the side entrance, Tucker Andersen tapped his code onto the keypad and waited until the iris-reader recognized him. When a soft *click* announced the door was unlocked, he walked in. Staffers moved briskly through the corridor, carrying folders color-coded to denote security levels. The old house seemed to vibrate with energy, and Tucker thrived on it.

In the reception area, Gloria Feit peered up from behind her big metal desk, slid her rainbow-framed glasses down her nose, and assessed him. "You appear healthy," she said tartly. She was in her late forties, a small woman with crinkled smile lines around her blue eyes. Wearing a black wool jumper and a long-sleeved white shirt, she looked more like a nun than a covert officer with a black belt in karate.

"What did you expect—a bullet-riddled corpse?" He unknotted his muffler and unbuttoned his wool overcoat.

"With you I never know," Gloria said airily. "Here's what we've collected so far about the Carnivore."

"Thanks." He took the stapled sheets she held out to him.

"Bridgeman's waiting for you." That was Scott Bridgeman, Catapult's new director.

Repressing a sigh, Tucker nodded.

"Tucker, I thought it was you." The familiar voice was behind him.

Turning, he saw Bash Badawi striding toward him. Bash was one of Tucker's infiltration artists. A lean, loose-jointed jock with straight ink-black hair, Bash had recently wrapped up a long-running operation in Rome. He had been home three weeks and was restless.

"Need any help?" Bash asked. "A mission? A quick trip to Peshawar?"

"You've got to decompress, Bash," Tucker warned. "Take it easy."

Gloria intervened: "Tucker, the boss wants to see you. Remember?"

"Okay, okay. I'm going." Tucker walked around her desk and tapped on the Catapult director's door.

"Come in."

Tucker entered. Scott Bridgeman had the best office in the three-story building, with large windows overlooking the tree-lined avenue. All of Catapult's window glass was bulletproof and distorted to prevent anyone from seeing inside or successfully using a demodulator to eavesdrop on conversations.

"Have a seat, Tucker." Bridgeman put down his pen. With regular features, wheat-blond hair, and bulging muscles, he was handsome enough to be a Calvin Klein model. Despite the handicap of good looks, he had proved to be deft in fieldwork, able to vanish into the background of almost any setting. The reverse was true at Catapult, where his presence was unmistakable and constant.

"Glad to." Tucker tossed his overcoat onto one of the chairs facing the desk and sank into the other. He was tired from all of the day's running around.

"Okay, so let's have the latest." Bridgeman leaned back, hands clasped behind his head.

Tucker described his noontime meet with the Padre in the movie theater. He explained how the barrel of armaments had landed on the Gaza seashore. "Of course, the Padre wanted something in exchange for the intel—the Carnivore. I asked Gloria to put together a preliminary report about the Carnivore." He started to slide it across the desk.

Bridgeman waved it away. "No, tell me."

"The short version is the Carnivore has been an international assassin for close to forty years. Sometimes he was useful to us. Sometimes not—"

Bridgeman sat forward. "The Carnivore turned up in the Library of Gold operation and delivered intel to you—even though only members of your team had access to it. How did the Carnivore get the intel? The answer has to be from one of your people. *My* people now. There was no other source. We've got a goddamned mole in here somewhere. Does this have you pissing your pants, Tucker? It does me."

Tucker was silent. Scott Bridgeman was just thirty years old, and yet he was running one of Langley's top clandestine units. Langley no longer had the wide array of experienced top management choices of years past.

Tucker responded patiently: "On the other hand, the situation could be innocent. There were people along the line who knew—people in the military, for instance. What's important is the intel was decisive in bringing the operation home. The Carnivore was a volunteer and unpaid, and his reward was to get shot up rather badly. Still, once I was back here, I opened an investigation into whether one of our people was collaborating with him. The investigation got sidetracked when some of our hotspots flared up. Of course I've told Gloria to reactivate the probe."

Bridgeman glared. "We need fast answers."

"Gloria knows that." Tucker considered whether to disclose the latest wrinkle, about Judd Ryder's imposter. Not even Gloria knew about it.

Beneath his blond crewcut, Bridgeman was studying him. His eyes narrowed. "Why didn't you take this job when it was offered to you, Tucker? You're a legend. You could be the one sitting here."

"Being assistant director keeps me in the office more than I like," Tucker said honestly. "With your job, I might as well chain myself to my desk." Fieldwork kept him sane. He liked the changes of scenery, meeting new people, the chance to test himself up front and personal against intelligent and dangerous enemies.

"How am I supposed to manage you, Tucker? You don't tell me what you're doing until you've already done it. I just got a call from Matt Kelley." Kelley was the director of the Clandestine Service. "He told me you'd been at the ME's and ordered them to keep the investigation into Judd Ryder's double a secret. Matt asked me whether I knew my arse from my ear."

That was Matt through and through, Tucker thought, his face expressionless.

"You used the excuse of national security, for chrissakes," Bridgeman went on. "You had absolutely no authority to do that. Besides, you know damn well Judd Ryder isn't clean—he got into some serious trouble in Iraq."

"But he saved us more than once in the Library of Gold mission," Tucker reminded him.

Scott's lips thinned. "He did blood work for army intelligence in Pakistan and Iraq. There's no way anyone can ever completely trust an assassin, not even one of our own. They have nightmares, flashbacks. They get jumpy and react crazily. They're unpredictable and get used to killing. You were lucky he was stable enough to be useful when you took him on as a contract employee."

"I've known Judd all his life. He's as stable as you or me."

Bridgeman shook his head. "There's bad family history there, too. His father turned out to be an international criminal."

"I doubt Judd knew anything about what his father was doing. Judd inherited ten million dollars from him, but instead of retiring to the Riviera or blowing it all on gambling or drugs, he started a foundation to build schools in disadvantaged places. He put the whole inheritance into it. And it's a working foundation, not one of those tax dodges. He personally manages the projects. He hammers nails and paints walls. He just got back from Baghdad, where he's started an elementary school in one of the poorest neighborhoods."

"Good for him. Send him back to Baghdad. I don't want him hurting Catapult." Bridgeman leaned forward, his jaw jutting. "You were protecting Ryder with the medical examiner, even though you knew I'd never approve. The murder of the double is a police case. I want you to call the ME, apologize, and tell him you were out of line."

"The ME's a showboat. He'll instantly go public about Ryder."

"Probably, but at least he won't drag Langley into it."

Tucker swallowed back his anger. "You're right—I should've reported what I was doing, but there was little time, and it doesn't mean I'm wrong. At least one international assassin—the Padre—is operating on U.S. soil."

"You know damn well it's the FBI's job to investigate inside our borders."

"We don't always share our intel with the Bureau, and vice versa. And when we do, there's often a time lag."

"The Padre is off the table. He hasn't done anything wrong here."

"That we know of," Tucker countered. "Worse, we don't know what he's got in mind, other than tracking down the Carnivore."

"He's given us valuable information." Bridgeman's tone was steely. "You have no real evidence he's out to wipe the Carnivore. And even if he is, the Carnivore could be thousands of miles away. Do you really want to waste our people's time on something as flimsy as this? Until you can bring me something that walks, talks, and bleeds, don't tell me one of your guesses is real."

Tucker looked down at his hands, folded neatly in his lap. He often sat that way when under attack. Some people crossed their arms, an unconscious gesture of self-protection, shielding their most vulnerable organ, the heart. Others put their hands to their throats or fiddled with their hair. Long ago Tucker had decided to appear relaxed, so he let his hands curl comfortably in his lap, which forced his shoulders to loosen.

The discipline of it distracted his mind from the assault and allowed him to focus.

Tucker spoke calmly. "You called me a legend. You said I could be the one sitting in your chair. If either of those is true, then perhaps I'm worth listening to on this issue. I'm going to approach it another way. . . . To be a good spy, you have to be smart, hardworking, and talented. To be a *great* spy, you've got to have one more quality—instinct. 'Gut,' if you will. I figure you have good gut." He had seen no evidence Bridgeman had any gut at all, but his goal was to put Bridgeman in a more receptive mood.

Bridgeman gave a slow nod. "Go on."

"My gut is screaming there's something very big going on here, and the Padre's hunt for the Carnivore is the tip of the damn iceberg. To begin with, they're titans in the underworld of assassins. They don't waste their time with turf wars. There's no money in it, and somebody's sure to die. When you work at that rarified a level, it could be you. So what's happened that's so big that it's provoked the Padre to go after the Carnivore?"

Bridgeman was silent.

"Next question, who killed Judd's double?" Tucker continued. "And who was the intended victim—the double or Judd? On the same day all of this happens, the Padre asks my help to find the Carnivore fast. The logical answer is the Carnivore killed the double believing it was Judd, because he was worried Judd could tell the Padre how to get to him. The Carnivore is obsessed with security. It's one of the reasons he's been untouchable for so many decades. He's used more pseudonyms than a brush has bristles. How about his real name? No way. His nationality? Please. This is the way I see it: The Carnivore knows the Padre is after him. He needs to eliminate any possibility the Padre can find him. The Carnivore's last job was with Judd, Eva Blake, and me. Judd claims the Carnivore didn't tell him anything about where he lived. He didn't tell me either. So that leaves Eva Blake. Judd is on his way to see her now. The Carnivore spent time with her. He could've told her, and if he did, then he's got to be worried she told Judd and maybe me."

"Are you thinking he'll come after you?" Bridgeman asked curiously.

Tucker shrugged. "What matters is something big is going on between the Padre and the Carnivore. Judd has already been dragged into it. Let's let him dig around and maybe save us some aggravation."

Bridgeman looked away. Tucker had made an important point, but Bridgeman seemed to be having a hard time agreeing.

"Matt Kelley can get the ME to back down," Tucker went on. "If you don't want to ask Matt to do it, I will." He had just pulled out his trump card and laid it firmly on the desk. Matt Kelley was not only the director of the Clandestine Service, he had also been Tucker's protégé some twenty years before. There was no way Bridgeman could let Tucker go over his head to Matt.

Bridgeman spoke as if he had just had a brilliant idea. "This is potentially too serious a situation to let the ME grandstand about it. How long does Ryder need?"

"A week."

"A week?" Bridgeman sat back and rubbed a hand over his face. "Christ. I'll talk to the ME and see if I can get it for you. But your boy, Ryder, better damn well move fast. His first day is closing out."

13

Montgomery County, Maryland

Houses and offices passed in a blur as Judd Ryder raced his pickup north on Route 650. Constantly checking the tracker Eva had left him, he drove at 80 miles per hour and watched for the state police. After fifteen miles the landscape grew rolling and rural, the four-lane highway narrowed to two lanes, and he still had not caught up with her. He gripped the steering wheel so hard his knuckles ached.

Finally the green dot on the tracker showed her vehicle had turned off the interstate. At a white-steepled church Ryder did, too, following east on a county road. That was when the moving dot on the tracker froze. As it remained motionless, he stared, riveted—her vehicle had stopped.

Relieved, he sped his pickup into a forest and then down across a stone bridge. Timbered hills rose around him, and he saw an entry not much wider than a residential driveway. Next to it was a small sign:

The Esti Hunt Club
Private—No Trespassing

Accelerating past, he parked off the road, slung on his pack, and walked back, the tracker in hand. Taking out his Beretta, he plodded into the forest. Winter sunlight shone down through the trees in silver shafts. From behind a large oak he assessed the hunt club's entry. Tall steel gate. Attached intercom. Closed-circuit security cameras high in trees on both sides.

His tracker showed the dot was moving fractionally. Eva must be walking around. Switching configurations, he called up a map of the region, but when he zeroed in, the geography grew hazy. He could make out only two rectangular buildings and what appeared to be smaller buildings, a blurred drive, and gray formless masses that were probably trees. He cursed silently. This area north of Washington was part of the nation's security zone, and the U.S. government forbade detailed public satellite views.

He slogged uphill, pushing through branches. His boots grew heavy with snow. At last he found a deer trail. Following it, he passed a deer blind. At the crest, he dropped to his heels and surveyed the hunt club below—two large lodges and several small cabins with steep shingled roofs. Two men dressed in padded hunting jackets and armed with Uzis stood outside a white Ford Explorer parked where the drive formed a wide oval in front of the lodges and cabins. One man was smoking; the other talked on a cell phone. They held their Uzis with confidence. There were no other cars, and all of the windows in the buildings Ryder could see were dark.

Shifting his gaze, Ryder spotted Eva stumbling off a lodge porch. She was hatless, her long red hair ablaze in the afternoon sunlight. An armed guard followed, shoving her. Ryder's jaw tightened. She fell to her knees and let out a cry. The guard grabbed her arm and yanked her up. Pushing her ahead, he hustled her into a small cabin and locked the door. Within seconds she was standing at the window, hands pressed against the glass, peering out. Her features were tight with fear.

It was unlike Eva to give an inch, yet she acted beaten. What had they done to her? Ryder's grip tightened on his Beretta. The hum of a powerful engine sounded from the drive, and in seconds a shiny black Cadillac limousine appeared. The windows were darkened, its occupants unseeable. As soon as it stopped, the driver's door opened and out stepped a man in a padded hunting jacket like those the three other men wore. He, too, carried an Uzi. He scanned the surrounding slopes.

Ryder crouched lower, studying the Ford Explorer, the Cadillac limo, the men with Uzis, and Eva in the window. He rose quietly to his feet. Using spruces and pines for cover, he started down the long hill.

14

The Padre was in a good mood. The sun was shining over his favorite hunt club, Catalina was making snowballs and laughing, and he was certain that one way or another he was going to have the Carnivore soon. Sitting inside his limo, comfortable in the soft leather, he touched a button and his window descended. He beckoned his longtime driver.

The man trotted over and crouched beside the window. *"Si, señor?"*

"Where is Judd Ryder?" the Padre demanded.

"Coming down. He has about fifty yards to go. He is wearing his dark peacoat, so when he stays in the shadows of the evergreen trees and keeps low, he is difficult to spot. His training has been excellent."

"He was military intelligence. Deep cover." The Padre had learned everything possible about Judd Ryder, just as he had learned everything about Eva Blake. One or both must know where the Carnivore was, and if they did not, then Tucker Andersen would deliver the information. But he did not want to wait for all of that to happen.

"We are ready for Ryder," the chauffeur assured him. "Where the forest ends, he must choose between crossing open space or using bushes for cover. Of course he will choose the bushes. He will not get past our Uzis."

"I want him alive," the Padre said sharply.

"*Por supuesto.*" He touched his cap deferentially.

The Padre smiled to himself, pleased, feeling a moment of warmth for his faithful servant. "*Bueno.* As a reward I will show you a very valuable secret, a strange wonder you will not see the like of again." He enjoyed tormenting his employees with what they could never have.

As his chauffeur watched, the Padre took from his trouser pocket a leather pouch. Loosening the drawstrings, he turned it over onto his palm, and out slid three smaller leather pouches. He opened one, showing a large, uneven chunk of limestone. Excitement spread through him as he turned it over so the cuneiform symbols showed.

He held up his hand. "Do you know what this is?"

The man frowned, puzzled. "No, *señor.*"

"It buys freedom from a blackmailer, and it's the secret to millions of dollars."

The chauffeur's dark eyes grew as large as the bells of San Sebastian's Good Shepherd Cathedral. "So much for a rock?"

The Padre chuckled and returned it to its pouch. He did not mention he had only three pieces and needed to acquire the rest of the tablet to win.

Suddenly he felt restless. He looked across the circular drive. The woman stood motionless in the window, a statue of misery.

He gestured at her. "Bring her out. I am weary of waiting for Ryder. Seeing her will inspire him to come more quickly."

As the chauffeur trotted away, the Padre checked his iPhone, but there was no message from Tucker Andersen. Disappointed, he sat back again to survey his secluded haven. Whenever he'd had business in North America, he had treated himself to a visit here, indulging his love of fishing and hunting. All of that was before Catalina, before his new life with her. She filled the void his many activities had filled before.

As he watched her bend over to scoop up snow, her wide smile and childlike delight, he thought again about his mother, Esti. He had named this place for her—the Esti Hunt Club. He sighed deeply.

Gazing up, he saw his man bringing the woman from the cabin. The Padre opened his limo door and stepped out into the crisp air. Stretching, he studied the hillsides. He wanted Ryder. Now.

Turning to the chauffeur, he pounded his fist once into his palm. The signal told him to hit the woman. That would bring Ryder tearing down the slope.

Puzzled, worried, she peered first at the Padre, then at his four men, and finally at his young wife. But Catalina had laid down on her back on the snowbank beside the limo and was swinging her arms and legs, making a snow angel.

The chauffeur nodded, faced the terrified woman, and pulled back his fist. The Padre did not see what happened next. Instead, he felt one excruciating nanosecond of pain, and then he felt nothing. A sniper bullet had exploded his skull. The rest of the sniper rounds fell like a deadly rain on his wife, his men, and the woman who looked like Eva Blake.

15

By the time the last shot was fired, Ryder knew the source was one of two snipers working in concert among the trees at the top of the hill to the north. Although they were at least a half mile from their targets, their accuracy was pinpoint. The tally—five males, two females. So fast it was over before any of the armed victims had a chance to aim and return fire, not that they could have seen the shooters. Not that their Uzi rounds could have reached that far. There had been nothing any of them could have done. Nothing Ryder could have done.

I couldn't save Eva. I couldn't save her.

Ryder plunged down the wooded slope, his boots sinking into the snow, his heart aching. A black crow shrieked and flapped low across tamped animal tracks, a narrow trail. Ryder jumped onto it, running and sliding and falling and running again. The trail followed an ice-coated creek that streamed down through the forest.

Almost out of the trees, Ryder saw a man leave one of the lodges and dropped to watch. Like the others, the man was dressed in hunting clothes and carried an Uzi. A sixth man. A survivor. He must have been indoors the entire time. Without a glance around, he went from one victim to another, kicking away weapons, testing for vital signs. He showed no shock, not a moment of remorse, no surprise.

Moving quietly downhill another twenty feet, Ryder hid behind a hedge of juniper bushes then crab-walked along it to an opening where he was behind the man. When the man closed in on two male corpses near the Explorer, Ryder sprinted to the rear of the limo. Dropping low, he waited. The man moved to the last two victims. The more distant was a teenaged woman, lying on her back in a snowbank. She had been making a snow angel and died smiling, a bullet between her eyes. The man hurried past her to a stout, older man, who was sprawled beside the limo's passenger door.

Ryder studied the corpse's coarse features. With grim satisfaction, he nodded to himself. He had at least one answer—the dead man was the Padre, whom he recognized from the surveillance video Tucker had e-mailed. Thinking back, Ryder remembered the snipers had begun shooting only when the Padre had climbed out of the limo, and the Padre had been the first killed.

He focused again on the last man, who was sitting on his heels above the Padre. He held his Uzi in one hand while he fished through the Padre's jacket pockets with the other. It looked to Ryder that he expected to find something important.

Standing up, Ryder fired a single round into the driveway beside the man. The noise was like a thunderclap in the winter hush.

The man jumped up and whirled around. He had a head shaped like an anvil, big and angular, as was the rest of his body.

"Put your weapon down!" Ryder shot a second bullet into the driveway. Brick chips sprayed, cutting the man's cheeks. "Now!"

"*Mierda!*" Swearing in Spanish, he set down his Uzi. Standing erect again, his eyes widened, as if he recognized Ryder.

"You know me. Tell me what's going on here," Ryder said. When the man hesitated, Ryder fired a third round so close the bullet blew snow off the man's boot.

The man's words tumbled out. "You are Judd Ryder. The Padre made us memorize your face." He gestured at the guards. "They were tracking you. I did not know you were here so soon."

"How were they tracking me?" Ryder demanded.

"The Padre put a bug in the tracker you found in Eva Blake's house. That way he could follow your progress here and interrogate you when you arrived."

Ryder swore loudly. While he had been electronically dogging Eva, her kidnappers had been dogging him. And now Eva was dead. A bitter taste filled Ryder's mouth. "Toss me your billfold."

The man produced a canvas billfold from his back pocket. He flung it onto the drive.

Ryder scooped it up, opened it, and saw an international driver's license in the name Tomás Lara. "Okay, Tomás. Is this about locating the Carnivore?"

"The Padre believed you or Eva Blake could say how to find him."

"Was it the Padre who had me doubled?"

Lara gave a slow nod. "You have powerful friends. It was a problem that they might go looking for you, so the Padre found a way to cover for a while that you were missing. But then you arrived a day early from Baghdad. The Padre did not have everything ready to snatch you." He gave Ryder an earnest look. "It is not necessary to shoot me. I will leave as soon as I fetch something from the Padre. It will be as if you and I never met."

Ryder gestured at Eva and the teenaged girl. "Unarmed. Innocent. No reason to kill them unless someone's afraid they'd identify you—or what you're taking. You're working for the snipers. Who are they?"

Sweat broke out on the man's forehead. "Eli Eichel hired me. He partners with his brother, Danny. They were the shooters. Eli is retired Kidon."

Ryder paused. He had expected the Carnivore to be the man's employer. Kidon was Mossad's highly regarded kill department, renowned for orchestrating successful wet jobs around the globe. And now a

Kidon-trained assassin and his brother had killed six people and Eva so they could get their hands on something the Padre was carrying.

"Keep searching," Ryder ordered.

Lara sat back down on his heels. He pulled a leather pouch from inside the Padre's coat. Using his teeth, he loosened the drawstring and spilled three leather bags onto his palm. He opened them. Each contained a chunk of limestone.

Ryder frowned. "What are they?"

"Eli said they are special rocks. See, there are marks on them." He turned one over.

Ryder recognized the symbols. Cuneiform writing. "How are you getting them to Eichel?"

"I am supposed to phone him. Then he will say where to meet."

Ryder considered. "Tell him to come here."

The man's eyebrows rose in fright. "They will kill me if I betray them."

"I'll kill you if you don't. Make the call. Put it on speakerphone."

As if in slow motion, Lara took out his cell and tapped numbers.

Ryder listened as a man with a deep bass voice answered: *"Shalom."* The low growl of a car engine sounded in the background.

Lara took a deep breath. *"Shalom.* I have the rocks. They are just as you said."

"You've done well. Walk out of the hunt club and turn left—"

Shoulders tensing, Lara interrupted, his voice quivering. "Come here. Please. It would be better than someone seeing me on the roadway."

The bass voice sharpened. "You're afraid. Why?"

Ryder caught Lara's gaze and stared hard at him.

Lara sighed. "There are many dead people. Much blood. More than I—"

"We'll be there soon." The connection went dead.

Lara pocketed his cell phone, his expression wretched.

"You're Jewish?" Ryder asked, remembering the exchanges of *Shalom.*

"Yes, from Bilbao. Most Basques are like the Padre—Catholic. But plain-door synagogues have always been around; you just have to know where to knock. There is an old Basque saying—we know who the Jews are because we used to be Jews."

Lara's being a rare Basque Jew would give Eli Eichel a powerful link to him.

Ryder nodded. "Put the rocks away."

As the man bent over to do so, Ryder quickly lifted his knee and slashed the heel of his boot down hard onto his skull. With a thick grunt, he toppled, unconscious. Ryder scooped up the limestone pieces, put them into their individual pouches, and then all into the larger leather pouch. He buttoned them into his peacoat's inside pocket.

Taking a deep breath, he walked over to Eva. She was on her right side, crumpled like a broken doll, her face turned away. A bullet had severed her carotid artery. Her head lay in a pool of freezing blood.

Breathing shallowly, he crouched and cupped her face in his hands. She was still warm. Steeling himself, he turned her face toward him. Her eyes were open, such a beautiful cobalt blue. Her chin was soft and round. Her lips full and sweet. He remembered the violent deaths of comrades, friends, and family. Of his fiancée. And now, Eva. His eyes burned with grief.

Gently releasing her, he started to get to his feet, then stopped. The sunlight reflected on her unblinking eyes in such a way he saw she was wearing contacts. Eva had never worn contacts. Puzzled, he studied her. He frowned. His heart rate accelerating, he cradled her head in his hands again and used his thumbs to feel around her cheeks, then around her lips. Her skin here was different from her cheeks, softer, more flexible.

Again he probed along her cheeks until he found a line, a subtle demarcation under his thumbs where one side of her seemed normal while the other was more dense, a bit rigid. He heard Tucker's voice in his mind: "The ME says the devices fit on snugly and are flexible, but when pressed they feel a little stiffer than human flesh." He pressed deeper until he found a slit, an opening, where the denser "skin" rose along the line of the natural skin. Using his fingernail, he tugged along the edge, slowly lifting up a rim of fake flesh. A prosthesis.

His gaze returned to her eyes. He pried off one of her contact lenses and stared at a pale blue eye. Not Eva's rich cobalt blue color. Not Eva. Not her.

He let out a long breath. Eva had been doubled, just as he had been. Lifting his head, he looked around at the bloody carnage and felt relief sweep through him. Somewhere Eva was alive.

16

As a cold wind swept down the timbered hills, Ryder looked at his watch. The snipers could arrive at any moment. Jumping up, he took out the tracker he had used to follow Eva's double and pried open the back. There it was, just as Tomás Lara had said—a paper-thin electronic bug the size of a shirt button.

He ran back to Lara, loosened the top laces of the unconscious man's boot, and pried open the lining. Sliding the bug inside, he pressed the lining back against the shoe and tightened the laces again.

Hustling from corpse to corpse, he looked for the tracker. At last he found it, a small handheld, under one of the fallen guards. Its miniature screen showed the bug as a motionless green dot, with data about longitude, latitude, and altitude. Now Ryder would be able to follow Lara electronically wherever he went.

Hefting Lara up onto his shoulder, he carried him to the Explorer, opened the rear door, and dumped him inside. He had the urge to beat the shit out of him, but he needed him to be able to talk when the snipers arrived.

He hunted through the vehicle and found rope under the front seat. He tied Lara's hands and feet. Checking his watch again, he swore. He had burned through ten minutes.

Picking up Lara's phone, he saw it was a disposable cell. He touched the MENU button and went to RECENT CALLS. The most recent had to have been to Eli Eichel, the sniper whom Lara had just phoned.

There was another number. Ryder dialed it. In moments he heard ringing—from a distant corpse. He ran, snatched the ringing phone from the dead man's hand, and answered the call. Now he had a line open between the two cells.

Putting Lara's cell on speakerphone, he slid it inside Lara's breast pocket. He held the other cell to his ear and aimed his voice at the one in the pocket.

He spoke in a normal voice: "One . . . two . . . three . . . four . . . five."

He smiled grimly. He could hear his voice with clarity. Now he should be able to listen to conversations between the snipers and Lara. He put the cell in the front pocket of his jacket where he could quickly access it.

Swinging on his backpack, Ryder scooped up one of the Uzis. It was not the semiautomatic version but instead its cousin, a far more efficient killer—a fully automatic weapon, illegal in the United States except for police and Class-3 dealers. The magazine was located in the grip assembly. He checked it—all twenty-five rounds were loaded. He grabbed two boxes of ammo from the back of the Explorer and shoved them into his backpack.

Slinging the Uzi over his shoulder, he gave a last look then sprinted past the limousine, around the line of juniper bushes, and back up into the forest. As he climbed, afternoon shadows spread black across the animal path and ice-covered stream. Winter birds chattered. Reaching the hilltop, he turned and looked back down on the scene of the massacre. For a moment he wondered who the dead women were and felt bad for their families.

The snipers had still not arrived.

He took out his Galaxy and dialed Tucker Andersen.

"What no-good are you up to now?" Tucker grumbled in greeting.

"Eva's been doubled, too," Ryder told him. "She wasn't at her condo, but there was blood and other evidence of a fight. I found her cell phone and a tracker there. It appeared she'd bugged herself so I could follow, and I did, to a place called the Esti Hunt Club." He described witnessing the slaughter and discovering prostheses on the woman whom he had thought to be Eva. "There was one survivor. He told me what we suspected—the Padre had planned to force me to reveal how to find the Carnivore. The strange thing is, the Carnivore wasn't the sniper. It was two other assassins—Eli and Danny Eichel. Apparently Eli Eichel was Kidon."

"First it's the Padre, then it's the Carnivore." Tucker's voice rose in frustration. "Now it's the Eichel brothers."

"Tell me about them."

"Eli is the leader. Early in his career, he tracked a key Iraqi scientist to Paris, slit his throat, stabbed him several times in the heart, and then made it look like a robbery gone bad—and the French police believed it. Just before that, Eli had gotten the scientist to reveal the location of Saddam's top-secret nuclear complex outside Baghdad. The result was, Eli got away without a trace, and a few days later the Israelis bombed the hell out of the installation. After several years, for no apparent reason, Eli left Mossad and began to freelance. Mossad handled it quietly. Losing someone as good as him is a bad outcome for an intelligence agency—unless, of course, the agency is using the former employee for off-the-books work. I've heard his brother, Danny, is strange but as gifted a sniper as his brother."

"I want photos of both. Every piece of information you have."

"I'll have Gloria assemble dossiers. What else did you learn?"

Ryder described the limestone pieces with the cuneiform symbols. "Lara didn't know what they were or meant, and I have no idea either."

"Eichel's just killed seven people to get them," Tucker said. "If he finds out you have them, he'll come after you."

"Probably. Do you want to send your people here to investigate, or are you going to wait for the locals?"

"I'll helicopter in a team," Tucker decided. "Where was Lara supposed to deliver the limestone pieces?"

"He's not delivering. Eichel is picking them up."

"I'll send backup for you."

"There's no time. You're too far away. And besides, I've bugged Lara so I can follow him, and I planted an open cell on him, too, to listen in on any conversations. He'll tell the Eichels about me, and I'm hoping they'll take him along to get as much as possible out of him. That way we can track them."

"I like it."

Ryder cocked his head, listening. The engine noise of a vehicle approaching the hunt club floated up the snowy hill.

"They're here," he told Tucker. "Before I go, I assume Eva's at the Farm. She needs to know what's happened and that she may be at risk. But if I call, they won't let me talk to her." Trainees at the Farm were incommunicado.

"I'll handle it," Tucker agreed. "Watch your back."

17

A light snowfall dusted the lawns and lampposts in Colonial Williamsburg. A tavern door swung open, and the aromas of strong ale and Virginia barbecue drifted out. Smiling and giving every evidence she was enjoying it all, Eva Blake moved with the throngs of tourists admiring the historic sights.

In truth, she was in field training, halfway through the CIA's six-month tradecraft school for spies at the Farm. Williamsburg was only a few miles away, which was why locals often served as unwitting participants in off-campus exercises.

A pair of enormous oxen plodded past, their bells jingling. Playing her role, Eva lifted her digital camera, joining other visitors as they snapped pictures. Then she turned and took more photos, this time of actors in period costumes and, finally, a row of picturesque houses with tall dormer windows.

Angled as she was, Eva again glimpsed the silver-haired woman a half block behind, pushing a baby carriage. The woman gave every appearance of being a grandmother taking her infant grandchild for an outing, except the buggy probably held a lifelike doll. Eva believed the woman was surveilling her. In Farmspeak, the woman was a shadow. And she was good at it, no doubt retired FBI or CIA.

Eva crossed the street. She wore a short brown wig over her long red hair, a quilted thermal coat, and flat-heeled black boots. With no makeup and her sensible clothes, she was more likely to be ignored than to be identified as a spy-in-training.

She repressed a smile. Her life was so different from when she was a curator at the Getty Museum, in Los Angeles. In those days there were gala fund-raisers, candlelit dinners to convince rich collectors to loan art, and of course the constant navigation through the piranha-infested waters of international museum work. She had loved it. But then it was the culmination of years of pulling herself up from her back-alley poor childhood, her alcoholic family, and her teenaged years as a pick-pocket. When you finally turned your life around, everything you accomplished was precious.

As she passed a bay window, Eva saw in the reflection the silver-haired woman cross to her side of the street. Eva did not change her pace or demeanor. Her job was to lull the woman with the normalcy of her own behavior, and at the same time to memorize the woman's face, clothing, choice of coffee and wine and chocolates—whatever details she could gather—for the report she must write tonight.

Passing a bookstore, she strolled into Merchants Square. All of the quaint buildings in the square had the style of the 1700s but were built in the 1900s. She was tired, done. She wanted to go back to the motel and have a long, hot shower. The problem was, her shadow had to be the first to quit. Then she spotted an unusual sight—a video store. She stared a moment. The store gave her an idea.

She pushed open the door. A bell tinkled. She paused near the cash register, viewing the videos under CLASSICS. The bell tinkled again. In the reflection of the glass counter she saw it was not her tail, but an older man in a shearling coat. She felt a surge of hope. Maybe the silver-haired woman had finally had enough and left.

No such luck. The bell sounded again, and this time it was the shadow pushing the baby carriage. Keeping her expression neutral, Eva headed

toward the rear of the video store. She glanced at titles in DRAMA, HOR-
ROR, and COMEDY as if she might want to rent one. And then she spotted
the sign she had hoped to find. It was overhead, small, discreet: ADULT
ENTERTAINMENT. Listening, she heard the wheels of the baby buggy
behind her.

Without a backward glance, Eva pushed through a beaded curtain
and entered a small room where the surrounding walls and a central
floor-to-ceiling rack displayed movies advertising titillating titles with
a variety of bold Xs. Bulbous naked breasts, steel chains, and black
leather beamed out at her. There was no one in sight. She hurried around
the central stack—no one was there either.

Running to the end, Eva rearranged movies so she could see through
a small opening back to the room's curtained entrance. When the cur-
tains rustled, she peeked out. The woman was backing in, pulling the
baby carriage. She stopped, leaving the carriage on the far side of the
curtain, one hand firmly on the handle. Her actions had just confirmed
two of Eva's suspicions—she was definitely her shadow, and she did not
want to be seen taking an infant into a video store's dirty-movie room.
Like Eva, she was not supposed to draw attention to herself.

The woman looked up and stared at a wall poster of a naked man
and woman sporting spiked dog collars, then at a couple wearing cel-
lophane G-strings. For a brief moment, her face darkened and she
gazed around as if she wanted to say something loudly. But breaking
cover was against the rules for her, too. She stood there another heart-
beat, trapped. Finally, she turned and left, the carriage's wheels sounding retreat.

Eva took a deep breath and chuckled. The woman might decide to
wait for her outdoors. Still, the temperature was dropping, and the
woman must be as tired as Eva. Peering out between the strands of the
beaded curtain, Eva assessed the store. She did not see the woman or
the buggy. She waited five minutes then walked back, stopping at the
THRILLER shelves.

The man in the shearling coat came to stand beside her and run his
fingers across a list of titles. His shoes were lizard-skin tasseled loafers.
His coat was three-quarter length, a pale bone color, beautifully made.

It must have cost at least three thousand dollars. His horn-rimmed eyeglasses sat solidly on his large Roman nose. His thick gray hair was artfully tousled. A dapper older man, he appeared relaxed and confident in his expensive coat and shoes. As sweat misted his forehead, he unbuttoned his coat, probably to cool off.

Amused, she realized she was assessing him just as she did her shadows. And then she saw he was watching, too—but other people.

"Tucker Andersen sends his regards," he said. His lips had barely moved, and his face remained in profile as he continued to face the shelves.

His quiet voice seemed to float on the air a few seconds before Eva computed he had spoken to her.

"Don't look directly at me," he continued. "You realize you've given Gretchen Hilton cardiac arrest. How she ever lasted in the field twenty years is beyond me. She'll get even with you, though. You can expect descriptive words like *unsavory* and *voyeur* and *sophomoric antics* about you in her report. Of course, there are some who will be delighted by her discomfort."

"Who are you?"

He slid the movie he had been examining back into its slot. "Frank Smith. That's my real name. I understand you're operating under the alias Debora Lane. Nice name. Let's go outside and walk while we talk. That way we'll minimize the annoyance of eavesdroppers, busybodies, and professional spooks like ourselves." Without waiting for her response, he walked past the counter and out the glass door.

Eva snapped up a *Washington Post* from a stack on the counter and paid the cashier. Pausing at the door, she scanned the sidewalk and trees. Seeing no sign of her shadow, she left the store, too. She did not bother to look for Frank Smith; if he were serious about talking with her, he would find her.

She turned back the way she had come to retrieve her rental car—all the trainees were required to use rental cars, at government expense. They were useful for changing identities and losing tails.

Before she had walked twenty feet, Frank Smith stepped out from the side of a building. How had he managed to hide himself so completely?

She turned to face him.

He gave an enormous smile. "Ah, yes, the Farm. By now you no doubt have done paramilitary training and conquered that ridiculous obstacle course. I assume you've created a bomb using Clorox, although I've never been certain exactly why we needed to know that—"

Eva walked toward him. As she forced a smile, she let her ankle turn just enough that she stumbled. Falling into him, she pressed *The Washington Post* against his chest. Hidden by the newspaper, her hand flew under his shearling coat, found a wallet, and with two fingers confiscated it.

Grinning, he grabbed her elbows, supporting her.

"I'm so sorry." She straightened. "I'm usually not so clumsy." The wallet was now safely hidden under the newspaper.

"On the contrary," he said genially as he guided her down the sidewalk. "That was an expert dip. I'd heard you were a pickpocket in your youth. You must've been quite successful, if that maneuver on me was any indication. Now you'll see I'm not carrying any additional papers under another name, and the ones in your hand are in order. Please do check."

Eva fought to keep surprise from her face, and annoyance. The only other person to make her had been Tucker Andersen, but then he, like Frank Smith, had been forewarned.

"I intend to." She kept her tone businesslike. Tucking the newspaper under her arm, she opened the leather wallet. Inside were credit cards, a Virginia driver's license, CIA identification, and a membership card in the Westwood Country Club in Vienna, Virginia.

"I'm a golfer," he explained, indicating the country club card. "Because of the sort of work we do, I've been fortunate to play some of the best courses on the planet. Of course, my favorite is St. Andrews. Scotland, you know." He rubbed his gloved hands together in delight. "And the whiskey is like velvet."

She handed him his wallet. He talked a lot but said little. "Why are you here?" she asked.

"Tucker Andersen needs you for a job. He's cleared it with the Farm, and I was ordered to collect you. Your supervisor is sending someone to retrieve your rental. I'll drive us to the airport. We're to wait there, ready to fly off at a moment's notice, when Tucker sends word where we're to meet him."

An excited thrill coursed through Eva. She owed Tucker. Her life in the museum world had exploded when her husband had betrayed her, lied to her, and used her. In the end, she had gone to prison for a crime she had not committed. But Tucker had offered her a reprieve because he needed her expertise in illuminated manuscripts. During the mission, she was able to prove her innocence. At the same time, she had discovered she had a talent for clandestine work, and that it gave her life meaning, a reason to go on. When the mission was over, she asked to join the CIA. The only problem was, she had fallen a little in love with Judd Ryder, and Judd wanted nothing to do with the CIA or any covert agency. She closed her eyes a moment, shaking off the hurt.

"I've not been told what it's about." He shook his head in disgust, giving her the impression he hated being kept out of the loop. If so, he was in the wrong profession.

Eva found her cell phone, a disposable one issued by the Farm.

Smith saw her. "Tucker has a new number." He relayed it. "Go ahead, call him. Might as well get it straight from the horse's mouth. No, no. Really. My feelings won't be hurt. Tucker will tell you exactly what I've told you."

Eva studied Frank Smith. Screw his feelings. She tapped the numbers onto the keypad. Lifting the cell to her ear, she listened to the ring. Soon Tucker's voice came on in a recording: "I can't talk now. Leave your name, number, day, and time, and I'll get back to you as soon as I can."

She left a message for Tucker, confirming she wanted the assignment.

18

Washington, D.C.

Tucker Andersen had spent much of the afternoon at his desk, going through Catapult mission reports. After the phone call from Judd Ryder, he sat motionless, hands splayed on his desktop, mulling what Judd had said about the Padre, Eli Eichel, limestone chunks with cuneiform writing, and a murdered woman who had been impersonating Eva. Finally he picked up his phone again and made a call.

"David R. Erickson," a strong voice answered.

"It's Tucker Andersen, David. I need a helicopter, and I need it fast for a short trip into Maryland. It has to carry a dozen people and medium-sized equipment. No big machinery. Can you do it?"

Erickson was a top "scavenger" in Langley's Support to Mission team, which built and operated CIA facilities, created and maintained secure communications, managed the CIA phone company, and hired, trained, and assigned officers to every directorate. As far as Tucker was concerned, he was a magician. Erickson found the unfindable—supplies, equipment, and personnel—often languishing unused and forgotten.

"It's your lucky day. A couple of choppers I liberated yesterday just arrived at Langley from Andrews." Ten miles southeast of Washington, Andrews Air Force Base was not only home to *Air Force One* and several air commands, it was the CIA's transfer point for VIPs and persons of interest. "One of the choppers is a Bell 412. Should work perfectly for what you need, and it's free until tomorrow. You lead too boring a life, Tucker. I'll call you with the details."

Tucker hung up and went to his coat rack. A knock sounded on his door. "Enter."

It was Bash Badawi again, wiry and casual in jeans and a black short-sleeved T-shirt. He watched Tucker put on his sports jacket. "Leaving?" he asked. "Aren't you the one who complains about being lashed to your desk?"

"I'm going down the hall to see Bridgeman," Tucker told him. "What do you want?"

"The same thing as the last time—something to do. How about letting me buy you a drink? You can tell me what you have going on."

"I may have a job for you," Tucker decided. "Wait here." He marched through the doorway and down the corridor.

In the reception area, Gloria was busy at her computer.

Tucker stood in front of her desk. "I need an audience."

"My, my. I'll check." She punched the intercom button. "Tucker would like to see you."

Scott Bridgeman's baritone announced, "Send him in."

Her eyebrows rose above her glasses. "I do believe you've charmed him."

"Hardly." Tucker headed for the Catapult chief's door.

Scott Bridgeman was tired and frustrated. He'd had a long day that had included another run-in with his number two, Tucker Andersen. The old spymaster behaved as if it were still the freewheeling days of the Cold War, before Twitter, Instagram, and Wikileaks could blow a black op and the careers of those involved into smithereens. Tucker's recklessness was going to backfire sooner or later and spray shit that could seriously hurt Bridgeman.

Bridgeman watched Tucker walk in the door. The old man's gray hair lay in an untidy fringe at the back of his bald head, and his chinos and sports jacket were, as usual, rumpled.

Controlling his irritation, Bridgeman gestured. "Have a seat."

Tucker dropped into a chair and crossed his legs. "You have word about the week Judd Ryder needs to investigate his imposter?"

"When I asked the ME for seven days," Bridgeman said, "he acted as if what I really wanted was to rip out his organs. So the answer is no. Ryder doesn't get a week. However, I did manage to get him three days. Be grateful for it. And he'd damn well better turn up something so I don't look like a jackass for going to bat for him."

"Maybe that'll be enough to figure out the basics of what's going on." For a moment Tucker looked appropriately appreciative. "I've got good news. The immediate problem between the Padre and the Carnivore is over." He described a two-sniper kill at a private hunt club in Maryland, the facts of which he said were Judd Ryder's eyewitness account. "The good end is we no longer owe the Padre anything, since he's dead. The bad end is he's no longer available as a source. On the other hand, it's possible there's evidence at the kill site about what was really going on between the Padre, the Carnivore, and the Eichel brothers. Eli Eichel was a notable Kidon."

"Eli Eichel, the Choirmaster," Bridgeman said.

"Yes. Which means we've got confirmation that international assassins are operating on U.S. soil. Second, there were pieces of cuneiform writing that the Eichels wanted from the Padre, which appears to be why the Padre and his people were killed."

Bridgeman felt a moment of relief. "So it could be something personal after all."

"Maybe. Maybe not. Third, one of the dead women was impersonating Eva Blake. Blake is ours, a trainee at the Farm."

Bridgeman gave a slow nod. "That's bad. Were there any other witnesses besides Ryder?"

Tucker shook his head. "No, just Ryder."

Bridgeman sighed. "What do you want?"

"A helicopter and a team to go to the site to do a thorough investigation."

"All right. Do it. But if you find nothing at the hunt club, this nonsense ends. We use common sense and walk away from Judd Ryder and some crazy internecine war among assassins. You go immediately to the ME and apologize so he can act like the public servant he is and inform the public."

"I understand."

But Bridgeman heard hesitation. He glared into his employee's eyes. "You've already ordered up a chopper, haven't you?"

Tucker gazed back evenly. "Of course."

Bridgeman fought an impulse to deck Andersen. "You have my authorization for it, and for the team," he said calmly. "But I want their report the instant you have it. And 'instant' means *instant*! Now, get the hell out of here."

19

Tucker hurried back to his office. When he opened the door, Bash was standing in front of the big window, hands clasped behind him, staring out. Turning to face Tucker, he had a hopeful look on his face.

"You've got a job for me?" he asked.

"Yes, you're leading a Langley investigative team. Sit down. I'll fill you in."

For the next half hour Tucker paced his office. To give Bash context, he described what had happened since Judd's phone call that morning describing his double and the double's murder. Bash stared off into space, sometimes closing his eyes, occasionally asking questions.

"In particular, I want hard drives, handwritten notes, GPS records. Anything that will help us understand the situation," Tucker finished. "Go give Erickson a call about that helicopter."

With a nod, the young spy vanished out the door.

Sitting down, Tucker called Dorothy Kunz. They had met when both were serving at the Athens station. While Tucker had stayed in the

Clandestine Service, Dorothy had transferred to various directorates. For the past five years, she had been chief at the Farm.

Kunz had a warm voice. "Yeah, Tucker. I know you want something. You never call unless you do. Someday I'm going to get you drunk again and pry all your secrets out of you."

He smiled. They had spent one liquor-filled evening together, but no secrets were shared. "I always thought you got me drunk because you wanted my body."

She laughed. "What are you looking for, Tucker?"

"You've got a trainee there I—"

"That would be Eva Blake. You were involved in us signing her up."

"I need to talk with her."

For the first time there was hesitation in Kunz's voice. "I'll check. I'm putting you on hold."

"Sure." Tucker turned to stare out his window at a line of barren maple trees growing in front of a wood-stake fence at the end of the Catapult property. Somehow they made him think of a line of soldiers, steadfast, ready for anything.

"Eva Blake has been in field training in Williamsburg." Kunz's voice sounded in his ear. "I thought I remembered, and of course I was correct—she phoned in not long ago to say she had a family emergency and had to leave immediately. She refused to give details. She said it was a personal matter, and she didn't know when she'd be able to come back."

Tucker sat up straighter. "That doesn't sound like Eva."

"Perhaps not, but it's what she did and said," Kunz confirmed. "It's a pity, because she was excelling."

"Which one of your people saw her last?"

"Gretchen Hilton. I checked with her. She was Blake's shadow today. She says Blake was doing a good job until she pulled a too-cute trick. She led Gretchen into the adult entertainment section of a video store while Gretchen supposedly had an infant with her. Gretchen was writing her up for it. Amusing, of course. Shows Blake's resourcefulness."

"Was Blake in touch with any of the other trainees?"

"We sent out queries. They said no. What's this about, Tucker?"

"Blake's been doubled. The double's dead now. Murdered."

"And you're not going to tell me more?" Kunz asked.

"We don't know anything more yet."

"Maybe Blake was being honest with us—she's got a problem in her family, and she's gone to take care of it. End of story."

Tucker nodded to himself. "Has the murder board met about her yet?" The "murder board" was a group of Farm instructors who decided, among other things, whether a trainee had done something that indicated they were unfit.

"They're investigating now," she said. "They'll discuss what they learn later today."

Tucker sighed. "Let me know what happens."

Ending the connection, he turned in his chair to peer out again at the long line of maple trees. Instead of soldiers ready for anything, for a moment they looked dead.

20

Montgomery County, Maryland

No other cars were in sight when Eli Eichel turned the gray Dodge van onto the drive leading into the Esti Hunt Club. He was smiling to himself, eager. Soon he would have three more limestone pieces.

"We're late?" Danny asked. He sat slumped in the passenger seat, playing a video game on his iPad.

As usual, it was just the two of them, the Eichel brothers. There was a time when Eli would have resented the loneliness of it, wished for a wife again, for friends.

"No, we're fine," he told Danny.

"I like it here."

"I know, Danny."

"There's no color." Danny looked up long enough to sweep his big hand across the windshield, indicating the grayscape of barren trees standing in white snowfields.

"Color depresses you," Eli said.

Danny sighed with pleasure. He was understood, and Eli knew that was all that mattered to his younger brother now.

Small and wiry, Eli had Levantine eyes and olive skin, and could pass for a Middle Easterner or a Creole, a southern Italian or a Corsican. He took pride in his physical advantages and used them constantly. He was sixty-five years old.

Danny was a decade younger, tall and hulking, with a thick body and an overlarge bony face anchored by a protruding jaw. When he was a child, he had been teased brutally for being so much larger than the other boys. In truth, the teasing was triggered by his lack of interest in them. He would not join their war games or soccer or other sports where his unusual size could help them win. Still he came home with bloodied cheeks, bruises on his back and legs, because he had let them beat him, unable to comprehend their emotions or confusion, himself unable to martial anger or outrage against them. He failed reading and history in school. He did not bar mitzvah. But within the family it was recognized he was blessed, and the rabbi agreed. Danny had one enormous God-given talent—he could build and fix anything. In particular, his eye-hand coordination was a marvel.

Ahead stood the club's lodges and cabins with their steep roofs. The white Explorer SUV and the black Cadillac limousine were parked in the same places they had seen from their sniper lair, and the corpses were lying on the drive in positions the living could not sustain. It was like all other kill zones, eerie.

"Wow." Danny stared out the windshield again. "We did all of them within seconds."

His eyes bright, Danny leaned forward, grasping the dashboard. He always got charged up by their kills, and this had been a highly accurate and efficient one. They had used the best rifles—Silent Assassins, the nickname of the British-made L115A3 Long Range Rifle, renowned for taking out insurgents in Afghanistan a mile away. Today's firing conditions had been nearly perfect, with clear visibility. The wind had died down just before the Padre had appeared. Only the low temperature could have been a problem, but they had accounted for it.

Eli stopped the van. Danny and he grabbed their AK-47s and climbed out.

Danny lumbered to the nearest corpse.

Eli assessed the silent buildings, the juniper hedges, the trees. There was no sign of his inside man, Tomás Lara. "Tomás!" he shouted. "Tomás, come out! ¿Como esta?"

Suddenly there was the noise of thumping. The SUV rocked, followed by shouts from inside.

Danny peered in a window. "Here he is, Eli. His feet are kicking, and he's yelling. He thinks he's angry, but I think he's frightened." At the age of twelve, Danny had been diagnosed with autism. Over the years, he had taught himself to assess expressions, skin colors, and eye contractions and dilations to deduce others' emotions.

"Thanks, Danny."

Nodding, Danny stepped back, and Eli opened the door. Lara lay on the floor, hands and feet bound. A big man, now he looked small.

Eli glared down. "What happened?"

"It was that bastard Judd Ryder." The man's eyes blinked rapidly. "He jumped me. He was going to kill me. I—"

"Where are the pieces of the tablet?"

"Ryder stole them. I could not stop him."

Eli glanced at his brother. "Check the Padre. See if he still has them."

With a nod, Danny trotted off.

Eli continued to study his man. The problem with buying someone's loyalty was you could never pay enough. There was always the risk someone would offer more or threaten them so much the money lost importance.

Danny reappeared. "The Padre doesn't have the pieces."

"Thank you, Danny," Eli said. He leaned his AK-47 against the SUV, took out his jackknife, and sawed the ropes that bound Lara's wrists and ankles.

"Muchas gracias." Pushing himself up, Lara leaned back against the vehicle's wall, rubbing one wrist then the other.

"Did Ryder know about the limestone pieces?" Eli asked, keeping his tone mild.

"Yes, of course. Why else would he take them?"

"How did he find out about them?"

"He did not say."

"Did he know about me?"

Lara shook his head violently. "No, no!"

"His information about the pieces came from somewhere. From the Carnivore, Seymour, Krot, or perhaps it was from the Padre himself?"

Lara looked away. "I think it must have been the Padre who told him. Yes, the Padre."

Eli felt an itch at the bottom of his spine. He turned to Danny. "Is he lying?"

Danny nodded. "It wasn't the Padre."

Lara's eyes widened. Sweat broke out on his forehead. "Then I . . . I must have been the one who said it. But I can help you find him. The Padre had him investigated. Everything that was learned is on the laptop in the main room of the lodge." He pointed with his thumb.

Without being asked, Danny broke into a lumbering run.

Watching Danny's back, Lara said eagerly, "I just remembered that Ryder must know something about the Carnivore. He asked whether the Padre was trying to find the Carnivore."

Eli said nothing. He simply stared down at Lara.

The man adjusted his sitting position. A drop of sweat slid down his temple.

There was the sound of running feet on the drive. Danny was returning.

"This was the only computer in the lodge." Danny showed them a Toshiba laptop.

Eli took it and handed it to Lara. "Find the material about Ryder."

The man opened the machine and searched. "Here is the file. You will see many pictures." He offered up the laptop.

Looking at the screen, Eli saw Ryder's name with documents listed beneath it—early childhood, college, the army, retirement.

"Put it in our van," he told Danny.

Again Danny left.

"How did the Padre find out Ryder or Blake might lead him to the Carnivore?"

Wiping sweat from his face, Lara was eager to help: "It was an equity kingpin named Martin Chapman. His relationship with Ryder is written in the report."

"Where is Chapman?"

"He has a horse farm here in Maryland." Lara related the location and described it.

Eli felt an odd ache and the beginning of a thrill. He aimed his AK-47.

Horror radiated from the man's face. *"No! Madre de Dios, no!"*

With a smile, Eli fired a burst into the traitor's heart. Blood exploded, spraying the SUV's seats, windows, and floor. Not bothering to close the door, he jogged away. The cold air felt fresh and sleek, a slipstream.

When he reached the van, Danny was waiting in the passenger seat.

"Call Karel," Eli told him. He jumped behind the steering wheel and tossed Danny his iPhone. "Tell him he can sanitize the place now. You and I are driving east, to see a man named Martin Chapman. He's going to help us find Judd Ryder."

21

Ryder stood in the snow high above the hunt club complex, listening to AK-47 gunfire reverberate across the hills. At the same time it sounded from the cell phone in his hands. Before that, he had heard the entire conversation between Tomás Lara and Eli Eichel, sent from the cell he had hidden in Lara's front jacket pocket. Now it appeared Lara was dead, and the Eichels were not taking his corpse with them.

Shaking his head with frustration, Ryder closed the phone and slogged off, leaving the hunt club behind as he headed through the pines and down the other side of the hill toward where he had left his pickup.

He phoned Tucker Andersen.

"Have you heard from Eva?" Tucker's tone was worried.

"Not a word. What's happened?"

"She called the Farm this afternoon to say she had a family emergency and didn't know when she'd be back. It could be the truth, but I'm not ready to believe it. I've sent a man to watch her house. I phoned her parents. They said they hadn't heard from her in a month. Does she have a boyfriend?"

"Not that I know of." Ryder kept his voice even while emotions pumped through him.

"I'm sorry about this, Judd. I know you're fond of her. It's entirely possible I'm wrong to be concerned, and she's fine. Now tell me what happened there."

Ryder paused, collecting himself. "First, the limestone pieces aren't random—they're part of a tablet, or at least that's what Eli Eichel said. I checked the three pieces I have. They fit together and seem to form a corner, but of course I don't have a clue what the cuneiform says."

"Just one more reason to wish Eva were here."

"Yes, maybe she could read it. Here's a shocker—Eli Eichel said the Carnivore, Seymour, and Krot know about the limestone pieces, too. Who are Seymour and Krot?"

Tucker swore. "This is getting to be a *Who's Who* of assassins. They're old war horses who got their starts during the Cold War, too. Seymour has used many names. He's formerly Islamic Jihad. Same with Krot. He's ex-KGB."

"Swell. I wonder whether they want the tablet pieces, too."

"And how many more pieces there are, and who has them?"

Ryder was halfway down the hill. "Before he left, Eichel shot his undercover man to death."

"Did he take the body?"

"No, dammit. I can't listen to any more conversations, and of course the bug's still with the corpse, which means I can't track the Eichel brothers either. I got the license plate number." He related it. "They stole a laptop from one of the lodges because it had background information the Padre's people had dug up about how to find me. Probably about how to find Eva and you, too. So now they're going to the source—the man who told the Padre we worked with the Carnivore—"

"Martin Chapman," Tucker said instantly.

"Yes, that arsehole." He heard the fury in his voice, then the sense of irreplaceable loss. It does not matter what others say, what the criminal evidence against your father is, if he put you on his knee and listened to you when you were young, took you fishing, never missed any of your football games, and told you he was proud of you even when you rebelled by choosing a different direction for your life, your father is still your father, and Judd had loved his. But his father had also been a member of a group of international businessmen led by Martin Chapman that had not only skirted the law but broken it many times, making large personal fortunes in the process. Still, his father had had a line he would not cross—he would not hurt U.S. security. When he discovered terrorist money might be flowing through the Library of Gold, the organization that was central to the powerful group, he had told Tucker. As a result, Chapman had ordered his death.

"You're planning to go to Chapman's place," Tucker realized.

Ryder took a deep breath, controlling his rage. "I figure it'll take me a couple of hours to get there. I'll be in touch."

22

Tucker Andersen was sitting at his desk at Catapult, reading the file on Danny and Eli Eichel, when the phone call from Bash came in. "Where are you?" he asked.

"At the hunt club." Bash's tone was strong and angry. "We were too late. The club's sanitized. No cars, no weapons, no blood, no bodies. No breathing people either. The place looks like any well-tended sports club after a snowstorm. We searched the buildings and didn't find any computers, files, records, or any sort of information to tell us more about the people that supposedly died here."

"Jesus." A knot formed in Tucker's chest. "What else?"

"I made some phone calls and tracked down the company that maintains the place. The manager said they were sent in a few days ago to put it in order. All their business with the owner is handled by telephone. His name is Sabino Zaragosa."

"That's the Padre's name."

"No surprise there. So now I've got a bunch of pissed-off Langley people on my hands. They want to know why in hell Catapult has wasted their time and government money sending them out here on a wild-arse chase."

Tucker hesitated. Not finding anything incriminating at the hunt club gave Bridgeman the excuse he needed to withdraw support for Judd and the investigation, and to tar Tucker with a very thick brush. Frowning, he sorted through events over the past few hours. That was when he remembered Judd had said he had planted an open cell phone and a tracking bug on Tomás Lara.

"I've got to make another call. I'll get back to you." Tucker hung up and dialed.

Judd's voice was tense. "Yes?"

"Check your tracker for the bug you left on Lara. I want to know where his corpse is."

"Shit. The body isn't at the hunt club? Hold on. I have to activate the tracker again." In seconds, he was back. "The bug's either been turned off or it's dead. In any case, there's no signal. What in hell's going on, Tucker?"

"The hunt club's been sanitized. I was hoping the cleaners had missed the bug you planted so we could figure out where the corpses and other evidence were taken. But then, hope is the last bastion of the frustrated."

Ryder sighed with disgust. "I bet I drove past the cleanup vehicles. About a mile from the hunt club's entrance, a flatbed truck carrying a street sweeper was parked nose to tail with a sanding truck that had a snowplow fronting it. I didn't connect any of it to the hunt club."

"The Eichels did a hell of a job covering their goddamn bloody tracks." Ending the connection, Tucker spun his chair around to his file cabinet, opened the bottom drawer, and took out a bottle of Jack Daniel's. As he poured himself a shot and downed it, warm memories of his previous boss filled his mind. At the end of an aggravating day they would meet in one of their offices to philosophize, analyze missions, and share a drink. Unlike his current boss, she had understood the terrible danger of being risk-averse in intelligence work. If you followed hidebound rules while facing an enemy who had no rules, you inevitably met disaster. She was not afraid to go where the outcome was uncertain.

What was driving Catapult's new boss bat-shit was that Tucker still operated that way—because it worked.

He got to his feet and paced. If he told Bridgeman the hunt club had been sanitized, Bridgeman would say the hunt club had never been the scene of a sniper kill, because there was no evidence—just Judd Ryder's oral report. And Bridgeman did not trust Ryder.

Tucker turned on his heel and marched back across the room. On the other hand, if he delayed telling Bridgeman, he would have a chance to prove Judd was right about the hunt club, about being doubled, about Eva's being doubled, and that international assassins were operating in-country—which was what scared the bejesus out of him.

He paused at his desk, poured himself some more Jack. Drinking it, he could almost see his former boss in the shadows of his office, hear her voice: "Dammit, Tucker, you know Bridgeman isn't going to give you a break on this. Do what you have to do."

Nodding to himself, he sat and dialed Bash Badawi, picturing his aggravation as he stomped around the hunt club.

Bash answered at the first ring. "What do you want me to do, Tucker?"

"Fly your people home to Langley," Tucker ordered. "Tell the pilot his next assignment is to ferry me back to Maryland, but to a different destination—Merrittville. If he needs to refuel, he should do it as soon as he lands."

There was no hesitation. "Want some help in Merrittville?"

"Not this time." Getting himself into trouble by bucking Bridgeman was one thing; getting his people into trouble was an entirely different matter.

"Merrittville," Bash repeated thoughtfully. "Doesn't Martin Chapman have a place near there?"

"Sometimes your memory is too good."

"Are you going to Chapman's? Will the Eichels and Judd be there, too?"

"Yes to your questions, but you don't get any more. And keep what I just told you to yourself. I'll see you at Langley." Feeling marginally better to have made a decision, he drank more Jack. Then he dialed Judd Ryder again.

"What in hell's going on, Tucker?" Judd wanted to know.

"I'm flying out to join you. Are you at Chapman's yet?"

"I'm about fifteen miles away. Why are you coming?"

"I'll fill you in when I get there. I'll be bringing dossiers on the Padre, the Carnivore, Eli Eichel, Krot, and Seymour. I'm hoping there's a clue in there about this situation. I'm commandeering one of Langley's choppers. There's an old airfield outside town. Meet me there."

After giving Judd directions, Tucker capped the bottle, set it back inside the file cabinet drawer, and put on his heavy wool overcoat. He strode out the door and down the hall. He could hear the tapping of Gloria at work on her computer keyboard.

He stopped at her desk.

She looked up. Her forehead crinkled as she saw his overcoat. "You're going out again? It's not on your schedule."

"I'm impressed you still think I have a schedule, and that if I had one, I could stick to it."

"Being an optimist keeps me young." The smile lines around her eyes deepened.

"I like getting old. I'm good at it. I've got the printouts of the reports on the Carnivore and the Eichel brothers that you assembled. Now I need ones on the Padre, Krot, and Seymour."

"No kidding. Krot and Seymour, too. But don't worry. I'm not going to ask."

"Good. And I want up-to-the-minute satellite photos of Martin Chapman's horse farm and the country around it. Building plans, too, if you can get them. Send everything to my secure handheld. I need all of it in an hour."

She took off her glasses and stared at him. "Where are you going?"

"To Langley."

"And then you'll be back?"

"Not until late." He glanced around. "When the chopper I requisitioned for Bash returns to Langley I'm going to nab it and head north, too. Judd and I are planning a surprise visit to Martin Chapman. It's better Bridgeman not know anything about any of this, at least not yet."

She nodded. "So Bash's report about the hunt club was bad news?"

"Like the *Titanic*."

ELI EICHEL

[T]hose who do not have power assassinate to get it, and those who have power assassinate to keep it.

—*The Assassination Business,* by Richard Belfield

23

Montgomery County, Maryland

Eli Eichel stopped the Dodge van at a reinforced wrought-iron entrance gate. Above it arched an ornate wrought-iron sign:

The Chapman Farm
Arabian Horses

He rolled down his window and touched the intercom button.

A voice answered instantly: "Good evening, sir. What can we do for you?"

"I'm a friend of the Padre's," Eli lied. "I'm here to give Mr. Chapman an update on Judd Ryder."

"I'll relay your message."

Closing his window, Eli looked up, studying the place. On the other side of the gate, a wide drive climbed past mounds of snow and picturesque wood corrals to a plantation-style mansion that was as white and fancy as a wedding cake. Fronted by stately columns, the house boasted railed porches across each of its three stories. The compound was highly secure, with closed-circuit cameras and electrified concertina wire atop the granite wall that surrounded the property. A sentry dressed in white patrolled among the buildings. Unless an outside light shone directly on him, the man was almost impossible to see against the snow. Soon Eli spotted a second guard, also wearing white head-to-toe.

"I estimate the mansion is twelve thousand square feet." Danny was gripping his knees, staring through the windshield. "Since it's fundamentally a box, it's easy to do the math. Would you like me to tell you the size of the other buildings, too?"

"Yes, I'd be interested in that." Long ago Eli had given up trying to understand why Danny was fascinated by such things. In any case, the exercise would keep Danny occupied.

"I'll start with the next biggest building," Danny said. "The barn. It's ten thousand square feet—perhaps it contains a riding ring. After that is the garage. It's five thousand square feet. He must have several cars. Then there's . . ."

Eli stopped listening. When the voice sounded again from the intercom, he rolled down his window.

"Go to the main house," the voice ordered. "You'll be met and searched."

Eli drove the van up the slope, passing under bright lights.

"I can't take any weapons inside, can I?" Danny said.

"No. They'd just confiscate them if you tried. And we don't want any fights, at least not yet."

They parked at the top of the circular drive. As they climbed brick steps, the front door opened.

"Come in, sir. My name is Troy." The speaker was an enormous man probably in his early thirties, at least six foot five, broad-shouldered, narrow-hipped, and dressed in a dark green sweat suit. Weighing close to 250 muscular pounds, he carried an M4 and wore across his chest a bandolier crammed with rounds.

The bandolier was ridiculous overkill, Eli thought to himself. But then, it fit in with what Eli had learned about Chapman. Behind the big guard stood two more guards—older and smaller—also wearing green sweat suits and bandoliers, also carrying M4s. They frisked Eli and

Danny, then led them into a three-story foyer dominated by a life-size painting of an older man. His thick silver hair was brushed back in waves, crowning an unlined, untroubled face. There was something noble about his erect carriage and the directness of his gaze. From his research, Eli recognized him—Martin Chapman.

With Troy in the lead, they climbed a curving staircase to the second floor and turned down a corridor. The tables and chairs along the wainscoted walls appeared to be authentic antebellum.

Troy tapped on a paneled door. There was a soft *click,* indicating it had been unlocked from inside.

He pushed it open, gestured, and they entered a softly lit library. Thousands of leather-bound books peered down from three towering walls. As he looked up, Danny's breath exploded in small excited bursts, while Eli simply stared at the mass of volumes covered in deep brown, rich red, and glossy black leathers. It was a majestic sight. Exhibition cases stood around the room, also displaying leather-bound books.

Across the room, a tall man stood up behind a giant carved desk. He was the live version of the man in the painting. Behind him were French doors that opened onto the porch and the deepening twilight. He was dressed casually in wool trousers and a neatly tucked-in Pendleton shirt. His expression was stern.

"My name is Chapman." He walked toward them with the graceful gait of an athlete.

Eli shook the mogul's hand, noting the neutral grip, a sign of self-confidence; the insecure either gripped too hard or had no grip at all. "You've got quite a library here."

A flash of pleasure appeared on Chapman's face. "How do you know the Padre?"

"It'd be more useful to tell you what I know about you and Judd Ryder's father," Eli said. "For months you've been worried Ryder was going to come after you for killing him, which is why you've got such intense security." He gestured at the three guards who stood against the rear wall with their bandoliers and M4s.

Chapman laughed as if he had just heard a good joke. "You're a man who likes tall tales. I had nothing to do with the man's death. Tell me who you are. It's only fair, since you seem convinced you know a lot about me."

"My name is Eli Eichel, and this is my brother, Danny. I realize you can't easily terminate someone who's a threat to you, so we'll do it for you. All I need is help finding Ryder."

Danny had been ambling around the room, gazing at the walls of books. He announced to Chapman, "You have eleven hundred forty board feet of bookshelves."

Chapman's eyebrows rose in surprise. "How did you figure that out?"

"A simple calculation. Once you know how long a shelf is, you multiply it by the number of them on the wall, and that gives you the total for that wall. There are three walls of books, and all are of equal size, so the figure then must be tripled."

"I didn't see you measure any of the shelves," Chapman said. "How do you know how long they are?"

"It has to do with the waves." Danny's expression was almost doting; he had found an interested pupil. "I see three waves for every foot. Waves are pieces of air that wrinkle. So I just wait until I see the wrinkles. The farther I am from a line, the harder it is to see them, but if the light's decent and I have time to wait, I can be pretty accurate."

Chapman said nothing. He simply stared for a moment, then turned to Eli. "Is he an idiot savant?"

"No, autistic. What's really important is he's a gifted sniper."

Chapman's gaze narrowed. "Independent?"

"Yes, both of us, for more than thirty years. But we're comfortable with other means of assassination, too."

Chapman watched Danny continue to roam the room.

"What will he do next?" Chapman asked.

"If you'd like to know the wattage of your lightbulbs, individually or collectively, he can tell you—or the depth of your rugs, or the average width of your books, or how quickly he can use Krav Maga to kill the three men guarding your door." In Hebrew, *krav maga* meant "close combat." Brutal and efficient hand-to-hand combat, it was stressed at Mossad's two-year training course at their school in the city of Henzelia, near Tel Aviv.

Chapman gestured at Danny. "He's Mossad?"

"No, I was. After Henzelia, a few of us were sent to a special camp in the Negev Desert to become executioners. Bullets, blades, bombs, poison, the garrotte, and of course the body, especially the hands. After I resigned, I taught Danny everything I knew."

"And you resigned because—?"

"Danny had become a serial killer. He'd murdered three men in Tel Aviv and a woman in Jerusalem. He was fascinated by the mechanics of execution, but he needed to learn to do it right, and to make money at it. Otherwise he wasn't going to survive. I've always taken care of my little brother."

Danny slid a book out from one of the shelves. He balanced it on his fingertips as if his hand were a scale and he were weighing the book. His hands looked big enough to clasp cinder blocks, almost dwarfing the leather hardback.

"Is what your brother told me accurate, Danny?" Chapman asked.

"I like perfectly clean kill shots with minimum spray." Danny curled then flicked his fingers upward. The book flipped over and landed solidly again on his fingertips.

Chapman nodded to himself. He faced Eli. "You have my attention. Both of us know you don't want to eliminate anyone to please me. You need to find Judd Ryder for your own reasons."

"The answer is simple—Ryder stole from me. My brother and I were hired to scrub the owner of three pieces of a rare cuneiform tablet," Eli lied. "Instead, Ryder did the hit then swiped the pieces."

"Who did Ryder kill?"

"The Padre."

Chapman's pale eyebrows rose. "The Padre's dead?"

Eli suppressed a smile. "Yes, as well as his wife and the employees he brought with him."

A moment of terror flashed across the mogul's face. "If Ryder could get to the Padre—"

"It's more than likely he can get to you, too."

Chapman looked away. "He tried once. For some reason he changed his mind at the last minute."

Eli had not known that, but he could use it: "Now that he's bloodied himself with the Padre, whatever internal censor stopped him from doing you is gone. You're as good as dead."

The mogul asked stonily, "Where have you looked for him?"

"I sent people to his row house on Capitol Hill. His mother's estate in Chevy Chase. Eva Blake's place in Silver Spring. They talked to neighbors, but nothing useful developed. I understand he was close to Tucker Andersen, the CIA man." He was repeating the reports the Padre's men had turned in to describe their search.

"There's no way Ryder can get past my security." There was a long moment of silence as Chapman looked away, seeming to collect himself. "When you arrived, you acted as if the Padre were still alive. Either you were lying then—or you're lying now."

Eli smiled. "I said what was necessary to get inside to meet you. Danny, what do you think?"

His broad back to them, Danny had reached above his head to caress the thick gold lettering on a book spine. Without looking back at them, he said, "Mr. Chapman doesn't care whether you're lying. He just wants to liquidate Ryder. He should pay us a lot because he's so scared his spit is dry."

Eli chuckled.

Chapman was expressionless. "Let's be clear . . . you'll eliminate Ryder in exchange for information about where he is?"

"Absolutely. And I keep the cuneiform pieces."

"Done." Chapman walked to his desk, his stride long and purposeful. He checked his Rolodex and dialed. "Senator Leggate, please. Martin Chapman calling." The mogul tapped the toe of one of his boots on the parquet floor. "She's not? Patch me through to her cell." His tone grew cold as he continued, "Then as soon as she gets reception, tell her to call me." Chapman hung up, his expression irritated. "She's back in Colorado, meeting constituents in some remote mountain resort. She's due to helicopter into Denver in a couple of hours. She knows to return my calls quickly. She'll phone from the air."

"Why Senator Leggate?"

"The answer is Tucker Andersen. If anyone knows how to find Judd, it's usually Tucker. The two are close friends. Senator Leggate is on the Intelligence Committee. She doesn't have to guess where the bodies are buried at Langley. She'll have ways."

"Why didn't you contact her for the Padre when he was looking for Ryder?" Eli asked.

"How do you think he found out Ryder was in Iraq?"

Eli nodded. Contacts were everything, for both billionaires and assassins.

24

As a cool afternoon wind whipped across the tarmac, Eva Blake followed Frank Smith up the staircase into a Dash 8 twin-engine plane. Holding about thirty passengers, it had a standard configuration of a central aisle lined with rows of two seats on either side. Frank and she were the only passengers.

Frank closed and secured the door. There was a sudden hush, and for a moment Eva felt as if she were in a time capsule, suspended, waiting for the unknown. Suddenly she was nervous. For what exactly did Tucker want her?

Frank hung their coats in the forward closet. With a courtly gesture, he indicated she should precede him down the aisle. She chose a seat above the wing, and he sat across from her. Dressed in charcoal-gray wool slacks, a gray-and-white herringbone jacket, and a pale blue button-down shirt, he looked every bit the professor.

"How long have you been CIA, Frank?" She peeled off her brown wig, and her red hair tumbled to her shoulders. She sighed with relief. A wig was like wearing a heating pad shaped like a skullcap.

"Too long, and not long enough," Frank told her. "As a round figure, let's say thirty years. One of the greatest tragedies I've witnessed is that Langley's only famous spies seem to be the failures and the traitors. Pity, when so much crucial work is done by the vast majority who must remain unsung. Still, I'm not near my expiration date yet, so I hope to be in use long enough to see the public perception of Langley improve."

Eva studied him, the large elegant nose, the good bone structure, the solid body. There was something familiar about him. She watched his gestures, listened to the timbre of his voice.

"Here's a little insider intel." He waved his hand grandly, taking in the aircraft. "This is a Dash turboprop, as you no doubt noticed. If you were in Afghanistan a few years ago, you would've seen her or one of her sisters bristling with unusual antennae. That's because Langley was secretly using them for 'special' transportation. That's just between you and me and the exit row, of course."

She asked where he had been stationed and the operations on which he had worked. But no matter how she phrased her questions over the next few hours, she never got real answers from him. He seemed to be the ultimate spy—charming, anecdotal about irrelevant topics, and close-mouthed about what mattered. As they sat on the tarmac of the Williamsburg airport waiting for word from Tucker, the pilot served soft drinks and sandwiches. Frank worked on e-mail. She had no computer, but the pilot brought her newspapers and magazines. Thinking about what Tucker might have in mind for her, she scanned through them, noting that the bloody lead-up to the election of Iraq's next prime minister dominated the news.

At last the cockpit door opened, and the pilot walked toward them, carrying a satellite phone.

"We have a message from Tucker?" she asked eagerly.

Nodding, he touched the button that activated the speakerphone.

The voice was a woman's, and her tone was authoritative. "My name is Jane Squires. Tucker says you're to fly to Merrittville Airport in Maryland and wait there for instructions."

Frank Smith's voice boomed, filling the aircraft. "What's this all about?"

"Someone named Martin Chapman," the woman said.

Eva felt a burst of adrenaline. "Is Chapman involved in something we can get him for?"

"Ask Tucker when you see him." Squires hung up.

The pilot snapped his phone shut and announced, "We'll take off as soon as I get clearance." He walked back to the cockpit.

Frank focused on her. "You seem to know something about Martin Chapman."

Eva's chest was tight. She glanced down at her hands, saw they were clenched. She took a deep breath. "He set me up so it looked as if I killed my husband in a drunk driving accident. I spent three years in prison. Not jail, *prison*." Without thinking, she was back in the Central California Women's Facility, a harrowing world of steel bars, guards, and violence. She thought she would lose her life, then her mind. Instead it had hardened her, made it easier to tune out what she did not want, made it possible to give up what she thought she needed.

"Tucker got me out to help him with an operation," she went on, "and that's where Chapman came in again. He sent people to kill a colleague and me, and we were shot up rather badly. I don't like it when a criminal doesn't pay for his crimes, but most of the people who could've testified against Chapman died. Then, when the operation ended in Greece, Chapman's lawyers brokered a deal between the Greek and U.S. governments. Chapman and his cronies paid off Greek officials, who agreed not to prosecute them, and the U.S. backed off because the CIA had been caught operating on Greek soil illegally."

Frank frowned. "That's terrible. Was the colleague you mentioned Judd Ryder? Before you ask, I naturally did my homework about you."

"Yes." In her mind she could see Judd's face, feel the warmth of his smile . . . and she was back in Los Angeles four months ago. Her house had been sold, and her things were packed and on their way to Judd's place on Capitol Hill, where they would live together. It was one of those perfect Southern California evenings. The sun was setting in a dramatic swath above the glittering lights of the city. Judd and she stood on the balcony of their room at the Chateau Marmont. He leaned close, his breath spicy. She lifted her lips, and he cradled her chin and kissed her.

Heat spread into her belly and legs. She pushed him back into their room, and they hurried to their bed.

Afterward, they returned to the balcony, holding hands, their flesh moist, the aroma of good sex lingering around them. There are rare times when one is in the right place at the right time, doing the right thing with the right person, and that was how she felt. They were together. They were happy. The mood was right to tell him.

"Tucker phoned," she said. "Langley has accepted me. I'm to start in two weeks, first at headquarters, then I go to the Farm."

"You're sure it's what you want?"

"Yes, but I want you, too. We're bigger than our differences over this."

He gazed at her, his expression somber. "It'd ruin me, Eva." He turned back into the room and walked through the shadows to the pile of clothes on the floor.

She followed him. "I don't understand."

He dressed. "The truth is, I was an assassin. A hit man, a closer, a clean-up man, a janitor, an executioner." He said the words as if he were pounding nails. "With you in the business, it'd be a daily reminder of what I did. What I was. What I could easily slip back into again."

"But you were working for the government. It was your job."

He shook his head hard. "I came to like it." And he was gone, the hotel room door closing softly.

Now she was sitting on an airplane, waiting to fly off to meet Tucker for a new mission. She closed her eyes and inhaled. She had never stopped missing Judd. She wished she could let him know Chapman had resurfaced, but Judd would not be back from Iraq until tomorrow.

25

It was twilight when the plane took off, heading north. For a long while Eva looked out her window, unseeing, then she slept. When she awoke, it was night, and they were flying over a vast expanse of snow-mantled hills and streams. The lights of a town sparkled ahead. By the size of it, perhaps fifteen thousand souls.

"Merrittville?" she asked Frank.

He nodded. "The airport is on the north side. A little terminal, a control tower, and just two runways. The runways are large enough to land a 737. They've become a low-hassle backup for planes that might've otherwise touched down at Dulles or National or even Baltimore. Discreet, too."

She said nothing, understanding. Movie stars, political celebrities, and well-known scoundrels would find the airport useful when dodging the press, divorcing spouses, or even the law.

"Nap well?" he asked.

"I did. And you?"

"No rest for the wicked." He lifted his head and smiled.

She admired his ability to appear serene while her insides were quivering.

The plane made a wide loop, and the landing strip appeared ahead. Touching down, the craft taxied to a fenced-off area marked for private planes. After the engines turned off, the pilot emerged again from the cockpit. He was carrying his phone again.

Eva straightened in her seat. "Has Tucker called?"

He shook his head and touched the speakerphone button.

"This is Jane Squires." It was the same woman's voice. "Tucker sends his apologies that he can't personally talk to you. He has a message for you, Frank. He had me arrange a rental car for you. It's waiting at Peebles Air and Land Transportation. You should be able to see the place from your plane. Your orders are to drive to Martin Chapman's house."

She related the address.

Frank wrote it down.

Puzzled why she was not included, Eva memorized it.

"Tucker will call while you're en route to discuss exactly where you're to go and what he wants you to do, Frank," the voice continued. "As for you, Ms. Blake, Tucker sends his regrets. He says you're to wait on the plane. He knows you have a personal interest in this matter, but as it turns out, he doesn't need your special skills at this time."

"But I—" Eva tried.

"He said you'd argue. Have you graduated from the Farm yet?" the woman demanded.

"Of course not, but—"

"That's Tucker's point. He's ordering you to stay put. This could be more dangerous than he anticipated, and you're not fully trained."

Suddenly there was a vacuum of sound. Squires had hung up. Eva stared down at her knotted hands, wanting for a moment to strangle Tucker for getting her hopes up.

"Well, well." Frank shot her a sympathetic look. "Sorry about that, Eva, but you know how Tucker is. The thing to do is to remember you're at the beginning of your career. There are a lot of operations in your

future, more than you'll ever be able to remember. Take it from an antique like myself—missing this one will pale against the number you'll
be sent on."

She gave a stoic nod. She felt raw with disappointment. She wanted
Chapman.

She watched Frank put on his coat and hurry out the door and across
the tarmac to the long metal building that housed Peebles Transportation. Soon he was out again and trotting past a row of what looked like
rental cars to a Chevrolet sedan parked in a dark spot between overhead lights. He climbed inside. As he drove away, he passed beneath pole
lights and she could see the car was black. Before the red taillights could
disappear into the night, she memorized the license plate.

26

Merrittville, Maryland

Growing bored, Eva gazed out her window, watching the few taxiing planes and the occasional pilot, passenger, or airport staff person cross the tarmac. A Dassault Falcon 7X docked a distance away. It was the only trijet in the private section. That was as exciting as it got.

As she leaned back and closed her eyes, she heard in her mind, *You're not fully trained*. She still was bothered by what was going on. It was not only that she had worked closely with Tucker in the past, but also that she had done so well, Tucker had personally recommended her to Langley. The more she thought about it, the more difficult it was to believe he would bring her this far then decide she did not have the chops for the job.

What was going on?

In surveillance training, the one mistake guaranteed to get you booted out of the Farm was missing a surveillance tail. Was she missing something here? *You're not fully trained . . .* it was the word *trained* that was important. *Training.*

Her eyes snapped open as she remembered the whispered rumors that there would be two particularly difficult exercises at the Farm. In one, the trainees were "captured" and thrown into a sham POW camp as terrorists. They underwent hours of interrogation, sleep deprivation, and isolation, first to coerce, and if that did not work, to force them to give up the name of one of the other terrorists—one of their fellow students—because it was vital the students learn the limits of their endurance. In the second exercise, the Farm ran a surprise operation on each trainee: Staff and sometimes retired or active officers created a situation that looked real from every aspect. It would be so well executed any normal person would believe it. In spookspeak, the operation was called a movie. The trainee's job was to detect and give evidence of the truth.

If it was illogical for Tucker to sideline her, then this whole situation could be a movie. Her frustration about not being able to make Chapman accountable was well known, and Langley had an entire department dedicated to creating identities—"Frank Smith" could easily be an alias.

Eva drummed her fingers on her armrest. Langley demanded its spies follow orders, but it also prized entrepreneurship. The line between the two was hair-thin, and what was left unsaid was that undercover officers were expected to know when to break the rules. If this really were a training exercise, she needed to reveal it.

She heard the cockpit door open.

It was the pilot—Jack—buttoning his black pilot's jacket. "I'm going out." He reached into the forward closet and grabbed a down jacket.

"Where are you headed?" she asked.

"Next door. The owner's an old friend."

She nodded. "I think the intent of Tucker's orders was for me to stay here at the airport within hailing distance, don't you?" Without waiting for him to respond, she went on, "I'm starving. I saw a pizza sign next to the Peebles building. How about I get us some?"

"Sorry, Ms. Blake, but you've got to stay here. You don't want to get kicked out of the Farm for disobeying orders." Jack added kindly, "I'll swing past for pizza. What can I bring for you?"

She made up an answer then watched as he turned the wheel on the door, lifted a lever, and pushed outside. Cold air gusted in, and the door shut.

Standing up, she paced the aisle and mulled the problem. The thing was she had heard nothing directly from Tucker himself—just from some woman named Jane Squires who claimed to work for him. Since Tucker had brought her all the way out here to the middle of nowhere, the least he could do was tell her what the mission was about. On the other hand, if this were a movie, he might know nothing about it—and she would be able to unmask it as a training exercise.

Hurrying back to her seat, she dug her Farm-issued cell from her shoulder bag and dialed Tucker's new number, the one Frank had given her. Soon the recording of Tucker's voice sounded in her ear. Disappointed, she ended the connection without leaving a message.

She considered a moment then tapped onto the keypad Tucker's old number, the one he had given her months ago. The phone rang three times. Eagerly she listened to the connection being made, but then to another recording of Tucker's voice. Jabbing the OFF button, she stared at the cell. The messages were identical. Quickly she again dialed one number then the other. Recordings answered both times. She listened carefully. Not only were the words the same, so were the inflections, the emphases, the rhythms.

Pacing the aisle, she hugged herself. It was possible Tucker had made a tape of his message and used it for the new number. But it was equally possible the Farm had made a copy of Tucker's recording and put it on Tucker's supposedly new phone number for Frank Smith to give to her—and she was in the middle of a movie.

She stooped to peer out the window. The door to the trijet was open, and Jack was stepping inside. As Eva watched the door close, she decided she would rather go down for being enterprising than for being an idiot.

She dialed Peebles Air and Land Transportation. "I need to rent a car," she told the man who answered.

"You like a lot of horsepower?" he asked, then began to describe a Ford V-8 Mustang he had on the lot.

"Here's my credit card number," she interrupted. "E-mail me the paperwork."

"I get it. Sure." In a small airport that served those who for a variety of reasons wanted to avoid the big airports around Washington, he probably had heard stranger requests.

Giving him her information, she put on her coat. As she slung the strap of her bag over her shoulder, the documents arrived on her cell phone. She signed and sent them back.

Then she phoned him again. "Leave the car by the gate with the motor running. I'll be able to see it from here. I'm on my way." With one hand she rotated the wheel on the cabin door.

"Hey, no can do. Can't leave the car running. I'll wait there with the key." He hung up before she could argue.

She shoved the door's lever and stepped out into the frosty night. Pulling her coat tightly around her, she hurried down the staircase.

"Eva!" The voice was a bellow behind her.

She looked back.

Jack, the pilot, was sprinting toward her. "Dammit, Eva, you don't know what you're getting into! Come back!"

She ran toward the waiting Mustang. A young man stood next to the driver's door, holding up keys in his gloved hand and smiling.

Before he could say anything, she snatched the keys. "Thanks!" She swung open the door, jumped inside, and ignited the engine. Throwing the car into gear, she pressed the gas feed and took off, tires spitting snow.

Checking her rearview mirror, she saw the kid standing confused, alternately watching her and Jack. Jack was gripping the fence with a gloved hand, his face red, breathing great white clouds. He was talking urgently into his cell phone. No doubt reporting her to the Farm. To hell with him. She was going to find Tucker.

Eva sped the powerful Mustang across Montgomery County's frozen countryside. She was tense, wondering what she was going to find at Martin Chapman's place. Traffic was light. The moon shone brightly, turning the rural highway bone gray in the night. Listening to her GPS's instructions, she watched the road.

When her cell phone rang, she picked it up and saw the caller ID was useless—"Private Number."

She considered then finally answered. "Yes?"

The voice on the other end of the line announced in warm tones: "Eva, this is Jack, your friendly pilot. Don't hang up."

She stiffened. "I'm not going back to the plane." She jammed the cell's red OFF button.

She drove past stands of snowy woods interspersed with houses, lights on, people gathered around dinner tables, sitting in front of televisions. "Private Number" called again. She did not answer. As she pressed the sports car onward, time seemed to stretch into eternity. When the GPS finally announced she had reached her destination, she slowed. The sign over the entrance confirmed it was Chapman's place. The drive was wide, rising to a towering manse fronted by Greek-style columns.

As she continued past she glimpsed a closed-circuit camera in a tree on the far side of a high security wall, then another camera. They were aimed at the wall but could also show the road. She made no more changes in her speed—she wanted to do nothing to attract attention. As she watched for sentries, she drove around the corner. She had to decide what to do. She shot a sharp glance at her cell phone. Then she snapped it up and dialed her voice mail.

There was a message from the pilot, Jack. "Dammit, Eva, call me!" He left his number.

She punched it into her phone's keypad.

Jack answered instantly. "Come to your senses, Eva. Get your butt back here."

Glaring at the two-lane road ahead, she announced, "This isn't a movie, is it, Jack. It's a real damn operation. Why have I been cut out of it?"

There was a surprised moment. Then: "You're not equipped. A lot's riding on it. It's as simple as that."

"Bullshit." She waited silently for him to say more.

Finally she heard him sigh. "Goddammit, Eva, where in hell are you?"

"I'm driving along the west side of Chapman's place. I see a service entrance ahead."

"Okay. So now you have a choice. Turn back, or if you insist on continuing, you've got to promise to do exactly what you're told. Follow orders."

"I'm not turning back."

"Say it."

Gritting her teeth, she echoed, "I'll do exactly what Frank or Tucker tells me."

"And don't forget it. Drive a mile past Chapman's service entrance then return and park the Mustang across from it. I'll tell Frank to watch for your car, but I haven't heard from him in a while, so I don't know whether he's even alive. I've given you your orders. Don't screw up and get someone killed." He ended the call.

Driving with one hand, she gripped her cell in the other until it hurt. Was she really that bull-headed? She peered out at a great sea of moon-glistening white—the snowy plain across from Chapman's property. It made her think of cross-country skiing and snowmen, of childhood. But her childhood had been shaped by a drunken father and a distraught mother. She had been the one who had held all of them together. She had learned a lot of lessons then.

Shaking her head, she checked her odometer then did a u-turn. Cruising back, she parked across from Chapman's service entrance. As she killed the car's engine, she studied the imposing gate. Was there movement on the other side? She waited another minute. Then she saw a side gate next to the kiosk had at some point been opened. It was ajar.

She slung on her shoulder bag, put her cell on MUTE, and opened the car door. The only sound was the hum of cars on the distant road. Heart pounding, she jogged across the street and slid through the gate's narrow opening. And hesitated. Scanning, she noted the driveway up to the compound, the spruce trees on the left that spread high into the horizon, the buildings on the crest.

She glanced back at the open gate, decided not to close it, and walked tentatively forward.

And froze. Dressed in a white jumpsuit padded against the cold, a white ski mask covering his face, a man suddenly appeared from around the kiosk. He was armed with an M4, and from the expert way in which he held it, he knew exactly what to do with it.

27

Montgomery County, Maryland

Sprawled on the front seat of his pickup truck, the doors locked, the heater warming him, Judd Ryder had been sleeping when the unmistakable chop of helicopter blades awoke him. Sitting up, he yawned and shook his head. He had no idea whether he had succumbed to jet lag or just general exhaustion, but whichever it was, he was weary. What a day. He had been on the run since at least eight o'clock this morning.

Forearms on thighs, he watched through the windshield as the helicopter landed a hundred feet in front of him on the road. Once a runway, the road and tarmac around it were maintained by the state for parking large machinery like dump trucks. Tucker jumped out, ducked, and hustled through the cold, his long overcoat flapping and big feet slapping the asphalt. The spymaster was a welcome sight.

Tucker climbed into the passenger seat and slammed the door. "Good to see you, Judd."

"Any news about Eva?" Ryder did a one-eighty with the pickup and headed off.

"I got a call from the Farm. They're convinced it was Eva who phoned in, and maybe they're right. They checked with Eva's parents and found out there wasn't any family emergency. They called her brother and sister, too. Ditto. As you know, there are serious rules about recruits lying and leaving training without permission. The murder board voted."

"She's out?"

"Yes, and we still don't know where she is."

Ryder grimaced. "Damn!"

"I know. I feel the same way. At least I can tell you the tag number for the van Eichel was driving belongs to a Toyota SUV."

"So Eichel swiped a Toyota's plates and put them on his van."

"Appears so. I've asked the Maryland State Police to watch for it." Tucker eyed him. "Where are the limestone pieces?"

Ryder paused the pickup at the intersection with the county highway. "There's a gallon of water in the bed of the pickup, Tucker. Get it, will you?" When Tucker did not budge, Ryder insisted: "It's important. Please get the goddamn jug."

"It'll be ice, not water." With a sigh, Tucker jumped out and returned in a cloud of arctic air. Slamming the door behind him, he dropped hard onto the seat, one gloved hand grasping the neck of the plastic jug. "It's frozen solid."

"You asked where the limestone pieces were."

Tucker grinned. "You clever bastard." He held the translucent bottle up to the street light. "Can't see anything inside."

"Good. I pulled off the highway a couple of times to rotate the bottle to make sure the rocks ended up in the middle." Ryder pressed the accelerator, and they entered traffic. "Five more miles and we'll be at Chapman's place."

"We've got a stop to make first. The satellite photos showed his spread was a fortress, but we think we've found a way to get in. I'll explain when we get there."

"Okay." As they passed farmhouses and corrals, he felt Tucker assessing him. He glanced over, saw the intensity of his gaze. "What?"

"You didn't ask what kind of security Chapman has," Tucker said. "The details."

"I figured you'd fill me in if it was important."

"Not good enough, Judd. It's the sort of question you always ask, because the information is critical. You know already. At some point you must've studied his protection." He did not pause for Ryder to deny it. "The only reason you'd do that is because you were intending to liquidate him. But Chapman's still breathing. What happened?" His brown eyes peered somberly through his tortoiseshell glasses at Ryder.

Suddenly the hot air blasting into the pickup was stifling. Ryder turned it down. "I surveilled Chapman for weeks, but he had a security detail that stuck to him like epoxy. Finally one night he went to a sex club, and he was in there so long I could see his guards were losing their edge. Finally at three A.M. he came out, and for a few seconds I had a clear shot." But just then, in his mind, he had seen his mother crying. At first he had thought it was because she missed his father, and then he had realized she was crying for him, for the killer he had become. "I tried my damnedest to pull the trigger." He shook his head. "I couldn't make myself do it. So here I am, caught up in something I never expected or wanted, and Martin Chapman is probably deep into it, too." Focusing on the traffic, Ryder changed the subject. "Why are you here? I expected you to send someone lower down the food chain to help me."

"The first reason is Bridgeman. If he can get me fired, every day will be Christmas for him. But he'll have to find some other way to do it when you and I uncover what in hell is really going on with these damn assassins." He took out his handheld. "I brought their dossiers, or at least as much as Gloria could collect in the time I gave her. I've already told you some of the background on the Padre and the Eichel brothers, so let's talk about the Carnivore."

"When Eva and I were with him in Turkey, he told us he still took jobs but only occasionally. He sounded semiretired."

"Yeah, that's my take, too. But maybe he's tired of it all."

"He didn't act tired when we were working together." Ryder remembered how the assassin had almost killed him and Eva.

Tucker changed the subject. "Langley must've had extensive records about him at some point, because Gloria found references to them. She tried to track them down but ran out of time. I never had any personal contact with him in the old Cold War days, but I remember hearing he was useful on occasion. Translated, that means we hired him for jobs we couldn't or wouldn't touch. By the nineties I wasn't hearing his name much." He peered at the handheld's screen. "This is from his dossier. . . .

"'He may have at least one U.S. parent, since reports from informants indicate he has an American accent when speaking English. He also is fluent in at least four other languages, most with no accent—German, French, Italian, and Spanish.'"

"He speaks Arabic, too," Ryder said.

"Makes sense. I think he was involved in some jihadist face-offs in the eighties, so he'd know Arabic if for no other reason than to protect himself." Tucker continued reading:

"'His real name is allegedly Alex Bosa. *Bosa* could be Hungarian, Italian, Portuguese, Spanish, or from any Central or South American nation, such as Cuba. It is believed, however, to be Italian.'"

"Bosa was one of the names he was using back when he was with Eva and me," Ryder recalled. "Do you have photos of him?"

Despite their past contact with the Carnivore, none of them had seen the assassin's real face because of his disguises.

"Not a single photo," Tucker said. "He's been called the Assassin Without a Face because there aren't any visuals of him. It's a hell of a handicap to anyone who wants to find him."

"What about his targets?"

Tucker scrolled through the document on his handheld. "Here's one.

"'In 1981, Minister of Finance Jacques-Claude Metarsque died when he drove his car off a cliff in Normandy. His blood alcohol level was so high that the coroner ascribed the event to an alcoholic blackout. However, our Belgium asset "Salsa" reports it was an assassination.

"'An insurance executive wanted to stop Metarsque's insurance reform, which was expected to cost the executive's company close to 100 million francs. Metarsque wouldn't drop the proposal. So the executive took matters into his own hands and secretly hired the Carnivore.'"

Tucker looked up. "As you can see, an 'accident,' thanks to the Carnivore. And it was effective for the employer—the insurance reform died, and no one has been able to resurrect it."

Ryder nodded. "Did I ever give you his rules?"

"What do you mean, 'rules'?"

"He told Eva and me the reason he'd survived so long while most of his colleagues had been killed off was self-discipline. He had terms, and every prospective employer had to agree to them or he wouldn't take the job no matter how much money they threw at him."

"You know the rules?"

"Yes, he gave them to us, but of course it had to be his way. He talked to us as if we were trying to hire him: 'When it's time to make the hit, I work alone. That means you must be gone, and your people must be gone. You must never reveal our association. You must never try to find out what I look like or who I am. If you make any attempts, I will come after you. I'll do you the favor of making it a clean kill out of respect for our business relationship and the money you will have paid me. After this, you will never try to meet me again. When the job is finished, I'll be in touch to let you know how I want to receive the last payment. If you don't pay me, I will come after you for that, too. I do wet work only on people who shouldn't be breathing anyway. I'm the one who makes that decision—not you. Do you agree?'" Ryder gave a cold laugh and shook his head, remembering.

"Imagine some car executive or socialite or politician listening to that," Tucker said. "They'd be sitting in a pool of their own sweat by the time he finished. The rest of the assassins are survivors, too, which tells you they're just as tough. And hardened. Okay, let's move on." He scrolled down the screen of his handheld. "Here's one about Eli Eichel.

"'In 1987, British citizen Madonna Millman was killed by a sniper shot between her eyes as she walked down a Mayfair street. She had been a witness against a Yamaguchi-gumi crime boss in Kobe, Japan, and managed to escape to London after testifying.

"'According to an impeccable source, the gang tracked her to London but wanted to lessen the chance any of the Yakuza family would be charged with her murder. They also wanted to send a warning to anyone considering breaking their code of silence.

" 'They hired Eli Eichel to do the wet work. . . .' "

Ryder let out a long stream of air. The Yamaguchi-gumi family was one of the largest crime organizations in the world, operating not only in Japan but across Asia and into the United States.

"Her murder was all over the newspapers," he recalled. "She was pregnant. The baby didn't survive."

"And no one was ever arrested." Tucker set his handheld on his knee and peered grimly out at the night. "There were more assassinations and terrorist acts in the 1980s than at any other time in history when there wasn't a major hot war. Everyone was targeted—children and grandmothers, passengers on airliners and cruise ships. And this was done by political, religious, and independent terrorists and assassins of all kinds. They were erasing the line between guilt and innocence and destroying ethical and moral norms. Does that sound like what we have today? Of course it does. There aren't any more boundaries. Anyone and everyone is vulnerable."

They were silent.

Judd finally asked, "Did you find any clue in your research about what connects the assassins with the cuneiform pieces?"

"I wish. I studied the dossiers. I checked for mutual jobs, for being employed by the same person if not simultaneously then at different times, for being in the same place at the same time, for shared suppliers, shared interests, shared politics, shared girlfriends, anything. One of our problems is that independent assassins are particularly covert. With no large organization to protect them, they have to be particularly secretive. Their employers demand anonymity. So the answer is no, I couldn't find anything that linked them. And I also couldn't find any links to limestone pieces, cuneiform writing, or ancient tablets."

Disappointed, Ryder said, "Have you come to any conclusions?"

"Yes. There are too many top assassins involved for this to be just about pieces of a cuneiform tablet. Something big is going on. I can feel it, smell it."

"Agreed. But what in hell is it?"

Tucker nodded. "Exactly."

"Where is this place you want me to stop?" Judd asked.

Tucker indicated a large single-story building ahead. A sign over the driveway announced LONG PLAINS FEED & SUPPLIES. "We're here. Doesn't look like much, but it's our ticket into Chapman's."

28

Their arrangements finished, Ryder kept watch, his Uzi on his lap, as Tucker drove them to Chapman's horse farm in a delivery truck owned by Long Plains Feed & Supplies. It was a large truck with a full load. The cab was aromatic with the earthy odors of hay and alfalfa. The owner of the feed store had kept the truck on the premises until they arrived, and then he had loaned Tucker a winter jacket displaying the store's logo. Under the jacket in Tucker's shoulder holster was his favorite pistol, a 9-mm Browning.

"That's Chapman's house." Judd nodded at a white mansion on a hill.

Tucker glanced up. "The house looks as if it's hatching the hill and little white cupcakes are going to Pop-Tart out of the ground."

Ryder repressed a smile. "The Eichels have arrived," he pointed out. "That's their van parked in front."

"I can hardly wait to meet the bastards."

"Check out the house lights."

The windows on either side of the front door showed bright light, while the rest of the first floor was dark. The top floor was completely dark.

"From what I saw when I was surveilling the place," Ryder went on, "the rooms on the first floor are lit only erratically and go dark at eleven P.M. The rooms on the third story are generally not lit until after eleven P.M., indicating someone going up to bed."

"That leaves the second floor," Tucker said. "There's a lot of light spilling out of four of the French doors."

"Just the way it was the last time I was here. The lights were usually on there until almost eleven o'clock. I was never able to get any architectural plans for the house, but there's got to be some kind of big room behind those French doors, and it's Chapman's favorite. Maybe his office or den, and he sits up there until bedtime, working, reading, or watching TV."

"Or 'entertaining' Eli and Danny Eichel." Tucker stared at the hill's flat summit. "Did you see movement near the house?"

Ryder stared, spotting a shadow cast out from the house's northwest corner, followed by a man in some kind of white snowsuit. "He's a guard. In the summer, the outdoor ones wear green sweatsuits. Looks as if he's wearing a bandolier. That's new."

"A bandolier?" Tucker repeated. "Chapman must be scared as shit."

"I see another guard back around the barn," Ryder commented.

"Great."

Tucker swung the delivery truck onto the rural road that ran alongside Chapman's property. On the left spread open fields, milky white in the moonlight. On the right was the horse farm's high wall, a long stone testament to wealth and fear.

"Time to get down," Tucker said.

Ryder picked up the container of frozen water from the floor and fit himself and his gun down into the foot well. He set the container up on the seat while Tucker reached behind, pulled out a blanket, and threw it over Ryder. It stank of horse.

"There's a wrought-iron gate at the service entry," Tucker said. "I'm going to punch the intercom button to let them know I'm here with the goods." He stopped the truck, and a draft of cold air seeped in under the blanket—Tucker had rolled down the window. Ryder listened as he announced: "Delivery for Dean Jennings." Jennings was the head horse trainer.

A voice came back with a question. "Where's Tim?" Tim Wayne worked for the feed store and usually made the delivery to Jennings, according to the store's owner.

"Poor bastard has the flu," Tucker explained. "My name's Jon Jacobsen. We brought you some extra roughage for the horses. It'll help 'em through this wicked cold snap."

"Okay, Jon," the voice decided. "Come on in. I'll tell Dean you're here."

Tucker drove again. Ryder felt the nose of the truck rise—they were heading up the slope to the compound. He breathed shallowly under the blanket, trying to minimize the stench.

"We're passing the stand of spruce trees," Tucker said.

In his mind Ryder could see the forest spreading up into the horizon. Earlier, when he had examined Tucker's satellite photos, he described seeing Chapman riding horseback into the woods. Studying the photos, they identified a horse trail Tucker could use tonight. Beyond the trail, at the rear of the property where the land was flat, were Chapman's airstrip and a hangar more than large enough for his Learjet. The photos, which had been taken earlier today, showed someone out on a snowplow, clearing the airstrip. That was Chapman for you—always prepared.

"A guard's walking down the driveway toward us," Tucker continued. "He's toting an M4 and wearing a bandolier and scanning all around. He keeps looking at the truck."

"Is it safe for me to stick my head out so I can breathe?"

"Yes, but stay down."

Pushing back the blanket, Ryder took a deep breath and saw Tucker's expression was bored, the complete pro, as he kept his gaze on the drive. Ryder tilted his Uzi up toward the window.

"Chapman's security must've warned him Tim has a replacement tonight," Tucker said, barely moving his lips. "He's stopped. He's checking out the store logo on the door. Now he's looking at me." He turned and gave a friendly wave. "He's gone." His shoulders relaxed a fraction. "Gave me a nod, which is as good as gold."

Lowering his weapon, Ryder felt the truck level off.

"We're at the top of the drive," Tucker said. "I'm taking us around to the rear of the house."

According to the photos, there was a point behind the house that was sheltered by the garage and out of sight of the barn. Near the middle of the house was the door through which Chapman would leave to get quickly into his waiting limo. From what Judd had been able to see, there was a lot of traffic in and out of the door, so it should be unlocked. That was where Tucker was supposed to let Ryder off.

"Christ." Tucker's voice was strained. Again his lips were nearly motionless as he talked. "A guard's coming around the corner of the garage."

"Does he have a clear view of the door into the house?"

"Fuck, yes."

Tension filled the truck. Tucker was supposed to slow the vehicle to a crawl, but that would make the guard suspicious.

Tucker gave a tight smile. "He just walked off toward the barn." He touched the brakes, slowing the vehicle, and grabbed the frozen water bottle from the seat. "Get the hell out of here before someone else shows up."

But Ryder was already opening the door. The truck was still moving. Holding the Uzi with both hands, Ryder stumbled out. Tucker leaned across the seat, pulled the door shut, and sped up again, heading to the barn.

Ryder sprinted to a lace-edged window. Flattening next to it, he peered inside and saw a short hallway. No one was in sight, then a door on the right opened, and out stepped a muscular man dressed in the dark green sweats Ryder remembered. Carrying an M4, he also wore a packed bandolier across his chest. Yawning widely, he walked away down the corridor and opened the door at the end.

As soon as he disappeared, Ryder slipped indoors. To his left was an archway framing a butler's pantry and on the far side a kitchen counter showed. He could hear pots and pans clattering. He paused at the door where he had seen the guard leave. He pressed his ear against it, listened, then cracked it open. It was a small locker room. Stepping inside, he closed the door.

Piles of folded green sweatshirts and matching sweatpants were stacked on a table. Across the room stood a glass-covered gun case. Inside hung four M4s and four bandoliers. There was room for six more M4s and bandoliers, which suggested that besides the two outside guards, there were four more in the house or elsewhere, so armed for overkill they could be advertisements for gun magazines. Smiling grimly, Ryder went to work.

29

Covered in blankets, a dozen Arabian horses whinnied and stamped the ground outside Chapman's large white barn. As handlers led them in a side door, Tucker backed the delivery truck up and jumped out of the cab. He needed to unload quickly so he could join Judd in the house.

A stringy man in padded winter coveralls walked toward him.

"Are you Dean Jennings?" Tucker said.

"I am. And you are?" Dean studied the Long Plains Feed & Supply jacket Tucker wore.

"Jon Jacobsen." Tucker gave him the explanation about the illness of the regular driver. "Where do you want your supplies?"

Dean took him inside. The earthy odor of horse manure sharpened the air. Tucker noted needlenose cameras observing from the rafters as two men tended, fed, and watered the horses. Although the grounds were not under observation, at least the interior of the barn was. But then Chapman was raising a small fortune in thoroughbred Arabians.

As soon as Dean showed him the storage area, Tucker hurried back outdoors, opened the truck's rear, and dollied the first batch of supplies inside. Horses stuck their heads out of the stalls to watch him pile sacks of feed. As he stacked bales of hay, his handheld vibrated. He snatched it from his pocket and saw it was Judd.

Dean had been observing, arms crossed. He radiated disapproval.

"The wife," Tucker explained.

As Dean gave a slow nod, Tucker silently read:

> Short hall inside door. Guards' locker room on right.
> Will change into a uniform and look for 2nd-fl room.

Tucker did not like the idea of Judd investigating without him. He texted back:

> In barn. Wait for me.

Stuffing the phone back into his jacket, Tucker rolled the dolly over to Dean. "How about you or your men giving me a hand? My wife's on my butt. I got to get home."

His feet planted solidly, Dean shook his head. "Tim never needed help."

The man was so laconic he probably had no blood pressure, Tucker decided. His best course was not to argue. "No problem."

Silently cursing, he pushed the dolly back outside and resumed unloading. The minutes passed slowly. Sweat streaked his face. By the time he rolled the last crate inside, his arms, shoulders, and back ached. He stored the dolly in the truck and slammed the door. With a wave of his hand, he got behind the steering wheel, closed the door, and started the engine. Fighting the urge to speed, Tucker drove past the garage and main house then downslope. In two minutes he was at the stand of spruce. Some hundred yards ahead were the service gate and protective granite wall.

Checking his mirrors, he killed the truck's headlights, downshifted so his red brake lights would stay dark, and searched for the opening in the woods he had spotted when they had driven past earlier. The trees had looked young and thin, and despite his slow speed, they seemed to blend together, a solid mass.

It came upon him suddenly, a narrow black tunnel fronted by saplings. The hole looked barely wide enough for what he needed. He yanked the steering wheel hard to the right and floored the accelerator. He smashed through the trees, bending and snapping branches, the snow geysering up in great waves coating the windshield and side windows. Lurching against the seat belt, he felt the front end ram into something. The back tires spun.

Turning off the ignition, he wiped sweat from his forehead and set the jug of frozen water on the floor, reached behind him, and grabbed a balaclava and snowshoes. Rolling the black balaclava down over his head, he adjusted the face hole over his glasses.

He opened the door and strapped on the snowshoes. God, it was cold. He took out his Browning and stepped onto the snow, the snowshoes sinking only an inch. Moonlight shone in luminescent streaks down through the trees, giving the woods an unearthly glow.

Closing the door, he slogged forward to check what had stopped the truck—a bank of snow. The fender was burrowed into it. Needled limbs poked out. There was a downed tree under there somewhere. Snowshoeing back to the truck's rear, he discovered the tires had dug themselves deep holes. Driving out of here was going to be dicey, if they could do it at all. He would worry about that later.

With a glance at the moon, he got his bearings and snowshoed off, pushing back branches and ducking needles. A gust of wind curled up and around him, spraying him with snow. He found the riding trail Judd and he had spotted in the satellite photos and moved onto it, increasing his speed. As he climbed, he watched through the trees for headlights, flashlights, moving shadows. The cold bit his flesh.

He paused within the forest to observe an open area that sloped up toward the compound. Bushes and trees made long-shadowed silhouettes. And then he saw a line of oval depressions—snowshoe prints. Holding up his Browning, he moved toward them, the snow muffling his progress, and stopped abruptly. Hidden just inside the treeline was a large mound that seemed not to belong there.

Tucker peered up the slope. The garage was dark, no light to indicate anyone was there. He studied the oval prints of snowshoes. There were three sets. Two people—one following the other—had come down the slope from the garage. Then one had dragged the other into the trees and returned uphill.

Tucker moved until he could see the mound's face. He recognized him—the sentry who had walked down the drive when Judd and he had first arrived. Blood frozen on the side of his neck shone darkly in the moonlight. Beneath it was a narrow black well in the snow, where the man's lifeblood had poured out.

The wound was a neat slice, a single well-placed thrust of a blade into the jugular. The man had probably been followed here, or forced here, then knocked unconscious so he would not yell or resist, and finally—and expertly—stabbed to death.

He stood. Where was the victim's M4? Stepping from the woods, he searched for the rifle along the treeline. There was no sign of it. Either the killer had taken it with him or he had flung it deeper into the forest. He looked up the hill again. No one was in sight, no guard, no horse trainer. If this were the sentry's patrol area, it was now without security. But who had killed him?

Taking out his handheld, he texted Judd:

> Sentry killed near spruce forest. Expert knife to jugular.
> Know anything about it?

Wary, watching all around, Tucker hurriedly climbed toward the compound, following the snowshoe prints. Lights shone from windows in the main house and the barn, while the garage remained dark. Somewhere in the distance a coyote howled.

When he finally reached the garage, Tucker was sweating and shivering at the same time. Still following the prints, he went around to the rear. The snow was gray and pounded flat here. He was assessing the prints when his handheld vibrated again. A response from Judd:

> No. Still in locker room. Hurry.

His back to the garage, Tucker stood where he had a 180-degree view of open space, trees, and a parking lot behind the barn, where there were a dozen cars and pickups—probably the employees' lot. Farther away was Chapman's airstrip and the hangar, a blocky silhouette. A narrow road led to it from the parking lot.

To Tucker's left was a large wood cart, the kind for hauling small equipment or hay. Snow heaped high and untouched on it while the snow on the ground alongside it was trampled. He moved closer, gazing down, following little speckles black against the snow. He checked under the cart. Another corpse in a white snowsuit lay there, face up, eyes open, iced over. Frowning, Tucker gazed around then crouched, examining the red blotch frozen on the dead man's neck—a single knife thrust to the jugular again. What in hell was going on?

He texted Judd:

Another dead guard knifed behind garage.

As he rose, the noise of one car engine then another crackled across the still hilltop. He hurried back to where he could see the employees' parking area. As he watched, steam curled up from the tailpipes of parked cars, and an SUV rolled off. Two bundled men ran from the barn to a car and fired up its engine, too. Members of the staff had finished for the day.

As he watched, his handheld vibrated again. He dug it out. Judd at last:

Figure 4 live guards inside. Watch out.

As the noise of approaching engines grew louder, Tucker hustled back around the barn and ripped off his snowshoes. Ramming them deep into a snowbank until they were out of sight, he ran full tilt across the drive to the mansion's rear door.

30

In the library upstairs, the three armed guards had not moved from their posts at the door, while Eli Eichel and Martin Chapman had taken to wingback chairs, drinking bourbon and branch water and waiting impatiently to find out where Judd Ryder was.

Chapman drank. "Are you married, Eli?"

Eli felt a dull ache in his chest. "Not now. My wife died thirty years ago, in childbirth. The baby died, too. Young love, young death, end of story." He remembered Madonna Millman, whom he had erased in Mayfair with a single shot between her eyes. He had not been told she was pregnant. He had always wondered whether he would have accepted the job if he had known.

"I'm married to a good woman," Chapman was saying. "Beautiful. Smart. Nice. She's usually visiting friends in St. Moritz or Cabo San Lucas or Paris. You get the idea. She thinks I don't understand the reason she travels so much is that she's lonely for me. I don't spend much time with her even when we're under the same roof." He shrugged. "It's my fault, my weakness. You must know about loneliness."

Before Eli could respond, Danny said, "Eli lives with me. He can't be lonely." He stopped beneath a large crystal chandelier. Staring up, he clasped his big hands behind him and muttered, growing lost in one of his calculations.

"I imagine all assassins are lonely," Chapman said.

"My money keeps me warm," Eli told him, "as I'm sure yours does you."

The phone rang. Chapman picked it up, checking the caller ID. "It's Senator Leggate," he said with obvious relief. Then into the phone: "Hello, Donna. I hope your investments with us are paying well." He listened. "I'm glad. We want to keep a fine public servant like you happy, and in the Senate. Yes, as a matter of fact, I do need another favor. It's Judd Ryder again. He's back from Iraq, but we don't know where." He paused again. "Thanks, Donna." Then his tone hardened. "I expect to hear from you quickly."

Washington, D.C.

Scott Bridgeman had been working quietly in his office at Catapult headquarters. He rubbed his eyes and peered out the window at the snowbank that city plows had dumped into the front yard. It was cold as hell out there, but going home to his wife was even colder. He shook his head, miserable. He checked the clock on his desk. He was not leaving until he was damn sure she was sound asleep. Another four hours at least.

Leaning back in his executive chair, Bridgeman stretched, trying to control his anger. Ever since he got the assignment to run Catapult, he had been working like a demon to inject discipline and accountability into the unit, while Tucker Andersen continued to defy him. Anyone else would have called in by now with a report—even a preliminary report—about the findings at the hunt club. Not Tucker. A half hour ago Bridgeman had looked for him, but he was not in his office or anywhere else in the building, and the day staff had gone, including Gloria. He had left a message on Tucker's handheld, but of course Tucker had not called back.

He was just about to call Gloria when his phone rang. God, he hoped it wasn't his wife. With relief he saw it was Senator Donna Leggate.

"Hello, Mr. Bridgeman. It's a pleasure to be in touch again." She had a strong, deep voice.

A smoker, he remembered, and a famous one at that. "Of course, Senator Leggate. I appreciate all of your support for Langley's efforts. How can I help you?" Anyone inside the Beltway who knew anything knew she was not to be crossed. At the same time, as one of the senior members of the intelligence committee, she could be politically advantageous.

"I'm trying to locate the same former military spook—Judd Ryder," she said. "Mr. Ryder is in-country but no one seems to know where. I thought someone on your staff might be useful again. You know, his link with Tucker Andersen. If you can find out quickly and without bringing me into it, I would be much . . . obliged."

This was new, he thought with excitement. The pause before the last word told him she was offering him a favor in the future. In the turbulent political waters of Washington, a simple, convenient favor could be a life raft.

"As you know, I'm delighted to do anything I can," he said sincerely. "Tell me where you are now with the matter involving Ryder." The request was *pro forma*—he needed to make sure the reason she was asking was neither illegal nor unethical. Standards were crucial to him, no matter the cost.

"Of course. Sorry, I should've started with that. The situation has become an embarrassment for my constituent. As you may remember, he's a banker, and he's been trying to locate Ryder because Ryder's father left a sizable account in one of his Denver branches. My constituent still hasn't been able to reach either Ryder or his mother. Finally, in frustration he called me again. We need continued discretion in this matter. I believe there is, ah, some concern that the money might have an illegal source, and Judd Ryder could know more than he should about it. We don't want to warn him, do we?"

"Certainly not." It would be sweet to have his suspicions confirmed that Judd Ryder was shady. "You're a good friend of Tom O'Day, aren't you?" he asked. "I'm a great admirer of his." Tom O'Day had been Langley chief only a few months, but already word had spread he was knowledgeable, fair, and had the ear of the president.

"As a matter of fact, I am. I enjoy him and his wife, Marie, a lot. Perhaps you and your wife would like to join us for dinner one night?"

"Delighted, Senator," Bridgeman said instantly. "I'll get back to you ASAP."

The senator ended the call.

Bridgeman sat motionless at his desk, hand resting on his telephone receiver. He snapped it up.

Using the keyed-in Catapult directory, he dialed Tucker's handheld and got the recorded message again. "Dammit, Tucker, call me!" He hung up. The last time he had discovered Ryder's whereabouts for the senator, it had been because he had joined a conversation between Tucker and Bash Badawi. The question about Ryder had been easy to slip in, and Tucker had shown no suspicion. Bridgeman smiled to himself. Badawi was leading the hunt club investigation. He looked up Badawi and dialed.

"Yes, sir?" Badawi sounded appropriately deferential.

"Are you still at the Esti Hunt Club?"

"No, sir. I'm home. Do you want me to come back in?"

Bridgeman ignored the question. "Why don't I have your report?"

"I haven't written it yet. I gave it verbally to Tucker."

"I want to hear it, too."

"Yes, sir." Badawi started talking.

Bridgeman sat back, surprised. "Let's be clear. You found no corpses. No blood or other signs of violence."

"That's right. As I said, the place had been sanitized."

Or nothing had happened there at all, Bridgeman thought to himself. He drummed his fingers on his desktop. "Where's Tucker now?"

"He said he was going to Maryland, to Martin Chapman's farm."

Bridgeman frowned. "Why?"

"Don't know, sir."

Bridgeman remembered a rumor that Chapman had ordered the death of Ryder's father.

"Is Judd Ryder going to Chapman's place, too?" Bridgeman asked.

"Yes, sir."

Are they going there to confront Chapman? Bridgeman wondered. He ended the call then dialed Senator Leggate. He got right to the point: "Judd Ryder and Tucker Andersen are, or soon will be, at Martin Chapman's place in Maryland."

"You're certain?" She sounded as surprised as he had felt.

"Absolutely."

"You're a man of your word. I'll get you together with the O'Days."

"Thank you for the opportunity to help you, Senator. It's been a pleasure."

Hanging up, he sat motionless, digesting. He'd had two good wins. First, he had scored big with Senator Leggate, and second, he had caught Tucker operating outside CIA protocols—way out. This time, Bridgeman had him by the short hairs.

31

Montgomery County, Maryland

After inspecting the guards' locker room in Chapman's mansion, Ryder changed into a green sweatsuit, slung a bandolier across his chest, and chose an M4 from the gun cabinet. He checked the weapon then paced the guards' locker room, waiting for Tucker and responding to his texts. Every second increased his chances of being discovered. There was a clipboard hanging near the door. It listed the guards' schedule. Finally he snatched it and left, following the route he had seen the yawning guard take down the short hall to a closed door.

Opening it, he saw a long, deserted corridor that extended across the building's rear. It was just wide enough for a serving cart—the staff's passageway. An air of emptiness enveloped him. It felt almost as if no one lived here. Despite the mansion's vast size, no floorboards creaked, no voices conversed. Guards, cooks, the Eichels, and Chapman were on the premises, but still there was an eerie silence.

He needed to get up to the second floor. To the left were doors that opened into the front of the house, where there would be some kind of grand staircase. To the right he could see near the end of the corridor what he needed—a stairwell. It would be the servants' stairs, much less high profile. But before he could reach it, he had to pass an open door-way. Light from it spilled into the corridor, and now at last there was noise. It came from that room—the sound of a chair squeaking.

He decided to check the front staircase. But before he could turn away, a guard stepped from the room pointing an M4 directly at him as if he had known he was there. The guard's wiry brown eyebrows were lowered over dark eyes that had the thick look of sleep. His cheek was creased as if it had been resting against something. He was the same man Ryder had seen leaving the locker room earlier. He seemed to have just awakened from an on-the-job nap.

"Who the fuck are you?" he demanded.

"I'm the new man," Ryder spoke firmly. "Did you write these damn orders?" He raised the clipboard that listed the guards' schedule.

"Troy didn't say we had a new man."

"Troy should've told you." Ryder figured Troy was probably the shift manager. He infused his tone with outrage. "He said I could work in-side tonight." He shook the clipboard at the guard. "But this has me pa-trolling outside. It's colder than a polar bear's cheeks out there. Check with Troy. I want to talk to him, too. Is he with Mr. Chapman?"

The guard's gaze narrowed. "I'm calling Troy. Move." He jerked his head at the room he had just left.

With a shrug, Ryder walked down the corridor, past the man, and into the room. It had to be the security center. The distant wall held surveillance monitors. One screen displayed the hall Ryder had just entered, which explained how the guard had known to come out with his M4 raised. Others showed the horse farm's perimeter wall and the interiors of the barn and garage. The mansion's first floor was also covered. Other than themselves, the only people in sight were in the kitchen, where a chef and a sous chef were stonily at work, their backs to each other. None of the rooms on the second or third floor showed, only long corridors lined with paintings, decorative tables, and closed doors. The house looked almost as vacant as it felt, which suggested the action had to be somewhere behind one of those up-stairs doors.

"There's too much turnover here," the man said irritably, studying Ryder. "Can't keep track of the hires. Damn Troy."

Ryder made his voice hearty—and conspiratorial. "Yeah, if I was you I'd be pissed, too. My name's Roger C. Graves. Call me Rog. What's yours?" As Ryder talked, he noted three file cabinets, a worktable with folding chairs, and a long, narrow desk beneath the monitors. There was no outside window.

"Matty Perkins. I babysit the security screens." Keeping his gaze and weapon on Ryder, he walked toward the desk.

Planting a friendly smile on his face, Ryder followed, narrowing the gap. The phone was sitting on the desk to the left of the chair, which was on casters. It should roll easily.

"Hold it." Matty snapped up his M4 and aimed between Ryder's eyes. "Keep your distance. What d'you think you're doing?"

Opening the back door, Tucker hurried into the mansion's warmth. His eyeglasses clouded over. Pulling off his balaclava, he removed the glasses and flexed the frozen fingers of his gun hand.

His vision was hazy, but he could see he was in a short hallway, just as Judd had described. He padded forward, passing an archway that led into a kitchen. From the opening sounded the distant thud of a cleaver hitting a butcher block. Putting on his glasses again, Tucker saw a closed door on the right—again as Judd had said. It should lead to the guards' locker room. Cracking it open, he scanned and stepped inside. Where was Judd?

Tucker texted him again. As he waited for an answer, he tossed the locker room, finding only the usual deodorant, shaving lotion, and un-derwear. Worried, he sat down on a bench, took off his boots, and mas-saged his aching legs and feet. Plowing uphill through the snow had been harder on him than he had expected. And now that he was warm-ing up, his legs ached even more. He had fond memories of being twenty-five. Hell, forty-five.

Putting on his boots again, he left, heading down the short hall. He looked at his handheld—still no text from Judd. Judd had always been a wild hare, and probably this time was no different. Or at least he hoped it was, and Judd had not gotten himself into a dark hole of trouble.

32

In the security center, Ryder watched Matty's thick eyebrows lower in suspicion and his eyes narrow. Ryder had moved too close.

Ryder stepped back, positioning himself on the other side of the rolling desk chair. "Guess I wasn't thinking."

"Damn straight you weren't."

As Matty glared, Ryder glimpsed what he did not want to see—one of the screens showed Tucker walking down the short hall, Browning in hand, still wearing his feed-store jacket. Fortunately, Matty had not seen Tucker yet.

Trying to keep the guard's attention on him, Ryder asked, "You going to call Troy or not?"

"Yeah." Matty's focus shifted to the phone. He took a step to the only place from where he could comfortably reach it—the other side of the desk chair.

Ryder kicked the chair hard. It flew forward on its wheels and clipped Matty's side, throwing him off balance. Ryder dropped the clipboard, hefted his M4, and rammed the butt into the man's temple. Blood spurted. Matty reeled, his head thrown to the side. Ryder ripped away his weapon, but Matty was reaching behind, pulling out a knife. Ryder slammed his M4 into the man's skull again.

Matty crashed back against the wall. His eyes were open, glazing in an unmistakable look of pain and confusion. Blood washed down the side of his face as he closed his eyes and fell limp. His fingers unfurled. He was unconscious.

With the butt of his M4, Ryder smashed the security equipment, taking the surveillance cameras offline. As he turned to go to Tucker, the phone on the desk rang. He hesitated. If he did not answer, whoever was calling would be suspicious. On the other hand, if he *did* answer, the caller might be "Troy," and Troy apparently was the authority on who should and should not be in Chapman's house.

After listening at the hall door, Tucker stepped into a long corridor. A phone was ringing ahead from an open doorway. Before he could move, the ringing stopped, the room went dark, and Judd stepped out and closed the door. Judd looked quickly around and ran toward him.

"What's happened?" Tucker asked in a low voice.

Judd stopped in front of him. "I had to knock out the security chief and smash the security monitors."

"Dammit, I told you to wait for me."

Judd shook his head. "You were gone so long I could've asphalted a highway to Baghdad. Besides, you're not in charge this time—remember? Did you learn anything about the dead sentries?"

Tucker did not answer. Behind Judd a guard in green sweats had just burst out of the stairwell and was running toward them, M4 ready. Tucker felt a jolt of energy. But before he could move, Judd shoved him back through the doorway. As Tucker slammed against the wall, Judd crouched, spun, and fired a burst from his M4. The explosive noise reverberated. In the kitchen, someone shrieked, and pans hit the floor with a loud metallic clatter.

Positioning his Browning, Tucker returned to the corridor.

The guard's chin was lifted as if he had just been punched. Blood drenched his sweatshirt. He staggered two more steps, dropped hard to his knees, then fell forward onto his face. Judd was already sprinting toward him.

Tucker followed, listening to feet rushing away from the kitchen. From the sound of it, the staff was jumping ship.

Judd squatted beside the wounded man. The metallic stench of blood rose in the air. The guard's face was turned toward them, one eye visible. It was closed. His breath was ragged.

"Damn," Judd said with a sigh. "Lucky to be alive, but unconscious."

"How did you know he was behind you?"

"I heard him running, and I saw you react. You're slow tonight. Are you all right?"

"It was damn cold outside, in case you didn't notice. Let's move."

With a businesslike nod, Judd was back up on his feet and running. Tucker worked to keep up. They were nearing the rear staircase when he heard low voices from the opposite end of the corridor. He listened, gauging how many were coming.

"Three," he told Judd in a husky whisper. "They'll be in sight in seconds. We ought to be able to take three."

"We want at least one alive and conscious." Judd turned back and tried the knob of the door they had just passed. Locked.

Tucker tried the one they had been approaching. Locked, too.

Judd passed him. There was one last door, and it was nearly opposite the staircase. Judd pushed it open. Tucker glanced back long enough to see the corridor was still empty. Judd pointed at Tucker then at the door. Tucker nodded. As Judd ducked up into the stairwell, Tucker plunged through the doorway and into darkness.

33

Sitting in a wingback chair in the library, Eli Eichel tapped the toe of a boot impatiently. Martin Chapman sat across the coffee table from him, drumming his fingers on the arm of his chair. Suddenly there was the noise of gunfire, a series of loud cracks that seemed to reverberate against the walls of books. The gunfire came from below.

Eli jumped to his feet. "We need weapons!"

Chapman jabbed a finger at Troy, the big muscular man who was the lead guard. "The gun cabinet." He jerked his head toward the west wall of books. "Do it!"

As Troy ran, Chapman looked at the remaining guard and ordered, "Call Kyle. Find out why the gunshots. With luck he's caught Ryder and Andersen." Chapman had sent Kyle downstairs to find out why the chief of security had not answered his phone call.

With Eli and Danny Eichel at his side, Chapman hurried across the expansive room.

As usual, Danny's large face was placid, but there was a flash in his eyes. "What's happening?" Unless he was personally interested in a subject, he ignored it. The gunfire had gotten his attention.

"Judd Ryder and his CIA pal Tucker Andersen are here," Eli told him.

"What's wrong with that?" Danny said reasonably. "We want Ryder, so it's convenient if he comes to us. It's efficient."

Eli glanced up at his brother, hiding his annoyance. "The gunshots are what's wrong."

"Kyle isn't answering his cell, sir!" the door sentry called out.

So the man they had sent downstairs was off the grid, too, thought Eli.

"Keep trying, dammit." Reaching the bookshelves, Chapman glared at Troy. "How in hell could Andersen and Ryder get past your security?"

Troy straightened all the way up to his impressive six-foot-five height. "I don't know, sir. But there are five of us in this room, plus there will be six new men in the house any minute to start their shift. I called to tell them what's happened. Even if the rest of our people are down, there are eleven of us against two of them." His shoulders seemed to grow more broad, and his muscular face took on a feral caginess. "They can't win."

"I want Ryder alive," Eli reminded him sharply.

"Yes, sir. Everyone knows that, sir."

"You asked about weapons," Chapman said and gestured at Troy.

Expecting a secret door in the bookshelves, Eli watched the big guard press his thumb against a spot inside one of the uprights. There was a moment of silence, then the floor beneath Eli's feet began to move. Swearing, Eli stepped away.

Danny leaped back as if a rattlesnake had lunged at him.

As Eli watched the floor, a six-by-five-foot section lowered some five inches. Dividing in half, the two parts slid silently away from each other. He felt a wave of excitement as a dozen gleaming M4s came into view. Arranged uniformly, the weapons lay in a rifle rack inside a polished wood cabinet. Boxes of ammunition were stacked alongside them. For Eli, the weapons were a sight more beautiful than a Michelangelo painting, more impressive than a Cambridge degree, more inspiring than a rabbi's sermon.

"This is how protection is secured," Chapman advised. "Preparation is key, but preparation no one knows about."

Danny grumbled, "I'd rather have my Kalashnikov."

But when Troy handed up the first M4, Danny was the one who grabbed it.

34

While Tucker hid in a room across the corridor, Ryder hunched at the base of the servants' stairwell. Listening as footsteps padded toward them, Ryder took a small mirror from his pocket and extended it—there were three men. One was in the lead; the two others followed single-file, moving warily, knees bent, pistols up. They wore neither green sweats nor white snowsuits but instead ordinary street clothes—jeans and shirts. Their cheeks were red, their skin shiny, as if they had just come in from outdoors. They were probably with the next shift of guards, and somehow they knew there was trouble in the house.

With a gesture, the leader directed the second man toward the kitchen door. Then he and the other continued on through the shadows. Ryder could almost smell the tension.

At the door that led to the short hall, the lead gestured again. But as his man started toward it, it opened, and the second guard reappeared, apparently having gone into the kitchen at one entrance and leaving from the other. Shaking his head to indicate he had found no one, he grinned and held up three M4s, probably taken from the guards' locker room. In moments, all were armed with the rifles.

Little is more unnerving than the sound of M4s being cocked. As the ominous noise filled the corridor, Ryder checked across it, to his right. No light showed in the room where Tucker had ducked. The guards would reach Tucker before they reached him, and he was worried Tucker might not hear them.

But as he stared, the spymaster's face appeared and faded back into darkness. A pale hand gave a thumb's-up signal. Tucker was saying he was on top of the situation—not to worry. But Ryder liked neither his wan color nor that he had reacted slowly to the guard who had run at them earlier. Tucker was not moving as fast or as agilely as he usually did.

Tucker's door closed slowly, leaving a two-inch opening.

Peering into his mirror again, Ryder saw the trio had broken into a run, focused on the guard he had shot. The lead dropped beside him and bent his head low. Even if you despised a brother in arms, you did not want him to go down—it reminded you, reminded everyone, that all of you were vulnerable.

Above the lead, the two others surveyed the corridor.

Jumping back up to his feet, the lead glanced at them and shook his head. He spoke quietly into a cell phone.

"Kyle's unconscious . . . nothing we can do for him . . . downstairs back hall. Yeah, sure. If they're still here, we'll find them."

The lead cautiously opened the first door they came upon—the security office, where Ryder had knocked out Matty and broken up the security equipment. The man slid inside low, M4 first. Within seconds the office was alight, and a snort of disgust sounded. Soon he reappeared, his expression sour.

The trio ran again. One after another, they opened the next two doors and inspected. Ryder glanced across to Tucker's door just as it closed completely. He texted Tucker:

They r coming.

The guards closed in on Tucker's room. The lead turned the door-knob and pushed. But instead of swinging open, the door slid off its hinges and slammed heavily down into the dark room, bouncing twice, making two loud *bangs*. From the depths of the lightless room, three gunshots rang out.

All three men were hit, the lead in the knee, another in the shoulder, and the third on the right side. Blood sprayed.

Ryder slid around the corner, putting him behind the wounded guards as they scrambled for position. The lead had dropped to his belly and was pulling his M4 around to shoot. The guard with the side wound threw himself against the wall beside the door, propping himself up so he could peer inside and fire. The third was closest to Ryder. The back of his beige flannel shirt was soggy red—the bullet must have gone all the way through. He was stumbling away, to where Tucker could not see him.

As he took in the situation, Ryder heard two sets of footsteps hurry-ing downstairs. He made a tough decision: If Tucker and he were to survive, there was little chance they could keep one of the trio here conscious and available for questioning, not with more arriving.

Two of the wounded men were shooting into the dark room. Bright muzzle flashes responded. The man with the shoulder wound who was out of the line of fire seemed to hear the footsteps on the stairs, too. He swung his M4 around—and spotted Ryder.

Ryder shot him in both thighs. The noise attracted the attention of the two others, and they turned. As they fired, Ryder did, too, explo-sive bursts from his M4. He had known precisely where they were, while they had shot on the move, looking for him.

His bullets cut ragged lines across their mid sections. As they went down, the man he had shot in the thighs managed to squirm around, lift his torso up onto his elbows, and fire. The rounds burned past Ryder's right ear and slammed into the wall. Plaster dust exploded.

Before Ryder could return fire, one of Tucker's bullets hit the shoot-er's rib cage. It must have pierced his lungs. He exhaled loudly and dropped, gasping.

There was no way Tucker could know about the men coming downstairs, and Ryder did not have time to tell him. Instead he grabbed the clipboard he had confiscated earlier, jumped up, and sprinted to the foot of the stairwell.

Dressed in regular clothes and armed with handguns, two men were about halfway down. More relief guards. They must have come in the front door. They quickly registered his uniform and clipboard—then frowned at his face.

"Who in hell are you?" one demanded.

Before he could ask another question, Ryder interrupted. "We've got a bad situation here. We were able to take down four of theirs, but there's got to be ten more out back. A couple of our people are completely out of action, including Matty and Kyle."

The second one's eyebrows went up. "Jesus Christ."

"They'll be inside any moment," Ryder warned.

The first man gave a curt nod. "Let's get this problem taken care of before it gets any worse."

As the men rushed downstairs to help, Ryder asked worriedly, "What about Mr. Chapman? We've got to protect him. Is he on the second floor?"

The first nodded. "In the library as usual."

A shoulder slammed Ryder aside, and Tucker was beside him, firing bursts of three rounds into each man. Surprise then pain contorted their faces. Wounded in the chests, they wove and fell.

Tucker gave him a sharp look. "We know where Eichel and Chapman are now. Let's go."

35

The narrow stairwell was claustrophobic, the stench of cordite stinking the air. Ryder and Tucker climbed. Ryder saw Tucker was sweating so much his eyeglasses had slid down his nose. With an irritated expression, the older man shoved them back up.

"You win a gold medal for those last two guys," Ryder said in a low voice.

"I figured they probably had their guns on you."

"You figured right."

There were soft sounds above. Ryder peered up again. The doorknob was turning. Tucker saw it, too. The rotation was slow and deliberate, cautious. Without speaking, they separated, flattening back against opposite walls. They aimed their M4s.

The door opened. But instead of more weaponized guards, in the frame stood a woman with long red hair, wearing a thermal winter coat. The unbuttoned coat showed jeans, a pullover sweater, and a cardigan, Eva's favorite winter clothes. She just stood there, hands helpless at her sides. No weapon. No purse. A strained expression on her oval face.

Ryder stared. His heart pounded. "Eva," he breathed. For a moment he was overcome by memories, the little things about her that delighted him so. And now here she was, standing there, waiting. And in trouble.

Tucker peeled himself off the wall. "Christ, Eva, what in hell are you doing here?"

"Have you lost your mind?" Ryder's fear for her erased relief. "We've got to get you out of here!" He sprinted up the stairs.

"Hello, Judd. Tucker." Her voice was too hearty. "I'm really sorry to do this to you—"

The men froze as two armed guards appeared on either side of her. One guard wore a regulation white snowsuit, his face unseeable behind the usual matching white balaclava. He was pointing an M4 at her, his eyes shining black and hard. Wearing khakis and a plaid shirt, the other one aimed an S&W 9-mm at Tucker and Ryder.

"Let's go, Ryder," said the one in civilian clothes. "You, too, Andersen."

So the gunman knew their names. They were expected, which explained why the second shift had arrived ready to fight.

"Move it," the man in the snowsuit ordered Eva.

When she did not go instantly, he grabbed her arm. She shook it. He pushed his M4 into her side. Her face collapsed. She let him pull her out of sight.

Ryder ran up the last few steps. His throat was dry, his chest tight. Keeping his eye on the S&W, he heard Tucker breathing hard behind him. At the top of the stairs, they stepped onto plush carpeting the dark color of blood. The hall was wide, with antiques placed along the wainscoted walls. A few feet distant, the man in snow gear released Eva's arm.

"Come here." He nodded at Ryder and Tucker. "Give me your weapons."

"I'll take them," said the other. "You've got your hands full with her." He gestured at Eva.

The man in white hesitated, then nodded.

Without comment Ryder and Tucker turned them over to the guard wearing indoor clothes.

Tucking them under his arm, he asked the man in the snowsuit, "Why in hell don't you take off those snow clothes? You've got to be hot."

"If you'd been outside as long as I was tonight you'd want to bake, fry, and broil yourself any which way you could. I can't get the cold out of my bones."

The other man gave a curt nod of understanding. "Okay, cocksuckers. Gotta search you. You're mine, Ryder. Don't try anything cute. You won't like the price your friend Blake pays."

"You"—the guard in the snowsuit nodded at Eva—"sit on the floor. There. No, dammit, you're in no position to argue. *Do it.*"

Her face a thundercloud, Eva slid down the wall beside a sideboard. Calming his feelings for her, Ryder gave her a quick smile of encouragement. She closed her eyes a moment and smiled in return, a small one, but real.

While hands roughed him up, Ryder thought about summer camp on the Chesapeake the year he turned twelve, long swims in the cold bay, pounding nails into siding as he helped to build a shelter. He glanced over at Tucker, who had a faraway expression on his face as he endured being frisked, too.

"Shit, all he's got is a billfold and a smartphone," said the man in white, who had done Tucker.

"Yeah, that's what mine has, too. Let's go, morons. Time to meet the boss."

Tucker was having trouble getting his jacket zipped. With a shrug, he gave up.

Ryder and Tucker walked ahead, the S&W at their backs. Eva and the guard in the snowsuit brought up the rear. Somewhere a clock ticked, one of those monotonous noises that made jumpy nerves worse.

"Stop, fuckers," the guard behind them ordered. "Turn left and face the door. Ryder, stand in front of the peephole."

The wooden door was broad, paneled, classic. Judging by its location, it opened onto the room Ryder and Tucker had seen alight from the road. He faced the peephole.

The guard in khakis pressed a cell phone to his ear. "I've got Ryder. And I've got Andersen and Eva Blake, too." There was a pause. "Of course I'm damn sure. They match the photos you e-mailed. Check out Ryder in the peephole. He's alive, just like you wanted."

36

With Ryder in the lead, they walked into a bibliophile's dream. Thousands of books lettered with decorative inks and paints filled three tall walls. Ryder stared. His father had had a private library like this, a library that both of them had loved.

Turning away, he focused on the men who were waiting with their M4s. His gaze locked on to Chapman. The mogul's silver hair was swept back in waves, and he was as aristocratic-looking as ever. His stance was relaxed, his smile confident, as if handling both a multibillion-dollar equity firm and a lethal M4 were everyday tasks. Fury rose bitter in Judd's throat. A painful sense of loss swept through him, for his father, for Eva's years in the penitentiary. For the many people Chapman had ruined or killed.

Lined up next to Chapman were the Eichel brothers. Eli Eichel—olive skin, small, wiry, a deadly fox. Danny Eichel—huge, cagy, aiming his rifle with one large hand. On either side of the trio stood two guards.

Behind Eva, Tucker, and Ryder were the pair of guards who had brought them. They blocked the door—the only escape route back into the corridor.

"Welcome, gentlemen." Chapman inclined his head toward Eva. "And lady. Have you met my other guests? These are the Eichel brothers, Eli and Danny."

Eli Eichel was having none of it. "What is this bullshit?" He glared at the guards. "Did you search them?"

"Yes, sir," the one in regular clothes replied. "No hidden weapons, and no limestone rocks either. Just cell phones and the usual billfolds et cetera."

Eichel turned his dark gaze onto Ryder. "You've got the Padre's pieces from the tablet. Where are they?"

Ryder frowned and lied, "What tablet? What pieces?"

Danny had been watching Ryder. "He's hidden them someplace."

"It's a good guess, if I had them," Ryder allowed, "but that's all it is—a guess."

"He's a liar," Danny said. "The pieces are in his car."

"That's logic, not clairvoyance." Ryder layered indignation into his tone. "The only thing left in our delivery truck—not a car—is the smell of pizza and beer."

"We'll decide that for ourselves," Eli announced. "Danny." The single word was a command.

Danny grinned and lumbered toward Eva. "She'll tell us where it is." His neck was so thick and short his bowling-ball head seemed to grow directly out of his bulky shoulders. But unlike the rest of his thuggish appearance, his black eyes showed intelligence. When he had looked at his brother, his gaze had been accommodating, tender. Now Ryder saw inevitability in his eyes, destiny: He was a killer. Killers killed.

Ryder's throat tightened. "She doesn't know."

"Maybe not, but you do," Danny said reasonably.

Eva stepped back. "Judd said he doesn't have the pieces."

Danny stopped and studied her. "I'm six meters away from you, or almost twenty feet," he told her. "From now on I'll slow to a rate of five kilometers an hour, or 1.39 meters per second. That's about 3.1 miles an hour, which is the average human walking speed. I will need only 4.32 seconds, more or less, to reach you. In that time Ryder has a chance to change his mind and tell us where the tablet pieces are. If not, I'll erase you."

Eva angled her body, bent her knees, and lifted her hands, preparing for defensive sword-hand strikes. She exuded defiance. She was not a small woman. Still, Danny dwarfed her.

Ryder had had enough. He moved in front of her. "Back off, Danny."

She stepped up beside Ryder and resumed her stance. "We'll do this together, Judd." She turned flashing eyes on Danny.

A voice boomed from the entry door, filling the library. "Enough, Eli. Call off Danny. Tell us where your portion of the tablet is, and perhaps we can convince Ryder to do the same."

Surprised, all turned. But instead of homing in on the voice, their gazes went instantly to the sentry who was dressed in a plaid shirt and khakis. He was sitting on the floor, slouched back against the door, eyes open. Blood was gushing from a mortal gash to his carotid artery, soaking his clothes. While they had been riveted by the tension between Danny and Eva, the man in white snow gear had eliminated the guard in the same manner as the two outdoor sentries had died.

The speaker, his white clothes sprinkled with blood, stood over his victim, aiming his M4 across the library at Eli Eichel.

Eli moved forward, focusing his M4 back at him.

Except for Tucker and Eva, everyone had been caught off guard. Tucker quickly produced a 9-mm Walther PPS from inside his jacket and trained it on Chapman. At the same time, Eva pulled an M4 from beneath her long padded coat and pointed it at Danny.

Judd noted that Chapman and his guards were standing off alone, spectators in a contest that apparently had nothing to do with them. Judd itched for a weapon. *Think for yourself. You have responsibilities—live up to them.* Judd yanked the M4 from Eva, slammed his shoulder into Danny, and squeezed the trigger, laying a line of automatic fire across Chapman and his two guards.

The rounds ripped through the men's torsos and burst out their backs.

Books exploded from the shelves behind them. Shredded paper rained down. But all that Judd saw was one perfect moment of retribution—Chapman's death. He had corrected a mistake. For a brief moment, he felt peace.

There was an immediate response. Danny lunged at Judd, and Judd hit the floor so hard he released his M4. Gasping for air, he rolled, chasing the weapon.

"Stop!" the voice roared from the killer at the door, the man in white. "Ryder is under my protection."

The library was suddenly still.

"Eli, tell your brother to back off." Again it was the voice from behind.

Danny's hulky shoulders quivered. "Eli?"

"Do it, Danny," Eli told him. "You can have fun later."

With the deliberation of a dance master, Danny took a step back, then another and another, his M4 pointed down at Ryder.

Ryder snatched up his M4 and got to his feet.

Eva was staring at him, shock in her eyes. "Jesus, Judd."

He shrugged then turned to the man in white at the back of the room. "What's going on here?"

Eva frowned at the man, too. "You waited a long time, Frank. That's not how we planned it."

"You *planned* this?" Judd said.

"Yes. I met Frank at the service gate, and he filled me in."

Now Ryder understood how Eva and Tucker must have gotten weapons: "Frank," the sentry in snow clothes, had given Eva the M4 earlier, and then when he supposedly searched Tucker for weapons, he had slipped him the Walther.

Ryder did not know who Frank was, even when he peeled off his white balaclava and walked toward them. He had a large Roman nose and thick gray hair that showed the vestiges of having been carefully tousled. A man of moderate height and stocky build, there was something dapper about him, about the casual but confident way he moved and held his M4. Despite having apparently scrubbed three men tonight, he seemed completely relaxed, and somehow the more dangerous for it.

His gray beard jutting, Tucker glared at Frank. "Thanks for the Walther. But who in hell are you, and what are you doing in the middle of my operation?"

"What?" Eva said. "Tucker, you asked for Frank's help—"

"Like hell I did."

Frank Smith said nothing. He was gazing steadily at Eli Eichel.

The corners of Eli Eichel's mouth twitched.

Frank Smith gave a wicked smile.

Eli laughed. It started small then turned into guffaws. "Dammit, you've done it again." He laughed more, enjoying the joke. He glanced around at Eva, Tucker, and Ryder. "Don't you know who saved you?"

The man in white lifted two fingers and touched his forehead in a brisk salute to the three.

Frowning, Ryder searched his memory for the gesture. . . . And then it was vivid.

Eva inhaled sharply. "My God, he's the Carnivore. Frank Smith is the Carnivore."

37

As Eva watched, the Carnivore laughed. "There are few times in our profession when one is amused," he told Eli Eichel. "I wondered how long it would take you. How did you know?"

"After all these years, I damn well better know," Eli said. "First, it's the Walther PPS you gave Andersen—your favorite pistol. But others like the same gun, so that wasn't enough. The clincher was your walk. You're tough, because you change yours with almost every role. But I remember you were using your 'Frank Smith' walk when we ran into each other in London in 1986."

The Carnivore's face froze. Whatever had occurred then, he had not liked it. Without moving his M4 from Eli, he glanced at Judd, Eva, and Tucker. "Good to see you haven't forgotten me. On the other hand, knowing me hasn't turned out to be the best luck for you. I'm in a hurry, so here's the bottom line. This isn't a reunion. It's just a momentary intersection of needs. You can call me Alex. Alex Bosa."

Eva calmed her pounding heart. "I thought you looked familiar. Why didn't you tell me what was going on?"

"I'd hoped to be able to send you back to the Farm without anyone ever knowing I was here. The Padre found out you were due R and R soon, and he was set on kidnapping you and Judd. He created doubles for both of you to buy him plenty of time to question you. His backup plan was to let it be known he was holding you so I'd get wind of it and try to rescue you. But then I killed Judd's double, and Judd came home early from Iraq and went looking for you." His gaze swept the three of them. "I owed you for saving my life. This is payback."

Eva knew the Carnivore had rules, and within their context he was ethical although seldom moral. One of his rules was to treat like with like, which was why paying back was a priority. Still, she'd had no desire ever to see him again. Dealing with the Carnivore was like having a flesh-eating piranha in your fish tank—exotic, but too close for comfort.

"He's right," Judd told her. "The Padre was trying to find him. He thought he could get the information from you or me, and he went to Tucker, too, hoping to trade for it." He addressed the Carnivore. "No one else has said it, so I will. Thanks for the help."

The Carnivore looked him up and down. "I thought you were out of the business."

"I thought I was, too."

"You'll live longer if you quit," he advised. "But after what you just did to Chapman, I don't know that you can."

Judd's face seemed to pale, Eva thought, but his expression remained unchanged, neutral.

Tucker interrupted: "How many of you assassins involved in this thing with the cuneiform pieces are in the United States?"

"To my knowledge, only those in this room," Bosa told him.

They checked each other from the corners of their eyes, two old pros who disliked each other.

Tucker snorted. "That's three too many."

Done with him, Bosa confronted Eli Eichel: "You and I need to talk about Burleigh Morgan. Do you know who planted the bomb under his car?"

"I'm telling you nothing unless you give me your limestone pieces," Eli said coolly. "You can't really care about the money. You're rich anyway."

"My reputation and life are on the line, too, but perhaps you're right." He slid his hand inside his snowsuit and withdrew a cloth box about three inches thick. It looked like some kind of microfiber material, the sort that molded itself to its contents. "I have four of the pieces, as you may remember." He walked to the library table, set down the box, and lifted the lid. "They're yours—in exchange for all of your information. No lies. No omissions. Agreed?"

Eva had no idea what the two men were talking about, except that it seemed to involve some deal that had gone terribly wrong.

"Agreed." Eli padded to the table and grabbed what appeared to be two of Bosa's rocks. He raised them to chin level. Using his thumb, he turned them over and around, examining them. Then he put them back and repeated the process with the last two. His face inscrutable, from his jacket he pulled a padded cloth bag that appeared to contain other items—more limestone pieces perhaps. Humming a little tune, he slid two of Bosa's pieces into the bag, signaling he accepted Bosa's offer.

So fast his hand was almost invisible, Bosa scooped the remaining rocks into his microfiber box, closed the lid, squeezed the Velcro shut, and returned the box to his pocket. "You can have the rest when I'm satisfied you've told me everything," he said. "Start with Morgan. Do you know who wiped him?"

Eva remembered reading the account of the infamous old international assassin Burleigh Morgan climbing into his gull-wing car in Paris and the driver's seat exploding under him. Not only had the bombing meant certain death, it also seemed deliberately dramatic to catch the attention of media worldwide, which it had.

"Morgan was too damn good, too well liked," Eli reasoned. "Worse, he knew too much. But no, it wasn't me that killed him. Hell, it could've been a disgruntled former employer for all any of us know. If you and the Padre hadn't carried him out, he would've died on the museum grounds. He's been living on borrowed time."

Bosa shrugged. "Somehow you found out the Padre was going to be at his hunt club, so you had time to set up for a sniper shoot. Knowing how close-mouthed he was, you either turned one of his people or planted one of yours inside his organization."

"I convinced one of his team to help me," Eli admitted. "He was feeling underpaid and unappreciated. I took care of both problems."

"You've eliminated him?"

"Of course."

"Which one of us are you working with?" Bosa asked.

"He's working with me," Danny said possessively.

Bosa did not even glance at him.

Eli Eichel hesitated, seeming to debate with himself. "I've been collaborating with Krot. He's the one who told me about the man inside the Padre's organization. My job was to take care of the Padre and retrieve his pieces, which I'll get from Ryder as soon as you and I finish our business. At the same time, Krot's job has been to find Seymour. As far as we can tell, Seymour dropped off the face of the planet in late 2003. I think his share of the tablet was four pieces. Do you have any idea where he is?"

Eva felt Tucker stiffen beside her. The Carnivore had said the three assassins in this room were the only ones he knew to be working in country, which meant that if "Krot" and "Seymour" were assassins, they were outside U.S. borders.

"No idea where Seymour is," Bosa told him. "Where's Krot?"

"At a hotel in Vienna, the Inner Stadt. Don't remember which one."

"Where are you now in the mission?"

"With your pieces, the Padre's, mine, and Krot's, we'll have more than half the tablet. Want to come in on this? It may take all of us to find Seymour and pin him down. He's one ruthless son-of-a-bitch."

"Not like us at all." There was irony in Bosa's tone. "I'll think about it."

Eli gave a slow, suspicious nod. "I've told you the truth. You owe me those last two pieces. Hand them over."

Bosa said nothing. Did nothing. No one moved.

The library table was on the room's west side, where the Carnivore and Eli Eichel stood beside it, facing each other. To the east, Judd, Tucker, and Eva were together, while Danny was positioned to keep his weapon trained on them while periodically checking on his brother.

Emotions flashed across Eli Eichel's face—fear, anger, hatred, and then nothing.

"Krot's not in Vienna," the Carnivore said quietly, too quietly. "He's in Marrakech, and you damn well know it."

As Eli started to snap up his M4, Danny yelled, "No!"

The Carnivore fired a single burst into Eli's throat. At such close range, the rounds nearly decapitated him. He reeled, then toppled.

"Brother!" Danny screamed as Eli's body hit the floor. He ran to Eli, blindly spraying automatic fire around the room.

The Carnivore fired again.

The bullets landed in a small circle in Danny's chest, above his heart. His head snapped back then fell forward. His great bulk propelling him, he lumbered two more steps and crashed to the floor, inches from Eli.

Judd was already moving, checking bodies, picking up weapons.

Bosa let his M4 drift down to his side. An iPhone appeared in his hand. He spoke into it: "Come and get us, Jack. We're done here. I turned on the lights to the landing strip. You shouldn't have any trouble. Hurry."

Eva heard Tucker moan.

"Oh, my God," Eva breathed. She knelt beside the old spymaster and raised her voice: "Tucker's down. Head wound. It looks bad!"

38

Judd ran back to Tucker. One of Danny's wild bullets must have hit him. Tucker was lying on his belly, his head turned to the side, the Walther near his hand. His tortoiseshell glasses had fallen off. One lens was cracked. His eyes were closed. Blood spread down his cheek, matting his gray beard.

Eva held her cardigan sweater against his head, trying to control the bleeding.

"Open your eyes, Tucker," she was saying. "Come on, I know you can do it. Open your eyes!" She glanced at Judd, her expression grim. "His pupils are different sizes. It's typical of head injuries. We need to get him to a trauma unit."

Bosa had been talking on his iPhone. Ending the call, he said, "The Merrittville Hospital has the closest one. Jack can fly us to the airport in ten minutes. One of my people is a medic. He'll do triage on the way."

Judd tapped numbers on his smartphone, calling Gloria Feit. It was late, past two A.M. Gloria and her husband, Ted, were probably in bed.

Still, her voice was strong when she answered. "This better be good, Judd."

"Tucker's been shot in the head," he told her bluntly. "He's alive, but he's not moving, not talking."

"Oh, God, no." There was a pause. When she spoke again, her voice was controlled. "What can I do?"

"We need an ambulance to meet us at the Merrittville airport to take Tucker to the hospital." He got a description and tail number for the plane from Bosa, then relayed the information to Gloria.

"Taken care of." Her line went dead.

Bosa had been searching Eli Eichel. He pocketed Eli's limestone pieces.

Judd flung books off a free-standing bookcase and carried two empty shelves about six feet long to Tucker and set them on the floor beside him. Judd and Bosa picked up Tucker and laid him on the makeshift stretcher.

Judd's phone rang. It was Gloria again. "I've alerted the hospital that a classified federal employee needs emergency care. An ambulance is on its way to the airport. A police escort will meet the paramedics, and one of the cops will stay with Tucker until I can get our people there to make certain he has the help he needs and doesn't inadvertently blab any secrets. I've also called his wife, Karen. How'd this happen?"

"There's been a shoot-out at Martin Chapman's horse farm." Judd surveyed the havoc. "We haven't heard any sirens yet, but it's possible some of the employees who bunked out have notified the Maryland State Police. The cops won't know exactly who and what they're looking at here for a while. That'll buy us some time."

"And what will they see?" Gloria asked suspiciously.

"Corpses. A dozen or so guards, Martin Chapman, and the Eichel brothers."

"Oh, hell, a billionaire and two international assassins," she said. "Is Tucker's blood there?"

"Yes. And our fingerprints and DNA."

Gloria's voice rose. "Who is 'our'? And whose airplane is going to fly you to Merrittville?"

"Brace yourself, Gloria. We're working with the Carnivore again."

She took an audible breath. "Well, if Tucker can, I suppose I can, too."

"Eva Blake is with us," Judd added.

"Eva? It's a shame you've dragged her into this. Will Tucker's injuries get him enough sympathy so he can hold on to his job?" There was a pause, and in it he heard *if he survives.*

"Tucker went AWOL in a big way tonight," Judd said. "Add that to the infractions Bridgeman has been toting up, and it might be enough to force Tucker to retire. It'll help if Tucker's right about something going on that'll seriously hurt the United States."

"Shit." She paused. "You know I'll have to tell Scott Bridgeman."

"Can you delay?"

"I can weasel out of a lot of things, but I can't dodge a direct question from my boss. He'll find out everything eventually anyway. Let me know if I can help again."

Judd ended the call.

"Come on," Bosa snapped. "We've got to get out of here."

Eva zipped up Tucker's jacket and grabbed his eyeglasses.

"Ready?" Judd asked, crouching.

Bosa squatted and nodded. "Let's do it."

The men picked up the boards holding Tucker and moved rapidly across the library. Judd was in the lead, walking backward, while Eva continued to hold her sweater to Tucker's head. In seconds they passed through the library door and entered the brightly lit hallway, then down the staircase past the two guards Tucker had shot, and along the first-floor corridor where the rest of the corpses lay. Judd's boots grew sticky with blood. Looking at violent death was like a worm crawling up his spine.

He rerouted his thoughts: "Was it you who knifed the two outdoor sentries?" he asked Bosa.

"Who else?" Bosa said.

"What are you talking about—what sentries?" Eva asked.

Judd told her about Tucker's text messages describing two corpses in the snow, their carotid arteries sliced.

Bosa nodded. "One of them had spotted Tucker, then the other saw me." He glanced at Eva. "All of this happened while I was reconnoiter-ing."

"Why are you here, Eva?" Judd asked.

She described how the Carnivore had tricked her into joining him in Williamsburg, and then how she had escaped his plane and driven here. "He met me at the service entrance, armed to his eyeteeth and wearing the white snowsuit with the balaclava over his face. He had a plan—he'd pretend he'd captured me so we could get into the main house. That worked, and then we learned you and Tucker had broken in. So he vol-unteered to be part of your welcoming party, and you know the rest."

The door to the short hall was open. Again they hurried, passing the silent kitchen and the guards' locker room, where Judd had left his things. The building reverberated with the powerful roar of approach-ing jet engines.

Bosa lifted his head, listening. "Jack is circling the plane. Let's put Tucker down."

"Jack is Alex's pilot," Eva explained to Judd.

They set the backboard on the floor.

Bosa went to stand beside the window.

Judd stepped into the locker room, peeled off the green sweatsuit, and put on his own clothes. Then he hesitated, realizing his hands were shak-ing. He held them up, empty, and stared at them, the big knuckles, the large palms. His hands were shaking just as they had when he'd had the chance to shoot Chapman and decided not to. But this time he had given himself no time to reconsider.

Shaking his head, he buttoned his peacoat and strode back into the hall.

Eva was sitting cross-legged on the floor beside Tucker, her head bowed over him as she wiped blood from his face. The entry and exit wounds were leaking now, not flowing. Tucker was motionless as a gravestone.

Judd looked down at them, feeling his love for Eva. He admired the tenderness she showed Tucker, her bravery and daring. There was some-thing about her that connected with something inside him that made it hard for him to be away from her, and painful to be with her.

Bosa opened the door. A cold wind swept in. "The SUV is in sight," he announced. "Let's get the hell out of here."

"Are you going to hunt down Krot after you drop off Tucker?" Judd asked.

"Yes," Bosa said. "Want to join me? I could use the help."

"Tucker believed that whatever was going on with you and the other assassins had to be about more than an ancient tablet," Judd told him. "Was he right?"

"Of course."

"I'll make you a deal like the one you made Eli Eichel," Judd decided. "Fill me in completely, and I'll go with you."

Bosa crouched to pick up his end of the makeshift stretcher. "Agreed."

Judd crouched over his end. "To Marrakech?"

"To Marrakech," Bosa confirmed.

Carrying Tucker, the men went out into the bitter cold.

KROT

For secret assassination . . . the contrived accident is the most effective technique. When successfully executed, it . . . is only casually investigated.

—*CIA Assassination Manual, 1954*

39

The night wind numbed Eva's cheeks and burned her nose. To the north, the parking lights of the Carnivore's plane glowed across the snow. The SUV arrived, white clouds of steam billowing from its tailpipe.

As choreographed as a ballet, Bosa's two men—the driver and a passenger—jumped out of the vehicle, opened the tailgate, slid the boards holding Tucker inside, and closed up. The driver and Bosa sat in front, while Eva and Judd took the bench seat behind them. In the far back was Bosa's second man, checking Tucker.

All of this was accomplished in less than sixty seconds.

About Bosa's age, the two men were bundled in thick coats and armed with AK-47s. Bosa, Judd, and Eva still had their M4s.

The driver threw the SUV into gear, hit the accelerator, and the vehicle rushed off. He glanced at Bosa, who sat beside him. "Christ, Alex. You really can pick 'em. That was one hell of a hike from the plane to the garage. We sweltered in the heat."

"Sure you did." Bosa waved a hand from the driver back to Judd and Eva. "This malcontent is George Russell."

His eyes on the driveway, George spoke over his shoulder: "Good to meet you." He had a muscular face and gave off of a sense of restlessness, a man who liked to be working his body, on the move.

Bosa indicated the man who was examining Tucker's wound. "And this is Doug Kennedy."

Doug peered up briefly and nodded. A gray-streaked brown ponytail dangled from beneath his black watch cap. He had a high forehead, wore nickel-rimmed eyeglasses, and shot them a warm smile.

As they drove past the garage, Judd told Bosa, "I left my cuneiform pieces in a delivery van we hid in the trees. We need to go back to get them."

"You mean the ones you put inside the bottle of ice?"

Judd did not change his expression. "So you found them."

"I couldn't figure out why you'd be carrying it around, so I turned on the engine and melted the ice. Not too bad a hiding place. Found this in the delivery van, too." He gave Judd his backpack.

"How did you get onto Chapman's property?" Judd asked. He went through the backpack. All of his belongings were there.

"One of my *compadres* discovered a map from the 1950s. It showed a concrete culvert. For some reason, the culvert fell out of use, and over the decades nature hid it. So I simply located it again. Not hard, with a GPS."

The SUV hurtled into the parking lot and accelerated across it.

Eva had been watching Doug inspect Tucker. Deathly pale, Tucker's skin resembled crepe paper, an old man's skin. His slender body was limp, fragile-looking.

"How is he?" she asked anxiously.

"I've been palpating his skull to check for instability, and it feels normal." Doug reached inside a bag near his feet and took out two sterile packets. He ripped one open. "His facial bones seem stable, too." He applied a bandage to the front of Tucker's head and another to the back. "Has he said anything or moved?"

"No." Eva's throat tightened.

"He's breathing on his own, and there's no drainage from the ears, nose, or eyes. Both are good signs."

"I've heard that ninety percent of gunshot wounds to the head are fatal," she said evenly. "Is that true?"

"Yes, but that doesn't mean Tucker isn't going to be among the ten percent who survive."

They were silent. Moonlight shone through the window, illuminating Judd's face as he peered off into the distance. She found herself studying his intensity, the bunched muscles in his jaw, the steady gaze. The cold had made his skin ruddy, deepening the fine lines on his forehead and around his eyes, too many lines for a thirty-four-year-old, but they were earned, and she liked that. She liked the thick unruliness of his hair, and his hazel eyes—they could be brown one moment and blue the next. Now his face was like marble, hard, emotionless, but when he allowed himself, it softened and she could see a gentle man, a man who was unafraid of himself. She liked that complexity, but the man she saw gun down Martin Chapman was new to her, and she did not know yet what to think of him.

"What sort of evidence does Bridgeman have against Tucker?" she asked.

"A lot originated with me." Judd described the murder of his double and then Tucker's persuading both the medical examiner and Bridgeman to keep it quiet so he could investigate. "The only reason Bridgeman went along with Tucker was because Tucker convinced him international assassins were working on U.S. soil and it was in Catapult's best interests to find out why and what they were doing. But then the Eichel brothers made the hunt club pristine, which left only Tucker's word that the Padre had cut a deal with him to find the Carnivore, and only my word about our doubles and the massacre at the hunt club, which meant only circumstantial evidence of assassins. So Tucker came looking for the Eichels here—without Bridgeman's knowledge, much less his permission."

The wind had risen, and the SUV swayed as it left the parking lot for the drive to the landing strip.

"But what about the gunfight tonight?" she asked. "The Eichels' bodies are in Chapman's library. That should prove Tucker was right about them being in-country."

Judd shook his head. "It doesn't save Tucker, and it's probably even worse for us. I'm a civilian with no authority to be there, so I could be perceived as just as bad as the men we left dead. Remember, there's well-known history between Chapman and me—and I'm the one who ended up shooting him. A good case could also be made that you abandoned your Farm training to help me wipe him."

Eva thought about it. "I made a commitment to the CIA, and I intend to keep it. Once Tucker is safely in the hospital, I'll rent a car and drive back to the Farm so I can explain what happened. That way I can speak on Tucker's and your behalf and maybe even save what's left of my career."

Bosa rotated in his seat, his knee up on the divider between him and the driver. He assessed Eva. "I have a better idea. Stay with us." He couched it like an invitation, but she did not believe for an instant that was all there was to it. "It's in your best interests."

"The reason you want both of us along is you're worried we'll go public with what we know," she accused. "A group of top international assassins fighting over pieces of a cuneiform tablet has got to be mighty interesting to the press. They'll be sniffing up your arse, and for a man who's gone to a great deal of trouble to stay unknown, unseen, and unfindable, that's got to disturb you."

Bosa smiled. There was something almost innocent in his expression, guileless, as if he were a man who had compartmentalized his life so well that when the killer in him receded, an almost grandfatherly man emerged.

"All of that's true, but I'm worried about you, too," he told her.

The killer might actually believe the sincerity in his voice, Eva thought.

"The Padre and Eli Eichel have already tried to terminate you and Judd," he continued. "What makes you think Krot and Seymour aren't reaching out to contacts right now, searching for you, too, also thinking they can find me through you?"

Eva shook her head. "I'm going back to the Farm."

"You won't be welcomed," Judd warned her. "Did you call in this afternoon to say you were dropping out because of a family emergency and you didn't know when you'd be back?"

"Absolutely not!"

"Then someone else did—someone who claimed to be you and sounded like you. Tucker told me the murder board has voted, and you're out. Fired."

For a moment she was stunned, speechless. Then she turned on Bosa. "Damn you! You did this to me!"

He shrugged. "My people hadn't been able to track down the Eichel brothers. I wasn't going to release you until I was sure you were safe from them. One of my *compadres,* a female and a gifted mimic, called the Farm only when it was clear I wasn't going to be able to slip you back in. You might consider readjusting your attitude—if you weren't alive, you couldn't be mad at me."

"Hell. Screw all of you!" Eva grabbed her disposable cell and dialed the number she had been told to memorize her first week at the Farm. Staring out at the night, she listened as it rang three times.

A woman answered: "Yes?"

"This is Eva Blake. I'd like to speak to Dan Lord, please."

"There's no 'Dan Lord' here. You must have the wrong number."

Eva recognized the voice—Judith Mignogna, a fellow recruit. "Please, Judie. It's Eva. I've had an emergency, and I need to explain it to my instructor. That's Dan. You see, I was kidnapped late this afternoon in Williamsburg, except it wasn't a true kidnapping. This is my first chance to call in."

"Kidnapped?" Judie's tone was alarmed. "Then you should phone the police. I'll hang up so you can do it right away. Good luck." The line went dead.

Eva stared at her cell phone, absorbing the fact she had been cut off. Silent, they watched her.

Gathering herself, she hit the REDIAL button. Again the phone rang. But this time it rang and rang. She remembered Bill, a fellow trainee whom the murder board had voted out last month. Security had arrived as he was eating dinner, told him the result of the meeting, and escorted him off premises. He was out of the Agency with no job and no place to live. The Agency was tough, but that was one of the reasons it remained one of the best in the world.

Eva listened to one more ring then hung up. For a moment she felt invisible. It was hard to breathe. With her CIA career ahead of her, life had made sense.

"They don't believe me," she told them quietly. She avoided looking at Judd.

No one said anything.

Putting away her cell phone, she focused on the Carnivore. "You could've let Chapman kill us. That would've eliminated any problems we'd cause you later. Why didn't you do that?"

"Because I might not have survived in Chapman's library without you. Unfortunately, I owe you again. On the other hand, you owe me. Let's not make a habit of it. Come with us, Eva. There's nothing left here for you."

She leaned back, feeling painfully adrift.

As they neared the plane, the roar of the three jet engines was impressive. Blue ground lights outlined the runway. A staircase was in place.

She had to decide what to do, but her thoughts kept returning to Tucker. He had a strong sense of himself and did not seem to worry much about what anyone thought of him. He had a hard time hiding his impatience with fools, but he made an effort to obey protocols. Sometimes he succeeded. Then there was his covert background—from London to both Berlins, from Moscow to the Middle East. He had been not just successful, but also honored. And he had believed Judd that the Eichels had ambushed the Padre and his people. He had been right. But then, he placed a lot of trust in "gut," the extra sense that came from a combination of experience and talent. And now she had a strange sensation. Something inside her was telling her to go with Bosa.

"All right," she said to the Carnivore. "I'm in."

40

Vibrating with power, the Carnivore's plane was the sleek, silver-skinned Dassault that Eva had spotted at the Merrittville airport. A trijet, it was decorated in expensive taste, with beige wool carpet, ivory-colored leather seats, and cherry cabinetry. Bosa liked not only comfort but also class.

She headed toward the rear. "This is all yours?" she asked over her shoulder.

He was right behind her. "Every one of its fifty thousand parts. Paid a fortune for it. I could say it was a necessary business expense."

They stopped at one of the passenger seats where he unloaded his pockets.

"What about the turboprop that flew you and me to Merrittville?"

"Rented," he said. "Langley doesn't have expensive planes like this for regular duty. I figured you might know that."

The cockpit door opened, and Jack stuck out his head, his cap at a jaunty angle. "What took you so long?"

Bosa ignored the jibe. "Get this bird off the ground. We've got an appointment with an ambulance."

"That's not all we have," Jack reminded him. "Hello, Eva. I'm glad you were persuaded to join us."

"Blackmailed is more like it."

Giving a knowing chuckle, he returned to the cockpit, and she hurried aft.

George brushed past her, heading in the opposite direction. "Got to make sure Jack doesn't think there's a foot brake and clutch on this flying saucer." Which she interpreted to mean George was copilot.

As she passed through the cherrywood galley, she heard the engines ratchet up for takeoff. The dining area had four more ivory leather seats, and in the rear of the plane was a three-place electric berthing divan, the open part covered with a white sheet. That was where Tucker lay, eyes closed. Judd was sitting nearby, leaning forward, elbows on knees, watching as Doug worked on Tucker.

Judd's expression was gloomy. He gestured, and she sat beside him. "Is there any improvement, Doug?" she asked.

"Sorry, no." Doug fastened an oxygen mask to Tucker's face.

"Drop into your seats, troops, and snap on those seat belts." It was Jack's voice on the intercom.

As everyone strapped in, the trijet rolled off. Aware of Judd sitting close to her, Eva turned away and leaned her cheek against the window, gazing out. The moonlit snowscape blurred as the aircraft increased speed and lifted off.

Using his stethoscope, Doug listened to Tucker's heart. He held Tucker's wrist, then pressed behind his ankle. "Heart and circulation appear normal." He studied Tucker's torso. "His bilateral chest expansion is good. He a runner?"

"Yes," Judd told him. "Three or four times a week. How did you know?"

"Lungs. Heart rate. Pulse. Thin but muscular. Being in good condition is always a plus."

Choosing supplies, Doug opened overhead and floor compartments containing what could be the contents of a mini paramedics van—

everything from splints and tubing to a portable defibrillator and a roof hook for an IV. "Alex believes in being prepared." Pulling up Tucker's coat sleeve and swabbing the arm, he inserted a needle for an IV. "Saline solution. Aggressive fluid resuscitation is standard."

"What do you think his chances of recovery are?" Eva asked.

"If the bullet damaged both sides of his brain or struck the brain stem, he's likely to have extensive permanent damage, or end up in a vegetative state, or die. But from what I can tell, the bullet appears to have stayed on the left side and missed the brain stem. There are just too many variables for me to say more than that, and of course I could be wrong." He hesitated. "The truth is, I'd feel a lot more optimistic if he'd open his eyes, talk, or move on purpose. That'd tell us the bullet didn't completely destroy the parts of his brain responsible for thinking, understanding speech, and having motor function."

Eva and Judd were silent.

Then Judd did something unexpected. He took her hand. "He'll pull through," he told her.

Without thinking, she squeezed his hand and nodded, her throat tight.

Doug glanced at them. "If I need help, I'll call. If there's a change in him, I'll call. Get out of here. You have other things to do."

Standing up, Eva and Judd peeled off their coats. As they hung them in a narrow closet, the trijet dipped and bounced. She grabbed for an overhead handhold and suddenly felt Judd's arm around her waist, steadying her. She listened to the faint hum of the engines. Her emotions whipsawed. And then his arm was gone.

They moved off, grabbing seat backs and the rail. Bosa was sitting in the forward cabin, an iPad on the retractable tray before him. His gray hair was no longer the artfully tousled arrangement of Frank Smith, but brushed straight back, utilitarian, away from his wide face. Drugstore reading glasses perched on the end of his Roman nose. He wore a long-sleeved black T-shirt and dark blue jeans. His stocky figure was intense, focused on whatever he was reading. Without looking up, he turned off the iPad.

Sitting across from him, Eva and Judd swiveled their chairs to face him.

He peered over his reading glasses at one, then the other. "Yes?"

"Are we seeing the real Carnivore at last?" she asked. "Every other time you've been in some disguise."

"This is the me you're getting for this operation," he told her. "How's Tucker?"

"Not good," Judd said.

"He's alive. Take the batteries and SIM cards out of your phones so they can't be traced." There was a Staples shopping bag next to his seat. He reached in, pulled out new cells, and tossed them at them. "These are disposable and can be used for international phoning. They're also smartphones, so you can e-mail and do research. Memorize your numbers and everyone else's, too. I made a call for you, Judd. The delivery van you left at Chapman's place will be picked up in a few minutes and taken back to the feed store. Whatever's personal in it will be transferred to your pickup, and the pickup parked in your garage, the keys in a holder under the driver's door. Questions?"

"Yes." Eva gestured at the microfiber box on his retractable tray. "We want to know about the tablet pieces. Talk."

41

As the trijet flew east, Eva watched Bosa lay out the limestone pieces on his seat tray. "I have Eichel's three pieces. The Padre's three. And my four. Ten altogether. Krot and Seymour have the rest—and maybe Morgan's two pieces, too." He turned them upside down. "As you can see, I've numbered the backs to make fitting them together more efficient."

When he turned them right side up, nearly half the unfinished tablet appeared, a puzzle in pale gritty limestone. About twenty inches long, it was eighteen inches wide and nearly two inches thick. He rotated the tray so it faced Eva and Judd.

Eva leaned close, once again the art historian and manuscript curator. Some pieces were chipped, and there were gaps near the middle and top where others were missing. The cuneiform symbols were mostly clear.

Bosa watched her. "Can you read cuneiform?"

She looked up. "Not as much as I'd like. I studied it when I curated an exhibit about the transition from pictographs to cuneiform. It can take a lifetime to become truly expert."

"Can you tell whether the tablet is authentic?" he asked.

They were silent as she assessed.

At last she looked up. "The artisan was skilled. He carved the wedges clean and deep. There's nothing amateurish about this. Generally, there are three different types of wedges—vertical wedges with the head at the top, horizontal ones with the head to the left, and slanting ones with the head either at the upper left or the center. Putting the heads in the wrong direction or in the wrong place is one of the most common mistakes forgers make. Another mistake is repeating groups of signs. They're being lazy or showing ignorance."

"The heads look to be in the right places," Bosa said.

"I don't see any repetitions," Judd added.

"Yes, the cuneiform symbols are correct," Eva agreed. "Also, we Westerners read books by turning the pages from right to left, but cuneiform is read from bottom to top. That's correct on this tablet, too. Of course, there are variations depending on the era and kingdom. From what little I know, the tablet appears to be authentic. Now, the problem is translation. I see the Sumerian word for 'war' on the tablet—the Sumerians invented cuneiform around 3,000 B.C. But which war . . . when, where?" She studied the lines and shapes, finally pointing to several symbols. "I think this means some kind of palace." She shook her head. "We need a real expert. I know people in L.A., of course, but that's in the opposite direction we're flying."

There was a moment of silence.

"Where did the tablet come from?" Judd asked Bosa.

"The Iraq National Museum by way of Saddam Hussein," Bosa said. "Iraq had laws against anyone owning antiquities, but Saddam took what he wanted and gave pieces away, even to foreigners. Of course, if someone else took something, Saddam had them shot."

"Okay, but why *this* tablet?" Judd tapped his index finger on the tray that held it. "Why have six assassins been fighting over it?"

"I'll start at the beginning, and then maybe I won't have to waste my time answering questions later. Do you know how Saddam began his political career?" When neither spoke, Bosa went on, "As an assassin—just like Eli Eichel, the Padre, Krot, Morgan, Seymour, and me. By the age of twenty he was doing wet work for the Baath party. By thirty-one, when the Baathists took over the country, he was known as a *shaqawah*, a man to be feared. His rise was spectacular. Eleven years later, he was president. At the same time, Iraq's neighbor Iran was on the verge of revolution. The Shah of Iran needed to hide his fortune. So Saddam hired an international financier who talked the shah into depositing a hefty chunk in the Central Bank of Iraq for safekeeping. The shah paid the financier a 1.5 percent handling fee. Saddam paid him, too—another 1.5 percent—but this time it was to transfer the shah's money out of the bank and into Saddam's personal numbered accounts in the Cayman Islands and Credit Suisse in Switzerland."

"Did the shah or his family recover any of the money?" Judd said.

"No, and the ayatollahs couldn't get it either. And while they were fighting over the shah's money, Saddam was next door, turning Iraq into his personal piggy bank. He took a cut of everything made, sold, or stolen. A few of his closest family members managed it all until his paranoia got so bad he wanted to be the only one who knew all the parts. That's when he sent for a master of financial deception—"

"The financier who stole the shah's money," Eva guessed.

Bosa nodded. "His name was Rostam Rahim. His mother was English, but his father was Iraqi. He lived primarily in London. Rahim brought in five 'assistants,' each a sophisticated moneyman in his or her own right. They set up a six-part network using more than seventy banks."

"So together they had the whole financial picture," Judd said.

Eva nodded. "Six assassins. Six financiers. Six *dead* financiers."

"You've nailed it," Bosa said. "Each of us took out one financier. That left Saddam as the only person to know the location of every piece of his wealth."

"They did one hell of a job hiding it," Eva said. "As I recall, even after Saddam was toppled, the U.S. government could find only a few billion dollars."

"Right again," Bosa said. "Somewhere between forty and seventy billion dollars are still missing. Saddam's family, bankers, and governments have been searching for years. It's turned into the biggest—and quietest—treasure hunt the world has ever seen."

"I wonder where all of it is?" Eva mused.

"Not in one place," Judd said. "It's probably still spread around. Imagine the power of the person who finds the various hidey-holes."

The pilot's voice sounded on the cabin speakers: "The ambulance is waiting at the airport. Prepare for landing."

"We'll be back," Eva told Bosa.

With her in the lead, she and Judd returned aft. Tucker was as they had left him, motionless, an oxygen mask on his face and an IV in his arm. They strapped themselves in. There was a light jolt and a sense of drag on the plane. The wheels were down.

Eva reached for Tucker's hand. It was warm but limp.

Judd leaned close to him. "This is just *sayonara* until the next time, old friend. We'll miss you in Marrakech."

Eva looked out the window as the plane stopped. "We've arrived, Tucker. There's a staircase rolling toward us. Your ambulance is waiting." She smiled at him as if his eyes were open and he could see how much she cared for him. She had to try one last time: "Tucker, flex your hand. Please."

A tendril of cold air touched her cheek. She peered down the aisle and saw Jack had opened the craft's door.

Judd saw it, too. "We don't have much time. The paramedics will come for him soon." He took Tucker's other hand.

Eva leaned close, her lips almost touching the old spymaster's ear. "You've been shot in the head. Do something—anything—we're asking. It'll mean you can still think, understand speech, and move on purpose. Come on, Tucker, you need to know for yourself."

"I'm going to squeeze your hand again, Tucker. Then you squeeze mine." Judd compressed it.

They waited.

"Did I feel something, Tucker?" Eva asked, excited.

Very slowly the index finger of Tucker's left hand straightened, held a second, and collapsed.

Eva closed her eyes. "Thank God."

Judd heaved a sigh of relief. "Congratulations, you old SOB!"

42

Aloft, on the way to Marrakech, Morocco

Climbing to 27,000 feet, the Carnivore's trijet approached America's coastline. Judd watched out the window as the winking lights of civilization ended and the black Atlantic Ocean spread before them. The only sound was the muted strum of the craft's engines. He was alone in the cabin with Eva: Bosa was in the galley with Doug, while Jack and George were in the cockpit, the door closed.

Eva was resting her head back against her seat. She looked tired, but then all of them were. It had been a long day.

"I'm puzzled, Judd." She sat up, folded her hands in her lap, and peered down at them. "You told me you couldn't be with me because you hadn't liked what you'd become in Iraq and needed a different life for yourself—different from all of the reminders you'd have with me. But just a few hours ago, you killed Chapman and two of his guards when they weren't a threat to us—at least for the moment. Are you happy you did it?"

"*Happy* isn't the word I'd use. I'd say a weight was lifted from me. It was as if time stopped. The noise receded. I felt at peace."

"I don't like the sound of that. *Peace.*"

"If it's any comfort, it was a cold peace, almost as if I was removed from the world. Why won't you look at me?"

She lifted her head. "Four months ago you told me you didn't want to kill again, and now you've just erased Chapman. That was personal, right?"

He frowned. "If he'd had the chance, he would've killed us. I traded his life for ours. Doing Chapman was necessary."

She hesitated. Then: "Do you have flashbacks about the black work you were doing in Iraq and Pakistan?"

"No. Why?"

"If you had them, would you tell me?"

"Of course," he said. "Sure."

Her expression said she did not believe him.

Then he understood and felt a pain close to his heart: "You're afraid of me. You're afraid I'll hurt you."

Her expression was unforgiving. "I didn't know you'd done clean-up work in Iraq," she reminded him. "You waited until I'd fallen in love with you to tell me. That was bad enough. Now you say you found a 'cold peace' wiping Chapman. You felt 'removed from the world.'"

"Eva, please. Those were just my emotions in a very special set of circumstances. They're not who I am. Certainly not the way I think about you. I'd *never* hurt you."

When she said nothing, he changed the subject. "How do you feel about being kicked out of the CIA?"

"Terrible. My career as an intelligence officer ended before it could begin. And I hate that it looks as if it's my fault. How do you feel about it?"

"Relieved. You're free now." He wanted to tell her he loved her, to hold her in his arms again. He took a deep breath. "Do you at least trust me enough to work with me again?"

She seemed to think about it. "We were a good team last time," she decided.

It was a start. "Then we'll keep it at that. Partners. Nothing personal."

43

Marrakech, Morocco

Francesca Fabiano had come to Marrakech again, drawn back by a dream of something she could not name, something good. Pyotr Azarov told her he did not trust dreams, but she forgave him. She knew dreams had power, especially when one paid attention.

When she had explained it to him, he had listened attentively, his gaze sober.

"You're better off using your brain than your emotions," he advised. "You have a good brain, you know."

It had all begun yesterday morning. As usual she had left her hotel on Avenue Hassan II and walked to the intersection with rue Mauritania. Both streets were a madhouse, with unmuffled cars and trucks, whining mopeds, and the occasional bellowing camel.

She waited at the curb for the traffic to stop. Near her, a young couple linked arms. Then a man carrying an English version of a Marrakech guidebook arrived and stood between her and the couple. He glanced at her and smiled.

She felt something shift inside her. Something wonderful. It was not just his good looks, although he was a striking figure with a shock of black hair silvered at the temples and a strong chin shadowed by a little vacation beard growth. His sunglasses were black as sin. Perhaps six feet tall, he gave off a feeling of athleticism in his beige slacks, open-neck white shirt, and sturdy leather sandals. He was probably in his fifties. She had just turned forty. Not an impossible age difference. He wore no wedding band.

Keeping her expression neutral, she looked away. There were many good-looking men on holiday in Marrakech. She would never see him again.

She focused on the bedlam in the street. A donkey was pulling a cart of vegetables down Hassan. It was staying close to the sidewalk to avoid the worst of the traffic. But then a pickup swerved, and a taxi driver leaned on his horn. The donkey's ears lay back and he bolted, his hoofs pounding the pavement, the cart swaying, the driver's face turning beet red as he yelled in Arabic and tried to control the animal.

Francesca jumped back and stumbled. Pytor caught her. That was Marrakech for you, she thought later. Where else would you meet a handsome man and fall in lust because of a freaked-out donkey?

"Are you all right?" He had a warm voice.

His arm was still around her back, supporting her. Each of his hands held one of her arms. They were firm, strong hands.

"I'm fine," she said. "Thank you. That was quick of you."

He smiled, and this time she smiled back.

"That's me," he said. "Speedy Gonzales. You know about Speedy?" When she shook her head, he explained, "He's a cartoon mouse. The fastest mouse in all Mexico."

She liked him. And she liked that he was concerned about her. She taught kindergarten in Portland, Maine, where female kindergarten teachers tended to marry early and well. Apparently some men—the kind with jobs and a future—had fantasies about them, which made the profession a slam dunk for women who wanted marriage. But she had not.

The stranger was holding her a little longer than he needed to, she realized.

"You're trembling." His forehead furrowed. "You could've been hurt. You need to sit down and relax. Let's go to that outdoor café." Releasing her, he gestured. "That's where I'm staying—the Hotel Fashion."

"I'm staying there, too." Wow. "You saved my life. My name is Francesca Fabiano."

"I'm Pyotr. Pyotr Azarov." He spelled the first name. "You pronounce it 'Peter,' though."

"Russian?"

"Cossack, from the Ukraine." He was built like a Cossack, with the very good shoulders, the broad chest, and the long athletic legs bred to tame wild horses.

They sat at a small round table and ordered *caffè lattes* and hot croissants. They slathered the croissants with butter and jam then looked at each other and laughed, surprised each had wanted the same breakfast.

Pyotr drank his latte. "Imagine that, a blond Italian from Maine."

"My people came from Milan, in northern Italy," she lied. "There are a lot of blondes and redheads there." Self-consciously she ran her fingers through her short hair, pushing it behind her ears. It was so pale it looked bleached white. She had a heart-shaped face, too, and a nose that turned up at the end.

"Yes, I remember that now." He studied her. "It's strange, but I feel we've met before."

"Impossible. But I wish we had."

Francesca and Pyotr took one of the shiny green *calèches*—horse-drawn carriages—to Marjorelle Gardens, the former home of Yves Saint Laurent. They strolled along shady paths, enjoying the vibrantly blooming trees and flowers.

He kept glancing at her. "Do you realize you're beautiful? I have a feeling you don't know that."

Surprised, she looked away. "Thank you."

"You're here alone?" he wondered.

"Yes. I've traveled here five times now," she said. "My mother worked here for a couple of years back in the eighties." That was her biological mother, not the good-hearted woman in Maine who had ended up raising her and who she told the world was her mother.

"Did she work in the airport duty-free shop?" he asked casually.

She felt her eyes widen with surprise. "How did you know?"

"Oh," he said airily, "that's just one of the jobs Americans did back then in an outpost like Marrakech."

44

As night approached, Francesca and Pyotr took a taxi to Place Djemaa el-Fna, Marrakech's outdoor marketplace, and hurried into Chez Chegrouni and upstairs. The aroma of couscous made Francesca salivate. On the roof terrace, they chose a table at the railing where the view across the teeming market was panoramic.

"I've been told Djemaa el-Fna is Africa's largest marketplace," he said.

She inhaled. "It's an amphetamine rush to the senses."

As they ate traditional *tajine* slow-cooked stew, the sun set in a tangerine glow. "You really grew up in Maine?" Pyotr asked curiously. "I know this is crazy, but there was a woman I once knew named Roza Levinchev. It was a long time ago, and I was a young man, but I'll never forget her."

Francesca could hardly swallow. Her mind was in turmoil. She busied herself with her food.

"Our families were living in a little city called Bedford," he went on. "As it turns out, almost every state in the United States has a town called Bedford. Anyway, this Bedford was in the southern part of the old

Soviet Union, near the Baltic. It was never on any map. Probably still isn't. Do you know what I'm talking about?"

She widened her eyes. "No. That doesn't make sense. Why would a Soviet city be named Bedford?"

He set down his fork. "We bought our groceries at Safeway, got ice cream cones at Dairy Queen, and ate quarter-pounders at McDonald's. I was a bachelor so I lived at home. My mother watched *As the World Turns* on TV. My father and I read *The New York Times* and the *Financial Times*—they were on our doorstep every morning. We spoke America's version of English. Our teachers taught us American history, American music, American literature." He looked around for eavesdroppers. "Bedford was a first-class school for Soviet spies, sleepers, and moles."

It was her turn to set down her fork. "Who are you?" She stared at his handsome face, at his lying Cossack eyes. The shit had been wooing not her, but her past.

"I think you're Roza's daughter—Katia. You don't remember me at all, do you? Well, it's no surprise. You must've been eight or ten then. It was a long time ago, and I've had several cosmetic surgeries. Your mother was a star student, but you probably know that. As I recall, you and your mother got assigned to Washington, D.C. Later I heard she was in Marrakech, working in the duty-free store, but what she was really doing was helping to move arms, ammo, and explosives with the PLO. The PLO did a lot of dirty work for us in those days." He gave her a compassionate look. "It must've been terrible for you to lose her. It sounds as if she set up some kind of situation in Maine to take care of you while she was gone. I heard her remains were found in her car at the bottom of a cliff in the Atlas Mountains. If it's any comfort, we were sure she didn't kill herself. She must've been burned, and the CIA took her out."

Katia leaned forward. Her voice was low and hard. "I don't know who in hell you are or what you want. I do know you've just made up a story so far-fetched that the only solution is for you to see a therapist. See one often."

She started to push back her chair, but he reached across the table with both hands and grabbed her forearms. A little thrill started up her spine, but she stopped it cold.

He spoke in a rush. "I assume you're a sleeper, but I'm not here to activate you. I've told you things about myself I haven't told anyone in decades. See what you brought out of me? Please, give me a chance. I mean it. I want to retire. *I'm not activating you.*"

She shook free and stood. "You're a lunatic. Stay away from me."

Francesca—Katia—needed to walk, to think, to clear her head. She strode past the marketplace's stalls, hardly hearing the blare of Arabic music, ignoring the whirling dancers. There was a tourist, a woman, with gray fluffy hair, a softly lined face, and a digital camera who seemed always behind her, sometimes close, sometimes distant. It was a coincidence, she told herself. But because of Pyotr, she was feeling paranoid.

A veiled woman held out a flat basket, her bracelets jingling. "Moroccan dates," she crooned in French-accented English. "Moroccan dates. The finest you will find anywhere—"

Katia rushed past and into the souk. She was moving so fast she broke into a sweat.

The older woman with the digital camera bumped into her. *"Pardonnez-moi!"*

"C'est pas grave." Katia hurried on. There were some two miles of convoluted passageways. She was getting confused.

Then Pyotr was at her side, walking with her and leaning over to speak in her ear. "Stop. Please, Katia. I'm sorry. I'm really not here to pull you back into the business. Will you give a fellow Russian, an old compatriot, a chance? I know this must be very hard on you—"

A dark wave of loneliness swept through her. She turned. Somehow Pyotr's arms were around her.

He held her tight, and she sank into him and wept into his white shirt. She could smell his aftershave, feel the prickles of his vacation beard on her forehead. She could hear her mother's voice calling long-distance from Marrakech. "I love you, Francesca. I'll see you soon. Be a good girl." Always in English. Never in Russian.

"It's all right," Pyotr murmured in Russian. "There, there." He gave her a gentle squeeze. "There, there."

When she finally pushed away, Pyotr handed her a big white hand-kerchief. She glanced around, realized people were staring. There was that gray-haired woman again, the one with the camera who had bumped into her. Had she been photographing them? She was shooting a tall clay pot now.

Katia wiped her eyes and blew her nose. Pyotr took her arm and led her back. As they walked through the souk, he slid his arm around her waist. There was something more protective about the gesture than sexual.

She had been thinking. "You didn't just recognize me, did you, Pyotr? You must've known I'd be here in Marrakech. It's no coincidence we're staying in the same hotel."

Guilt flashed across his face. "You're right. I was standing on the corner, trying to figure out how to introduce myself to you, when the donkey bolted, and you stumbled and I caught you. I wanted to meet you—Roza's daughter. I always admired Roza, and I wanted to touch base with my past. I had a small hope you'd remember me."

"I'm not a sleeper," she told him, "I was too young to be trained to be one." But then in Russian: *"Kharashóh, Pyotr. Shto vam núzhna?"* All right, Pyotr. What do you really need from me?

"Your friendship," he said solemnly. "Will you be my friend? With you, I thought I could talk about the old times." His black eyes were tender. "I could use a friend, and I thought maybe you could, too."

She was falling in love with Pyotr. This was crazy, she told herself. *Crazy.* He had pretended they were meeting accidentally. In other words, he had lied to her. But now that he had explained, it made sense. Or maybe she just wanted to believe him. She was excited and giddy and . . . crazy. Falling in love was making her nuts.

He was telling her again he was out of the spy business and not in Marrakech to activate her. *"Vi panimáyitye minyá?"* he asked finally.

"Da. Da. Yes, Pyotr. Of course I understand what you're saying." And then she heard herself say, "I believe you. Really I do. And I'm relieved." She meant it.

Back in the hotel, he accompanied her up to her room on the third floor. His room was below, on the second floor. She unlocked the door, opened it, and turned to face him. Her heart was pounding so loudly she was afraid he could hear it.

"You'll be okay?" His black Cossack eyes devoured her.

It was hard for her to speak, so she nodded. Her chin lifted, she studied him. She wanted to stroke the bristles of his beard, move her fingers down his throat, slide them under his shirt. She wondered what his skin tasted like.

As he leaned toward her, she reached into her room, fumbled across the wall until she found the switch, and turned on the light. She grabbed the door jamb for support. "I've got to go in. I need to . . . go to bed."

His lips were so close she could almost feel them on her mouth.

"May I see you tomorrow?" he said. "Will you spend the day with me again? I have to leave early the next morning. I would really like more time with you."

She felt her cheeks flush. "Yes. Breakfast in the café again. Nine o'clock." And then before she could change her mind, she stepped back into her room. "Good night."

Closing the door, she could see the smile on his face fade. He was disappointed she had not invited him in. She could not believe he was leaving Marrakech so soon.

45

The next morning, Katia and Pyotr met again at the little café for lattes and hot croissants. Sitting beside newspaper racks, she saw headlines about the terrible bombings, kidnappings, and murders in Baghdad. She closed her eyes, willing away memories. When she opened them, she saw Pyotr's happy smile.

The traffic roared, and the sun climbed the sky. They caught a taxi to a grand old Berber palace, now the Museum of Moroccan Arts. She found herself glancing around, wondering whether she would see the older woman with the camera who might have been following her last night.

The air was cool inside the museum. The art, furnishings, and architecture were a stunning mix of Spanish and Moorish.

"How long have you lived in the States?" Pyotr asked curiously.

"Since I was fifteen. I wanted to move to Marrakech with Mother, but she insisted I finish my education in the States. A widow who'd been like a grandmother to me had left Washington and gone to Maine, so Mother sent me to live with her. That's where I grew up. I love teaching kindergartners. And I love the woman I came to call Mom. But now that I look back, I realize I've been terrified someone would find out who I really was. It was better to never let anyone get close."

He stopped her beneath a tiled archway. Turning her to face him, he put his hands on her shoulders and looked gravely down at her. "I know exactly who you are, Katia Levinchev. It's an honor to have met you again after all these years."

At twilight they caught another taxi. Riding through the streets, they passed old Moroccan architecture standing side by side with modern buildings. For Katia, it was like an omen—the old and the new interwoven seamlessly.

There was a closed glass window between the driver and them, so they had privacy. "What about you?" she asked. "Tell me about your family."

"The ones in Bedford were trainers. My true family was back in the Ukraine. I envied you because your Bedford parents were real." He shook his head, then brightened: "Perhaps you can clear up a mystery. What about your father? As I recall, his name was Grigori. I'd been in Bedford a year when he vanished."

Her lungs tightened. "He left during the night. I kept asking Mother where he was, when I'd see him again. She said she didn't know." Her father, Grigori Levinchev, had been a great undercover agent.

"Didn't he get in touch with you when your mother died?" Pyotr asked.

"I never heard from him again." It was a lie. She turned her face away.

The taxi stopped, Pyotr paid, and they left the chaotic traffic for the serenity of Café France, where Pyotr had made a reservation. White linen covered the tables. The silver and crystal sparkled. They ordered roasted salmon caught that morning in the North Atlantic. The sommelier poured a Pinot Gris from Alsace.

"What did you do after you left the training village?" she asked.

"I can't tell you. You know that. It was a long time ago. Who cares? Ancient history. You don't mind, do you?"

She did mind. "You know about my life. I know almost nothing about yours."

He gazed out the window at the passing parade of Moroccans and tourists. His profile hardened. Finally he shrugged. "All right . . . I studied six months at our school for sabotage in Prague, and then I was sent back to Moscow to learn psychological warfare and media manipulation at Patrice Lumumba University. That's where Ilich Ramírez Sánchez had studied on scholarship."

"Carlos the Jackal."

"Yes. He was a legend by then, but I heard he'd been a party boy in school—smart but lazy. When I graduated, Moscow was selling weapons to groups like the Red Brigades and the IRA and training them at camps across the Middle East. I was deep into it. I suppose you could say I was a troubleshooter."

Their dinner arrived. Pyotr looked at it, but his initial enthusiasm seemed to have waned.

When the waiter left, she asked, "Troubleshooter. What does that mean?"

He peered at her gravely. "I'm gambling you'll be all right with what I'm about to say. I'm trying to make a full and honest disclosure, and . . . it's not pretty." His glass was empty. He offered her more wine. When she shook her head, he filled his glass and drank. "We were dealing with violent people. Sometimes the only response was violence. Lubyanka brought me in to eliminate the worst ones." Lubyanka was the KGB's headquarters, in Moscow.

For a moment she was taken aback. But what had she expected—the KGB was not a gentlemen's garden club. "You were an assassin?"

"Yes." He shook his head with disgust as he continued: "First we treat allies like our friends, and we invite them to Moscow and feed them caviar. And then suddenly they're our enemies, and we liquidate them. I was risking my life for communism and the Motherland. Where did it get any of us? There was no change. We still helped anyone who'd sabotage the Middle East peace talks. We still funded both Iran and Iraq, first to keep their war alive, and then to keep their relations with the United States tense. We kept proxy wars going in Africa, and a million people died. We were on a treadmill to nowhere." He sat back, radiating anger and frustration. "It was stupid. *I* was stupid."

"Lubyanka allowed you to retire?"

"I'd stashed plenty of money and several identities, so I dropped out of sight and changed my appearance. I was good at that sort of thing." He was silent, his head cocked as he assessed her. "You can call me names and leave now. Go ahead. I'll understand."

She looked away. "What happened after that?"

He hesitated. "I went independent, like Carlos and Abu Nidal. I was skilled, experienced. My services were in demand from all sides. I was called Mole."

"Krot," she whispered, translating from the Russian.

"Yes. I am Krot."

46

It was past midnight when Katia and Pyotr left the French restaurant. The night was warm and soft. The traffic was quieting. Across the street, people were standing around an ice cream cart, eating and talking. Then Katia saw the woman with the bouncy gray hair and spidery-lined face. She was shooting pictures of hands, mouths, food.

Katia slowed. "Do you know who that woman is, the one who's taking the photos?" She nodded across the street. "I think she was following me last night. She may have photographed you and me when we were in the souk. Maybe before then, too—in the marketplace."

He peered at the woman. "I don't remember her. Does she worry you?"

Katia felt safe with Pyotr. Despite his violent past, or maybe because of it, there was something about him that made her feel taken care of.

"No," she decided. "She's probably just a tourist."

A fortune-teller called out from an alley. "Come. Find out how many years of happiness you will have together, love birds. Come, come." Stooped, she beckoned with both hands. Gold rings covered her arthritic fingers, and tiny gold cymbals chimed from her ears. "You will not be sorry. You will learn your good future!"

Pyotr gave her dirhams. "You're much too young to be out so late."

She laughed, and the money vanished into the red sash at her waist. "I am much too old to care. Here, let me see, young miss. Your palm, please."

But Katia put her hands behind her back and shook her head. "Dreams are better than predictions, but thank you."

As they walked on, Katia peered back over her shoulder. The ice cream cart was as busy as ever, but she no longer saw the photographer.

"Where do you live, Pyotr?" she asked curiously.

"In a wood chalet at the top of a high green valley in Switzerland. The views take your breath away. The bells of the dairy herd are my only alarm clock. My idea of heaven."

Ten minutes later they arrived at their hotel. The outdoor café was closed, the little tables vanished. They strolled through the lamp-lit lobby and rode the elevator up to her floor. Even though they were not touching, she felt heat radiate from his body, calling her. She ached to have sex with him, but it was not a good idea.

Soon they were at the door to her room. Unlocking it, she opened it onto darkness, emptiness. The loneliness of her life was almost palpable.

She turned. "Thank you for two wonderful days."

"That sounds like good-bye."

"I didn't mean it to. I just meant it's been wonderful."

"There you go again. That sounds like good-bye, too." There was disappointment in his eyes. "You're worried about me. Who I was. Whether I'm the same person today. A contract killer. Whether I could kill again."

"You've given me a great gift," she told him. "You showed me the poverty of my life—and that I can change it. Love is what my dreams were telling me I could have. It's what I came to Marrakech to find out."

There was a small smile on his lips. If he had changed the way he claimed, he was a remarkable man. He was also handsome, elegant, strong-looking, virile. She could not believe she was getting rid of him.

She stepped back and forced herself to say the words. "I'm tired. I have to go in now. Again, thank you for everything. I'll never forget you."

He gave a slow shake to his head, the small smile still on his lips. "Let me ask you a question, although I'm sure of the answer. Did you love your father? Do you still love him?"

She frowned. What a weird question, especially now. "Of course."

"Do you still miss him?"

"What are you getting at?"

"I'll take that as a yes." He looked both ways along the carpeted hall.

She looked, too. They were alone.

When he spoke again, it was quietly and in Russian. "Let me educate you about who you are, Katia Levinchev, daughter of Roza and Grigori Ivanovich Levinchev. I asked you about your father because I was trying to find out whether you knew what Lubyanka had assigned him to do after he left Bedford training village. He and I partnered occasionally. Lubyanka made him into a political assassin, too. He went independent a year before I did."

She said nothing. Was there a corner of her mind that had suspected this? About a decade after his disappearance, her father and she had talked several times a year, especially on their birthdays. For her, each time was special. The clouds in her life would vanish, and the sun would warm her.

"I respected him," he went on. "If you loved and trusted your father, perhaps you can give me a chance. He and I are no different."

For a moment she felt numb. What was left to her? Returning to her mother who was not really her mother, to a kindergarten class to teach American children when she was not really American, to a few friends who had always known who they were and never questioned it.

She made herself breathe. She liked the way he looked at her, his gaze steady but concerned. His nose was a little crooked, and she liked that, too. Odd that he had not had it straightened. She admired that about him—he seemed not to mind imperfection, even in himself.

He took her hand and covered it with his own. "Let me fall in love with you, Katia."

Shivers of pleasure spread up her arm and down into her belly.

He pulled her to him. Her head fell back, and she sank into his muscles and heat. She lifted her mouth hungrily, and he kissed her long until she felt weak and had to pull away.

He walked her back into her room, kissing her ears, her throat. She ran her fingers down his cheek, over his beard stubble, and down his throat. Somehow the door closed behind them, and the little bed light came on. Fumbling, she unbuttoned his shirt. His mouth went to her shoulder, wet and probing. She arched back, and he slid off the straps of her sundress and pulled it down over her breasts.

She could feel her nipples harden. Fingers trembling, she unzipped his pants, and then he was against her, hard, pushing her into the wall. She shook with need. He flipped up her skirt and slid his hand between her legs.

She moaned, eager to greet the inevitable.

47

At three A.M. Pyotr untangled himself from the hotel bed sheets. The only illumination in Katia's room was moonlight slanting in from where the drapes did not quite touch the wall. Listening to her regular breathing, Pyotr slid out of bed and padded across the carpet, picking up his clothes. He had a short errand.

Dressing quickly, he left, running along the hall to the staircase then down to the second floor. He was inside his room in seconds, changing into a black zippered jacket, black pants, and black athletic shoes. He slid his PB "silent pistol" into his shoulder holster. Based on the famous Soviet Markov gun, it had been his favorite small arm since his days in the KGB.

He peered out the door and sprinted to the stairwell again, traveling down another flight, to the first floor. Through the closed door to the lobby he could hear the television broadcasting what sounded like an old French movie.

He opened the door, padded along another corridor, and pressed his ear against the kitchen door. Silence. Opening it, he stepped into darkness tinged with the aroma of cinnamon and cloves. He had scouted the kitchen earlier. With the aid of moonlight from a high window, he headed straight to the rear door. As expected, it was bolted from the inside. It was a solid bolt, but he was not trying to break in. Sliding it open, he was soon outdoors and hurrying along the brick alley.

Her name was Doktor Hanke Bűrger, or Sarah Rosenblatt, or Señora Agrifina Cortez. Or tomorrow, just plain Jane Smith. She was in a very good mood, because the Carnivore was regularly wiring $5,000 payments into her Liechtenstein account for her reports on the tall man with the black hair staying at the Hotel Fashion under the name Pyotr Azarov. She had no idea whether Azarov was his real name, and she did not care. Her assignment was simply to follow him and report in detail whom he saw, where he went, what he did, and whatever conversations she could listen in on.

Standing in a dark doorway across the street from his hotel, she finished her thermos of hot green tea and honey and smiled at the tally on her Droid. So far she had earned $20,000 for this one assignment, a lucrative gig.

She yawned and checked her watch. Surely by now Azarov and his girlfriend were inside for the night. She was so tired she ached. Surveying the sidewalks and street, she left the doorway and headed toward her *riad,* the little hotel where she was staying. The nighttime traffic was intermittent.

As she passed a grassy area between two buildings, she had a sense of being followed. It was not so much that she heard footsteps, it was almost a change in energy. She glanced in a store window, hoping to see whether she was right. The only reflection was her own, her narrow face, her dark hair pulled loosely back in a ponytail.

"What did you do with her?" The voice came from behind. A man's voice. She recognized it—Pyotr Azarov.

Glancing over her shoulder, she pulled out a small Luger and sprinted. All she could see were palm trees, buildings, and parked cars. She could no longer hear him, and she did not sense him behind her either. Not slowing, she angled into an alley, dodging cans and crates, then through a side gate she had discovered three days earlier, in case something like this happened.

Azarov was waiting on the other side. His feet were planted solidly, and his PB pistol with sound suppressor was pointed at her. She stopped quickly, hunched over, her body still in running position. Her heart thudded against her ribs. She started to raise the Luger, but as if from nowhere his forearm slashed it from her hand.

Keeping his gaze on her, he scooped it up. "What did you do with the old woman who was fronting for you? The one who was taking photos to distract me from noticing you?"

Thinking quickly, she reached for her pocket. "Are you going to rob me? I'll give you my billfold. There are a lot of dirhams and euros in it—"

"Christ, woman, don't be stupid." Azarov was tall and muscular. There was a darkness in his eyes she did not like. "What the hell did you do with your gray-haired employee?"

She drew herself up. "Vivienne flew back to Paris tonight. Her vacation's over, and she has to report to work tomorrow."

"You killed her," he decided. "Did you leave her body where the authorities would find it quickly?"

"I didn't—"

He swore loudly. "Damnation, you've really fucked things up. I'm going to have to figure out how to convince Katia I didn't do it. Who do you work for—the Carnivore or Eli Eichel?"

"The Carnivore, not that it matters. I wasn't able to find out anything about you," she lied. "He fired me tonight. How did you make me?"

"Honey, if you have to ask, you're in the wrong business."

Her lips peeled back. "I'm sorry I ruined your little plans . . ."

She did not hear the single gunshot, but the impact of the bullet was like a sledgehammer to her forehead. She felt herself stagger back. Then blackness shrouded her.

48

Aloft, over the North Atlantic Ocean

Alex Bosa walked down the trijet's aisle, carrying a tray with six sandwiches on three china plates. "I'll finish debriefing you as we eat," he announced.

"How long until we reach Marrakech?" Eva asked as she chose the plate with turkey sandwiches. She had not realized she was hungry. She ate eagerly.

"It's an eight-hour flight. We arrive in the afternoon."

"Talk fast. We need to get some sleep." Judd grabbed rare roast beef sandwiches and chewed.

Sitting in his usual seat across the aisle, Bosa put the last plate on his lap, also roast beef. He took a large bite. "I'll start with Burleigh Morgan. A bomb exploded under his sports car a few days ago in Paris. He was the central figure in this situation. He was a Brit, and in the sixties, the Brits had plenty of oil interests in Iraq, so when the Baath party took over the country and needed someone to partner with Saddam for some hits on British oilmen and officials, they hired Morgan. Flash forward forty years, and Saddam needs an outsider to honcho the wet jobs on his financiers—"

"He went to Morgan," Eva said.

The assassin nodded. "And Morgan came to us. All things considered, the money was so good it was hard to refuse—four million dollars a corpse. The problem was, afterward Saddam wouldn't pay the second half of what he owed us. Naturally, we decided to scrub him. But Saddam varied his routine and used body doubles, sometimes five at a time. They were so good, when one brushed his teeth supposedly Saddam was the one who went to bed." He paused, his voice tight with anger. "All we could do was wait for an opening. We finally got it in 2003, when it was clear the United States and friends would invade Iraq. Saddam was going down."

The trijet bounced and swayed. Bosa looked out his window, his brow furrowing as if considering how to stop the forces of nature. "Morgan found out about a valuable cuneiform tablet Saddam had stashed in the Iraq National Museum. The tablet was supposed to be worth at least twelve million dollars as an antiquity. So we broke in and confiscated it. The problems began when the Republican Guards shot up Morgan so bad he dropped it, and it smashed into bits. All of us took pieces. Since we believed its value was as an artifact, we never got around to agreeing about the details of having it assembled."

"It's been a dozen years since then," Judd pointed out. "What's changed?" Finishing one sandwich, he picked up the other and ate.

"We received anonymous, untraceable e-mails that described one high-profile wet job by each of us," Bosa told them. "The information was accurate and included contact information for both employers and targets as well as details of the hits themselves. Several jobs, including mine, are still believed to be accidents. None of us wants that e-mail read by anyone else. It could destroy the lives of our employers, and it could lead to our arrests. In any case, it'd make it damn hard for us since we guarantee our employers secrecy."

"Gee whiz, too bad," Eva said. "Your employers hired you to commit murder!"

Bosa peered at her gravely. "One of them was the U.S. government."

She sighed. "Of course."

"What's worse, the sender claims to have detailed fifty jobs each of us did—that's three hundred assassinations—in something he calls *The Assassins' Catalog*. The good thing is, he'll trade it for the tablet pieces. He says the tablet is a map to some ancient Mesopotamian treasure, and he wants it. He gave us five rules. First, if any of us drops out, he'll e-mail the *Catalog* to online blogs, TV networks, and international newspapers like *The New York Times* and *The Times* of London. So he's damn well blackmailing us. The second rule is one of us—but only one of us—can win the *Catalog*. Third, we have to kill each other off." Flushing with anger, Bosa jumped up and stalked down the aisle. "Fourth, each of us has to keep our tablet pieces with us so they'll efficiently make their way to the winner. And fifth, we have to check in every twelve hours to the blackmailer's anonymous e-mail address. It's a means for him to keep tabs on who's alive, and it gives the winner a way to set up a meet to exchange the tablet pieces for the *Catalog*."

"So the last man standing wins," Eva said. "He's set up a contest to find out which of you is best."

Bosa dropped back into his seat. "Over the years there's been speculation about that, but it's an impossible question to answer. All of us have strengths, and merely living as long as we have says we're damn good."

"You don't know who sent the e-mail?" Judd asked.

"When I say 'untraceable,' I mean it. I have a stable of black hatters that would make Russia drool. They couldn't find the source. I was in touch with Krot, and his people couldn't find it either. I have to assume the Padre and Eli Eichel were unsuccessful as well."

"You said the e-mail went to all six of you," Judd said. "That should've at least given you a way to contact each other."

Bosa shook his head. "The sender addressed the e-mail to us, but he sent it out individually. The first time I knew there was something to it was when Krot confirmed receiving it, too. He was in touch with Eli Eichel, and Eichel confirmed it to Krot. We already had certain loose alliances. For instance, I was working with Krot, while he was working with Eli Eichel. Because of Eli, Krot learned the Padre had doubled you, and he told me. Anyone who got in the way was going to get scrubbed, and that included both of you."

"So Morgan died when his car was bombed in Paris," Judd ruminated. "The Padre died at his hunt club in Maryland. You killed Eli Eichel and his brother in Martin Chapman's library. That leaves Krot, Seymour, and you. How good is Krot?"

"The best. I hired a surveillance expert to follow him. According to her, he's been playing tourist with a schoolteacher staying at the same hotel. There's no sign he's been searching for Seymour, even though his latest e-mail to me claims he's 'close' to finding him."

"Why Marrakech?" Eva wondered.

Bosa shrugged. "Don't have a clue. What's concerning me is I just got an e-mail from my surveillance woman reporting Krot was continuing his daily routine, but her e-mail arrived much later than usual. And even stranger, she didn't ask to be paid for her report. I have to assume her abnormal behavior and Krot's unexplained choice of Marrakech could indicate problems for me."

"Have you told Krot that the Padre and the Eichel brothers are dead?" Judd asked.

"Only that the Padre is, and I said I had the Padre's limestone pieces. If he thinks I've stopped looking for Eichel, he might suspect I'm planning to pay him a surprise visit. I'm not fond of walking into a propeller blade, and that's what Marrakech feels like. I could go in disguise—that's effective 99.9 percent of the time. But it's damn hard to fool colleagues. You saw how quickly Eli Eichel recognized me even though I was wearing Chapman's snow gear and my face and hair were different. We're vulnerable that way."

"So your second idea is us," Judd said. "You need us to help you."

"If you're as good as I think, Judd, you should be able to get close and scope out the situation," Bosa said. "I want two things. First, the location of Seymour, and second, a safe, controlled environment where Krot and I can meet." He gazed steadily at Judd, ignoring Eva.

Before Judd could say anything, Eva turned to him. He could feel waves of outrage sizzle from her.

"Judd, I need to know more about the mission, don't you?" Her tone was so naive she was almost batting her eyes.

Bosa interrupted sharply. "You're too inexperienced for this, young lady. I can't have any more fuckups. You're staying on the plane."

"Well," she drawled, "I'm not sure how anyone could fuck up more than you have, Alex. First, you can't collect money that's owed you. Don't you have a rule about wiping anyone who stiffs you? You do, and you couldn't pull that off either. Then you let Morgan drop the tablet and break it. Hmm. And finally, when you realized one of your 'colleagues' was coming after Judd and me, you had to hustle your arse to 'save' us, which you couldn't really do without goddamn kidnapping me and ending my career."

Bosa glowered at her.

Judd interrupted. "She's got a point. She's a beginner, but she's a good one."

Bosa raised his eyebrows, considering her.

She glared at him. Her blue eyes were silvery with outrage.

Bosa pursed his lips, looking irritated. Then he made a noise in his throat that sounded to Judd like the beginning of a chuckle. "All right, Eva's in," he decided. "Now, about Krot . . . here are photos my surveillance woman took of him and the girlfriend." He passed copies to them.

Leaning together, Eva and Judd studied the small blond woman and the tall, black-haired man. There were individual shots and one of them together.

"Nothing here to show how deadly he supposedly is," Judd said.

"Right," Bosa agreed. "He's registered in the hotel under the name Pyotr Azarov. She's Francesca Fabiano, but after a while he started calling her Katia. They both speak Russian. He seems to be genuinely fond of her, but you can't trust it. His specialty is unusual—he has an uncanny ability to meet other people's emotional needs. He's manipulative in the extreme. It's a talent he's used time and again to position his victims so he can easily terminate them."

49

Washington, D.C.

At precisely 7:55 A.M., Scott Bridgeman parked his car and marched into Catapult headquarters. Gloria was sitting at her desk, sifting through color-coded files and making neat stacks. At the same time, she kept glancing up, watching him walk down the hall toward her.

"Morning, boss," she said.

"Morning, Gloria." It paid to be nice to Gloria. She knew more than anyone what was going on in the building and often inside Langley itself. "Send Tucker to my office." He headed past her, toward his door.

"Can't do that, boss. Sorry."

He stopped. She was usually cheerful, but not this morning. He studied her unsmiling face. Her reluctance was palpable.

"Why not?" he said.

She stood, straightened her tartan skirt, adjusted her red pullover sweater, and walked to his office door. Opening it, she said, "We'd better talk privately."

He had a moment of nervousness. Her skin looked almost gray. He headed past her. "Are you scared, or did someone die?" It was a joke. Probably some nasty memo had come over from the seventh floor. Gloria could take things personally.

As he stood behind his desk, she closed the door and turned.

She clasped her hands in front of her. "Tucker Andersen has been shot in the head. He's in the trauma center at Merrittville Hospital up in Maryland. His wife, Karen, is there. I sent a two-man Catapult team to bird dog Tucker. The hospital's done an MRI. Other tests, too. The last time I talked to Karen, the doctors were performing emergency surgery on him. He'd begun to hemorrhage inside his skull, so they needed to reduce the pressure on his brain. I'm hoping for a call soon about how the operation went. I haven't told anyone here yet."

"Jesus." He sat in his executive chair. "Christ."

"We don't know whether he'll survive. They're hoping for the best."

His voice hardened. "The last I heard, Tucker and Judd Ryder were on their way to Martin Chapman's place."

Her eyebrows shot up. "You knew about that?"

He ignored the question. "Is that where he was shot? I want all the details. Everything."

She sat, folded her hands in her lap, and related the story.

He listened with growing outrage. Among the dead were Martin Chapman and the Eichel brothers. Eva Blake was involved, as was the Carnivore. Blake, Ryder, and the Carnivore had flown off somewhere, leaving a mess of dead bodies.

"You know this is exceedingly bad, don't you, Gloria?" Bridgeman said.

She looked down at the toes of her black pumps. "Yes, sir."

"Have the Maryland authorities figured out Catapult's involved?"

She shook her head. "I've been keeping tabs. At the moment, they have several theories. One is Chapman's guards stopped a robbery, and the robbers ran before the authorities could get there. There are a lot of valuable things in his place. They're hoping Chapman's attorney has an inventory and can tell them what, if anything, is missing. Another top theory is that it was a revenge killing for one of Chapman's equity deals. He wasn't exactly an angel to the people whose companies he bought or to the banks when one of his big house-of-cards deals crashed, especially since he somehow always made a profit."

Bridgeman heaved a sigh. "Langley knows?"

"Of course not. That's your decision."

"Where are they?"

"Judd and Eva? I don't know."

He stared at her.

She moved uneasily in her chair. "Honestly, I really don't know."

He nodded. "If they call, tell me instantly. Now it's time for damage control. It's unlikely they're staying in the United States. Makes them too vulnerable. Notify Interpol. Tell them we want Judd Ryder and Eva Blake for possible involvement in a multiple homicide that includes two international assassins, and that a third assassin is likely roaming around somewhere with Ryder and Blake. All are armed and dangerous—the usual warnings. Send photos, bios, everything you have. We want them shut down as quickly as possible. That's it. Get to work."

Gloria did not move. "Tucker was right—international assassins were operating inside the country. He could be right, too, that it's just the beginning of something very bad. Shouldn't we find out what they were up to?"

"Tucker lied so much I doubt he knew when he was telling the truth. But there isn't a hint they were doing anything illegal except killing each other off. And in some quarters, fewer assassins is a good thing."

"And Martin Chapman's death?"

Bridgeman shrugged. "Chapman was shot and killed. It could've been Tucker's bullet."

"If it was Tucker's bullet, then it was self-defense. The whole thing in the library could've been an attack on Tucker, Judd, and Eva."

"Or the reverse. It could've been them going after Chapman. Unfortunately, Chapman's not alive to tell us, and it's hard to believe anything Tucker, Ryder, Blake, or the Carnivore claims."

Her eyebrows rose. She changed the subject. "Would you like me to gather the staff in the lunchroom so you can tell them about Tucker's head injury? If you'd rather not, I'll talk to them. They're going to be upset."

He frowned. "Of course I'll do it," he said firmly. "It's my job. Let me know when everyone's there." He would praise the legend of Tucker, not mention the shell of an intelligence officer the old man had become.

Gloria nodded and opened the door.

Bridgeman spoke again: "You'll notice I didn't ask you why you didn't call me as soon as you got off the phone with Ryder. That's a dereliction of your duty. I'll let it go this time, but don't *ever* give me reason not to trust you again."

50

Marrakech, Morocco

Katia felt like a cat, purring and stretching in bed. She sighed contentedly. They had slept long. It was nearly noon.

"Hello, darling. You're awake?" Pyotr was coming out of the bathroom stark naked, toweling his hair dry.

"Yes." She snuggled back down, peeking over the covers and staring at his long lines, the spray of black hair on his chest, his curly pubic hair black, too, and his cock at half mast. "More?" she asked.

He had been walking to the window to check the day. Abruptly he turned. Wadding the towel, he stalked toward her, head lowered, grinning widely. He hurled the towel at her. "You're going to wear me out."

She rose up and caught the towel. "I don't think so."

Pyotr left to go to his room to put on fresh clothes while she showered. By the time he returned, dressed in a pressed white shirt and bone-colored linen slacks, she was out of the bathroom and wearing her favorite blue sundress.

"You're beautiful." He handed her a pink rose. "I stole it from a vase in the hallway, but as long as it remains in the hotel, it's not stealing, right?"

"Don't expect me to absolve you of your petty sins." She grinned. "Thank you anyway—I love it."

Not only Pyotr had arrived, so had breakfast. Well, brunch, Katia thought. They'd had a long night of off-and-on lovemaking and sleeping. Sitting across from each other at the little table by the window, they drank their lattes and devoured their croissants.

"I'm going to get fat if I keep eating croissants," she warned.

"Not likely. But if you do, there will just be more of you to love." He smiled.

"Were you always so handsome?"

He laughed. "No. The cosmetic surgeries helped. Why?"

"I would've thought anyone who wanted to go unnoticed would've had surgery to make them look as plain as possible."

"Under ordinary circumstances you'd be right. My last surgery was just after I retired, and being somewhat attractive made me seem less likely to have been in my profession."

"Are you growing a beard?" She reached across the table and stroked his holiday stubble. The hair was longer now, springy and soft.

"I'll wait until winter to cultivate a beard. I hope you'll like it."

She had a catch in her throat. Was he saying—

"You look stunned." He was grinning again. "What did you think? Of course we'll still be together this winter, and next winter, and next." He frowned. "Unless of course you don't want to."

She tested her emotions. There was no way she had enough sense right now to test her brain. "I'd like that. One day at a time, okay?"

He sat back, his latte cup in one hand. "I need to talk with you about something that happened last night. I didn't want to scare you, but I was worried about the woman who was taking pictures of you. I figured if she were really following you, I might be able to spot her outside the hotel. So I got up around three o'clock and went out. I didn't find her, but I did find her employer, the person who was the real surveillor. She was operating under the name Laura Billingsley. She'd hired the older woman to take photos as a distraction, because it was me she was following, not you. Billingsley ended up killing her, probably because she was the only witness to what Billingsley was doing."

Katia covered her mouth with her hand. She was speechless, horrified.

Pyotr inhaled. "Billingsley had done a good job on me—she knew who I was, and she'd overheard enough of our conversation to know we speak Russian and you have two names. She pulled a Luger on me. I had to shoot her. She's dead."

Katia gasped.

"My past haunts me," he said quietly. "I try over and over to leave it behind, and then something like this happens."

She was silent.

"Katia? Darling?"

She stood shakily. "Give me a moment."

Her legs were weak. She walked into the bathroom, closed the door, and leaned back against it. She took several deep breaths then went to the sink and ran cold water. Leaning over the basin, she splashed her face until it numbed. She grabbed a towel and held it to her skin. It smelled of Pyotr. She muffled a sob.

Staring into the mirror, she wondered how her mother had handled learning about her husband's clean-up work for the KGB. Had she felt as if she had just received a gut punch? Or had she accepted it as filling an honorable need for the country. But Pyotr no longer had the excuse of patriotic duty.

She stared longer, her eyes narrowing as she struggled to remember what else Pyotr had said. Her memory seemed to have stopped once he told her he had shot the woman. That was when it came to her—the woman was dangerous. She had been armed. Pyotr had simply done what he needed to save not only him but her.

As if it had been a sudden summer thunderstorm, the horror passed. She was surprised at how calm she felt. She could handle this.

Opening the door, she saw Pyotr pacing across the room, his hands clasped behind his back. He turned, questions in his eyes.

"Thank you for telling me, Pyotr," she said. "Is there any way you'll be connected to Billingsley's death?"

"I don't think so. I left her body in the souk. The police have few friends there." Gazing worriedly at her, he walked to her, his hands helpless at his sides. "You're all right with me then? You forgive me?"

"Of course, darling. It's good you knew what you were doing. You survived, and you cleaned up the mess. Now we can get on with our lives."

"Not quite yet." He took a small backpack from the bottom drawer of the bureau. "This was Billingsley's. Want to help me go through it?"

"Of course."

He unloaded it on the table where they'd had breakfast. They sat together.

First was a Luger. "This was what Billingsley pulled on me." He inspected the weapon. "There's a round in the chamber. She was prepared." He picked up a tube of lip gloss, opened it, and pressed all of the gloss out onto a napkin. "Nothing hidden inside." He handed her the map of Marrakech. "See if she wrote anything on it, will you? Notes, a highlighted route, anything."

As he opened the wallet, she spread out the map. She studied the street grid then the list of street names. "No handwriting or marks of any kind," she announced.

The wallet was black microfiber and appeared to be brand-new. He counted the cash. "She was carrying six hundred euros and five hundred dirhams plus a credit card and driver's license in the name Laura Billingsley." He looked at his watch and grimaced. "It's two o'clock. Time for the news."

He turned on the TV and rotated it so they could watch from the table. National news was beginning, discussing politics and crime from Tangier to Casablanca and Tarfaya. The report was in Arabic mixed with French and occasionally English. Pyotr translated some of it for her. Finally a local newsreader appeared. The first item was a fatal skiing accident in the mountains.

When a colored drawing of a young European woman with a narrow face and long brown hair appeared on the screen, Pyotr said, "That's her. The police think she died in a robbery."

"Why was she following you?"

"She was hired by a former colleague of mine who operates under a variety of aliases. Generally he's called the Carnivore. He's an independent assassin. I think he's planning to neutralize me."

She gasped.

He held up the Droid from Billingsley's backpack. "I read through the e-mail reports she made to him. I didn't want him to know she was dead, so I reported in as if I were her. I've stayed in touch with him as myself, too. If Billingsley were reporting to the Carnivore about me, then she must've told him about you, too. He might come looking for you to find out where I am."

She frowned worriedly. "What are he and you involved in?"

He jumped to his feet and paced, for the moment anxious and out of place, a Cossack without a horse. He turned. "Let's get out of the hotel. The walls are closing in. Then we'll talk."

They gathered their things. He slid his pistol into a shoulder holster and put on a jacket. She stared at the gun then at him, at his almost nonchalant expression. Her skin prickled uncomfortably. They rode the elevator down to the lobby and were soon out in the shadows of late afternoon.

He hailed a taxi. "We've got some time, so let's be sightseers again. It's fun with you." As they climbed inside, he told the driver, "Maison Tiskiwin."

He seemed to know just what to do, what to say. She had needed to get out of the hotel, too. The traffic was thick and noisy, as boisterous as Marrakech itself.

"Tell me what's going on." She studied Pyotr's dusky face.

He nodded. "A few years ago six of us participated in a series of hits for Saddam Hussein." He described Saddam's billion-dollar horde and the financiers who had hidden it for him. "The man Saddam brought in to manage the wet jobs was Burleigh Morgan. His target was a Swiss financier. Mine was an investment banker from Moscow. Eli Eichel had a Saudi. The Carnivore did a banker from Liechtenstein. The Padre wiped a financier from Rome. And Seymour got the financial mastermind himself—Rostam Rahim. I'm going into all of this detail so you'll know I'm not holding back anything." He reached inside his jacket, removed an aluminum box, and put it into her hand. "Tell me what you think this is."

She unhooked the latch and opened it. Inside were four padded mounds. She peeled back the Velcro enclosing each. Puzzled, she said, "They look like chunks of limestone with some kind of funny carving on them."

"Yes, they're pieces of an ancient cuneiform tablet, a very valuable one." He had been glancing out the rear window. Now he stared.

She peered back, too. Twilight was spreading across the city, purple in the waning light.

"Did you see that black Mercedes?" His voice was tight. "It was an E350 with Algerian plates." When she shook her head, he continued: "I thought it was following us, but it turned the corner."

Now she understood: "The real reason you wanted to leave the hotel was to find out whether we were still being followed."

"I'm sorry, darling. I didn't do you any favor by falling in love with you."

51

Maison Tiskiwin was a large Moroccan house of graceful arches and old tiles, stuffed with art and artifacts illustrating the legendary Gold Road, the caravan route from the Atlas Mountains to Timbuktu. Pretending to study the exhibits, Katia found herself nervously watching the guards and other visitors. Pyotr was covertly scanning, too.

"Besides avoiding the Carnivore, what are you trying to accomplish?" she whispered.

"I've got to find Seymour," Pyotr told her quietly. "During the Cold War, he was Islamic Jihad. Your father, Grigori, met him in Athens when they cooperated on a job. It turned out to be the beginning of a relationship good for both organizations and eventually a friendship between the two men. Then when your father went independent, Seymour did, too. . . ."

She did not hear what he said next. She struggled to find an explanation for why he had just told her about a close relationship between her father and Seymour.

He peered down at her, questions in his eyes. "I need your help, Katia."

Fury exploded through her. "Bullshit." With effort, she kept her voice low. "You son-of-a-bitch. The only reason you came to Marrakech was because you thought you could use me to find my father, and then you could use him to get to Seymour."

"That's partly true. But what I told you earlier is true, too—I wanted to reconnect with Roza's daughter." His expression was somber. "I wanted to meet you. We share a history few others know even exists. What I didn't count on was falling in love with you."

She looked around. Two couples were gazing at displays of belts and scarves, but they were also shooting glances that told her they knew there was a problem. Her voice rose: "You brought me here so I wouldn't make a scene." She spun on her heel and marched back toward the museum's entrance. How could she have been so stupid. So naive.

Pyotr was at her side, a shadow she did not want.

"Please believe me, Katia," he whispered. "I love you. I really love you. I want to marry you."

"Liar."

"You know I'm telling the truth. There's more. . . ." He leaned down, talking in a hushed, almost mesmerizing tone: "Grigori and Seymour dropped out of sight in 2003." He took her hand and pulled her to a stop, facing him. He pressed her hands between his. "I know Grigori was in touch with you. He said so. He loved your mother, and he loves you. There's no way he'd cut you off. Where is he, Katia? Where is Grigori? I really need to know. I'm sure he can tell me how to find Seymour."

She tried to keep the bitterness from her voice. "First you pretend we've never met. Then you tell me you're retired. You saw my loneliness and used it to get close to me. You were so nice, so handsome, so com-passionate. But all of it was for one reason . . . because I'm Grigori's daughter—not because I'm Roza's daughter. Because you wanted to find Seymour—not because you loved me. Now I know why you're called Mole. You're underhanded, a master manipulator. No one ever sees your true motive—until it's too late." She yanked her hands from be-tween his. "But it's not too late for me." She stepped back.

"Oh, God, Katia. I didn't mean to hurt you. I'm sorry."

There was so much despair in his face she almost flinched.

He gestured at the exhibit beside them. On display were magnificent necklaces, bracelets, and rings. "You sparkle more than any jewelry, Katia. Whoever would've thought I'd find someone as wonderful as you to love. You're right that I came here because I hoped to convince you to help me. But once I met you, everything changed for me. You're beautiful and sweet and we fit together. I really was retired until this mess about the tablet came up. Can you ever forgive me for asking you to help me find your father?"

She gave her head an angry shake. "Let's go."

Silently, they walked through two more rooms and out the museum's front door. Night had arrived, glistening black punctuated by vehicle lights, streetlights, and the occasional flash of a cigarette lighter.

Pyotr surveyed the traffic and clumps of tourists and locals.

He stiffened. "Did you see a black Mercedes? It slowed as it passed."

Her throat tightened. "The car that was following our taxi?"

He grabbed her arm. "Yes, run!"

They tore down the sidewalk, weaving around pedestrians, jumping out of the way of a bicyclist. He craned, watching the cars rushing in both directions. Abruptly he pulled her behind a fruit cart. The donkey looked back and brayed. They crouched and watched the street. Then it appeared, the black Mercedes E350 with license plates from Algeria, driving toward them, illuminated by streetlamps. It was almost on them.

"I can't see the driver's face," she said worriedly.

The brim of the driver's cap was pulled so low, just his mouth and chin showed. He kept glancing across at the sidewalk. Pyotr said nothing, focused on the luxury car. Again the vehicle slowed, then it glided past.

As soon as it was out of sight, they ran again. Hugging buildings, they ducked under awnings, and, when the Mercedes appeared a third time, they dashed into a recessed doorway. The car vanished. He grabbed her hand. They ran another thirty feet into a store selling French goods and out a rear door into a dirt alley. It was like a tunnel, lined with buildings and overhung with balconies. Slowing, they checked around.

Katia was shaken. She had never had to run for her life. She hugged her purse close. She found herself admitting, "I'm afraid for you. Will the Carnivore stop if he can't find you tonight?"

"Probably not, but I'll be fine. I've been at this a long time, remember."

She nodded, but she had a sick feeling in the pit of her stomach.

At the alley's opening, they moved into a dark shadow against the wall where they could watch for the Mercedes. He wrapped his arms around her, and for a moment she resisted. She felt the beat of his heart, solid, reassuring.

"We can't stay here forever, and we can't go back to our hotel because the Carnivore knows about it." He took out his iPhone. "I know a place that'll be safe for us." He tapped in a phone number and spoke to some-one named Liza, asking for a room. "Yes, we're registered at Hotel Fash-ion." After a pause, he gave Katia a nod, indicating they were all set. When he said good-bye, he dialed again, this time alerting the hotel to be prepared for Liza's man to pick up their luggage.

Leaving the alley, they walked at a fast clip around the block. With every car that approached, Katia had a few seconds of fear that it was the Mercedes. Staying on back streets, she was soon lost. Her anxiety grew as Pyotr hurried her along a stretch of old buildings with deeply cut windows.

"Where are we?" she asked.

"The back of the souk."

"I've always entered from the marketplace."

He was looking around alertly. "This part is older, more residential, if you can call it that. You won't find an array of goods for sale, or the friendly smiles. We'll be at Liza's place soon."

52

They were a nice-looking couple in their thirties, approachable. Mr. and Mrs. Roman. She was a pretty redhead, her long hair pulled back in a ponytail; he had light brown hair and a weathered face. They smiled at each other when they talked. Looking around the lobby of the Hotel Fashion, she commented on the intricate tile work, and he was impressed by the comfortable furniture. They left the registration desk and sat on a sofa near the hotel's glass entry doors to wait for their friend—Pyotr Azarov.

"Bloody inconsiderate of Pyotr," the husband, Greg, grumbled loudly. His English accent was thick. "Leaving us high and dry as a martini without a clue when he'll be back, the wanker. I *need* a martini."

"Now, now, dear." The wife, Courtney, patted his arm. She was obviously American. "He's just out having a good time. What are vacations for, if not to have a wonderful time?"

They sat down on the sofa, and she put her large straw shoulder bag on her lap. It was heavy—inside was her Glock. She was wearing a dark blue blouse in some sort of light summery fabric tucked into matching trousers. With the sleeves of a yellow sweater tied around her neck, she looked sporty. He wore an eye-bruising Hawaiian shirt decorated with huge green palm fronds and orange hibiscus flowers. His jeans looked designer, but it was hard to tell—the Hawaiian shirt fell sloppily over them, concealing the 9-mm Beretta holstered at the small of his back.

As would be expected, the comings and goings and registrations of more guests soon attracted attention, and Judd and Eva—"Mr. and Mrs. Roman"—became part of the background.

From the sofa, they watched the lobby doors. Eva's chest was tight. Every time the doors opened, she grew more tense.

After two hours, she was ready to jump out of her skin.

Judd had been glancing at her. "Waiting is always the worst. Let's find out how Tucker is. I'll call."

"Yes." They had phoned twice and heard he needed surgery.

"Hello, Gloria," Judd said into his burner cell. "No, don't worry. I'm not going to tell you where we are. Hold on. I'm putting you on speakerphone so Eva can hear. How's Tucker?"

Judd and Eva hunched over the phone, their heads bent, their shoulders touching. As they watched hotel guests come and go, they listened to Gloria's low voice: "He hemorrhaged, so the doctors operated to reduce the pressure on his brain. They removed part of his skull. It's apparently standard procedure when the brain swells a lot. They froze the piece of skull and hope to put it back in his head once he's better."

Eva took a deep breath. "That sounds ominous."

"He came through the operation fine, and they're watching him closely," Gloria said noncommittally. "I know you want to keep in touch to find out how he is, but Bridgeman has declared war. He ordered me to notify Interpol to look for you. I haven't done it yet, but I'll have to pretty soon. He didn't think to ask whether I'd heard from you, but it's only a matter of time."

"What will you say?" Judd asked. *Will you lie for us?*

"I don't know. I've got to go. Stay safe." And the line went dead.

Someone new had arrived at the registration desk. A short man with skin the color of dry mud, he wore a black baseball cap and a long white linen *djellaba* embroidered with black thread. He was speaking Arabic

with the clerk. Judd was fluent, and Eva had been studying it. She heard
the names Pyotr Azarov and Francesca Fabiano and something about
suitcases. The desk clerk made a call. The man in the baseball cap turned
to survey the room.

Judd stood up and reached his hand back to her. "Let's go outside,
honey, and get some fresh air. My arse is going bloody numb from
waiting."

"Hasn't affected its fine shape, though," she said brightly. Standing,
she slid the straps of her straw bag up onto her left shoulder so her gun
hand would be free.

They pushed through the doors into the cool air of evening. Taxis
and pickups cruised past. They walked to the curb.

"What were they saying?" Eva whispered.

"His name is Hata, and he's here to pick up Krot's and his girlfriend's
luggage. They're staying somewhere in the souk tonight."

"Let's bug his car so we can follow the luggage." She dipped into her
straw bag, took out a small case, and popped it open. She offered him
the microtransmitter that lay inside.

He waved it away. "It's better if you do it. I'll set you up."

The glass door swung open, and Hata backed out, pulling a brass cart
loaded with two roll-aboard suitcases, a valise, and a shopping bag. In
three quick steps, Judd reached the door and held it open for him.

Eva heard him ask the man a question in Arabic—something about
help you.

But Hata shook his head. *"Mish be eed."* His car was not far away.

As Hata pushed the baggage cart off down the sidewalk, Judd ambled alongside. Hata barely reached Judd's shoulder, but the short man's
stride was long, aggressive.

Eva followed. She heard Judd say "vacation" and "tourist." He was
asking which sights to see. Hata answered with few words, while Judd
played the chatty Brit, gesturing and holding forth. Hata turned the cart
toward a black Citroën parked with two tires up on the sidewalk.

Eva closed in, but there was still no way she could plant the bug without Hata's seeing her.

Hata took out a key chain, touched a button with his thumb, and the door to the Citroën's trunk lifted. He turned back to his cart just as Judd grabbed the shopping bag and one of the suitcases.

With breathtaking speed, Hata pulled a stiletto from inside his *djellaba* and aimed it at Judd's heart. The needlelike point caught the lamplight and flashed.

"Thief, thief!" he bellowed in Arabic.

Judd backed up, talking quickly, still holding the suitcase and shopping bag as he led Hata away from the car.

Eva stepped off the curb and ran. Vehicles rushed past, spinning up dust.

Furious, Hata was dragging the cart after him, leaning forward, stiletto in hand, determined to strike. Judd kept dancing backward, balancing the suitcase and shopping bag, and spitting words out like a nail gun. From what she could understand, Judd was trying to convince Hata he should accept Judd's help.

Brushing past the car's rear fender, Eva pressed the bug low against the rear passenger window. As it slid down into the door frame and out of sight, she sprinted away. Hata's and Judd's dangerous dance had not slowed. She raised her chin, caught Judd's eye, and nodded.

Judd hurled the suitcase and shopping bag at Hata.

Screaming obscenities, the little man leaped out of the way while tissue paper and silky slips, bras, and panties exploded from the bag. Cursing a string of oaths, he dropped to his knees to gather up the garments.

Eva saw Judd dash off. As she raced around the block toward their rental car, she smiled to herself. Now they would find Krot.

53

In the medieval souk, smoke from charcoal braziers drifted past shuttered windows, the odor oily. Streets twisted in a snakelike maze. Katia looked around with relief—the passageway was too narrow for the Mercedes to follow. Perhaps they were safe at last.

"Who exactly is the person you phoned—Liza Somebody?" Katia asked.

"Her name is Liza Kosciuch," Pyotr told her. "She grew up in Warsaw and Leningrad. We've known each other since the old days. Her inn is private, the sort of place the police ignore and others fear. No one talks about it. No one can find it even if they've heard rumors of its existence." He gestured. "This is it."

They stopped at a three-story building, where a small round window near the top of a short door was covered by an ornate iron grille that appeared strong enough to bar a prison cell.

Pyotr knocked, and soon the window opened. Behind the grille appeared the face of a middle-aged woman. Her cheekbones were high, her nose straight, and her chin square. Deep lines cross-hatched her cheeks. She must have been a great beauty in her day.

"Ah, is you, Pyotr." She had a heavy Russian accent.

"Hello, Liza," he said. "Glad you can take us in."

"Naturally."

The face retreated, and the window closed. As Pyotr found his wallet and counted out ten hundred-dollar bills, the door opened.

Liza beckoned. "Come."

Bending over to pass through the doorway, they left the drabness of the souk for a bright foyer with a high ceiling, sunny yellow walls, and a tile floor that was a mosaic of blue and green. Katia looked eagerly around. An antique silver samovar shone atop a mahogany table. But the centerpiece was Liza herself. Her luxuriant silver-gray hair was pulled back in sterling clips, and she was dressed in a baby-blue Donna Karan jogging suit.

"I appreciate your help." Pyotr tried to hand the greenbacks to Liza.

She waved him off. "Is always pleasure to see you, Pyotr. And who is this beautiful woman?"

"Katia Levinchev," Pyotr told her. "Katia, meet a Cold War heroine."

Liza laughed and waved a dismissive hand. "Welcome to safety."

As Pyotr returned the money to his pocket, Katia studied the foyer. Perhaps eight feet wide, it extended twelve feet to a generous arch through which a corridor showed. Inside the arch stood a silent, heavy-set man with shoulders like boxcars. He carried some kind of rifle. His eyelids blinked slowly as he watched them.

"Spartak, you remember Pyotr," Liza told him. "This is his lady friend. First lady friend he ever show me."

Spartak nodded. "Da." There was a straight-back wood chair behind him. Sitting down, he laid the rifle across his lap, one hand firmly on the grip.

"So, Pyotr, you look good," Liza said. "Any more big changes since Switzerland?"

"As a matter of fact, yes." He took Katia's hand, lifted it to his lips, and kissed it. "I want to marry Katia."

"Oh? You are crazy new man. What next—babies?" She laughed. "But what about you?" She turned to Katia. "Will you marry this broken-down old assassin?"

"I'm thinking about it." The truth was, despite everything, she did want to marry him.

"I hear hesitation," Liza decided.

Katia shrugged. "We still have things to talk about."

Liza's eyes narrowed, and she studied them. "Is wacky world we live in. Cold War made sense. Grab happiness while you can." She turned to Pyotr: "Your room is ready. Your luggage is here soon. I will call when Hata is close." She handed him an electronic key. "Enjoy." Opening a door next to the samovar, she disappeared.

His gaze bored, Spartak said nothing as they passed him.

More tiles paved the hall. To the left, the top half of a Dutch door was open, showing a spotless kitchen. At last Pyotr stopped at a simple wood door, no peephole. "This is ours." Using Liza's electronic key, they entered to the romantic music of Sergei Rachmaninoff. It filled the room.

"Oh, my God." Katia walked inside, listening excitedly. "Piano Concerto Number Two."

Locking the door, Pyotr grinned at her. "Rachmaninoff himself is playing. There's nothing like great Russian music played by a great Russian composer. It was recorded in 1929." He sat on the love seat, watching her.

"How did you— Oh, never mind."

As the music soared, she wrapped her arms around her breasts and closed her eyes. Each note seemed to resonate within her, and in her mind it was spring in Bedford, with the linden trees leafing and tulips blooming along Main Street. She had finished her homework, the dinner dishes were done, and they were watching television. Papa and Mama were on the couch, his arm around her, and Katia was sitting on the floor between them, feeling their legs pressed against her shoulders. It was a sweet feeling, the tactile sensation of protective love.

At nine o'clock, she had gone off to bed. Then something unusual happened—Papa said good night not only in the living room, but came into her bedroom as well.

"You are happy in school?" He sat on the edge of her bed.

"I like it."

"No, you're not happy." His blue eyes scoured her face, looking for the truth of her.

"I miss home," she admitted.

"Of course you do. Your mother and I do, too."

He had a simple face, nothing distinctive about it, but a good face, a solid peasant face with a snub nose and round cheeks and curly brown eyebrows.

"Always remember you come from Stalingrad," he told her. "Two million Soviets and Germans died there in World War Two. The city survived and became great again. When you have problems, think about their resolve and their sacrifices, and you'll come through like Stalingrad, still standing." He looked down at his hands. "Have fun, too. You have a good life ahead of you, my dear Katyusha."

He kissed her on the forehead and both cheeks. With a big smile, he stood. In the doorway he turned and gave her a cheery wave.

But she did not see him again for years. For a few seconds, she could still feel the security of his presence, could still smell his old-fashioned aftershave, Old Spice. Her throat tightened. But then the music ended.

54

The room was quiet except for the warm crackle of the fire in the stone fireplace. Katia saw Pyotr was watching her from the love seat, head cocked, smiling tenderly.

She sat beside him. "My parents loved Rachmaninoff's music."

"Liza always has something Russian playing for me. Kind of her."

"But you don't pay for the room."

He hesitated. "Years ago we happened to be working in Athens at the same time. I got word she was in trouble. I arrived in time to help."

"You saved her. You feel safe here, don't you." It was a statement, not a question.

"Yes. I'm sure no one followed us, and Liza's security is cutting edge." He paused. "Liza's right, I've been going through a lot of changes. Getting older can do that to you. Affairs come and go—I never wanted any of them to last. But with you, Katia . . . I'd do anything to slow down time, stretch every moment." He lifted her hand and kissed the fingertips. "It feels to me as if we belong together. You understand my past, what I was. I love you for more reasons than there are stars in the sky, and I think you love me." He paused. "But if you can't believe in my love, we should end this right now."

Her lungs tightened.

"Will you tell me how to get in touch with your father now?" he asked gently. "I just want to find a way to reach out to Seymour."

She looked away and bit her lower lip. "Papa is dead. He died seven years ago."

For a moment he appeared stunned, then discouraged. "I'm sorry, Katia. I'm really sorry. Did you ever get to see him again?"

She fought an impulse to rip open the door and run. Instead, she folded her hands in her lap, entwining her fingers, holding herself together. "Yes. Once. We met in Vienna. It was . . . it was incredible."

For a few seconds she was with him again, smelling the Old Spice he had put on just for her, feeling the gentleness of his hands. They had laughed together, the joy of it all, the bittersweet pain, too.

"He was dying of esophageal cancer," she told him. "He'd smoked all his life. He wouldn't let me go back with him to where he lived. He said it still wasn't safe. He was so thin and pale, like a piece of chalk. He said someone was taking care of him. I can't remember for sure now, but I think he called him Seymour." Reaching into her purse, she found notepaper and a pen. "I'll give you the contact information, but it may not be good anymore." She uncapped the pen and began to write.

"Can't you just tell me?"

She gave a hard shake of her head. "No, getting in touch with him was always very secret. I don't know why, but I'm not going to start questioning it. Here's the phone number."

He leaned close. "Baghdad?"

She nodded. "He'd been in Baghdad for years. Whoever answered spoke Arabic." She pointed to the words with her pen.

"Is it a real business?"

"I don't know. Next you say, 'I need to buy some wrenches' in Russian. That was when I'd be told he'd call me back at a specific time. I don't know where this will lead you—or maybe it's just a dead end."

He studied the instructions. "Got it."

"Good." Wadding up the paper, she walked to the fireplace and tossed it into the blaze. She turned.

He smiled. "I love you," he said simply. "I know that was hard."

A phone rang. It was sitting on a writing desk next to his elbow.

He answered. "Yes, thanks." Then to Katia: "Our suitcases are here. We can pick them up in the garage."

55

Alex Bosa sat in his darkened trijet on the tarmac of Marrakech-Menara Airport, checking local news on his iPad. It was not long before he discovered why his surveillance expert had not reported on schedule—she was dead, shot sometime between three and four o'clock this morning.

Crossing his arms, Bosa mulled. Her murder explained the lapse before her most recent e-mailed report. Whoever had written it had been motivated to pretend she was still alive. The logical deduction was Krot had wiped her then impersonated her to lull Bosa into thinking nothing unusual was going on in Marrakech.

Bosa felt his iPhone vibrate. He checked the digital identification—Sacher Torte.

Bosa answered immediately. "You have news?"

"More than that . . . an answer." There was an unusual amount of steel in the timbre of the old voice, which told Bosa something had happened—or was about to. "I did some digging into the woman Krot's been romancing. From everything I could learn, her American identity started some twenty-five years ago. Before then, she was a cipher. So I ran her face through several Cold War data banks of known spies. Here's the shocker—she looks a lot like Roza Levinchev. Remember Roza? She was married to Grigori Levinchev, the bastard. I'm going to forward the photos and background to you. On top of the physical resemblance, the young woman's arrival in Maine coincided with Roza's assignment to Marrakech."

"Jesus." Bosa closed his eyes in frustration. "So Krot's involved with Grigori's daughter. If I remember correctly, Grigori and Seymour worked a lot of jobs together even after they left their organizations."

"Indeed they did. But the daughter is registered at the hotel as Francesca Fabiano."

"The woman I paid to tail Krot said he called her Katia."

"Roza's daughter was named Katia. Grigori was crazy about her."

"How do you know all this?" Bosa demanded.

"Seymour. He told me years ago." There was a pause. "Guess I'm getting senile. I should've remembered the relationship."

Bosa repressed a sigh. They were all getting older, but this was the kind of mistake that could have far-reaching consequences. "Does Katia Levinchev know where her father is?"

"Why else would Krot bother with her at this point? He's taken her into the souk, poor deluded woman. But the two kids—Judd and Eva—have planted a bug on the car that picked up their luggage. Clever."

"Where in the souk?"

"Don't know yet."

"Find out!"

Bosa ended the connection and sat in the low light of the plane. Jack, George, and Doug were in the dining area playing Texas hold 'em. Letting the hum of their voices grow distant, he closed his eyes. He had slept well on the flight, but he could think better in the darkness.

Making a decision, he opened his eyes and punched in the number to Judd's disposable cell. He listened to it ring twice.

"Yes?" Judd sounded distracted.

"Where are you?" Bosa demanded. "What are you doing?"

"We're following the car that picked up Krot and the woman's luggage. Eva's driving. I'm monitoring the tracker. We've got the Citroën in sight. Christ, there's some kind of a parade going down the street."

"A wedding procession." It was Eva's voice.

"Put your cell on speakerphone," Bosa said. "You both should hear this."

In a moment, Judd said, "Done. What's up?"

"The real name of the woman Krot picked up is Katia Levinchev," Bosa told them. "Her father is Grigori Levinchev, an old KGB assassin. Levinchev and Seymour have been tight for years. Katia's father may know where Seymour is."

"So Krot's turned up a lead. That's good news."

"Maybe. The problem is, the woman I sent to surveil Krot is dead, and he's probably the one who killed her. Plus, we don't know whether Krot and Katia are a couple, or whether Krot has kidnapped her. Go in prepared."

"You still want us to try to set up a meeting with him?"

"Yes, if you can. And if you can't . . . use your best judgment."

56

Judd alternately watched the tracker and the traffic while Eva drove. Across the street, the wedding party was dancing and singing down the block. Donkeys pulled wood carts piled with gaily wrapped gifts. Dressed in satin gowns, the bride's attendants twirled as musicians played drums and pipes.

Judd rolled down his window. "Smell that?"

Eva rolled hers down, too. "Marijuana."

"Yup. It's called *kif* around here. We're at the back of the souk. That's it."

He gestured to the left, across the traffic to where buildings stood shoulder-to-shoulder, two and three stories high, gray and faintly sinister in the streetlight.

"There's the Citroën." Eva nodded.

It was slowing for the parade. A garage door began to roll up in the sheer wall of dirty buildings.

"Has to be an automatic door opener," she observed. "That seems sophisticated for the souk."

"Agreed. Check out the mini surveillance cameras up in the eaves. They're high end, too. Let's stop here. I'd rather confront Hata in the garage than on the street. If we move quickly, we may be able to get inside and take charge of the situation before anyone can react to the cameras."

As the Citroën drove into the garage, Eva parked the car.

He gave her a look. "Don't do anything stupid," he warned. "Let's go."

Dodging traffic, they ran across the street and landed against the garage wall. They took out their pistols—his Beretta, her Glock.

Eva stared at the garage door. "It's getting so low we're not going to be able to get under. Let's move!"

Before Judd could respond, she dropped to her heels and crab-walked inside. Swearing silently, he followed.

57

Inside the quiet inn, Katia and Pyotr followed the blue-and-green tile floor down the hallway toward a large steel door. He slid the bolts and opened it. Headlights blinded her. She raised her hand, shielding her eyes, and listened to the rumble of a powerful automobile engine coming to rest. The headlights went dark, and overhead fluorescent lights turned on. The vehicle's engine stopped. It was a black Citroën.

Pyotr and she were standing on a large platform above the two-vehicle garage. As they walked to the rail, the door opened behind them, and Spartak appeared, cradling his rifle. He inspected the area then stepped aside. Liza hurried past him, carrying a pistol. Two guards followed closely.

Her expression tense, Liza stopped at the top of the steps. "We have uninvited visitors," she told them. "Stay up here."

Pyotr slipped his PB pistol from his shoulder holster. "Need help?"

"No. Is covered."

Motioning, Liza led the men downstairs and past the Citroën to the big door. She divided them in half—Spartak and she on one side, and the two other guards on the other. All moved back into the shadows. Seconds later, two strangers—a man with light brown hair and a red-headed woman—slid in under the closing door, pistols up and ready. Their expressions were wary.

"Now!" Liza ordered.

She and her people converged, their weapons aimed down at the crouching pair. The couple exchanged a glance and stood, swinging their pistols slowly around, but they were outnumbered and outmaneuvered.

Liza cocked her head, studying them. "Before you ask, you do not get to know my name or what this place is. Unless you behave yourselves, you will not leave alive. So, to begin, you must answer two questions: Who are you? What are you doing here?"

To Katia, the man did not appear at all intimidated. He was lean and muscular, an outdoorsy sort, with a craggy face. His nose was strong, his jaw solid. A good-looking man if you liked them unfinished. He wore a Hawaiian shirt.

Staring across the garage at Pyotr, he said, "My name is Greg Roman. We have a message for Krot—Pyotr Azarov. That's you."

As soon as the man identified him, Pyotr changed—the warmth he had been showering on Katia vanished, replaced by a chilly emptiness. She stared at him.

Pyotr did not even glance at her. He was focused on the strangers. His voice deepened. "Yes, I'm Krot. Who's your message from?"

The redheaded woman interrupted: "My name is Courtney Roman. Are you all right, Katia?"

The woman was probably in her early thirties, Katia judged. Pretty enough, with an oval face and blue eyes. There was an air of confidence about her.

The question brought Katia up short. She had made peace with Pyotr's lies, and she had been happy. But now Pyotr was different. His handsome face was a mask. His eyes were flat, without depth.

Breaking her gaze away, Katia cleared her throat. "I'm okay."

"Krot wants to find your father," the woman warned. "He's already killed once. You're in danger, especially if you refuse to tell him."

Katia frowned.

Pyotr was getting impatient. "Did the Carnivore send you?"

The man nodded. "He wants a meeting."

"Agreed, but only under certain conditions. *My* conditions." Pyotr did not query, or discuss. His voice commanded.

Katia felt a surge of fear, then fury with herself. "Pyotr!"

He scowled, not looking at her but instead watching the man and woman. "Yes?"

"You're playing weasel-and-rat with the Carnivore. Do you honestly care? If you could vanish so well the KGB couldn't find you, then you sure as hell ought to be able to hide from a few assassins who don't have nearly the same resources." Katia's voice rose. "There'll always be one more meeting. One more threat you think you have to take care of. I can't live the way my mother did. I can't keep worrying about you—and me. Stop this. Stop it now, or I'm going back to Maine." She heard the strength in her voice and realized she meant it.

His eyes still on the man and woman, Pyotr told her, "That sounds good in theory, but a lot's at stake, and it's not just money."

"You're right," Katia retorted. "The stakes are huge. Your life. Your future. *Our* future. Make a decision. This stupid game—or me."

The garage was silent. She was aware everyone was staring at her. She had surprised them. *Good,* she thought. *Fuck all of them and their miserable lives!*

The fingers of Pyotr's free hand twitched nervously. "I don't want to lose you, Katia, but I need to do just this one last thing with the Carnivore—"

"Horseshit. Good-bye." She spun on her heel and marched back toward the door and pushed it open.

"Wait!" Pyotr's voice sounded like the Pyotr she knew. "I'll quit looking for Seymour. No, I've quit. Right now."

She turned. "How do I know you mean it?"

He holstered his pistol, walked to her, and took her hand. "Let's leave."

She hesitated only a moment. "Yes. I'd like that."

Holding hands, they walked down the steps into the garage.

"As you can see, Mr. Roman, my plans . . . *our* plans . . . have changed,"

Pyotr told the man. "Let's be clear. The Carnivore doesn't want a meeting with me as much as he wants my tablet pieces and information about how to find Seymour. I still don't know where Seymour is, and I'm quitting the business for the last time. Both are the truth. Here, take my cuneiform pieces." Moving slowly, he reached inside his jacket and removed the aluminum box. "This will prove I'm done. In fact, I'm so done that if *The Assassins' Catalog* is published, I don't care."

"What about your father, Katia?" the woman asked. "We'd like to talk to him."

Katia found herself bristling. "You can't do that. Ever."

"Let's take the Citroën, Katia." Pyotr pulled her toward it. "Our suitcases are already in the trunk. That makes it easy."

"Yes. What a wonderful idea. *Yes*."

Pyotr turned to Liza. "I'll send you cash for the car, old friend. Do you mind parting with it?"

Liza was smiling an amused smile. "I do not mind. Go, go. *Prashcháytye. Zhiláyim vam shchástya!*" Farewell. We wish you happiness. "Hata, open the garage door. Our friends are leaving."

As the door rose, Katia and Pyotr climbed into the auto. It smelled of fine leather. He started the engine. They looked at each other. She could not believe her dream finally had come true.

"I'm so happy," she told him. "I've heard it said you can't choose love; it chooses you."

He pulled her across the seat and kissed her.

She let herself sink into him. "Wow."

He grinned. As he backed the car out of the garage, Katia waved good-bye. The group lowered their weapons and waved back. Soon the Citroën was in the street, and Pyotr was turning the steering wheel to drive off.

Neither Pyotr nor Katia saw a gunman sprint up on the driver's side of the car. The man carried an F2000 bullpup assault rifle set to automatic. He wore a bulky black jacket and a motorcycle helmet with a dark face shield.

Katia screamed. Krot reached for his pistol at the same time he whipped his head around.

The gunman made it a rule to avoid looking into the faces of his victims. But this time was different. He owed Krot the respect of letting him know who was taking him out. He lifted his face shield.

When Krot saw him, his eyes widened in shock. "But I'm out of the game," he mouthed.

"Nothing personal," the assassin answered as he fired.

58

The street behind the souk was cast in evening shadows. Judd and Eva had been heading out of the garage when the helmeted gunman fired into the Citroën. They saw Krot's face explode, and then Katia Levinchev's. Blood sprayed through the car and out the broken windows. The gunman had not aimed at Katia, so the rounds that hit her had to have gone through Krot's head first. Eva's heart seemed to stop.

The gunman spun on his booted heels and raced off.

"You set them up!" Liza screamed at Judd and Eva from the doorway. "You're dead, dead!" She aimed her gun.

But they were already tearing off after the killer, who jumped on a motorcycle. As the man kicked it into gear, Judd threw himself at him. But the bike bolted off, and Judd grabbed air and hit the street. Swearing, he started to scramble up.

"Stay down!" Eva snapped. She was crouched, Glock in both hands, firing, as the motorcycle angled sharply into the oncoming traffic. She paused, then had a clear shot as the motorbike wove around an SUV. She fired twice more. One bullet put a hole in the bike's tail and the second came close to the killer's left arm. The motorcycle swung in front of the SUV and out of sight.

"Let's follow him!" Their car was on the other side of the street. She could do a U-turn and—

"Stop, Eva!" Judd scrambled up.

"What?"

He turned back toward the garage. "We'll never catch him. I've got another idea." Hurrying, he held his Beretta down close to his thigh where it was less noticeable. "Liza may be able to help us find Seymour."

She caught up with him. "In case it's slipped your mind, she just threatened to scrub us."

As they neared the garage, Hata drove the Citroën back inside. He stared straight ahead, his profile wooden. There was a streak of blood on his cheek. Neither Liza nor any of her other men were in sight.

Watching warily, Eva and Judd followed the Citroën. The car's trunk opened silently, and the metallic odor of fresh blood drifted out. There was Krot's corpse, tucked in neatly, curved like the letter C.

Liza stepped out from the shadows, carrying a full highball glass. She glanced at Krot's body and drank. As she lowered the glass, she sighed then addressed them. "I saw you try to stop the prick that killed them. Is not necessary to wipe you. Do not give me a reason."

Hata climbed out from behind the steering wheel. His white linen *djellaba* was bloody and matted with gore, and his expression was grim. One of the guards opened the passenger door and lifted out Katia. The guard curled her body into the trunk with Krot's.

Liza looked away and drank.

Hata returned to his driving post again, and the guard got into the passenger seat. Hata backed the car out and drove off down the street.

"Where will they leave Katia and Krot?" Eva asked.

"In the souk. At least they will be together. Is best I can do for them." Liza drank again.

Eva hesitated. "I'm sorry."

Liza gave a Slavic shrug. "Part of the business."

"Did either of them say how to find Seymour or Katia's father?" Judd asked.

"No. Are important men?" Liza asked.

"Maybe," Judd said. "I noticed you've got security cameras to spot anyone trying to break in. That tells me you're seriously concerned about security, and that you may have extended your concern to indoors."

Liza's eyes narrowed. She said nothing.

"We can offer you one thousand dollars for any recordings you have of Krot and Katia—video, audio, whatever."

Liza's face darkened. She seemed to think about it. "Is more likely for two thousand."

"Done." He pulled out his wallet. His Beretta in one hand, the wallet in the other, he thumbed it open so she could see the hundred-dollar bills.

"I should have asked for more." Liza turned away. "Spartak, watch they do not steal anything."

A tall, muscular man with a bowling-ball head appeared on the landing. He was carrying a Radom Beryl carbine. Saying nothing, he aimed it at Judd.

Liza hurried upstairs and into the building.

The next few minutes were tense. Spartak continued to aim at Judd, while Eva and Judd pointed weapons at Spartak. No one spoke.

At last, Liza returned, sauntering down the steps into the garage, carrying a CD and her refilled highball glass.

She held up the CD to Judd. "So, American, here is the audio of everything that was said in their room. It is noise activated. Give me money."

Judd took the CD and turned over the cash.

Liza counted the bills. "Nice doing business with you." She nodded at Spartak, and he lowered his weapon.

Judd grabbed Eva's arm and hustled her out. Lamplight cast the street in a ghostly glow. They waited for an old Volkswagen bus to pass and then ran to their car and climbed inside.

Shoving the transmission into gear, Eva drove off, passing the place in the street where the motorcyclist had killed Krot and Katia. "It's terrible Katia died. She wasn't involved in any of this."

Judd nodded. "You did a good job going after the gunman. He planned the assault well and moved fast. He was a pro."

Judd did not hand out praise lightly. As she nodded thanks, he slid the disk into the car's player and punched the ON button.

Static sounded, then music by Rachmaninoff. As they drove on, they listened.

59

L ife was to be lived linearly, or so Eva had always believed. But now
as she listened to the recording of Pyotr and Katia's conversation,
she was thrown back in time to the almost palpable love they had for
each other. Against all common sense, Eva found herself rooting for
them to survive.

Pyotr was talking: *"Will you tell me how to get in touch with your
father now? I just want to find a way to reach out to Seymour."*

"Papa is dead," Katia admitted. *"He died seven years ago."*

"Jesus," Judd breathed.

Katia described meeting her father a final time, and the diagnosis of
cancer. *"He said someone was taking care of him. . . . I think he called
him Seymour. . . . I'll give you the contact information, but it may not be
good anymore."*

Eva felt a surge of excitement.

But instead of Katia's giving instructions, there was a long pause.

In the car, Judd decided, "I think Katia's not talking because she's
writing it out for him."

"Bad luck for us," Eva said, frustrated.

At last Katia spoke again: *"Here's the phone number."*

A few seconds later, Pyotr asked, *"Baghdad?"*

"He'd been in Baghdad for years," she confirmed.

Katia told Pyotr what to say when he dialed the number, then the phone rang, and the couple left the room. The recording ended.

In the car, Eva and Judd were silent.

"Poor sods," he said at last. "At least they died fast."

"Some consolation. Like choosing the flavor of your poison."

He nodded. "Pyotr may have been a master emotional manipulator, but in the end, it sure looks as if his own feelings took over. He let his guard down when they left the garage. He got them both killed."

They drove southwest on Avenue Guemassa past groves of citrus trees. The number of camels, donkeys, and carts were few. Ahead loomed the modern Marrakech-Ménara International Airport.

Eva sighed. "All we salvaged out of this mess was incomplete directions to Seymour, and no guarantee he's still in Baghdad. Are you sure you want to go back to Bosa's plane and report in?"

He glanced at her. "Other than the usual risk of working with him, did you have something else in mind?" He leaned back against the door and crossed his arms, studying her.

As she drove, she focused on the street and changed the subject. "I didn't see another tail on the Citroën while we were following it, did you?"

"No. Go on."

"Pyotr said he was sure no one had followed them into the souk. So if no one followed them, and no one besides us followed the baggage, how did the motorcyclist know to be at the garage door, ready to kill Pyotr?" Without waiting for him to respond, she continued. "Of course, Liza could've called the motorcyclist to alert him, but I doubt she'd betray Pyotr."

"Your deduction?"

"Someone followed *us*. The only person we told what we were doing and who had reason to terminate Pyotr was the Carnivore. He knew we were waiting at their hotel. He knew our rental car was around the block. When we talked to him on the phone, he might not have been on the plane. He could've been staking out our car. What I don't understand is how we missed a motorcycle on our tail."

"If he planted a transmitter on our car just as we did on the Citroën, he would've been able to stay out of sight as he tailed us." He hesitated. "There's something I'm missing. A piece of logic, maybe."

"I don't think the Carnivore lied to us about anything . . . at the same time, I'm equally sure he hasn't told us the complete truth. What worries me is he may wait so long to fill us in that he'll put us in danger. Sometimes I wonder whether he considers us expendable."

"He went to a hell of a lot of trouble to save us from the Padre," Judd said.

"He could've changed his mind since then."

Judd nodded. "Still, unless you know something I don't, the Carnivore remains our best lead."

"Yeah, but he's about as trustworthy as a hedge fund manager with an insider tip."

They left the car in the rental agency's lot. Gray clouds floated overhead, hiding the moon. Scanning, they hurried across the tarmac.

"The plane's engines are running," Judd noted. "He's eager to leave."

They broke into a jog.

The door opened, and Alex Bosa walked out to the top of the staircase. The craft's interior light glowed around him. "Glad you made it," he said as they climbed the staircase. "I've been watching for you." It was hard to see his expression in the darkness, but his voice was as strong and authoritarian as ever. "Is Seymour in Baghdad?"

"He was a few years ago," Judd said. "How in hell did you know about Baghdad?"

"Come inside. I'll tell you."

BURLEIGH MORGAN

[A]ssassination remains hardly a dying institution worldwide. Political assassination exists and has existed ever since humankind formed a body politic.

—*Encyclopedia of Assassinations,* Carl Sifakis

60

Aloft over North Africa

Bosa hustled Judd and Eva onto the trijet, drew up the staircase, and locked the door. The accelerating growl of the engines told Judd the craft was in final preparation for takeoff.

Bosa stuck his head into the cockpit, where Jack was in the first officer's seat with George, his copilot, beside him. "Baghdad," Bosa ordered.

As the aircraft rolled across the tarmac, Eva, Judd, and Bosa rushed to their seats and strapped in. Bosa was on one side of the aisle in his usual place, his iPad beside him, his collection of cuneiform pieces on a tray on his other side. Across from him, Judd and Eva turned their seats so they could see him and each other.

Once they were in the air, Bosa said, "Tell me what you learned." His large face seemed weary. Still, he favored them with a smile.

Eva looked Bosa in the eye. "Why did you kill Katia Levinchev, Alex?"

He frowned. "It wasn't me. Tell me what happened."

"Both Krot and Katia are dead," Judd said. He related the events in Liza Kosciuch's garage. "No one but you knew about our rental car and that we'd bugged the Citroën that was carrying Krot's and Katia's luggage to them."

"Ah, I see," Bosa said. "You think I followed you."

"I can understand wiping Krot," Eva said. "But you should've been careful of Katia. She wasn't part of this. She was a bystander."

"I'm sorry about her, but I didn't do the hit," Bosa told them. "You've got to remember Krot had a lot of enemies, just as I do. You can't be in our business without them, and some are extremely powerful. That's just one reason I maintain tight security. I haven't told you any lies, and I'm not going to start now."

As the plane climbed the night sky, Judd glanced thoughtfully out the window. There was something wrong with what Bosa had just said, another piece of logic missing—or maybe the same one.

Bosa broke the silence: "Let's listen to the CD Liza sold you."

Loading the disc, Judd fast-forwarded, and soon they heard again Krot and Katia discuss her father, his death, and how she had contacted him.

"We have the code Katia used to reach him," Judd said, "but no phone number."

For a moment, Bosa sounded discouraged. "I didn't know Grigori Levinchev was dead. That's a blow. He was by far our best link to Seymour."

"You were going to tell us how you found out Grigori was in Baghdad," Eva reminded Bosa.

He nodded. "Once I knew Katia had been using the name Francesca Fabiano and lived in or around Portland, Maine, I contacted a source who was able to acquire three phone numbers she'd had over the last ten years—two land lines and one cell. Then he pulled her computerized phone records and discovered the only calls she'd made overseas were to Baghdad, and all were returned from Baghdad. There were a dozen Baghdad numbers. Eleven belonged to disposable cells, so they were untraceable. The twelfth belonged to a land line—someone in Baghdad had used that number to return her call. That was seven years ago, so maybe it was the time she and Grigori arranged to meet. In those days, the number was blocked, but of course the phone company had the name and address of the owner—the Save Iraq League, a political party. I dialed the number. A nightclub answered."

"The SIL is closely aligned with Iran," Judd remembered. "It's vying with the current prime minister's party for control of the country."

"Grigori Levinchev was Russian," Eva said. "Why would he be in Baghdad and using the phone line of an Iraqi political party?"

"Because he was friends with Seymour, probably," Bosa said.

"Is 'Seymour' his real name?" Eva asked.

"I doubt it." Bosa crossed his arms. "I heard he was born in the United States to an Iraqi mother and an American father and was raised in Basra in southern Iraq. There were a lot of stories about him after he joined Islamic Jihad, one more outlandish than the other. . . . He was a descendant of Mohammad. . . . He was a South American pretending to be Muslim. . . . He was the most bloodthirsty killer the jihad ever had. . . . He saved the lives of a thousand children. . . . He could vanish like a puff of desert sand. On and on. He wore the lies like gold medals. Seymour was restless, though, and I had the feeling that nothing was ever going to be enough."

As Eva and Bosa had talked, Judd dug Tucker's handheld out of his backpack and scanned through it. "I have an old photo of Seymour. It was in one of the dossiers Gloria put together for Tucker."

In his twenties, Seymour was a striking man. His build was heavy, rugged, while his clean-shaved face was cherubic, almost sweet. The burly body of a football player topped by the face of an angel.

Judd passed the handheld to Bosa. "Is that him?"

Bosa examined the picture. "He was overweight the last time I saw him. The face is in the ballpark but not the same—could be because of plastic surgery. You can see his confidence. And the way he tilts his head back and to the side shows some of his charm. Yes, I'd say it's him." He passed the handheld to Eva.

"He doesn't look a bit like one would expect an assassin to look," she decided. "The worst he seems capable of is returning a book late to the library."

Bosa smiled. "Such naïveté."

She shook her head. "Any lingering assumptions I had that assassins were the same have been fully trashed—except that they're all cold-blooded killers." She avoided Judd's gaze.

"She's auditioning me for the list," Judd explained to Bosa.

Bosa shrugged. "One does what one's good at."

"I'm just trying to figure things out," Eva said.

Cocking his head, Bosa assessed one then the other, finally settling on Eva. "We're all ages, nationalities, personalities, and personal lives. Years ago I had a wife and child and lived a 'normal' life. I grocery-shopped, kept in touch with my sister, took my family for outings, and of course left town occasionally for business. Everyone thought I ran an import-export company, and I did, minimally. I enjoyed that life."

"What happened?" Eva asked.

Bosa took a deep breath. "My daughter—Liz—grew up, married a bad man, and I eliminated the problem. Liz found out I was responsible for the death, and then she discovered what my business really was. By then my wife was doing wet work with me. Liz walked out of our lives. Later, when my wife was killed on the job, I'd hoped Liz would come back." He sighed heavily. "Liz disapproves of me."

"Do you ever see her?" Eva wondered.

"No." There was a long silence, then briskly: "Let's see where Krot's cuneiform pieces fit in." He pulled the tray table toward him.

As Judd opened Krot's aluminum box and removed the padded chunks, Eva peeled back the Velcro coverings, and Bosa found each's place in the puzzle of the shattered limestone tablet. They studied the result. Six pieces were still missing. Judd could feel Eva's intensity as she focused.

"Can you translate it now?" Bosa asked.

She shook her head. "I'm not good enough. If you'll take photos of it, I'll e-mail them to a friend at the Getty Center. She's an expert."

"Right." Bosa stood, positioned his iPad, and started photographing the tablet from different angles.

Judd watched, noting the assassin's efficiency. There was deliberation in his movements, also a sense of leaving nothing to chance. The uncomfortable feeling Judd had had earlier returned. There was something about Bosa's denial. Minutes ago, Eva had asked, "Why did you kill Katia

Levinchev?" and Bosa had replied, "It wasn't me." Then when Eva persisted and told Bosa he should've been careful of Katia because she was a bystander, Bosa had said, "I didn't do the hit."

Suddenly Judd understood—Bosa was right . . . he literally had not shot them with his own hand. He said to Bosa: "While we were following the Citroën to the souk, you called to give us Katia's real name and that her father was tight with Seymour. You didn't know any of that when we left the plane, or you would've told us. So either you were in Marrakech, too, and found out there—or whoever gave you the information was there."

Eva stared at Judd, impressed. "You're right."

Judd said nothing, his gaze fixed on the wily assassin. "Well?"

"Took you long enough." Bosa gave a brief smile. "Would you do an old man a favor and grab me a blanket, Judd? My legs are getting cold. You should go, too, Eva. Get a blanket for yourself. We keep them in sick bay." He gestured aft.

Eva's eyes narrowed. "You don't really want a blanket, do you?"

Bosa shrugged. Then he chuckled.

Judd and Eva were on their feet and moving. The trijet had been flying smoothly, so the trip down the aisle took seconds. They passed through the galley, where Doug was making sandwiches. His black watch cap was gone, and his brown-gray ponytail hung loosely down his back.

Eva reached the door first and opened it. Judd peered over her shoulder. Lying on the same divan Tucker had used was a skinny old man with a prominent nose and neatly trimmed silver mustache. His silver hair was pulled back, a ponytail lying down over his chest, coiled on top of the blanket. Despite his advanced age, or maybe because of it, there was a tough look about him. He snored lightly.

Judd and Eva turned as Doug came up behind them. He smiled, entertained, but said nothing.

They looked at him, then at the man on the bed. The faces were different, but there was a resemblance in the men's bone structure and something about the cockiness in their expressions. And then there was the unusual fact both wore ponytails.

"A relative?" Eva guessed.

"He's the one who told Bosa about Krot and Katia?" Judd wanted to be sure.

Doug nodded. "My father. He and Bosa go back a long time."

On the double jump seat was a large bundle with a blanket tossed over it. Judd pulled off the blanket, revealing a bulky black motorcycle jacket, a black motorcycle helmet, and an F2000 bullpup assault rifle.

Recognizing the items, Eva said angrily, "He's the one who shot Katia."

"And Krot, too," Judd said.

He studied the sleeping man, all bone and sinew. His skin was almost translucent. Still, he had tailed them to Krot's hideout in the souk, waited outside for the chance to eliminate Krot, and then mercilessly done it. That showed a lot of motivation, maybe the kind of motivation inspired when someone forced you into a deadly game of last man standing.

"You don't have the same surname, do you?" Judd asked Doug.

"No. My mother loved him but she wouldn't marry him," Doug told him. "Now that I'm older, I understand why. You'll see what I mean. Right now, he's exhausted. He's had a long day. Actually, several long days. His sports car was blown up in Paris. The kid he sent to bring it to him was the one who died. Dad didn't bother to correct the coroner about the victim. The whole thing made him pretty mad. Dad liked that car a lot."

"Christ, he's the sixth assassin." Judd stared at the sleeping man. "Burleigh Morgan is alive."

61

Judd and Eva quickly returned to the cabin, where Bosa was leaning forward, working on his iPad. They dropped into their seats across from him.

"So you and Morgan have been collaborating all along," Judd said.

Bosa looked up. "Morgan got in touch with me after the attempt on his life in Paris. We decided it was smart to let him stay dead. He went to Marrakech, rented a Mercedes, and started following Krot. When he called me with what he'd discovered, I relayed it to you. Morgan was necessary, and you were necessary. Morgan wasn't going to hurt you, and he wasn't able to handle the situation by himself. Christ, he's closing in on eighty years old. When he got to the plane, he said you were on your way back and he'd fill me in later. He crashed, and I haven't seen him since. There was no point in telling you about him until I had to."

"Watch it, sonny boy." Grasping seat backs, Morgan swayed down the airplane's aisle. In motion, his wire-thin body seemed supple, not the bag of bones it had appeared in repose. His face was drawn and weary, but his eyes glinted. "I can still bloody well beat the crap out of you, Alex." He fell into the seat next to him and peered across the aisle at Judd and Eva. "Alex is an uncivil bloke. Should've introduced us. Glad to meet you both. You realize you're in love, don't you?"

Judd recoiled, feeling a strange sensation in his stomach.

Eva looked away.

Morgan chuckled and peered up at his son, who had followed him with blankets. "Dougie, I need some food."

Doug opened the blanket over Morgan's lap. "Sure, Pops. Right away." He handed another blanket to Bosa, who spread it on his legs.

"Don't call me Pops," Morgan grumbled.

"No problem, Gramps."

Muttering under his breath, Morgan focused on arranging his blanket.

Doug gestured down at him. "Now you see why my mother wouldn't marry him."

"She was an idiot," Morgan announced. "But great legs and boobs."

Doug sighed. "He never learned any manners. But then, he started out as a bullet man in London's old East End. A few years later he shot his boss to death at Ronan Point and knifed his boss's boss in an alley near what's now South Quay Station."

"I got ambitious," Morgan explained.

Doug continued: "He offered to do occasional work for the remaining boys if they'd let him make his own way in the world. He was twenty-five. They said get the fucking bloody hell out of here, we'll call you when we need you—and he went independent."

Morgan nodded. "I never looked back. And I damn well don't have any plans to retire, either. I'm more trouble than a war horse. I'm the bloody war."

With a roll of his eyes, Doug returned to the galley.

Eva glared at Morgan. "Why did you kill Katia? You're a pro. You could've made a different decision."

Morgan shot her an appraising look. "Krot was bloody damn dangerous. I wasn't going to get a second chance. So I took the chance I had.

It's over. Done with. Can't change it. Walk away from it, Eva, or it'll weaken your ability to do what you have to do in the future."

Morgan had just admitted accountability, but not responsibility. Eva leaned back in her seat, seeming lost in thought.

Before Morgan could respond, Jack's voice came over the loudspeakers: "Cairo International ahead, folks."

Cairo was an unscheduled stop. "Are we scrubbing our trail?" Judd asked.

"Right," Bosa confirmed. "We'll switch planes so our flight plan to Baghdad shows we came from Cairo, not Marrakech."

"Are you worried that if Seymour is in Baghdad, he's somehow found out about us?" Judd wondered.

"What I worry about is getting lazy," Bosa said, "and dead."

The trijet circled over the metropolis. The Nile River was a black ribbon, glossy, splitting the sparkling city in two. Landing, they rolled to a stop beside a Gulfstream IV business jet. They transferred their things aboard, choosing the same seating arrangements, with Bosa and Morgan on one side of the central aisle, and Judd and Eva on the other. Reading the maintenance reports, Jack and George walked around the craft, tugging, prodding, doing a thorough inspection.

After more than an hour on the ground, they took off again. There were no clouds, and the stars shone brightly. Judd turned away from the window. An idea had been percolating in his mind for some time. He sat forward, clasping his hands between his knees, and studied Bosa and Morgan. "Considering the lengths you six assassins go to maintain operational secrecy, who could possibly have found out enough about your work to compile an encyclopedia of your contract kills? And who besides you knew about the cuneiform tablet? The only answer I can see is one of you must be the e-mail's author. It's one of you who's blackmailing everyone else to play this sordid game."

Morgan and Bosa exchanged a look.

"You tell them, Alex." Morgan's bony face was grim.

Bosa gave a brief nod. "Morgan and I have talked about this, of course. As far as we know, Seymour didn't contact any of us. The Padre, Eichel, and Krot were looking for him. Morgan and I have been looking for him. The blackmailer tried to blow up Morgan, so Morgan isn't the blackmailer. I know I'm not the blackmailer, and Morgan knows it, too, because I could've wiped him many times, including when he came limping back to the plane tonight. From the beginning, he and I figured whoever sent the e-mail starting the game could be one of us. Now that it's down to Morgan, Seymour, and me, it sure looks like it has to be Seymour. There's a logical reason he didn't contact any of us—he didn't need to. We've been reporting in to him every twelve hours, we just didn't realize it was him. Morgan and I think he's been waiting until there's only one of us left. When he gets that report, he'll make up some lie that he—Seymour—is dead, meet the 'winner,' and ambush him. That way Seymour gets the cuneiform tablet, keeps the *Catalog,* and has the satisfaction of knowing the rest of us are no longer taking up space."

"I thought you assassins made a lot of money," Eva said. "Your plane is worth what, Alex—forty million? Is Seymour so broke he needs the twelve-million-dollar tablet?"

"God knows why he's made so much trouble," Bosa said tiredly. "Seymour's a piece of work. I want to surprise the bastard, but first we've got to find him." He tapped his iPad. "I went on Google Earth to check out the building associated with the last phone call from Baghdad to Katia. It's clear why the SIL moved—all that's left is a big hole in the ground. Then I found a historical photo, and it showed a five-story apartment building. The SIL could've had a storefront on the first floor, and Grigori Levinchev was renting a place upstairs. Maybe Seymour was, too. So I searched for the building's owner. Of course, there are almost no records of Baghdad real estate online, so I went to my next question—where did the SIL move to? The answer is Saadun Street near Firdos Square and the Palestine Hotel."

Grabbing a remote control from his tray, he aimed it aft and tapped a button. The skin of the wall next to the galley door slid down, revealing a 48-inch LED television screen.

Bosa tapped his keyboard. "I'm linking my iPad to the TV screen. Let's see what we can find out about the SIL political party."

Google returned more than 100,000 references. There were links about its founding by Tariq Tabrizi and Siraj al-Sabah, its members, its ideology, interviews, analyses, programs for the poor, cultural events, and critiques by other politicians, academics, and foreigners.

When they reached the tenth page, Morgan finished his sandwich and put the plate aside. "Go back to the beginning," he told Bosa.

Bosa returned to the opening page.

Morgan leaned forward. "Can you make those pictures bigger?"

Three thumbnail photos showed people while a fourth displayed a stately white stone building fronted by Corinthian columns.

"Which photo do you want me to enlarge?" Bosa asked.

"I don't care a gopher's snout about the building. I want to see the people."

Without comment, Bosa put his cursor on the first photo and clicked. Immediately it enlarged. According to the caption, a group of thirty angry SIL MPs were storming out of a parliamentary session after they had lost a vote. In the lead was Tariq Tabrizi, who was running for prime minister now. In the next photo, Tabrizi stood at a podium making a speech. The last photo showed two men shaking hands. One was Tabrizi, who was congratulating the second man, a history professor, for winning the annual SIL leadership prize for his daily column in *The Iraqi Sword*. Besides a bronze plaque, he received a prize of €100,000.

Judd whistled. "That's one hell of a lot of money for an organization in a poor country like Iraq."

"Go through the pictures again," Morgan said. "I'm not sure what I wanted to see."

Bosa obliged.

"There's something about Tabrizi," Morgan said. "Can't say what. Is there any way to see him move?"

"Probably." Bosa clicked on VIDEOS at the top of the page.

A column of photos with descriptive text appeared. Bosa scrolled down the page. He opened one, and they watched a video of Tabrizi standing in parliament, shaking his fist. In others, he was cheering at a soccer game and greeting people at an outdoor market.

"Well?" Bosa asked.

"Keep going," Morgan ordered.

The next video showed a clear Baghdad day. Tabrizi embraced a Shiite cleric wearing a black turban then strolled with him down a sidewalk in front of the same white building from earlier. The men held hands, which Muslim men did with close male friends. A woman in a long black *abaya,* most of her face covered, stood at the curb watching. She was small, a good head shorter than Tabrizi and the cleric. A bearded man in a business suit walked into view and joined her. He was smoking a cigar, obviously enjoying it. As they stood there, the cleric climbed into the rear of a black limousine. They waved, Tabrizi waved, and the limo rolled away.

"Holy mother of Jesus, Alex, did you see what I saw?" Morgan asked, excited.

"Tabrizi?" Eva asked. "What is it?"

"I didn't see anything special," Judd admitted.

Neither of the assassins answered. The video continued to play: The would-be prime minister, Tabrizi, turned to the bearded man and the woman in the *abaya.* He said something, and all three walked back toward the camera. Tabrizi laughed at the camera. The bearded man laughed at the camera and waved his cigar. And then it was over.

"I'll be damned," Bosa swore. "I never would've guessed it. He's got that slight hesitation before he comes off the balls of his feet. He's not bothering to hide his natural walk. He's decided he's safe enough in Iraq not to always be on high alert."

"Yes," Morgan agreed, "and it's also the way he swings his left arm. It's a little crooked compared to his right one. And see how much he likes his cigar? Just like you, Alex. You two are cigar snobs. Again, bingo. We've found Seymour, bloody bastard."

Eva's voice rose. "Tabrizi—the presidential candidate?"

"No, no." Bosa shook his head. "It's the other one. The bigger man—the one with the beard. He's Seymour. I wonder what name he's living under." He clicked back through several still photos until he came to an unposed shot of six men drinking tea in a café.

"That's the bloke," Morgan said immediately.

The man he indicated had the same square face, short gray beard, trimmed gray mustache, and blockhouse body as the unnamed man in the video with Tabrizi and the cleric.

"According to the caption, his name is Siraj al-Sabah," Eva said. "Anyone know anything about him?"

"We ran into his name earlier when I was researching the SIL," Bosa remembered. "Tabrizi and al-Sabah founded the SIL."

Morgan gave a cold chuckle. "Who would've thought Seymour would be hiding out in Iraq. But then, a war-torn country that the world wants to forget is always a good place to lose yourself. And the pigdick's gone into national politics. He has what he always wanted—the limelight. It's a small limelight, but it's a hell of a lot bigger than any of the rest of us in our business ever gets."

Bosa nodded grimly. "Now we know. Siraj al-Sabah is Seymour."

62

Baghdad, Iraq

It was past midnight in Sadr City, home to more than two million Iraqis. The moon shone down brightly as Seymour drove onto Umreidi Street, notorious for its black market. Everything was for sale here, from alcohol to weapons, from pharmaceuticals to human organs. The street was quiet; most illicit activity happened inside the ramshackle mud-and-brick buildings.

As he parked, Seymour heard automatic gunfire crackle across the Tigris River from a wealthier section of the city. Violence roamed Baghdad's streets and alleys again. The mortuary classified victims by how they died—the beheaded were Shias killed by Sunnis; those whose brains had been power-drilled were Sunnis murdered by Shias. So many corpses washed up on riverbanks that people were afraid to eat the fish.

All of this was on Seymour's mind. After decades of wandering the globe, he had been back home in Iraq a dozen years. In the beginning, he had kept to Old Baghdad, where he could see vestiges of the capital city that once was, the richest city in all the world, the Baghdad of Mongols at the gates and of caliphs in their harems. He wandered the dusty streets with their picturesque sand-colored buildings, their overhanging balconies and oriel windows with woven screens of carved wood. He drank the sweet cinnamon-flavored tea and listened to the laughter of coppersmiths pounding out their wares. And now he had risen to the heart of this ancient country's tense political situation.

Leaving his car, he carried his Heckler & Koch 416 carbine and a nondescript suitcase heavy with cash. Scanning alertly, he moved off.

Despite his bulk, Seymour walked quickly and surely. He wore loose jeans, a long shirt and coat, and a traditional *kaffiyeh,* a checked cotton scarf, covering all of his head except for his eyes.

As he approached the house he needed, the door opened.

"Ahlaan." Welcome. Fatima stood in the doorway, her body hidden in a long black *abaya,* her head covered by a black *niqaab* scarf arranged so that only her dark eyes showed.

"A-salaamu aleekum," Seymour greeted her.

Her eyes smiled, and his heart pounded a little faster.

She retreated to the area that was the kitchen—a propane-powered two-burner stove and a wood shelf holding bowls and pots.

Four men in dark jeans and shirts sat on stools around a long wood table in the claustrophobic room illuminated by a single oil lamp. They, too, hid their faces behind *kaffiyehs.* In the underworld of Iraqi militias, it was safest to be anonymous, even to one's benefactors. An open laptop sat on the table before each, and Kalashnikovs leaned against the table within easy reach. All looked first at Seymour's H&K then at his suitcase.

"Our money is here at last." The one who spoke used the name Abdul Ahab, which meant Servant of the One. A former structural engineer, he specialized in military tactics.

"Let's see it." The second speaker called himself Ma'thur, the name of the first sword the Prophet owned.

But Seymour looked over their heads to the black-swathed Fatima, the name his wife used when undercover. "You've checked the plans?"

Again she nodded. "They're good." She listed the places in Baghdad and the rest of the cities in Iraq that would be involved. She'd had extensive KGB training in operations.

"We're set to go this morning," Abdul Ahab assured him.

But again Seymour consulted Fatima. "Are you satisfied?"

"I am."

With that, Seymour set the suitcase on the table. The four men leaned forward, watching. Seymour spun the rotors of the combination lock with one hand, while he kept his H&K ready with the other. When he heard the faint *click,* he pushed the latches with his thumb. The lid flipped up. Tidy stacks of greenbacks appeared.

He turned the suitcase so they could see. "Two million U.S. dollars," he told them. "As agreed."

They stared. There was a moment of silent appreciation.

Then Abdul Ahab pulled the suitcase to him and began dividing the cash. "Our expenses are large. You will deliver the rest tomorrow night." It was a statement, not a question.

"Do your jobs, and you'll have the money."

Each of the four men led a different Shiite militia cell, handling discipline and religious training and the problem of finding financing. Iran's ruling ayatollahs donated $5 million a month, but it was not enough to keep them in grenade launchers, mortars, ammo, stipends for martyrs' families, and food, housing, travel, and recruitment. Until Seymour had come along, they had supplemented their income with street crime, which had taken so much of their time that they had been forced to reduce the number of missions they could carry off.

"*Inshallah.* Where do you get such wealth?" Abdul Ahab asked.

The room grew tense. To them, Seymour was the key to a fortune, and a fortune was key to their being able to continue their militant crusade.

"Who's backing you?" demanded the man known as Antarah.

Seymour swung his H&K casually. They saw the motion.

"Come, Fatima." As she floated toward the door, Seymour backed to it. Despite an urge to tell all of them to go fuck themselves, he kept his voice calm as he repeated an old Mesopotamian saying: "When you ride a good horse, do you care in which country it was born? Of course not. Kill me, and your money stops."

Their shoulders sagged.

But then Abdul Ahab rallied. "Don't think just because you're the one with the money you have our loyalty. That belongs to Iran!"

"We wouldn't have it any other way," Seymour said.

He turned, and Fatima and he walked out into Baghdad, a city that would soon be theirs.

63

The Tigris flowed through Iraq like arterial blood. Tonight the river was calm and silvery. Wood boats anchored in the shallows tapped against each other, making a hollow sound. Seymour cradled his H&K carbine and stood in the shadows of an abandoned boathouse near Abu Nawas Street, keeping watch on the river. The earthen banks were a jungle of reeds and untended trees, perfect cover for tonight.

Hearing a rustle, he stepped back against the boathouse, his dark clothes and *kaffiyeh* blending into the shadow. He peered left, toward the street, which was above him here. His wife, Zahra, was hurrying down the slope, her *abaya* flowing. She covered her blue eyes with dark contact lenses, vanished under black cloth, and went out to do business with insurgents and terrorists under the *nom de guerre* Fatima.

"Any problems?" Zahra cradled a customized Ruger 9-mm semi-automatic pistol against her body. It was a blocky weapon, but she said she liked its ruggedness, strength, and reliability.

"None. Where are we with your arrangements?"

As they continued to wait by the river, Zahra told him about the Sunni leader of a network of sectarian death squads who was going to complete missions tomorrow. It had cost another $2 million.

Shiites and Sunnis were like Catholics and Protestants in that they shared many common beliefs, such as that Muhammad was God's messenger and the Koran was divine. The split began in 632 when Muhammad died. Sunnis believed Muhammad's successor should be elected. They won the argument, and Muhammad's close friend and advisor Abu Bakr became the first caliph. But others thought someone in Muhammad's family, in this case his cousin and son-in-law, Ali bin Abu Talib, should have succeeded. His followers were called Shiites. The wounds caused by the dispute deepened and continued to erupt into violence for the next 1,400 years.

The growl of a boat's motor drifted in from the quiet river, and a battered yacht came into view. Some fifty feet long, it had been "freed" during the 2003 looting by two fishermen: Khalif and his son, Abbas. They lived on it, and they made their living with it, including the occasional dinner cruise. Tonight's cruise had ended just before one A.M., as planned. Now the yacht was returning home.

Seymour cracked open the boathouse's door and spoke into the darkness. "It's here."

"Yes, sir," a voice answered from inside.

Zahra had passed him and was walking down through the reeds to the shore. Seymour left the door open and hurried after her. There was a flurry on the yacht as Khalif and Abbas dropped anchor among the other boats in the makeshift harbor.

"A-salaamu aleekum!" Seymour called. "We'd like to rent your yacht tonight!"

"Come back tomorrow!" Khalif yelled.

But his son was lowering a dinghy into the water. "He's too tired. I'm not."

A notoriously hard worker, the son scrambled down the rope ladder and rowed toward them. In his forties, he had a dark, deeply rutted face that told of a lifetime working in Baghdad's harsh sun. When the dinghy slid into the reeds, Seymour was waiting, his adrenaline pumping. He slammed his carbine's butt up under the son's chin then crashed it back into his throat, crushing his windpipe. The man collapsed.

"Abbas!" the father yelled through the darkness. "What's happening to you?"

"He's sick," Seymour shouted back. "We'll bring him to you!"

Zahra and Seymour climbed into the dinghy. Once she was settled, he rowed off, the dying man lying at his feet.

The father remained at the yacht's rail, the moon illuminating his worried expression. As they closed in, Zahra aimed the Ruger. Seymour looked over his shoulder to watch what would happen.

She fired once. A dark spot appeared on the bridge of the man's nose. He groaned, exhaled, and fell back onto the deck.

"Fine shot," Seymour told her.

"*Shukraan,*" she said modestly. But her eyes were shining.

They tied the dinghy to the yacht and climbed the ladder. Seymour checked the old man—dead. The varnish on the mahogany was peeling, and the seat cushions were faded. But the wheelhouse was large, and there would be plenty of room down below for storage. Equally important was the configuration of the deck. It was perfect—flat and spacious.

Seymour and Zahra stood at the rail together, holding hands as they watched a large rowboat cruise toward them. All that showed were the heads of three men and the silhouette of a tall tarped mound that would be parts for three special mortars.

"Let's check down below." She headed for the wheelhouse.

Seymour's iPhone vibrated. "I've got a call."

She stopped. "I'll wait."

There was no name on the ID screen. Frowning, he touched the TALK key but said nothing, waiting in the silence.

A woman finally spoke. "You are one suspicious fox, Seymour. Is me, Liza Kosciuch."

"It's been a while, Liza. What can I do for you?" He had known Liza since the eighties, when they had trained together in a PLO camp in Sudan.

"Is something I'm doing for you. Our old colleague Krot arrived with a lady friend tonight. Then a man and woman broke in to talk to Krot. They said their names were Greg and Courtney Roman and they were tracking Krot for the Carnivore. Krot gave them some special rocks—cuneiform rocks—and told them he was quitting the business. So he and his lady drove out of the garage. This is important . . . no one but us knew he was here. *No one.* I have excellent security, but even that did not matter. A motorcyclist ran up and shot Krot. The bullets went through Krot's head and into the lady's head. She died, too. The motorcyclist was wearing one of those all-over helmets that are darkened. No way anyone could see his face. Who do you guess it was?"

"Sounds like the Carnivore."

"Who else? He took off on his motorcycle. Greg and Courtney Roman chased him, but he got away. So they came back and bought the audio recording of what Krot and his lady had said in their room. I kept a copy. They're looking for you, Seymour."

He felt a jolt of excitement. "How much do you want for the recording?"

"Is free. I will give you video of Courtney and Greg Roman, too, since they are probably headed for Baghdad. I do this for Krot. I am hoping you will get that shit Carnivore. Give me your e-mail address."

He relayed it. "Is that all your news?"

"No. Krot's lady was Katia Levinchev."

Seymour's breath left his body. He willed himself to remain on his feet. He looked for Zahra. She was still waiting at the wheelhouse. She stepped toward him. Her expression told him she knew something was wrong.

He thanked Liza and said good-bye.

Zahra stared worriedly up at him. "What is it?"

"The Carnivore went to Marrakech to find Krot. He found him and shot him to death."

"Good. That's good. One less of them for us to deal with. What's wrong with that?"

"The problem is, Krot was having an affair with Katia."

Her hand went to her mouth. "How did he . . . she—"

Seymour grabbed her and pulled her to him, holding her tightly as he told her what had happened. "Katia died from the same bullets that got Krot. The Carnivore killed her."

The howl was a wild animal's cry of pain. He could feel it wrack her body. Her head thrown back, she howled again, at the stars, at life, at her mistakes. At irreplaceable loss.

"Shh, Zahra. Shh, shh." He kissed her cheeks and tasted the salt of her tears. "It'll be all right. We'll get the Carnivore. You'll feel better then. One way or another," he vowed, "the Carnivore will die."

64

The first hint of morning light rose in a pale yellow ribbon above the Tigris River. Across the city's rooftops from the highest minarets pealed the calls to early morning prayer: "Come to salvation. Prayer is better than sleep. . . ." Machine gun fire a block away disturbed the quiet, but the noise of gunfire was so common it was not worth noting.

Standing at the boathouse, Siraj al-Sabah watched two of his men ferry the last load out to the yacht swaying at anchor. The third man was working onboard. Soon the three would have everything packed out of sight below. The yacht was customarily anchored here, would remain here during the day, and tomorrow night his men would take it out for one of its cruises. Everything was going according to plan, except for Katia's death. That had been unexpected. Al-Sabah kept pushing it from his mind. Zahra was in their car, crying.

In the reeds, two bulbul birds sang sweetly to each other. As a child in Basra, al-Sabah had listened with great longing to their beautiful songs, an emotion that had stayed with him. For some, it was important to know who they were. For others, it was beside the point. And for the rest, the question had not occurred to them. Al-Sabah had never been interested in finding out. There was a small dark place in his mind that told him he did not want to know.

But now his life was changing in a way he had only been able to dream. When you grew up without a father or a mother, barefoot, no money, you learned that staying hidden was survival. That was the way he had lived all of his adult years, too—until now. At last he had come out of the shadows into a public life where he was admired, respected, envied. There was no way he was giving up that.

When the rowboat returned, his three men—Jalal, Hassan, and Mahmoud—jumped out and dragged it up onto the muddy shore. Each wore a pistol on his belt. They were in their early forties, seasoned and strong. They joined him.

"Everything's aboard and stored, sir," Jalal reported.

Jalal was a compact man built for speed but not endurance. Al-Sabah had allowed him to join his special guards on the recommendation of Jalal's uncle, who had died a few days ago in a firefight. Jalal had been there, too, but had walked away uninjured.

Al-Sabah nodded and turned to the second man. "Tell me what you are thinking, Hassan." It was a question he often asked, and they knew how to answer it.

"Because of you, I'm working for Allah and the future of Iraq," Hassan responded. "What's better than that?"

"Yes," al-Sabah said. "And what about you, Mahmoud?"

"Thanks to Allah, yes, I agree."

"Good. And what do you say, Jalal?"

There was a second of hesitation, of guilt. Al-Sabah saw it.

"I agree with Hassan and Mahmoud." A ray of morning light coming through the trees beamed on Jalal's face, the cheek muscles that were starting to droop, the mouth that had grown thin, the eyes that squinted from a lifetime in the sun. Baghdad's climate was not kind to the poor.

"That's not what I've been told, Jalal," al-Sabah said sternly. "I hear you've been talking to Prime Minister al-Lami's people."

Jalal stepped back. His eyebrows rose. "No!"

Al-Sabah followed, pulling Jalal's pistol from his belt. He pointed it at him. "You are courting Cala." Her father worked for one of Prime Minister al-Lami's top aides.

Jalal swallowed hard and stared at the gun. "I . . . I have the money to marry now," he begged. "Please—"

"Didn't it occur to you that the reason her father allows you to visit is because he knows you'll eventually tell him everything he wants to learn about us so you can continue to see her and hope he'll let her marry you?"

Jalal gave a violent shake of his head. "That's not true. I come from a good family!"

"You're a fool, a damn dangerous one. What should we do with him?" al-Sabah asked his two other men.

Hassan and Mahmoud were stiff with tension. Al-Sabah's rules were strict. Everyone knew what happened when someone broke them.

Before they could answer, al-Sabah turned on Jalal again. "What should we do with you, Jalal?"

A tear slid down Jalal's cheek. "I'm sorry," he muttered.

"Did you confess to your aunt that you killed your uncle because he was going to tell me what you were doing?"

"I didn't kill him! I'd never do that!" Jalal shook his head hard.

Mahmoud cleared his throat. "Jalal didn't have anything to do with his death," he said nervously.

Al-Sabah gave Mahmoud a withering stare. No one contradicted him, and Mahmoud knew that. Was Mahmoud getting restless, too?

Looking away, Mahmoud seemed to shrink.

Al-Sabah turned again on Jalal. "What should we do with you, traitor?"

"No, no! I didn't do it!" Jalal bolted, his feet making a hollow, sucking sound as he scrambled through the muck.

"Take care of him," al-Sabah ordered.

Hassan's eyes were dull with disbelief that Jalal could have been disloyal. Mahmoud's expression was grim. They aimed and fired. Two shots rang out. Jalal's arms flew up and his back arched. He took three more steps, started to turn, and collapsed. The noisy gunshots seemed to shock the waterfront. There was a sudden silence. Not even the bulbul birds sang.

As the men cleaned up, al-Sabah climbed the hill to where his car was parked next to the road. Getting in, he saw that Zahra had taken off her headdress, and her face was red and puffy from crying. She was sunk deep into her seat, looking limp and weak.

"How are you, dear?" He patted her hand. It was an inadequate gesture, but it was the best he could do.

Clasping a wad of tissues, she rested her head against his shoulder and sobbed, murmuring memories of Katia as a baby, her baby.

Al-Sabah drove them away from the river. He phoned Jabari and warned him about Mahmoud. "Mahmoud tried to save Jalal. In the end, he did the right thing and helped to execute him."

"I'll have him watched." Jabari Juader was his number two, a completely reliable man whose knowledge of Baghdad was as intimate as the veins in his body.

Ending the conversation, al-Sabah paused the car at a red light. He stroked Zahra's arm. As much as he wanted to, there was nothing he could do to repair her heartbreak.

"Can you stand to listen to Katia and Krot's conversation?" he asked.

She sat up, her face hardening. "Yes, of course. We need to know everything." She blew her nose.

He handed his iPhone to her. It was open to the attachment Liza Kosciuch had e-mailed. Zahra started the recording and put it on speakerphone. From Rachmaninoff's concerto to Katia's and Krot's warm statements of love, they listened carefully.

"Katia sounded so happy," Zahra whispered. "At least we have that."

He nodded. "The Carnivore is probably on his way here now. I forwarded the video Liza sent to Jabari with instructions to distribute it to our people and send out teams to cover the airport and train and bus stations. If Greg and Courtney Roman come, we'll find them."

"We won't know what the Carnivore looks like," she said worriedly.

"There are other ways to recognize him. The problem is, I'm the only one who can do it." Al-Sabah parked the car at the curb.

Starting the video on the iPhone, she leaned close to him. He inhaled her fresh lemon scent. They watched Mr. and Mrs. Roman—the tall, athletic man in the Hawaiian shirt, and the woman with the red hair, dressed in dark slacks and blouse—run across the street toward Liza's garage, pause against the wall, then duck under the lowering garage door.

"They're well armed," Zahra noted. "They seem confident. Competent, too."

"Don't worry, dear," he assured her. "We're better. Besides, we can't let them get away with murdering our Katia."

65

It was nine A.M. when al-Sabah strolled down the arcaded walkway of centuries-old Mutanabbi Street, the city's beating heart of intellectual and literary life. Old men in knit vests and a few old women in *hijab* sat in the open windows of the Poets' Café, arguing books and ideas while drinking strong tea from little cups shaped like hourglasses. The scent of fine tobacco was in the morning air.

Al-Sabah walked past and stopped a block away at a bookstall where he bought a copy of the *International Herald Tribune*. At exactly 9:04, the bomb went off in front of the café. The noise was thunderous. The façade exploded. Two wrens fell dead from the sky, killed when the blast sucked the oxygen from the air. Charred bodies and the smoking shells of dozens of cars littered the area.

Satisfied, al-Sabah tucked the newspaper under his arm and walked away.

In central Baghdad, Tahrir Square was a roundabout at the end of Jumhuriya Bridge. Six of the city's major boulevards met there, the vehicles circling at dizzying speeds. At the nearby bus stop, two rockets exploded, shattering glass and melting signposts. Thick dust and debris rained down. Survivors screamed and ran.

As Zahra left, she noted with satisfaction that police were sealing off the bridge. By the time she was a mile away, the normally bustling city center was silent except for the high-pitched shriek of sirens.

Tariq Tabrizi, candidate for prime minister, stood outside the smouldering ruins of the Ministry of Interior. Ceilings had pancaked into rubble. The air stank of ash and soot. Forklifts were removing the shells of burned-out vehicles. As Tabrizi lifted his head, news cameras focused on him. His long face was angry as he railed against the terrorist bombers—and against the current government.

"What more has to happen for the prime minister to know he should quit?" he raged. "This is the country's deadliest day in a year. Attacking a government institution like this ministry building is more than the terrible destruction you see around you." The cameras panned over the smoking hills of concrete, brick, and wood. "This is an attack on the state itself, designed to undermine our belief in our country and destroy our sense of unity. You said you'd keep us safe, Prime Minister al-Lami! Where are you now? Hiding under your expensive desk? Vote for me, people of Iraq. Elect a leader who will protect you!"

66

The situation in Iraq was worsening: The national elections were over, but they still had no prime minister. Without a prime minister, they had no cabinet, and without a cabinet, bridges could not be fixed, schools could not be rebuilt, and hospitals could not be repaired.

In the parliament building, politicians jockeyed, each party trying to gather a large enough coalition to take control of the new government.

In one of the meeting rooms, two of Iraq's most influential men exchanged customary pleasantries. After shaking hands, they pressed their palms against their hearts and sat on sofas facing one another. From a bowl on the coffee table between them, they nibbled green pistachio nuts. The sweet aroma drifted through the room.

They were very different in dress, one traditional Arab, the other modern European. Both were Shiites from the south. One was a member of parliament, an MP; the other was the cofounder of the Save Iraq League political party, which was backing Tariq Tabrizi for prime minister.

Siraj al-Sabah, cofounder of SIL, leaned forward over his bulk, clasping his hands between his knees. "It's always good to see you, my friend. Is there any chance you'd honor us by taking a position in a Tabrizi government?"

Gone was al-Sabah's *kaffiyeh,* and in full display was his square face and short gray beard and mustache. Somehow he looked scholarly. His hands were knobby, his nose flat, his black eyes steady. He was dressed for government business—a dove-gray Savile Row suit that emphasized the muscularity of his girth, a sedate green silk tie, and highly polished wing-tip shoes. He had checked the room for bugs before beginning the day's meetings.

"I'm delighted you ask," the sheik said. "If Tabrizi wins, I would like oil. After all, oil is the south's lifeblood." Sheik Muhammad bin Khalifa al-Hamed lifted his hands and gestured widely around his red-and-white–checkered headdress, drawing to him the room, the parliament, all of oil-rich Iraq. The sleeves of his *thawb*—his white robe—slid down, revealing his brawny forearms and gold Rolex watch.

Al-Sabah said nothing. He lowered his gaze. A respectful statue, he sat unmoving and unmoveable.

With al-Sabah's silence, a note of resignation entered the sheik's tone. "But if not oil, then finance. Definitely finance. If you're serious about wanting my people's votes for your coalition, I must have finance."

Al-Sabah looked up. "You deserve the Ministry of Oil or the Ministry of Finance. You could make something of them." It was not what you told people that mattered in politics, it was how you made them feel. For millions of Iraqis, loyalty lay first with the tribe. An endorsement by a popular tribal sheik like al-Hamed could make or break a coalition.

"Then it's oil?" al-Hamed said eagerly.

"My friend, I can't do that." Al-Sabah wanted to keep oil, finance, and the interior for himself. Those three ministries would give him the most clout.

The sheik's black brows lowered, hinting at anger. "You need me. Tabrizi needs me. Don't let me down."

Al-Sabah patted his hand. "We hope never to disappoint you. Let's talk for a moment about one of the tragedies of our people. Our date trees."

For five thousand years, southern Iraq had been famous for its dates. But the Iraqi date farmers were mostly Shiite, and Saddam Hussein was both paranoid and Sunni. When they finally revolted, his troops crushed them, and to make sure they never rose up again, he ordered some six million date palm trees cut down. Then the swamps were drained, killing the rest of the trees.

"Saddam wasn't satisfied killing Shiites." The sheik's voice rose with outrage. "He executed our date trees, too."

Al-Sabah nodded. "Remember how beautiful Basra was—the wide boulevards, the flower gardens and parks? Now it's a dump. Help our people, Muhammad. We need to be the date capital of the world again. If you do that, you will be an important international figure."

The sheik sighed heavily. "I want to say yes, but I have a large family to support. On the other hand, if it's oil or finance—" He shrugged, his meaning clear: With either ministry, he could skim and get generous kickbacks, while agriculture was, after all, just farming, a crippled giant unlikely to rise from its knees anytime soon.

Al-Sabah slid a large white envelope across the coffee table. "You must save our date industry, Muhammad. You'll be doing Allah's work."

The sheik picked up the envelope, lifted the flap, and peered inside. His eyebrows rose. Pulling out the sheets of paper, he scanned them and smiled broadly. They were unregistered bearer bonds totaling €1 million, about $1.4 million at today's exchange rate—highly liquid, with no record of the owner or the transfer of ownership. As good as cash, they were much easier to conceal and transport. He studied al-Sabah. "I hear I'm not the only one to receive an offer of a kindly gift from you. Where did you get such a fortune that you can be so generous? I ask only because I'm concerned you'll deprive yourself."

"My resources are a deep well," al-Sabah assured him. "Don't worry, my friend. Perhaps in six months you'd like another white envelope?"

"With the same contents?"

"Of course."

The sheik sat back, gripping the open envelope, still not committed. "What makes you think you can assemble the winning coalition? From what I hear, Prime Minister al-Lami has more promised votes."

Al-Sabah took from his briefcase a printout of the morning's online edition of *Al-Zaman* newspaper, one of the most circulation-rich in Iraq. He handed it to the sheik. "This is why our man will win. Read the first paragraph of the lead story."

Frowning, the sheik put on gold-rimmed glasses and read aloud:

"'Over a matter of hours, bombings and mass shootings struck government security forces and buildings in thirteen Iraqi cities this morning, killing at least two hundred and three people and wounding five hundred. In Baghdad, two ministries and four popular landmarks were bombed in shocking coordinated attacks. . . .'"

As if it burned his fingers, the sheik dropped the printout onto the coffee table. "We used to be a civilized people. What have we become?"

"Foreigners won't invest here because of the instability," al-Sabah reminded him. "And they won't order our goods and services because they're afraid we won't be able to deliver. If this keeps up, oil contracts will freeze, and we'll lose the revenue stream that's kept us afloat. Prime Minister al-Lami still hasn't brought us back up to the standards we had under Saddam. The attacks and kidnappings are worse than ever. Our country is dying. How long do you think we'll last as a nation if al-Lami is reelected?"

"You're right." The sheik licked the flap, sealing the envelope and the deal. "If you can talk an old desert nomad like me into taking on agriculture when I'd rather be out riding a camel, *you* should be the next prime minister." In a sudden swirl of cloth, he was on his feet. "Will I see you at the party at the Iraq Museum tonight?" The popular gala had become a ritual to honor newly elected MPs.

"Of course. I'm looking forward to it." Al-Sabah led him to the door. They kissed each other's cheeks in farewell, and the sheik left.

The conference room was quiet, peaceful. Al-Sabah strode to the coffee table and picked up the newspaper. He would need it for the next meeting, and the next after that. He smiled grimly to himself. The attacks had been as successful as he had hoped.

67

W omen's chatter filled Zahra al-Sabah's living room. In their designer-label jackets and slacks, cashmere sweater sets and skirts, the women looked like just what they were—upper-class homemakers and professionals. They were important in their own right or, far more often these days, claimed importance by being married to an important man. This was Zahra's monthly salon, where they discussed culture and history. But that would not be all today.

As the women sipped tea from fine china cups, they listened to young poets from the University of Baghdad's College of Arts recite their latest works, then, as the salon wound down, they talked about life in Baghdad, the new restaurants briefly opening on Rasheed Street, the nightclub closing on Sadun Street.

"Has anyone else gotten a fish pedicure?" The woman who spoke lived in one of the luxury high-rises on Haifa Street.

"You're joking, yes?" asked a neurosurgeon. Her family had moved back from Jordan in 2011, but she had been unable to find a clinic or a hospital that would let her be associated with it. That was one of the greatest problems today—fewer jobs for women.

"It's the truth," the Haifa Street matron said. "There's a tank full of carp attached to your pedicure basin. The pedicurist opens a little door, and the fish swim for your feet and start munching the dead skin. It tickles, but your feet feel fabulous afterwards. The spa spent ten thousand dollars to buy six hundred carp and ship them here. Can you imagine?"

Laughter spread through the room. For the moment, they were no longer the women who had arrived two hours earlier, drawn and frightened. In Baghdad, you grew accustomed to the fact that people died violently every day. You could see your friend, your aunt, your son in the morning, and attend their funeral tomorrow. It was the new normal, and it wore on everyone.

Zahra was sitting near the fireplace on a low ottoman and had been listening absentmindedly, her face a pleasant mask, betraying none of her grief. A short woman in her late fifties, she had graying blond hair smoothed back into a chic chignon. Her features were small and delicate, her nose turned up, and her blue eyes dazzling, the color of cornflowers. With her round figure and lively disposition, she was a popular guest at women's teas and parties. A convert to Islam, she spoke Arabic with a Russian accent. It had taken nearly five years for her to be accepted, but now that she was, seldom did anyone remark on how different she looked and sounded. At the same time, she never gave a hint of the covert life she led with her husband, Siraj, or their backgrounds.

Rallying, she changed the subject. "As you may know, there will be a celebration tomorrow night at the National Museum of Iraq to honor the new members of parliament. It's sure to be another grand affair, with live music and the finest food. If any of you haven't received invitations, please let me know. My husband will see that you and your husband are invited."

There was a rustle of approval. Zahra was one of the best connected women in Baghdad. Her favors were famous.

"Before we close," Zahra continued, "I want to tell you how worried I am. Iraq was supposed to host the Arab League summit this summer, but Saudi Arabia and Kuwait said our country was too dangerous for foreigners to visit, so Iraq lost the summit. Almost worse, the Gulf Cup soccer tournament was scheduled to be here in November, but it was canceled, too. These are two huge international insults—but they make sense, too. All of us know violence is shrinking our lives. There's less and less we can do and still feel safe."

The women nodded. All had lost relatives to kidnapping or violence. No family was untouched.

But the wife of a deputy minister warned Zahra, "We're admirers of Prime Minister al-Lami. My husband is campaigning for him."

"Yes, Jaida, I know," Zahra said cordially. "Still, please consider what I'm saying." She had been holding a printout in her lap. She lifted it. "I want to read you a news story from *Al-Zaman* this morning." It was a copy of the same one her husband had taken to parliament for today's round of meetings. After reading the first paragraph, she continued:

" 'In Taji, three explosives-rigged cars in a Shiite neighborhood went off within minutes of each other, killing eight and wounding twenty-eight in back-to-back blasts. A suicide bomber drove a minibus into a security checkpoint in Kut, killing three police officers and wounding five. A military patrol hit a roadside bomb in Tarmiyah, killing two soldiers and wounding six passersby. . . .' "

Looking up, she addressed the room. "When is the last time you felt safe in Baghdad? It was bad before, but ever since al-Lami took over, it's only gotten worse. Please talk to your husbands about this. It's time for a new prime minister. We need Tariq Tabrizi. He'll bring peace into our streets and homes again." She picked up a stack of pink envelopes and gestured with them. "I have a small gift for each of you, for considering what I've said."

"What's inside?" asked a woman sitting beside her.

"Look for yourself." Zahra gave one to her, then walked around the room, handing out the others.

The woman opened her envelope. "Dinars!"

"Yes. It's cash for you to donate to your mosque or favorite charity or to keep for yourself." Each guest was receiving 6 million Iraqi dinars, about $5,000. "It's just a sample of the affluent future our country can expect if Tabrizi wins. All of us will benefit, and I'll be able to continue to pass out pink envelopes at future salons. With Allah's guidance, we'll have prosperity at heights not seen since the 1970s."

A retired history professor smiled broadly, the money in her hand. "I remember the seventies. Iraq was so wealthy, obesity was a national health concern."

"Ali never gives me any money for myself," a second said. "This is *fabulous*. Thank you!"

The women talked and laughed. Zahra knew some, perhaps most, would "donate" their gift money to trips to Dubai to shop at Saks Fifth Avenue and Bergdorf Goodman. As she watched, several checked their iPhones for the time.

"Thank you for coming," she called out. "Please give Siraj's and my best regards to your husbands. Good-bye. Safe travels."

Servants brought in the women's *abayas* and *hijabs*. Chatting, they arose, covering their feminine clothes, hiding their coiffed hair, putting sunglasses over their glamorous eyeliner and shadow.

At the front door, Zahra hugged them and said individual farewells. With the exception of two, all told her their husbands were already considering changing their political allegiance. Like dark sailing ships, they glided toward the Bentleys and Volvos and Humvees parked along the palm-lined residential street, where their armed drivers were holding passenger doors open. The women had been sophisticated and magazine-pretty in Zahra's sitting room. They were wives, grandmothers, mothers, and daughters—women with responsibilities—and with each day of violence their fear deepened.

Now that her duties were finished, Zahra gripped the door jamb, awash with the pain of losing Katia. Through the years, Zahra had sent emissaries secretly to photograph and talk with Katia, without Katia ever realizing they were reporting back to the mother she thought dead. Knowing Katia had a safe life in Maine had been everything to Zahra. Her throat thickened, and she blinked back tears. *She'd failed Katia.* Her daughter's life had not been safe enough.

She forced herself to go inside. With each step, she told herself to grow stronger, that her spine must be steel. She still had her husband. She must focus on him now, help him to fulfill his dream.

68

If you were running for office in Iraq, one of your must-do appearances was on *Today's Lunch,* a daily TV, radio, and online show that boasted the highest midday ratings in the country, reaching some two million people. The show was hosted by Hydar Aadil, a chubby man with red cheeks, who approached each interview as if his guest were not being invited to his lunch table, but to be on it, served up in a boiling stew.

In the studio greenroom, al-Sabah and Zahra sat on folding metal chairs, watching through the glass, as Tabrizi arrived, fresh from noon prayers. He looked every bit the modern Iraqi politician in his dark blue pin-striped suit, starched white shirt, and blue silk tie. He was slender, whippetlike. Age lines crisscrossed his long, narrow face. His dark olive-shaped eyes were large, almost liquid behind rimless glasses. And his hair—more gray than black—had receded beyond the top of his head. Half Dome, some of his less-than-admiring colleagues called him.

The interviewer and the candidate sat across from one another. Aadil started the interview at full speed: "You're putting together a strictly all-Shiite coalition, Mr. Tabrizi. What about the Kurds and Sunnis? Are you telling the Iraqi people that if you're not Shiite, you're nothing?"

Al-Sabah saw Tabrizi start to bristle, but when he spoke, it was calmly, almost with kindness. "Of course Sunnis and Kurds will have positions in an SIL-led government. But first, Shiites need to pull together for the good of Iraq, and then we'll be able to bring in everyone."

The interviewer stabbed an index finger down onto the table. "Prime Minister al-Lami's coalition includes all minorities. New businesses are opening. Oil profits are growing. The stock market is righting itself. Iraqis are returning home after years abroad. There were pessimists and troublemakers who predicted the current terrorist attacks would stop everything. Obviously, they were wrong. The prime minister is doing a lot of things right."

Tabrizi did not hesitate: "Everything good that he's done is small. There's no sweeping change. Count the potholes in the streets—they're big enough to swallow tires. Dead bodies lie in the parks for days and are discovered by our children. We don't have reliable electricity, gas, phone service, or water. He can't even protect government buildings— today not one but *two* were bombed. Iraq will never be great again while mortars and RPGs and bombs and automatic weapons kill people and destroy property day after day after day. Do you disagree?"

"Of course not, but—"

In a show of power, Tabrizi faced the camera and spoke passionately to viewers: "I promise security . . . true security . . . to all the people of Iraq. Prime Minister al-Lami has put your lives and your children's lives in danger. Will you be the next to die because of his inadequacies?" There was an audible gasp in the studio for the baldness of his question. "If you want safety, tell your MP to vote for me. As your new prime minister, I'll lead you back into Allah's hands and into a better day worthy of our legendary history."

They left the television studios together, al-Sabah and Tabrizi in their business suits, Zahra between them in her *abaya* and headdress. The noontime sun reflected like white heat from the glassy high-rises around them. The trio went to Tabrizi's car.

Without a camera recording him, Tabrizi's expression returned to its usual severity. His face was like glazed concrete. In the center of his forehead was a callus. To al-Sabah, that was what really identified Tabrizi. Westerners might think the callus was a blemish, but to those in the world of Islam, it was a mark of piety. It meant Tabrizi had prayed several times a day, 365 days a year, for most of his life. At every prayer session he had prostrated himself at least twice, touching his forehead not to a rug but to a *turba,* a rough clay tablet made in the holy city of Najaf, as Shiites had done for centuries. Al-Sabah had seen Tabrizi look in a mirror and touch the callus, then smile quietly to himself.

As they walked, al-Sabah delivered their news: "The Carnivore is on his way here. We have visuals and names for two of his employees. We'll be able to track him through them."

"Good. We can end this at last. It will be a relief. What do you think, Zahra?" Tabrizi asked politely.

Her hands knotted. "We'll kill that bastard Carnivore."

Tabrizi winced. He did not approve of words like *bastard,* especially from a woman.

Zahra was so distracted by her grief she did not seem to notice, but al-Sabah did. He changed the subject: "Your interview was good, Tariq. It will help. We're close to having a majority coalition, but the prime minister is creeping up in numbers, too."

"Tonight, we'll crush him," Tabrizi said with conviction.

Al-Sabah nodded. Tonight's event would shock and terrify the populace, cow the MPs, and prove without any doubt that the current prime minister was inadequate to protect anyone, including himself.

As they reached Tabrizi's armored black limousine, the driver jumped out. He was a beefy specimen with a pistol on his belt. Al-Sabah knew he kept a fully loaded AK-47 on the passenger seat beside him.

The trunk opened. Inside was a large cardboard box labeled BOOKS. Al-Sabah surveyed the parking lot as the driver leaned over and opened the box flaps. Inside, stacks of greenbacks appeared on the left, and stacks of euros on the right.

Zahra reached inside and touched the cash.

"How much?" al-Sabah asked.

"What you said you needed—ten million dollars." Tabrizi smiled a real smile. His intense pleasure in the money was palpable. He had spent most of his life in the twilight world of international finance, where the big players seldom slept because somewhere around the globe markets and banks were open. When he was finally worth billions of dollars, he had found it too dangerous to continue. Quitting, he left London for Iran but felt lost without his old world, a rich man whose riches did him no good because he could no longer play the high-stakes money games that had made life exciting. He needed a new challenge, something hard, something complicated, something verging on the impossible. When you have all the money in the world, all that is left to want is what you cannot buy.

Then the Americans and Brits invaded Iraq. The invasion was the chance for which Tabrizi had hoped. He moved across the border to Iraq, to Basra, where he had grown up with al-Sabah, to pursue something so priceless it could not be purchased—governing an Islamic nation. He intended to become prime minister.

In some ways, it was like the old days for him—he was gambling again. Ballot boxes could be stuffed, but they might not stay that way. Votes could be bought, but someone else might come along and offer a higher price. He was an MP eleven years, long enough to learn who had profited by working with Saddam, who had collaborated with the CIA and MI6, with Iran or Russia or both, who was most corrupt, who had fomented revolution, and who had led death squads. If he were to become prime minister, he knew what his altruistic goal was: to make Iraq stable and safe and take it back to Allah.

Al-Sabah had been with him through all of it because of three simple facts: Tabrizi had needed someone he could trust, al-Sabah wanted the opportunity to have a public career, and he also wanted the enormous fortune his old friend had promised him. The money would be wired into al-Sabah's Cayman Islands bank account when Tabrizi became prime minister.

Al-Sabah's iPhone vibrated. Seeing it was Jabari, he answered.

"We've made flyers with a photo of Greg and Courtney Roman and a phone number to call to get a reward for finding them," Jabari told him. "Our people are taking copies into all the transportation hubs—airports, bus stations, car rental agencies, taxi servers—and they're staying on hand to watch. The ten-thousand-euro reward gets people's attention."

"Remember," al-Sabah warned, "the Carnivore's stock in trade is deviousness. Don't take anything for granted."

"It'd help if we knew what he looked like," Jabari said.

"No one knows. Just find the Romans, they'll lead you to him."

Al-Sabah relayed Jabari's report to Tabrizi and Zahra.

"Tell me as soon as you learn anything." Tabrizi climbed into his limo. "Good luck, and God bless."

Tabrizi's limo drove away as al-Sabah and Zahra climbed into their Land Rover. That was when they heard the first explosion quickly followed by a second. Smoke billowed up toward the blue sky. The afternoon bombings had begun.

69

Aloft over the Middle East

Sunlight flooded the corporate jet as it sped on toward Baghdad. Talking about the fact that Seymour had a new identity as Siraj al-Sabah, Eva, Judd, Bosa, and Morgan sat facing one another.

"Why do you think Seymour really started the game?" Eva asked.

Bosa uncrossed his legs and stretched. "As al-Sabah, he appears to feel safe from detection in Iraq, but if he wants to travel and work outside the country, then he's going to be a lot more vulnerable. He's got to be worried about us spotting him."

"You mean identifying him the way you did when you saw his walk and other motions on video," Eva said.

"People's bodies always betray them," Bosa explained. "Believably changing one's posture, gait, and gestures takes a lot of training, but none of us can maintain the changes indefinitely just as no one can stay on high alert indefinitely."

"Seymour was always a bossy bloke," Morgan ruminated. "But never stupid. My take is he created the game so we'd kill each other off for him."

Bosa gave a sober nod.

Judd had been listening quietly. "Tucker was worried this situation was a lot bigger than just six assassins fighting over pieces of a broken cuneiform tablet. I'm beginning to wonder whether the SIL has a role in it, too. We all know the international picture—Iraq and Iran are primarily Shiite, and together they're a political island surrounded by an ocean of Sunni-dominated countries. Tabrizi is a highly conservative Shiite. In fact, he was one of the Shiites who left Iraq for Iran while Saddam was in power. Now, for the first time, the SIL has a very good chance of winning the office of prime minister and all that comes with it—appointments, patronage, policy, power."

"You think Seymour started the game to protect the SIL," Eva said.

Judd nodded. "Seymour cofounded the SIL, so he's invested in it and probably has political ambitions of some kind. The last thing he or his party needs is for word to get out that it was created by a freelance assassin who's murdered hundreds of people for profit."

Holding up a bony finger, Morgan said, "I can see his slogan now— 'Vote for me, or I'll erase you.'" He grinned.

Bosa shook his head at the black humor, then he laughed.

"I never saw worse violence in Baghdad than I did over the past month," Judd went on, "and it was all in the buildup to the elections. Some assaults were obviously meant to intimidate Sunnis and keep them out of the political process—for example, jihadists were bombing Sunni polling stations. Other attacks, like the ones on Shiite religious sites, were meant to get the Shiite-dominated security apparatus to crack down harder on the Sunnis. The result was no party won a conclusive majority."

"And the violence is continuing while Tabrizi and the current prime minister fight it out over the winning coalition," Eva said. "If the SIL takes over Iraq's government, Seymour will be in line for any job he wants. Can you imagine him as ambassador to the U.N. and sitting on some kind of human rights committee? God-awful irony."

They were silent.

"Do you see any way Seymour could've found out we're flying to Baghdad?" Bosa asked Morgan.

"I'd like to believe we'll surprise him," Morgan said soberly, "but optimism where he's concerned is never a good idea."

70

They were flying at 37,000 feet. Judd gazed down, seeing only a sea of white clouds, the earth invisible beneath. In the cabin, Eva, Bosa, and Morgan were at work on their laptops.

Judd called his friend Bash Badawi in Washington. It was the middle of the night there, but Bash was at work.

"Bridgeman's locked down Catapult," Bash complained. "He's suspicious we're helping you. He's riding Gloria's tail like she's a surfboard. Everything has to go through him until you and Eva are brought in, and that includes all assignments, queries, and information searches. He's got us by the nuts. I can't help you, buddy. If I did, he'd be able to somehow backtrack to where you are."

"Terrific." Judd fought discouragement.

"But I've got some good news," Bash continued. "Tucker's hemorrhaging has stopped, and there are signs he's regaining consciousness. For the first time, doctors are sounding somewhat optimistic."

Smiling, Judd said good-bye and told Eva about Tucker.

As she listened, she took a deep breath and closed her eyes. "Thank

God." But then she sighed and pointed at the e-mail displayed on the laptop screen in front of her. "I didn't hear back from my cuneiform expert, so I e-mailed her assistant. He says she's in Death Valley investigating pictographs and won't be back until tomorrow afternoon. As a personal favor, he's going to try to find someone else to get started on the cuneiform right away, but we shouldn't expect much. As he says, some cuneiform is more difficult to translate than others."

The tap-tap of keyboards being worked on filled the cabin.

Crossing his arms, Judd thought about the situation in Iraq. Langley always had players in the field there, and right now they would be focused on the country's politics. Iraq was a critical player in the Persian Gulf, and the region was an area of enormous national interest to the United States. The problem was, Prime Minister al-Lami's coalition was fragmented and only erratically able to control the ministries, the military, and the security forces. The government's logistical and planning abilities were limited, too, making it incapable of any serious national defense. Still, it was in the best interests of the United States that al-Lami be reelected instead of a Shiite extremist like Tabrizi. Al-Lami's quasi-democratic regime might be short on stability and long on thuggery, and it might be unduly interfered with by the Iranians, but at least it formed the basis of a state that could evolve in a better direction.

The CIA station in Baghdad would have in-depth dossiers on everyone who was connected to the election, including Tabrizi's would-be kingmaker, al-Sabah. The problem was, by now the station also had Bridgeman's orders to capture Eva and him. There was no way he could get around that.

He cursed under his breath.

Checking the time, he saw it was almost noon in Baghdad. He dialed Hilu Wahid. Hilu owned a tour guide business—his male relatives did most of the guiding, and his wife ran the office. A top translator, he also worked for the U.S. Embassy, where he sometimes acted as unofficial go-between with Iraqi politicians, businesspeople, tribal leaders, and the media.

Hilu was connected, a fixer who moved in many circles.

After five rings, a brisk voice answered. *"A-salaamu aleekum."*

"*Masa'ah alkhier,* Hilu. It's your old friend Judd Ryder."

Hilu was instantly alert. "Didn't I put you on a plane back to Washington a couple of days ago, or am I hallucinating?"

"I couldn't stay away. I'll be in Baghdad in a couple of hours."

"I'd say welcome back, but I can hear in your voice you want something. You are a scamp, Judd. Hold on." There was a pause. "All right, I've got my reading glasses and a pad of paper. Talk."

"Tell me about Siraj al-Sabah."

Judd heard a sudden intake of breath.

"That dog," Hilu growled. "He has a mountain of ambition but a black heart. He thinks he can get anything by spreading money like manure. Al-Sabah and Tabrizi sometimes act as if Iran is somehow a better, purer country than Iraq because its ayatollahs say religion and government are the same. 'Islam *is* politics'—that's what they say." He muttered something under his breath. "Our Shiite imams are different. They say religion shouldn't bother with day-to-day government. There are other differences, too. Iranians speak Farsi, and we speak Arabic. They're Persians, and we're Arabs. In the old days, Iraqi fathers wouldn't give their daughters in marriage to Persians—it was considered shameful. We are *not* Iran, and I don't want to be. Iran wants to swallow us whole, but we're not going to let them do it!" Hilu's hard, angry breathing sounded in Judd's ear. "Is that enough background for you?"

"That's helpful, but what about al-Sabah's family? Where does he come from? Where did he get so much money?"

"Okay, okay. There's someone you need to meet when you get here. He works for al-Sabah and knows him personally. He'll give you an earful. He wants to leave al-Sabah's organization, but there are only two ways he says you can get out—you die in the field, or he has you killed."

"Good. Can you arrange it?"

"Of course. He's my cousin."

They said good-bye, and Judd slid his cell phone into his pocket. He had been so focused that he had not noticed someone had pulled the shades down on the jet's windows. Morgan was dozing in his chair, his gaunt head lying to the side, his beak of a nose in grand profile against the seat's pale leather back. Bosa's and Eva's eyes were closed, and they appeared to be sleeping, too. In the cockpit, Jack and George took a tray of sandwiches from Doug and exchanged some banter.

As Doug left, they slammed the door shut.

"Fly boys." Doug shook his head. "I'm going to lie down, too. Don't bother me unless there's blood on the floor."

As Doug headed aft, all of them opened their eyes and peered at Judd.

"What did your Iraqi friend say?" Eva asked.

Judd repeated the information from Hilu.

A couple of minutes later, Judd's cell phone buzzed. He answered quickly. "Yes?"

"It's Hilu, my friend. All is arranged. My cousin's name is Mahmoud Issa." He related the address. "He'll meet you at four P.M. I'll try to be there, too. He says to be careful. Very careful."

71

Baghdad, Iraq

Judd peered down at Baghdad International Airport. Ten miles west of the city, it was an island of concrete and steel in the dun-colored desert. As the jet circled toward landing, he could see a couple of jets taxiing, a few helicopters waiting, and four planes parked at the terminal.

As he looked around, a black cloud erupted in northeast Baghdad, then another billowed up in the downtown area. More bombings.

"Iraq's a dangerous place these days," Eva commented.

"Worse than ever," he told her. "Businesspeople and tourists are reluctant to come here. Now there are big empty spaces at the airport again where nothing is going on."

"It used to be an international hub," Morgan remembered. "Flying into Baghdad wasn't like flying into Frankfurt, but it was pretty damn impressive."

Bosa said nothing, just shook his head.

It was almost three o'clock. Judd and Bosa had a little more than an hour to get to the meeting with Mahmoud Issa. The rendezvous was in downtown Baghdad, and if the traffic were bad, they would not make it in time. Eva and Morgan were going to SIL headquarters to watch for al-Sabah. It, too, was in downtown Baghdad.

As the jet descended, Judd spotted two black SUVs parked together next to a chain-link fence skirting the airport's private section. Jack had called ahead and rented two Ford Explorer SUVs, both armored of course and both black, because black was a favored color in Baghdad to warn of power. The rental agency had taped keys under the driver's side back fenders.

Landing, they taxied past the terminal and toward a short line of private jets then parked, the motors decelerating. Their Gulfstream was the largest one there. A row of small-craft hangars stood off to the side.

Jack and George left the cockpit and pulled on their dark blue cashmere jackets, which matched their dark blue cashmere pants. Their shirts were crisp white, their ties matching—blue and orange stripes. They adjusted their flat-topped hats. Shiny gold wings were pinned atop their shoulders. There was a slight bulge inside each's jacket where their pistols were holstered.

"My God, you look like professionals," Morgan said.

"Naturally." Jack gestured. "If you please, George."

"Delighted." George opened the jet's door and let down the staircase.

Warm, dry air wafted into the plane.

Bosa handed Jack a wad of euros. In Jack's other hand were six passports—four were for Bosa, Jack, George, and Morgan and were as realistic as a small fortune could buy, one was for Judd from the selection of cover identities he had brought from home in his backpack, while the last one was more obviously fraudulent, despite Doug's fancy computer work applying Eva's photo.

Jack headed down the staircase. George followed.

Morgan and Bosa remained in their seats, while Judd and Eva peered out their windows at the transaction below. The customs inspector was a sharp-eyed man with a drooping mustache, a gray uniform, and brown loafers. His gaze was on the euros.

Judd watched as the man pocketed the cash. His smile was huge, but then the tip was probably two months of income for him. Without examining the passports, he stamped them and handed them back. He gazed up at the jet and waved. And then for the briefest of moments, his expression changed. There was surprise and some kind of recognition.

"What just happened?" Eva asked.

"I'm not sure," Judd said.

Bosa frowned. "Is there a problem?"

"We'll let you know," Judd told him.

The inspector started to back off. Jack put his hand over his heart and nodded, saying good-bye. The inspector rallied and placed his hand over his heart in response. Then he hurriedly walked away.

Jack pushed his hat up on the back of his head and put his hands on his hips, watching the customs official's retreat. He had sensed something had happened, too.

All of a sudden the customs man broke into a trot and put a cell phone to his ear.

Immediately, Jack and George ran, chasing him.

On the plane, Judd jumped up. "We've got a problem, Bosa."

Judd bolted down the staircase, Eva close behind. Their feet pounded over the tarmac. Ahead of them, Jack and George huffed, their arms pumping as they pursued.

Judd passed the older pair just as the customs official glanced over his shoulder. His eyes opened wide in alarm, and he put on a burst of speed.

But Judd was close. He accelerated and rammed his shoulder into the inspector's back. Propelled forward, the man stumbled, crashed, and slid belly first across the tarmac. Somehow, Judd kept his balance, ran past, and pivoted.

As he hurried back, Jack and George grabbed the man under his arms and hauled him up to his feet.

"What in hell was that all about?" Jack asked him in Arabic.

The customs official panted. His face dripped sweat. He reached inside his jacket and pulled out a crumpled paper.

Two shots rang out. The inspector's throat exploded. Blood and flesh spurted.

Judd grabbed Eva and pulled her down. Jack and George hit the ground, too. Peering up and around, Judd saw two men with automatic rifles standing outside the passenger terminal. They aimed again.

Suddenly a fusillade of gunfire exploded from the plane, ripping through the attackers' torsos.

Judd turned again, seeing Bosa standing at the top of the jet's stairs, a menacing figure, expressionless, an AK-47 in his hands. The attackers had been focused on the customs official. Bosa had been focused on them. Whatever the customs inspector knew, the attackers did not want him to tell it.

Judd scanned the area. No one else was in sight, but that would not last forever.

"We've got to get the hell out of here!" Bosa yelled from the staircase. "Jack and George, stash the bodies in one of those hangars."

In a flurry of activity, everyone rushed to do their jobs. Judd snatched up the inspector's cell phone and the crumpled paper then sprinted to the jet, following Bosa and Eva inside.

Morgan was waiting for them with their backpacks.

Bosa barked orders to Doug. "Tell Jack and George to fly this crate out of here ASAP, rent a new one, and fly back. This time they should land at Al-Rasheed. Text, don't call unless you absolutely have to."

Leaving Doug behind, they hurried down the staircase again. The bodies of the customs inspector and the two other men were no longer where they had fallen. Jack and George were at the row of small hangars, dragging them inside.

In the lead, Judd and Eva sprinted toward the gate in the chain-link fence.

"Where are the police?" Eva asked as they ran. "At least airport security should be here. They had to have heard the gunshots. There aren't even any sirens."

"Welcome to Baghdad," Judd said grimly. He gestured at the skyline, where two more plumes of brown and gray smoke spread upward. "Today's bombings are our competition for official attention. Otherwise, security would be crawling up to our hairlines. Right now, it's good for us. Later on, it might not be."

The lock on the gate had been shot out. Judd shoved the gate open, and they jogged to the pair of black SUVs, stopping between them where they were least exposed. He peered back across the tarmac—Bosa and Morgan were hurrying to catch up.

He opened the crumpled paper. "Let's see what set off the customs inspector."

It was a flyer. The centerpiece was a photo of Eva and him, crouched in shadows but peering up. Judd translated the first three lines from the Arabic:

> €10,000 REWARD
> *For the Location of*
> *Greg & Courtney Roman*

"Then it goes on to say we're in our thirties and either American or British," he told her. "There's no name to contact, but a local Baghdad number to call."

"When the customs man looked up at the plane, he must've recognized us," she said.

Judd was studying the photo. "This was shot at the back of Liza's garage. It's probably from one of Liza's security cameras. We told her we were hunting for Seymour, remember?"

"She could've easily sold the photo and information to him. Maybe a copy of the CD, too. God knows how many places the flyer's been distributed." Eva shook her head. "We just got to Baghdad, and we're already blown."

They stared worriedly into each other's eyes. Perhaps it was the constant strain of being on the run and now finding out the danger was intensifying. Or perhaps it was the frustration that came from two people in love whose paths had intersected for a few unforgettable days and then cruelly, by their own choices, diverged. Whatever it was, Judd was afraid one or both might die before he could tell her how much she meant to him, that he was a sorry-ass fool, that if he had to do it all over again. . . . He tried to control his pounding heart. Tried not to reach for her. But then he saw something shift in her gaze, a softening, and somehow tension left her face. She stepped into his arms. They stood there in the bright Baghdad sun sheltered between the two big SUVs, holding each other tightly as if nothing else mattered.

"God, you feel good," she murmured. "I'm sorry I doubted you."

"I'd never hurt you, Eva," he said earnestly. "You're more important to me than my own life—"

She touched her fingertips to his lips. "Don't say that."

"But it's true. I want us to be really *us* again."

Suddenly her arms were around his neck, and she was kissing him.

He pulled her into him, crushing her to him, tasting her lips, her mouth, inhaling her rose scent.

She broke away first. "Yes, when—not if—*when* this is all over, let's try again."

Then he felt her stiffen. She was looking past him. Bosa and Morgan had arrived, trotting sweaty-faced between the SUVs.

Morgan assessed the situation. "Your timing stinks, but you're cute."

"Get in the SUVs," Bosa ordered. "We've got work to do."

72

Her heart full of emotion, Eva watched through the windshield as Judd drove off in an SUV, with Bosa in the passenger seat. Their speeding rear tires sent gravel pinging against the chain-link fence. The two men were late for their rendezvous in Baghdad and worried their source might leave before they got there.

With effort, she turned her attention to Morgan. They were in the front seat of the other SUV. Morgan had insisted on driving, explaining he had been in Baghdad many times and was fluent in Arabic. He was probably right—but all he was doing was sitting behind the steering wheel and examining the cell phone Judd had found on the dead customs man.

"Let's go," she said impatiently. "Maybe we'll get lucky and spot al-Sabah at SIL headquarters."

But Morgan had not even turned on the ignition. "Not yet. I'm working on something. Ah, here it is. *Redial*." He tapped a button and lifted the phone to his ear. "Trouble!" he announced in panicked Arabic into the phone. "Need help!" He ended the connection.

He had sounded so terrified that she had felt her chest contract.

He glanced at her. "Pretty bloody convincing, aren't I?"

"Why did you make that call?"

"I want to see how many more of Seymour's people are around here and what they'll do." He opened his backpack and took out a canvas case.

"Now what?"

"Directional mike. Low self-noise, high consonant articulation, and good feedback rejection. Compact and top of the line. Takes video, too. Hope someone shows up." He rolled down his window and rested the mike on the side-view mirror. All of the windows in the vehicle were darkened, including front and rear windshields.

Jack had already flown the jet away. In the distance, airport personnel were working around the planes parked at the terminal. No one was near the private jets.

And then two men ran out of the terminal. They had cell phones in their hands. Both seemed to be dialing out. Instantly Morgan turned on the mike and aimed it.

The phone lying on the dashboard rang.

"One's calling here," Eva said. "The other must be dialing one of the guys who answered the inspector's call."

"That's what I'd do," Morgan said.

Abruptly the pair stopped and stared down at the tarmac.

As they talked, Morgan translated for her: "They believe they're looking at blood. They're wondering where the two other men are."

The men looked up and yelled what sounded like names. Surveying the area, they ran again toward where the rental jet had been parked. Again they stopped and peered down, this time at the place where the customs inspector had died.

"More blood," Morgan explained. "One of them is phoning someone named Jabari. It sounds as if Jabari's important in al-Sabah's organization. They're telling him the customs inspector found Greg and Courtney Roman, but now there's blood in two places, the jet is gone, and the Romans, the inspector, and the two men are missing." After more gazing around, the two new men looked down again. "There are some drops of blood. They're following them." Periodically glancing at the tarmac, the pair ran toward the small hangars. They tried doors. "They've found one with a broken lock," Morgan told her. "Guess why."

"George and Jack broke it so they could dump the bodies inside."

"Bingo."

Because the men were out of sight, there was no way the directional mike would work. Morgan and she sat in silence. He seemed relaxed.

"Aren't you worried?" she asked.

"About what? Two bungnuts who have to report in to a boss who really isn't the boss but works for a worse SOB than he ever dreamed of being."

The men reappeared, talking as they hurried to the terminal.

Morgan aimed the mike again. "They're leaving the bodies where they are," he translated, "and they'll tell the coppers they saw you and Judd kill them."

She felt a jolt of fear. "That's just wonderful. Now every policeman in Baghdad will be looking to welcome us."

Morgan waved at her to be quiet. The men were still speaking. "Ah-ha. Now we're getting somewhere." He listened, his gaunt face intense. "They're going to meet Jabari." He turned on the ignition. "They're parked near the front of the terminal. We'll follow. Call Bosa and tell him what we're doing."

73

There had been no bombings in downtown Baghdad for more than an hour. People emerged from shops and stores to peer around nervously then move briskly off, heading home, for errands, or perhaps to the local café. Walking toward a large Shiite mosque with a blue-tiled dome, al-Sabah passed a man with a pushcart kitchen who was slicing thin cuts of meat from a rotisserie for *shawarma*, flatbread sandwiches. The mouth-watering aroma of grilling lamb drifted along the sidewalk. A crowd was gathering. Doing ordinary things helped people to feel normal, al-Sabah noted. The human animal was predictable.

Skirting the group, he stepped through a door into a thousand-year-old Shiite mosque that had been built of stone laid upon stone secured not by mortar but by the finest craftsmanship. Continuing down a corridor, he knocked on a polished wood door and entered a small whitewashed room with large framed portraits of Imam Ali and his son Hussein, the founders of Shiism, on two walls and of Grand Ayatollah Ruhollah Khomeini, the leader of Iran's 1979 revolution, on a third.

Across the room, kneeling on the floor in the traditional pose, his back to the wall, was Ayatollah Abdel-Hussein Gilani. Looking up, he closed the Koran and rose. With his long gray beard streaked with snowy white, his high-bridged nose, and his black, intelligent eyes, Gilani was the picture of a Shiite patriarch. He wore a light gray robe, black loafers, and the black turban that told the world he was a descendant of the Prophet Muhammad. At the moment, his gaze was kindly and interested, but Gilani was a follower of Imam Khomeini, who believed all of God's authority was vested in the supreme leader and senior religious scholars.

They exchanged the usual affectionate greetings.

"*Allaa bil-kheir,*" Ayatollah Gilani said. God bless.

"Shall we walk?" al-Sabah, the courteous host, asked.

"Yes, let's do."

With a gracious gesture, al-Sabah invited the ayatollah to precede him into the corridor. Like Baghdad's oldest houses, the mosque was built around a courtyard rimmed by colonnaded porticos. And, too, like the oldest houses, the great building was inward-looking, sealed off from the street on the ground floor except for a single door in each of its four exterior walls, all of which fronted streets. Al-Sabah and Gilani, who was still carrying his Koran, walked beneath an arch and into the central courtyard, an emerald-green oasis of plum, apricot, and walnut trees with winding paths and hard-packed sand areas for prayer rugs. When they saw the ayatollah, the men who had been reading or praying retreated respectfully to the porticos and vanished into the mosque, leaving al-Sabah and Gilani alone.

It had all begun in 2003, when al-Sabah and his boyhood friend Tabrizi had founded the SIL political party in Baghdad, sharing a vision of Iraq once again at the heart of a powerful and important Shiite world. Al-Sabah had used his old Islamic Jihad and Hezbollah contacts to set up meetings with mullahs from Iran's ruling clerical class.

Over the next few months, both sides grew optimistic that it was possible in their lifetimes. Shiites who had found safety in Iran from Saddam's persecutions were returning to Baghdad to run the government, to open businesses, and increasingly to fight the Sunni sheiks and military men who did not want to give up the privileges Saddam had lavished on them. The American coalition was losing control of Iraq, while the country disintegrated into violence. For many it was disaster, but for al-Sabah, Tabrizi, and the Iranian mullahs, it was opportunity. That was when al-Sabah began working with Ayatollah Gilani to fund and train Shiite freedom fighters to come from around the world, especially from Iran, to put Iraq finally and irrevocably under Shiite control.

Nothing happened quickly in the Middle East, and certainly nothing as drastic as a political union between the Persians of Iran and the Arabs of Iraq, two ancient civilizations that had warred against each other. But now, at last, they were on the brink of success.

As if Gilani were reading al-Sabah's mind, he said, "One of my assistants told me yesterday, 'Iran's history is so magnificent that the world should listen to us.'"

"Yes, of course," al-Sabah agreed. "Iranians are nostalgic to be a superpower again."

Beginning with Cyrus in the sixth century B.C., the Persian empire had become the largest, most powerful kingdom the world had ever seen—the world's first superpower.

"Mesopotamia had also more than its share of glory," al-Sabah reminded him, his tone amused at the recurring debate between them. Neither expected to win, and in the process they somehow grew closer by sharing the storied greatness of their ancestors. "More than two millennia before your empire—in fact, in 3000 B.C.—we gave you writing. We gave you the wheel. We were the cradle of civilization. And by the way, we gave you the Arabic language, too—the language of the Prophet, blessed be His name."

With a smile, Gilani inclined his black-turbaned head. "And then our kingdoms came together. The Prophet brought us together."

In the seventh century, after Muhammad's death, the Islamic armies of the caliphs rode out of Arabia and conquered Mesopotamia and Persia. The vast majority of both countries converted to Islam. Over time,

Baghdad became Islam's capital and intellectual center, the wealthiest and most beautiful city in the world, where art, science, and philosophy thrived.

Al-Sabah and the ayatollah followed their usual path across the courtyard and through an archway into another corridor. It had been a warm afternoon, but the enormous mosque was cool. Pipes on the roof trapped the breezes and circulated them all the way down to the cellar. As they walked downstairs, al-Sabah could feel the whispers of fresh air slipping past the stone walls. It was almost as if the mosque were breathing.

"They are hard at work, as you will see." Al-Sabah opened one door after another, showing small windowless rooms where clusters of men sat at computers, alternately typing and sifting through documents and printouts. All were Shiites, some wearing the white robes and head cloths that marked them as Arabs, some in the long robes and turbans of Persians. The ayatollah greeted each group and blessed them.

As they left the last room, the ayatollah asked, "How is security?"

"As always, impeccable," al-Sabah assured him. "They are doing Allah's work. They won't betray Him." In addition, Shiite black hatters had created unbreachable computer security.

Still in the basement, they entered an office, another whitewashed room but large and with a bank of television screens turned to International Al-Jazeera and news stations in both Tehran and Baghdad. All were muted, with captioned translations in Old Arabic, the language of the Koran. In Tehran was a duplicate office where, on alternating months or immediately, if events demanded, al-Sabah and Gilani met to address concerns and continue negotiations and planning.

Two assistants quickly got to their feet, and again the ayatollah greeted and blessed them.

"You have the new opening to the constitution's preamble?" al-Sabah asked. It had been the cause of much heated discussion and had finally been approved at the highest clerical levels in Iran, and by both Tabrizi and al-Sabah, who, assuming all went according to plan, soon would be running Iraq's government.

The assistants handed copies to al-Sabah and Gilani. They read silently:

> May Allah guide us as we create a living embodiment of
> the Koran and the Hadith, joining our two great nations,
> Iran and Iraq, in an Islamic theocratic federation called
> the Union of Shiite States. Each nation will be partially
> self-governing, with the division of power between the na-
> tions and the central government to be spelled out in our
> constitution. Just as Islam was born of the fire and blood
> battles of Mecca and Medina when the Prophet, blessed be
> His name, stood fast against the infidels, Iran and Iraq will
> stand fast against all necessary obstacles to create our feder-
> ation. We hope that this century will witness the establish-
> ment of a universal holy government and the downfall of all
> others.

Islamic lawyers and scholars were working on a constitution in which
the two nations would be united under a Shiite central organization.
They would integrate their school systems to teach both Farsi and
Arabic. Citizens would have the right to cross their shared border without restriction. All cross-border tariffs and duties would be eliminated.
Additional highways and rail systems would be built to speed commerce
between the two states of the union. Groundwork would begin for a uni-
fied currency and economy. Each nation would have its own sharia
courts, but there would be a Union of Shiite States supreme sharia to
which questions and disputes would be referred.

As with NATO, the two states would share defense responsibilities.
Iran was far stronger militarily. It had established a military self-
sufficiency program in the 1980s, and today it not only bought but built
its own jet fighters, tanks, missiles, submarines, torpedoes, and drones.
It had the largest military in the Gulf region and controlled the Strait
of Hormuz, through which much of the world's oil passed every day.
Iran's proven oil reserves and natural gas reserves were sizable, but Iraq

had the advantage—its oil reserves were even larger. Together, they were sitting on most of the globe's oil and natural gas, with the result that the USS would have all of the wealth, influence, and power that came with such rich petroleum and gas reserves. At last, the world would again give them the respect they deserved.

Al-Sabah and Ayatollah Gilani exchanged gratified smiles.

"I'm satisfied," Gilani said.

"Yes," al-Sabah agreed. "I'm also satisfied."

They left the room together, walking side-by-side down the narrow stone hall.

Gilani stroked his long beard thoughtfully. "How are your plans developing for tonight?"

"In a matter of hours, it will all be over," al-Sabah assured him. "Tonight's action will shake my people to the core. There's nothing worse than to lose confidence in one's government, and Iraqis' confidence, which is already shaky, is going to evaporate. Our friend Tabrizi will be elected prime minister and appoint a cabinet of Shiites, either religious or easily controlled."

"My fellow mullahs are ready to move forward," Ayatollah Gilani told him gravely. "Everything depends on you now. What exactly is this 'action'?"

Al-Sabah hesitated. Then he quoted: "'It is He who makes the lightning flash upon you, inspiring you with fear and hope, and gathers up the heavy clouds. The thunder sounds His praises, and the angels, too, in awe of him. He hurls his thunderbolts at whom He pleases. Yet the unbelievers wrangle about God.'"

Gilani pressed his Koran against his heart. "Allah is ever all-aware. Yes, I understand. Muhammad was forced into a violent armed struggle against his enemies. We should expect nothing less."

They exchanged farewells. Wishing the ayatollah a safe journey back to Tehran, al-Sabah headed upstairs and out into the warm Baghdad afternoon. With each step he remembered his years in Islamic Jihad, when he had fought with sincere dedication to restore the caliphate to Shiite Islam; then there were his years as "Seymour," feared international assassin; and finally, now, there was his life in Baghdad and the happiness he had found here. He had come full circle. At last he was able to plant the roots of his boyhood dream of an all-powerful Shiism, and it would be right here in Baghdad, in the city of myth and legend. *His* myth, *his* legend.

74

It did not look like the Wild West, but it had the feel of it, Judd thought as he and Bosa stepped inside Sindbad's Oar. It was the new, hypermodern nightclub where they were to meet Mahmoud Issa. The nightclub was in Karada, an affluent area in central Baghdad.

Past the entryway, Judd could see tables and customers and a large, high-ceilinged room decorated with chrome, leather, and fake leopard skin. The noise of many voices, clinking glassware, and chairs scraping across the terra-cotta floor was bruisingly loud.

"Are you packing?" The young man wore tight jeans and an even tighter T-shirt. In one hand he held a walkie-talkie, the omnipresent sign of authority in Baghdad. He spoke to them in Arabic. "If you are, you have to check it." He waved a ticket. "We'll take good care of it and return it when you leave."

Judd simply nodded and handed over his Beretta and a fifty-dollar bill.

"Ohhhh, I'll take very good care of it, sir," the youth crooned. He gave Judd a ticket.

Bosa had said nothing, but Judd could feel disapproval radiating from his pores. Finally he handed his Walther to the young man. "I'll kill you if it's not waiting for me undamaged and unused."

"I'm sure you will, sir," the youth replied. "But then everyone else will kill me, too, if I don't have their guns for them. There won't be much of me left. I lead a very dangerous life." He turned and opened a narrow door. Inside were wall hooks holding an array of weapons.

A middle-aged man walked toward them from inside the nightclub. Muscular, he had an oval face and a cropped brown beard. His eyes were sunk deep in dark hollows. "No, Imad," he told the youth. "These are my guests. Give them back their toys." He smiled at Judd and Bosa and introduced himself. "I'm Mahmoud Issa."

"Yes, sir." And that was that. The young man returned the Beretta and the Walther. Reluctantly he offered Judd the fifty-dollar bill.

Judd waved him off.

"Thank you, sir!" He beamed.

Mahmoud led them into the nightclub, and they skirted the room. The patrons were mostly men. The few women wore head scarves. The tables were piled high with food, the spicy aroma enticing. Waiters in black button-down shirts and shiny black suits took orders and carried trays.

With Mahmoud in the lead, they climbed stairs and paused at the top where a wide balcony overlooked the dining area. Mahmoud studied the patrons below, his head moving every time someone new entered. At last he lit a Gauloise cigarette. "We're religious here in Iraq now—no alcohol, no pop music, no pornography, but smoking is tolerated. I'd been watching for you on our security cameras. Did you see anyone following?"

"No," Judd told him.

Giving a nod of approval, he tapped on a door. There was no door handle, no apparent way to open the door. "This is where our security gets closely controlled."

The door was opened by a man the size and shape of a side-by-side refrigerator. Inclining his head to show respect, the man stepped back.

Mahmoud gestured, and they walked into a softly lit room. Tiles painted in stunning mosaics covered the floor and climbed halfway up the walls. Tall narrow bureaus appeared to be made of mirrors, reflecting the rich furnishings and the men and beautiful women there.

While all the men appeared to be Arab, the women were black-, brown-, and white-skinned. There were brunettes and redheads and one blonde, all dressed in sheer, flowing *abayas,* their nipples and pubic hair on display through the silvery see-through fabric. The women served drinks, filled hookah pipes, and sat with their arms wrapped around the men, who were dressed in desert robes, business suits, or suede sports coats and baggy jeans.

"You're religious?" Judd asked. "Are my eyes lying, or is this a—"

"A very high-class whorehouse." Mahmoud laughed. "This part of my establishment obviously isn't religious, but it's high-security and safe for intimate gatherings."

"You work for al-Sabah?" Judd wanted to be sure.

"Yes." Mahmoud opened another door and invited them into a silent room with paneled walls and leather furniture, a masculine room.

"My office," Mahmoud said. "Please sit. Relax. Chivas Regal? This is the hour I indulge myself. You could say it's my daily ritual."

To their right were two heavy leather sofas facing each other, a chrome coffee table between.

Bosa lowered himself on the more distant of the two sofas, facing them. "I'll have a double." He set his Walther on his thigh, his hand gripping the hilt.

Judd sat beside him. "Double for me, too." He also took out his pistol, but in his palm was what appeared to be a tiny memory stick. They had stopped to buy it at a crowded market in the Sadriya district. It was a miniature digital movie camera that was motion- and voice-activated and both saved the movie and sent it wirelessly. Judd had set up a new Yahoo account to receive it. Hidden between his hand and his weapon, the recording end was pointed at Mahmoud. He could feel Bosa watching.

Glancing at their pistols, Mahmoud walked behind the other sofa where they had seen a cabinet. He stood facing them. There was a crystal decanter on top of the cabinet. The decanter's facets reflected the light in a rainbow of colors.

Mahmoud put out his cigarette and picked up the decanter. "When the great Abbasid caliph al-Mansur founded this city, he called it Medinat al-Salam, the City of Peace, but we've seen almost continuous war. I've worked for al-Sabah for years. It's thanks to him that I could afford to create all of this." He nodded around him. "He pays well, and I held on to my money."

"Why do you want to leave al-Sabah?" Bosa asked.

Mahmoud studied Bosa. "You are?"

"Alex Bosa," the Carnivore told him. "A friend of Judd's."

Mahmoud focused on Judd. "And you're a friend of Hilu's."

"Yes. Tell us why you want out."

"Because al-Sabah has gone too far," Mahmoud said. "I began working for him when I was young and angry and wanted to help my country. Now I'm older, and I'm a husband, father, and businessman. I see the bad place all of the violence has taken us. I want to grow my country, not destroy it. People here are all the time talking about the historic tension between Iraqi Shiites and Iranian Shiites, but Iran is trying to change that attitude, and al-Sabah and Tabrizi are helping to front a lot of it with bribes, blackmail, and ideology. It's obvious Iran is the rising power in the Gulf states, and the United States and Saudi Arabia don't have an easy counter for that. So, it doesn't matter how we Iraqis feel about Iran. Resisting Iran is going to be dangerous."

His face glum, Mahmoud removed the stopper of the decanter and poured the blended scotch into three rocks glasses. "What finally made up my mind is al-Sabah had one of my oldest friends killed just because he fell in love with a girl whose father works for the opposition—for the prime minister." Two angry spots appeared on his cheeks above his beard. "When al-Sabah ordered it, I shot Jalal." His lips thinned, and anguish crossed his face. Closing his eyes, he took a deep breath. "Few people know what I'm about to tell you. It's not only al-Sabah, but it's also his wife, Zahra, and Tariq Tabrizi. Of the three, al-Sabah is the brains. He does the negotiating and back-room politicking. Zahra is the organizer. She goes undercover and works with militants and insurgents to arrange attacks. And Tabrizi has the fortune that they've been using to buy our country. Tabrizi makes speeches and appearances. And it's all for one goal—they're determined to join Iraq and Iran into one nation. They're calling it the Union of Shiite States."

"Holy shit." Judd sat up straight. "Are you certain about this?"

"Yes. I've driven al-Sabah and Tabrizi to meetings with the Iranian mullahs. It seemed to me something big was happening, so I dug around. They're working with the mullahs to integrate Iraq with Iran." Mahmoud handed the drinks to Judd and Bosa. Taking a long swallow of his own, he described a joint constitution and steps for the two countries to integrate. "Al-Sabah is planning an attack, a massively destructive one that will force Iraqis to accept that the current prime minister has failed to stop the violence. With this one stroke, al-Sabah believes— and I think he's right—that the MPs will have to elect Tabrizi to be the next prime minister. Once that happens, Tabrizi and al-Sabah will use their money and political power to deliver Iraq into Iran's arms, and Iran will never let us go. You're an American, Judd Ryder. Tell the CIA about this. Tell the CIA to stop them, because I don't think our government can."

"When is the attack?" Judd asked. "I need all the details."

"It's tonight." As if for emphasis, Mahmoud jammed the stopper back into the crystal decanter.

The force of his action made the decanter shudder. Before he could say more, there was a tremendous roar. The cabinet beneath the decanter exploded. His body lifted and ripped apart. Stuffing and framework erupted from the sofa, and the frame bent and slammed against the chrome coffee table, and the coffee table crashed into Judd's and Bosa's legs, pinning them.

In a hidden place in his mind, Judd realized all of this had happened. Then he lost consciousness.

75

I t looks like the bloody devil came through here and laid his dirty paws on everything in Baghdad," Morgan rumbled, staring through the windshield. "This used to be a garden city. Beautiful architecture and unique brickwork. Fine houses with patios and courtyards and roof terraces. Now it's all security checkpoints, blast walls, and barbed wire."

"A lot of bullet holes in buildings, too," Eva said. "Watch it—they're turning."

The two men they had followed from the airport were driving a big black Hummer H3. It had been easy to see even at a distance on the highway, but now that they were in the city, it was squeezed in among other vehicles. Many were new—Land Cruisers, Pajeros, Beemers, and Jaguars. The city was dangerous, but it was not poor.

Honking his horn, Morgan nosed between a battered Cadillac and a new Peugeot. The Hummer was three cars ahead but in the same lane. It turned right. The two cars that followed drove straight ahead, and Morgan turned their Ford Explorer right, too.

———

Karar watched the Hummer turn, then the Ford Explorer with the female passenger whose face was on the flyer. Her name was Courtney Roman.

"They're still following you," Karar reported to the man driving the Hummer. "Do you see them in your rearview mirror?"

"I see them."

Baghdad's traffic was thick. Blood-pressure levels shot sky high. Drivers swore, their arms windmilling with frustration. But Karar had found a solution—a new Yamaha SMAX motor scooter.

Bouncing up over the curb, he drove down the sidewalk, bypassing two pickups and six cars. Young men were playing backgammon at card tables in front of a café. He whizzed past, kicking up dust and gravel. They yelled and shook their fists. He turned the corner. There were only a dozen cars on the street. The Hummer was going slowly, as if the driver and passenger did not have a worry in the world, making sure the Ford Explorer could follow easily.

"I don't like it." Morgan glared at the Hummer. "There's not much traffic here, but he's driving so slow he could be in a funeral procession."

Eva's elbow was on the back of her seat, and she was leaning over it, staring out the rear window. "There's a cherry-red motor scooter behind us. I swear I saw it behind us earlier."

"We've been made?" Morgan seemed to ask himself, not her.

"Doesn't look good."

The Hummer passed a clothing store, an appliance store, a toy store, and pulled into a parking garage.

"A trap!" Eva said.

"No shit. No way are we going in there." Morgan hit the accelerator.

An enormous bakery van careened out of the parking garage's exit. The impact felt like a bulldozer had just run into them. Air bags exploded, locking Eva and Morgan against their seats. She pushed against the bag. Pain shot through her chest—some of her ribs were maybe cracked. Morgan swore words she had never heard. He had a cut on his forehead that was bleeding down his cheek. Somehow he must have hit the steering wheel. She could not reach her Glock. Morgan was struggling, trying to get to his weapon.

Her door swung open.

Carrying an AK-47, a tall, rugged man with a long black mustache stared at her, then at the photo on the flyer he held.

"How nice of you to stop by, Courtney Roman," he mocked. "We're planning a party just for you."

SEYMOUR

[B]y one single [assassin] on foot, a king may be stricken with terror, though he own more than a hundred thousand horsemen.

—*Ismaili Poem in Praise of the Fidawis,*
by a thirteenth-century Persian poet

76

Zahra and Siraj al-Sabah lived in central Baghdad in the heavily
fortified Green Zone, once the infamous playground of Saddam
Hussein's family and governing elite, now the nerve center of Iraq's national government and home to embassies and the political elite. The
al-Sabahs' villa was on a street lined with swaying palms. Red bougain-
villea climbed the white walls, and glistening blue tiles blanketed the
driveway. The interior was comfortable, with hand-knotted carpets on
the marble floors, Western-style furniture covered in Iraqi-designed
prints, and antique tables from the Ottoman era.

It had been a long day, especially after a night of little sleep. Al-Sabah
had napped, while his wife had paced the house, mourning Katia. Now
he was home from meeting with Ayatollah Gilani and ready for a
drink. He was an observant Muslim in all things but this: If Muhammad could drink fermented camel's milk, then he was not going to de-
prive himself of the occasional cocktail.

In the den, Zahra was lying on a couch, an arm over her eyes, a wad of tissues in her hand. He walked around behind the bar. "Gin and tonic?"

She sat up, her face puffy, her eyes rimmed in red.

"Do you think I did the wrong thing?" she asked in Russian.

"If you mean about Marrakech, you didn't have any choice," he answered in Russian. "You were sanctioned. Lubyanka was setting up the 'accident' when we staged your suicide. I'm making you a drink. Alcohol will help. Alcohol always helps Russians."

It was a little joke, and she actually smiled at him.

Then she sobbed. "I was so ashamed. I couldn't tell Katia. How could I tell her what her mother had become? I wanted her to believe in a good mother so she could be one herself someday." She lowered her head, crying into the tissues.

He quickly mixed the drinks and carried them to the couch. He set them on the table then put his arms around her, holding her close. She buried her face in his chest, her tears soaking his shirt. The sobs and tears and great gasps of breath touched an old part of him, a lost part that once knew how to cry.

"Darling Roza, dear Roza," he crooned. "You gave her a good life. She was free to do and become anything she wanted in the United States. If you'd taken her to Marrakech, we would've had to fake her death, too, and she would've had to go into hiding with us. She was just a teenager. She wouldn't have been able to have any sort of normal life. And how could we expect her to understand much less approve of the way we were living? Her mother was not only an assassin, but she loved two men, and they her. Katia would've hated it. Hated you; hated all of us. Her good memories and love for you and Grigori would've died."

Roza—Zahra—pulled away and leaned her head back against the couch. Her graying blond hair was a maelstrom. Her lips were swollen.

"You're right." She closed her eyes. "I really fucked things up."

"No, circumstances did. All of us got caught in something bigger than us—the needs of our countries. And then the countries left us twisting in the wind. Imagine what hell her life would've been if we'd brought her to Iraq with us. She was used to the freedom of being a young woman in a Western country. That could've gotten her killed here, if a car bomb or IED or random gunfire didn't."

Roza nodded. Then she nodded again, as if telling herself to get on with it. "I'll have that drink now."

He picked up the martinis and handed her one. He touched the rim of his glass to hers, and they heard the musical clink of fine crystal. "To Katia Levinchev, our daughter." Not Grigori's daughter, *his* daughter. Neither Grigori nor Katia ever knew. It had been a hard thing for him to live with, but in the beginning it had been necessary because of the politics of the time, of the distrust in both their organizations if Roza had divorced Grigori and married him. Later the lie had been necessary to protect the girl.

"We did the best we could." She gave him a brave smile. "Now tell me how your meeting went with Ayatollah Gilani."

A half hour later a call came in from Jabari. "Good news. Mahmoud Issa is dead. The bomb went off in his office as planned. None of our people has said anything, but there's a new sobriety. They understand it was an execution—and why. We won't have any more attempts at defection. Also I got a phone call from one of the waiters. He swore he'd seen Greg Roman in the nightclub."

"You think he really saw Roman?"

"I sent people to check it out, but no one's been able to find out for sure."

"Unfortunate. It'd be nice to have an easy solution."

"But we're ahead with Courtney Roman." Jabari's voice was triumphant. "We staged a car crash and got her. An old man was driving. I took a photo of him. I've e-mailed it to you."

"Hold on."

Al-Sabah switched functions on his iPhone, checked his e-mail, and saw the familiar face of an angry old man with a long silver ponytail. Blood streaked his cheek. Trapped by a car's air bag, his lips were pulled back in a snarl.

Cursing, he reopened the line to Jabari. "It's Burleigh Morgan. Somehow he escaped the car bomb we set for him in Paris."

"What do you want us to do with him and the woman?"

Al-Sabah thought a moment, then he gave instructions.

77

Coughing, Judd regained consciousness. Plaster dust snowed down from the ceiling in Mahmoud's office. Bosa and he were covered with it. Elsewhere in the nightclub, women were screaming. Someone was gagging. Mahmoud's arm lay on the coffee table in front of them, tendons and veins dripping blood. Judd could see other body parts scattered around the room. While the bomb had detonated next to the wall with the whorehouse, leaving a large hole, Bosa and he had been protected by the cabinet and sofas.

"You've still got the miniature camera?" Bosa asked.

Judd lifted his hand from his pistol. There it was, the camera that looked like an ordinary memory stick. As it slipped off the gun, he grabbed it and put it in his jeans pocket. With luck, it contained the complete video of what Mahmoud had told them. "Sure do."

Exchanging a glance, the two men shook themselves into action and rushed out of the room, passing the working ladies and johns, who were motionless, stunned. White dust coated them, too. The bouncer was on his feet but seemed dazed. He flung open the door and ran out. They followed.

It was bedlam. People yelled and pushed for the exits. Judd and Bosa entered the throng, people pressing all around. The stench of fear-induced sweat rose in the air. And then Judd saw a flyer in the hand of one of the waiters. The man was surveying the crowd.

Judd turned sideways, his back to the man, moving with the crowd.

"I've got him!" A different waiter was looking directly at Judd from across the crowd, waving the flyer. He jostled people aside, trying to reach Judd.

"Holy shit." Judd looked for an opening so he could get out more quickly.

From behind, Bosa said, "I see him."

Judd looked back over his shoulder. Bosa had stopped moving. People cursed and shoved him.

The waiter's gaze was locked on Judd. But as soon as he started past Bosa, Bosa cold-cocked him. There was a flash of surprise on the man's face, then he collapsed. Bosa caught him and dumped him under a table.

At last Judd reached the counter where the young man had tried to take their weapons. He was still there, backed into a corner. Some men were fighting to get past one another to their firearms; others were waving euros and dollars, trying to buy them back.

Judd could smell fresh air. The nightclub's double doors were wide open.

"Judd!" The voice was loud. It came from somewhere ahead.

That was when he saw him—Hilu Wahid. Improbably, he was peering over the top of one of the doors. Police sirens were shrieking.

Hilu bellowed, "Judd! *Ya Allah! Ya Allah!*" For God's sake, hurry!

Propelled by the stream of people, Judd burst out of the doorway. Hilu climbed off the back of a man who looked strong enough to lift a bank vault. Hilu was perhaps five feet five inches tall, a chubby-cheeked, friendly-looking man with thick tufts of black hair on the sides of his head. He handed a wad of dinars to the man who had been his stepladder and thanked him politely.

"Where's your car, Judd?" As Hilu talked, his eyes kept moving, scouring faces, checking hands.

Bosa arrived, and Judd introduced them. Then the three walked off briskly, the smaller man between them.

"You're in trouble?" Judd asked Hilu.

"We're all in trouble. I hope you got a car that's armored and has plenty of horses under the hood. I just dropped by to make sure everything was going fine between you and Mahmoud. And then *boom*!" He threw his hands up into the air.

It was twilight. The streetlamps in this enclave for the wealthy blinked on, sending pools of yellow light across the sidewalks.

Behind them, police cars and ambulances were arriving, beacons flashing. But the three of them were now far enough away from the nightclub that the sidewalks and avenues seemed just normally busy, people strolling, shopping. They passed display windows showcasing the latest Paris fashions.

Hilu shook his fist at one window boasting designer-label suits for men. "The government is full of thieves. A lot of well-positioned officials and businessmen are getting disgustingly rich!" He walked a few steps muttering to himself. "I heard from the people coming out of the nightclub that Mahmoud was killed when the bomb went off. Is that true?"

"Yes." Judd described the explosion triggered by Mahmoud's putting the stopper back into his decanter.

Hilu shook his head angrily. "It had to have been al-Sabah who ordered the hit. Al-Sabah has spies everywhere. He must have heard Mahmoud wanted to quit. You'd think I'd be used to this. One more death in the family. Terrible. Mahmoud has—*had*—a wife and six children. And now, finally, he comes to his senses about leaving al-Sabah and what happens? He dies!"

They arrived at their rental SUV. Judd and Bosa climbed into the front seat, Bosa behind the steering wheel, while Hilu got into the rear.

As Bosa drove into the street, Judd opened his disposable smartphone and called up his e-mail program. There it was—the e-mail with the attachment of the audio-video of Mahmoud.

"Did you get it?" Bosa wanted to know.

"It arrived. I'll tell you in a minute if I can download it." He opened the attachment, and on his phone's digital screen appeared Mahmoud, putting out his cigarette and picking up the decanter.

"Are you going to tell me what Mahmoud said?" Hilu asked impatiently.

"I'll let him tell you himself." Judd handed the smartphone to Hilu.

The dead man's voice filled the SUV: "When the great Abbasid caliph al-Mansur founded this city, he called it Medinat al-Salam, the City of Peace, but we've seen almost continuous war. . . ."

Judd looked back. Hilu was silent, his eyes moist. The hand holding the phone trembled as he listened to Mahmoud talk about al-Sabah, Zahra, Tabrizi, and their plot with the Iranian mullahs. Finally the bomb exploded. The noise seemed to send shock waves through the car.

Hilu let out a long stream of air and handed the phone forward to Judd.

"Poor Mahmoud," Hilu said. "It's good you've got this recording. It's his testimony, isn't it? I always thought Tabrizi wanted to make us into a Little Iran. What they're doing scares the spit out of me. Think of the people they've killed to get to this point!"

Bosa pulled the SUV to the curb. Sitting in the shadows, they spent the next half hour phoning people to alert them about the forthcoming attack.

The first person Judd called was Kari Timonen, CIA station chief in Baghdad. "Is the attack coming from land, sea, or air, Judd?" Timonen's tone dripped sarcasm.

"I don't know," Judd admitted.

"So let's make sure I understand what you're saying. . . . An Iraqi strong-arm told you that one of the country's most respected politicians is planning a terrorist attack on an unnamed target, but there's no way to back up the information because your source is dead. Is this like the massacre at the hunt club in Maryland that you say you witnessed? The massacre that there's absolutely no trace of? Come on, Judd. No one who knows your background is going to believe you."

Judd had a sinking feeling Timonen was right.

"How about you drop by for a visit?" the CIA man suggested. "I've got an order to tag and ship you back to Langley."

Judd hung up. He thought about it then dialed his military intelligence contact. When the response was the same from him, Judd phoned an undercover FBI man who was working out of the U.S. Embassy.

Finally he lowered his phone. "I'm getting nowhere," he told Bosa and Hilu.

"I've notified my contacts," Bosa said. "Perhaps they'll be able to track down what the target is."

"Contacts as in former employers?" Judd asked.

Bosa shrugged.

"I couldn't get through to Prime Minister al-Lami," Hilu reported from the rear seat. "I left messages with his secretary and his assistant. I've tried the army and the Baghdad police, but they get so many warnings and threats that they just added mine to the piles." He sighed worriedly. "I was going to phone a few of my relatives, but word might get back to al-Sabah. Two of them work for him."

Bosa ignited the SUV's engine and drove into the street, joining the traffic. "We've got to find al-Sabah."

"That I can do," Hilu said.

Judd and Bosa sat silently, listening to the Iraqi make more calls.

"I've got him," Hilu told them at last. "There's a big gala at the Iraq National Museum tonight to celebrate the election of the new MPs. It's a fund-raiser for the museum, too. It starts at eight o'clock. Of course Tabrizi and al-Sabah will be there—it's too important for them to miss—and Tabrizi is supposed to speak. You guys want to get into the museum?"

"Yes," Bosa said. "I'll need a wheelchair. Al-Sabah and I worked together just enough that he might be able to recognize me by my walk."

Hilu exhaled. "You worked with al-Sabah. Who are you really, Mr. Bosa?"

"For you, a friend. Can you arrange passes, disguises, whatever else we need?"

"Consider it done." Hilu dialed out again.

"I'm calling Eva," Judd said. "We haven't heard from her or Morgan since she left the message saying they were following a Hummer." He tapped the number of her disposable phone.

A small voice answered, a little boy. Frowning, Judd passed the phone to Bosa. "It's not her. It's a kid, and I'm not good translating kid accents."

"*A-salaamu aleekum*," Bosa said into the cell phone. He continued in Arabic: "Let me speak to the lady who owns the phone." There was a pause. "Then I'd like to talk to your mother. All right, your aunt." He glanced at Judd and nodded, indicating the aunt was coming to the phone. "Can you tell me where the lady is who owns the phone you're using?" He paused, listening. "No. Yes. Thank you." Hitting the STOP button, he took out his cell phone.

In the silence, they could hear Hilu's low voice talking on his phone in the backseat, making arrangements.

Soon Bosa's cell phone rang. "Yes, it's me again. Thank you. Of course, keep both phones."

"Are Eva and Morgan missing?" Judd asked, his throat tight with concern.

Bosa nodded and closed his eyes. "Apparently so, otherwise they would've let us know they were going off the grid. Unbefuckinglievable. Morgan *is* getting old." His eyes snapped open. "The aunt and nephew were shopping at the open-air market outside Abu Hanifa Mosque. The kid found two smartphones under a fruit stand. The phones are scratched up pretty bad from hitting the cobblestones. Whoever grabbed Morgan and Eva dumped their cells in case we had the ability to trace them." He heaved a sigh. "I just hope they're still alive."

Judd was silent, feeling a cold wash of fear for Eva.

"I should've been a general," Hilu announced brightly behind them. "I've just orchestrated a magnificent campaign to get us inside the museum compound. We're going to have to change both of your appearances, but I'm hopeful we can make this work."

78

The river reeked, stinging Eva's nose. Garbage bobbed on the surface, visible in the light of the moon and the bright mercury vapor lights of a refinery near the beach. She was seated on the deck of a yacht near the bow, her back to a metal post bolted to the wood planking. Her hands were bound tightly behind the post. She struggled against them. The ribs on her right side ached. Inwardly she cursed.

"We should've disconnected the SUV's bloody air bags." Morgan was tied to a post six feet away from her. His cadaverous face was gray in the light.

"This is a new experience I would've happily skipped." She twisted her wrists, hoping the rope would loosen, but all she accomplished was giving herself rope burn and a sharp pain in the ribs.

Repressing the discomfort, she studied the riverbank. It was not moving, which meant the yacht was probably anchored. Judging from the gradual flow of the refuse and the location of the moon, the river was running west to east here. Downriver, a bridge carried traffic across to the greatest glow of light in the night sky—the city's center, to the north. Other than the refinery, she could see no other lights near them.

The six Iraqi men onboard were making such a racket that the bank along this portion of the river must be as isolated as it was dark. Three were opening wood crates on the deck with pry bars, hammers, and axes, and unpacking them quickly and noisily. Metal parts thudded and clanked as they landed on the deck. Eva wondered why the men had bothered to dress in dark clothing; anyone close enough to see them would hear them first.

One man handed small crates up onto the deck from the dory that had delivered Eva and Morgan to the yacht. Two men wrestled with what looked to Eva like an enormous sewage pipe, perhaps six feet long.

She had an unobstructed view of the Iraqis' operation because the deck between her and them was open and empty, no masts or super-structure except for the wheelhouse toward the stern. When they had arrived, there had been a dozen small tables, stackable chairs, and benches. While some of the men opened crates, others had quickly pushed the furniture to both sides of the deck.

"A party boat," Morgan had explained.

The crates emptied, the men broke into two groups of three and began assembling some kind of equipment.

"What are they doing?" Eva asked.

"See those long tubes? Looks to me as if the Iraqis are setting up mor-tars. If I'm right, they're huge, the kind you have to tow behind a truck."

Moments later, the three at one of the positions joined the other team and lifted a tube into a nearly vertical position. It was taller than the tallest of the men holding it, close to seven feet. While they stabilized it, the others secured parts to its side and base. Once the gun was up, they went to work at the other site.

"So you're a munitions expert now," Eva said. "I thought you only slit people's throats."

"I slit the throats of the disrespectful, so remember that." He was silent for a moment, perhaps mulling over Eva's sarcasm. "Let's just say I've made mortars a hobby and found them useful. The ones here look like 150- or 160-millimeter."

Once again the Iraqi men split up; some headed back to their individual guns while others returned to the unopened crates. As the men broke open the crates, Eva could see more cylinders, this time smaller—and they had fins. The men carried them to the mortar positions and stacked them.

"Strix smart rounds," Morgan told her. "The Swedes make them. Once they're aloft, their fins move to correct their trajectory. They can be laser- or GPS-directed. They're nasty, powerful things."

"What's their range?" Eva said nervously.

"Seven miles in neutral air—that means no wind. Normally each round carries thirty-two bomblets. If these are the new Iranian mortars, they can launch up to eight rounds a minute. That's faster than a sneeze. It'll be bloody rough on the receiving end."

"Have they said what they're shooting at?" She was frustrated because she understood so little Arabic.

"They aren't talking much. They seem to know exactly what to do, and they just do it. They've finished the mechanical assembly. They're moving on to what looks like the electronics. You can see a computer screen glowing at the base of each mortar." A minute passed. "One of them mentioned an embassy, but didn't name it."

"The direction of the tubes looks as if they're aiming into the city, doesn't it?"

"Crap. One of them just said the target was the U.S. Embassy."

"Oh, God, no!"

Morgan's expression was grim. "Have you seen the embassy?" When she shook her head, he said, "Never accuse a Yank of being modest. It's a heavily fortified compound the size of Vatican City. It's got high walls, guard towers, machine-gun emplacements, rings of security, and doors like bank vaults. There are more than twenty buildings, including apartments, a couple of gyms and swimming pools, shops, bars, restaurants, offices, meeting rooms, and its own power station and water- and waste-treatment facilities. If that sounds like the most expensive and largest and most secured embassy the world's ever seen, it's because it is."

"You think the mortars are big enough to do serious damage?"

He stared at her. "There are something like fifteen thousand people there, all crammed into one and a half square miles, and those mortars are serious enough to cut through heavy steel like it's butter. What do you think?"

"I think we'd better damn well do something!"

79

Bright with light, the vast exhibit hall in the National Museum of Iraq was filling with people. It was a very different scene from the one in 2003 when the six assassins broke in to steal the cuneiform tablet. The hall had rung with emptiness then, and the only illumination had been moonlight filtering down through high windows, barely touching the gloom. Looting had left display cases and shelves smashed and empty.

Tonight, that terrible time was nowhere in evidence. Ancient statues stood on marble pedestals, showcases displayed important artifacts, and glass shelves presented exhibits chronicling the illustrious history of Mesopotamia. Many of the guests were members of the Iraqi parliament and their spouses. There were also museum officials and local dignitaries. The third contingent was foreigners.

The scent of expensive perfumes drifted toward where Judd, Bosa, and Hilu stood in line, waiting to be allowed through the guards' checkpoint. They had already been inspected by backscatter X-rays to detect hidden weapons and explosives. To be unarmed made Judd more than a little uneasy. He scanned, hoping for an opportunity to relieve one of the guards of his gun.

At last they reached the front of the line, where a young sentry stood with a clipboard and a felt-tip pen.

"*Si*, yes. It is all true." Wearing a curly white-gray wig and gesturing with a conductor's flamboyance, Bosa peered up from his wheelchair at the museum security guard and lifted his VIP badge so the young man could more easily read it. "You are very handsome, Signore Guard. Do you sing?" With prosthetic inserts to widen his nose and makeup to tan his face and hands, Bosa was transformed into a nonexistent person: René San Martino, Italian maestro. "As Hilu told you, I am general manager of the Italian-American Heritage Chorus—"

"*Shukraan*, Mr. San Martino." Thanks. He checked off San Martino's name on a clipboard and turned to Judd. "And you are, sir?"

"I'm the American manager of the Italian-American Heritage Chorus," Judd lied. His light brown hair had been shaved off completely— he was bald. His eyebrows were dyed black, his hazel eyes darkened with contact lenses, and his mouth widened and enlarged with prostheses. "Brad Chastain, at your service, from Philly. We're hoping to—"

"*Shukraan*, Mr. Chastain." The guard found Judd's cover name, checked it off, and gestured to Hilu, who was on the manifest as their official escort. "You can go in." He beckoned to the next guests in line to step forward.

With Hilu pushing Bosa's wheelchair, they moved into the exhibit hall. Judd heard at least four different languages and, of course, Sunni and Shiite accents. The place was packed, the noise a rush of excitement.

Judd studied the layout. A temporary stage had been erected at the far end of the room. Halfway there, on facing walls, hung large screens to televise the speeches so those who were distant could have close-up and personal views. Audio speakers were fastened discreetly high in the corners. At the moment, they were softly playing Arab music.

Bosa was glancing across the room. "Hilu, do you see the small blonde woman to our right?" She appeared to be in her late fifties, an attractive woman with a round figure, turned-up nose, and blue eyes. She was chatting with two Iraqi women. "There's something familiar about her. Who is she?" Bosa asked.

"She's al-Sabah's wife," Hilu said. "Her name is Zahra. Very popular among the women. Usually she's veiled. The only times I see her without one is at an event like this."

"Zahra," Judd repeated. "In English, that's 'Rose.'"

"In Russian, it's 'Roza,'" Bosa said. "I'll be damned. She's Roza Levinchev—Katia's mother. I recognize her from the old days."

For a moment, Judd and Bosa were silent.

"All three of them must've been here in Baghdad," Judd said. "Seymour, Roza, and Grigori. Why didn't they tell Katia?"

"Roza apparently wanted her daughter to think she was dead," Bosa said. "Other than that, you'd have to ask her."

"And now she's Zahra, Seymour's wife." Judd shook his head.

"Let's follow her around, Hilu," Bosa said. "She'll lead us to him."

They angled to the right, always keeping Zahra in view as she greeted women friends. She chatted, she laughed, she touched their arms.

The crowd opened enough that they could see Tariq Tabrizi making his way toward a stage that had been erected at the other end of the room.

"Stop here," Bosa said.

Judd saw he was studying Tabrizi.

"Now I understand why Morgan was interested in Tabrizi when we were watching the videos of him and Seymour on the plane," Bosa said. "Seeing Tabrizi is like looking at a ghost."

"What do you mean?" Judd asked.

Bosa crooked a finger, and Judd and Hilu crouched together beside the wheelchair.

Bosa leaned close. "Hilu, listen while I talk to Judd." Then to Judd: "Remember how this whole mess started with Saddam when he hired a major financier to hide his fortune?" It was a rhetorical question, because he continued without waiting for Judd to answer: "The financier divided the money into six sections and hired five more financiers. Each stashed their portion. Only Saddam and the head financier knew where all of the parts were. So Saddam hired Morgan to put together a team of six assassins, each to eliminate one of the moneymen. Morgan can be an obliging sort, so when Seymour asked that his target be the top financier, Morgan agreed. Afterward, everyone reported their wet jobs were successful. Then when Saddam was executed, no one could find the bulk of his money. It was believed the information died with him."

"It's not *Saddam's* money," Hilu corrected angrily. "Many billions are still missing, and they belong to the people of Iraq."

"True," Bosa said. "In any case, the money isn't missing now. Tariq Tabrizi can tell you where it is. Every dirham, every penny, every euro. *All* of it."

Judd frowned. "What are you saying?"

"Tabrizi is the London financier who was responsible for hiding Saddam's money," Bosa explained. "His real name is Toma Asker— Professor Toma Asker. He was one of the highest-flying, most successful moneymakers and managers in Europe. Instead of erasing him, my guess is Seymour helped him to vanish because there was something in it for him—probably money and maybe the political arrangement we're seeing now between them."

"Tabrizi is trying to buy a new job for himself—prime minister of Iraq," Hilu said.

"Agreed," Judd told him. "We need to figure out a way to expose him."

As Judd and Hilu stood, the U.S. ambassador and the current Iraqi prime minister climbed on stage, followed by Tabrizi. Tabrizi shook hands with both men, then the three stood in a row facing the audience. It was apparent Tabrizi and Prime Minister al-Lami disliked each other, while the ambassador had placed himself between them. Cameramen were taping. Journalists were recording and taking notes.

Al-Sabah—Seymour—finally appeared through an archway. He entered the crowd, greeting and making brief comments. He was far more impressive in person than he had been in the video. His face was open, his beard and mustache trimmed closely, his head at a happy, cocky angle. He was smiling an inviting smile, and it seemed when partygoers spotted him, they moved toward him. He radiated the sort of charismatic energy that attracted people, made them want to talk to him, agree with him, follow him.

Close behind came a curly-haired man with a mustache and a muscular, athletic walk that spoke of strength and persistence. There was a bulge under his arm, and he surveyed the room as if looking for trouble. He must be al-Sabah's bodyguard. Judd's fingers itched, wanting his Beretta.

Al-Sabah was getting closer to them. Judd felt a moment of nervousness that al-Sabah might recognize Bosa and him, despite their disguises.

Just then, Judd's smartphone vibrated. *Hell.* He would check the call later. He slid his hand inside his jacket pocket and touched the button that stopped the vibration.

Bosa told Hilu to get al-Sabah's attention. Hilu called out al-Sabah's name.

Al-Sabah turned. When he saw it was Hilu, he walked toward him. "You are well?"

They pressed their hands against their hearts.

"Very well, thank you."

Bosa cleared his throat. Hilu introduced him to al-Sabah.

"I understand that you like the fine cigars," Bosa told him in his best Italian accent. He held up two fat cigars, each a rich dark brown color and encased in a glass tube. "You have met the HMR?"

Staring at the cigars, al-Sabah said reverently, "Gurkha His Majesty's Reserve."

"*Si, si.*" Bosa gave him a confidential smile, one gourmand to another. "A secret blend of premium tobaccos from all over the world covered by a rare aged Dominican wrapper and infused with an entire bottle of Louis XIII, an extraordinary cognac. As you must know, fewer than a hundred boxes a year are produced, but then their standards are the highest." Each cigar also cost about $750. The Carnivore liked the best, and so did Seymour. "I was fortunate to be allowed to purchase a box. I am happy to offer you a cigar. Care to join me outdoors to smoke? It is a grand and starry night."

Al-Sabah's gray eyebrows rose. He looked around. The American ambassador was introducing the two candidates. Cameras were whirring. Reporters were making notes. The audience was busy listening. Zahra had joined a large group of women.

"A pleasure," al-Sabah told Bosa, and seemed to mean it. "This way." He walked toward a patio door.

The bodyguard followed through the throng. Next came Bosa with Hilu pushing his wheelchair. Judd took one final look around and caught up with them.

80

The yacht bobbed gently at anchor. The six Iraqis continued their work assembling the mortars on the deck.

"I'm almost ready," Morgan whispered.

"What?" Eva looked at him, really looked. He was freeing his hands. "How did you—?"

He shushed her. "Don't stare at me."

Eva peered back at the Iraqis, who were concentrating on their mortars.

"They weren't expecting prisoners," Morgan continued, "so they used ordinary rope, and they're not trained guards so they didn't take my belt—with the razor blade in it. Before they tied me up, I dug the razor blade out and hid it between my fingers. We've got to warn Bosa and Judd what they're planning for the embassy. I want you to start making a row, get at least one of them to come here. I'll give you Arabic insults to yell at them. With luck, whoever comes will have a gun and a cell. When he gets close enough, kick him in the pills. I'll cut you loose.

While I search him for a gun, you search him for a cell. If you find one, run to the bow and jump over. Hold the cell high, and keep it dry. Then start phoning. If the guy doesn't have a cell, stay close until we can find one. Got it?"

"Why do I jump over the bow? The sides are closer."

"The bow is farther from them, and it's long and sculpted, which means it's got a decent overhang to protect you from gunfire. Of course, you're going to have to be smart and stay under it. Don't get entrepreneurial." His thin frame was intense, his gaze sweeping the yacht then studying the Iraqis. "As soon as you get a phone, *go*. Don't look back or wait for me."

"And what will you be doing while I'm running and phoning and treading water?"

"I'll be keeping them distracted."

"It's one against five. You won't have a chance. If I stay, too, we can beat them."

He glared at her. "Better still for you to listen to someone who's done this sort of thing before. I can handle five. Besides, our first priority is getting out the alert—more important than my survival, or even yours."

"You're an assassin. You kill people for a living. Why are you doing this?"

"I take pride in my work. That means I'm not a mass murderer."

Eva nodded. "Okay. what were those insults you promised me?"

"Stand up and yell as bitterly as you can, *'Ya khorg.'*"

"What's it mean?"

"'Asshole.' Move!"

Shimmying up the pole, Eva balanced on her feet. "Hey, *ya khorg*!" she shouted.

The Iraqis looked at Eva, puzzled, then at one another. Two shrugged. All went back to work as if nothing had happened.

"Bidde neek immak," whispered Morgan.

"Bidde neek immak!" The Iraqis looked at her again. *"Bidde neek immak!"*

Morgan chuckled and whispered, "That's 'fuck your mother.' You got their attention. Pick one of them and yell *'mos era'* at him. That's 'suck a dick.' "

She chose the nearest Iraqi and leaned toward him. *"Mos era!"*

Staring at her, the man folded his arms across his chest as if summoning patience.

"Now try *'yebnen kelp,'* " Morgan said. "That means 'son of a dog.' "

"Yebnen kelp!" Eva spat at the man.

The man turned to the others, said something, and nodded at Eva. He started walking toward her.

"Tfoo ala wishak," Morgan said, "and spit again. That was a good idea, especially now. It means 'I spit in your face.' "

Eva bellowed *tfoo ala wishak* at the man. She spat.

That did it. The Iraqi's eyes narrowed to angry slits. He reached into his back pocket and pulled out an automatic. Flipping it into the air, he caught it by the muzzle, ready to whack Eva. Head lowered, he paced toward her.

She spat one last time. This time some of her spittle splashed him.

She could see his face darken, his lips thin. He was seething. He was almost within striking distance. As he drew back his gun, he took one more step, and she braced, lifted her knee, and slammed her foot up into his crotch. It was a good, solid blow.

He groaned and sagged in pain, gripping himself. Smiling, Eva kicked him under his jaw. His head snapped back. Like a praying mantis, Morgan was on him. He slashed the man's jugular, spun around behind Eva, and cut the rope that bound her wrists. Reversing direction, Morgan returned to the shuddering body, crouched, grabbed the man's gun, thumbed the hammer back, and fired two rounds across the dying man at the men working on the mortars.

Eva dropped to her hands and knees and rifled through the man's pockets, searching for a cell.

Surprised by Morgan's sudden assault, al-Sabah's men were slow to reach for their weapons. Morgan's third shot hit one in the chest, slamming him down on his back. Morgan's next bullet got another one in the hip.

The men scattered, several scrambling aft toward the wheelhouse for cover. One sprinted starboard and dived among the chairs and tables, while another hit the deck, fumbling for his weapon. He was the closest. Morgan rushed him, firing twice before the man could train his pistol. The man's face exploded. Morgan rolled the corpse onto its side, revealing the man's automatic. Now Morgan had two pistols. He stretched out behind the corpse, using him for cover.

"Did you find a phone?" he shouted back at Eva.

"No!"

"Come here, I'll cover you." He fired at the man hiding in the furniture, then at the first target he saw by the wheelhouse.

An instant later Eva was lying next to him.

"Take this and shoot anything that moves." Morgan handed her one of the pistols.

The Iraqi hiding in the furniture fired wildly. One of his rounds shattered the railing behind Eva and Morgan, and a second buried itself in the deck.

Eva fired back as Morgan rolled the body, patting its pockets. She fired a second time, and her target dropped his gun and grabbed his thigh. She pivoted to her right and fired twice more, once at a man peering around the wheelhouse and once into the wheelhouse.

"Got it!" Morgan thrust a cell phone at Eva. "Fully charged."

"Good." She took the phone and gave him the automatic.

He fired at a man moving toward one of the empty crates. Missing, he fired again directly at the crate the man had disappeared behind. "Get the hell out of here!"

Eva hesitated, putting a hand on his shoulder. Morgan was trembling. His skeletal face was covered with sweat. Her throat tightened with worry.

He swung his head around and frowned. "No time for fucking sentiment. Run!" he bellowed.

Her heart in her throat, Eva scrambled up and zigzagged the twenty-five feet to the bow, bullets spitting into the deck and shooting up sharp slivers of wood. A hand on the railing, she vaulted overboard. She spread her left arm and legs wide and kept her right arm straight up, phone in hand. She hit the water hard, the cold swallowing her, pulling her under. Darkness engulfed her. And then she bobbed to the surface. She looked up at the phone and said a silent prayer of thanksgiving. It was dry.

She rolled onto her back and flutter-kicked under the bow. Treading water, she angled the phone to catch moonlight and saw the icons on this Arabic phone were identical to the American ones with which she was familiar. She dialed Judd's number. It rang twice, then went to voice mail. Frustrated, she waited for the *beep* signaling the end of the message. Automatic arms fire opened up above her, intermittent with the less-rapid fire of what she hoped was Morgan's weapon.

She spoke in a rushed voice: "Judd, I'm on a yacht in the Tigris. Al-Sabah's men are setting up big-time mortars on the deck to attack the U.S. Embassy. Looks like they'll start shooting soon. Don't return my call."

She thought for a moment. She had Gloria Feit's number, too. Tucker had insisted she memorize it. On the second ring, Gloria picked up.

"Gloria, it's Eva Blake. I'm in Baghdad. Actually, I'm under the bow of a yacht in the Tigris, treading water while I talk to you. Iraqi terrorists are getting ready to shell our embassy from the yacht. The man behind it is a local politician named Siraj al-Sabah." She spelled the name. "He's probably the assassin known as Seymour. Burleigh Morgan is on board, trying to stop them. If he can't, there's going to be a shelling." As gunfire sounded above, she lifted the cell. Returning it to her ear, she said, "Did you hear that?"

"Yes." As expected, Gloria was quick to understand. "How do I know it's you, Eva?"

"Judd Ryder and I got here this afternoon. Don't ask how. We left Tucker in a Maryland hospital with"—a burst of automatic weapons fire drowned her out—"a head wound. Judd's somewhere in Baghdad, but I can't reach him to get help."

"Where are *you*?"

"The yacht is in the Tigris south of the main part of the city, west of a bridge, and northwest of what looks like a refinery."

At that moment there was a fusillade of fire from above. The surface of the water erupted in a wide arc, crashing down on her. The Iraqis were shooting down, trying to hit her. In a moment they would fire under the bow. She had to move. She ended the call.

81

As soon as Morgan heard a solid splash near the bow, he exhaled, relieved. Oddly, none of the Iraqis had fired at him once Eva went overboard.

Frowning, he decided they probably had automatic weapons and had been quiet only because they were locating and loading them. If that were true, then the corpse he had been using for cover would be lousy protection. He had to keep the men busy so Eva had enough time to make as many phone calls as she needed. He looked quickly around. There was the furniture along both sides of the boat—flimsy cover at best—and there was the wheelhouse, but that was closer to them than it was to him.

And there were the mortars. Better yet, there were the piles of Strix rounds. The Iraqis could not shoot if he hid behind them for fear of setting them off or at least rendering them useless. On the other hand, hiding behind deadly munitions might decrease his chance of survival. He felt a rush—poor odds thrilled him.

He studied the rounds: The Iraqis had stacked them in two groups of eighteen—enough for a two-gun, two-minute attack, which would do enough damage that it could kill hundreds and take months to repair. Each stack was about a yard wide and twenty inches high. Decent cover.

He fired twice more at the wheelhouse, jumped up over the body, dashed across the deck, and hurled himself behind the munitions pile closest to the bow. *Christ, that hurt.* Pain throbbed in his arthritic knees and ankles, and landing lengthwise on the hardwood was like slamming into a bulldozer. With the back of his hand, he wiped sweat from his face. He massaged his left elbow.

With the crack of gunfire, bullets zinged overhead. He had been right—they were deliberately firing above him, avoiding hitting the ammo.

He knew what they would do next. Some would continue to fire over his head or to his left, away from the nearest mortar, to keep him down. Others would advance along the side of the boat on his left and right, trying to flank him. In fact, if they were smart, one or more would take to the dory, paddle around, and attack him from behind.

He peered around the right end of the Strix stack. Sure enough, someone was low-crawling along the port gunwale. A quick shot, and the man collapsed. By Morgan's count, that meant three were left. His odds were improving. Another burst overhead, after which he heard what sounded like a splash, coming from his left. It could not be Eva, not from his left. Morgan longed for a hand grenade. Another burst overhead. He peered around the left end of the stack and then again around the right end. Nobody visible. Another burst, probably to muffle the sounds of the man or men in the water. Morgan flipped over so his back rested against the Strix ordnance. The attack would come up over the gunwale, probably from the starboard because a shot from the bow risked hitting the projectiles.

A moment later a hand reached up and grasped a stanchion, at the starboard rail. It was dead even with the post Morgan had been tied to. He brought his right foot up under his buttock and rested his right pistol hand on his knee, training it on the Iraqi's fingers. A couple of seconds later a forehead appeared. Morgan fired, and the forehead splattered and dropped back out of sight.

An instant later, Morgan felt a hammer blow to his right midsection. He turned to see the man who had been hidden in the furniture aim his weapon again.

Morgan tried to swing his pistol to his right but could not get his arm to move. The man fired again, and a powerful impact to his right shoulder smacked Morgan flat on the deck on his left side. His right arm refused to work. He could not defend himself. The man was yelling something.

Morgan still had a pistol in his left hand. He managed to move his left arm so he could aim at the laptop hooked to the nearest mortar. He fired into the screen. He heard someone run past him toward the bow. He heard automatic gunfire at the bow. Now a man was standing over him, aiming a pistol at his face. The last thing Morgan saw was the man's finger contracting the trigger.

82

Washington, D.C.

When the phone went dead, Gloria got up from her desk and headed to Scott Bridgeman's office. The door was closed. She knocked once and opened it without waiting for an invitation. Bridgeman was on the phone. His youthful face looked at her with sharp disapproval.

"Hang up, quick," she told him.

His forehead knitted in surprise. He ended the connection. "This had better be good, Gloria," he warned.

"Go to our recorded calls." She pointed to his phone. "You've got to listen to the message that just came in."

He punched a couple of buttons, then put the conversation on speakerphone. Eva's message replayed perfectly, the gunfire loud and lethal.

"Dammit all to hell." He shook his head. "What do you make of it?"

"Don't take a chance, boss. Let me order up the satellite feed, and we can try to locate the yacht and confirm the mortars."

The National Reconnaissance Office oversaw the designing, building, launching, and maintaining of U.S. intelligence satellites, while the National Security Agency collected and analyzed foreign communications and signals intelligence. Catapult had been supplied with a direct feed of live satellite imagery. The satellites over Baghdad were so good they could read the playing cards at a poker game at midnight.

Without a word, Bridgeman rose from his desk and hurried out. Gloria followed as he headed down the hall to IT. He opened the door on a rumble of voices and clicking keyboards. Worktables arranged in neat rows housed a dozen secure computers and phones. The usual cans of soda, crumpled take-out sacks, and empty pizza boxes littered the area, impregnating everything with the salt-and-grease odor of fast food. The place radiated a sense of urgency.

Debi Watson, the manager, was studying one of the sixteen monitors hung on the opposite wall. A pretty young brunette in a short black skirt and pink sweater, she turned as soon as they walked in.

"Yes, sir?" she said.

"Show me the Tigris River south of the center of Baghdad, east of a bridge and northwest of a refinery," Bridgeman commanded.

"Bones Howe, this one's for you," she ordered.

A freckle-faced young man at a keyboard quickly tapped keys, moved a mouse, and indicated a screen above him to the right. "There she is. The Tigris."

On the monitor, the Tigris curled like a snake through Baghdad. He zoomed in, following Eva's directions.

"I'm looking for a yacht," Bridgeman told him.

There was a series of flashing screens and a boat or yacht appeared.

"That could be it. Zoom in more." Bridgeman leaned toward the monitor.

The boat's deck seemed to jump out of the screen at them. Visible were a couple of men working around two cylinders pointed up like cannons. There were corpses, too, that appeared to be lying where they had fallen.

"Thanks, Debi." Bristling with purpose, Bridgeman turned to Gloria.

"Call Kari Timonen in Baghdad," he commanded. "I'll phone Langley."

"We'd better warn them that Eva and Judd aren't the terrible villains we thought," she said.

Bridgeman hesitated. His face darkened. Then he gave a reluctant nod. "You're right."

They hurried out the door.

83

Baghdad, Iraq

Treading the dark water, Eva let the river carry the cell phone away. Thank God she had been able to reach Gloria. She looked up and around, studying the yacht. She was not sure how deep the keel was, but if she touched the river bottom she should be able to swim under the craft.

She exhaled hard, inhaled deeply, and dived. Two strong breaststrokes and her fingers sank into muck. She tucked her body to bring her feet down. Breaststroking and frog-kicking, she swam about ten yards, passing under the large black shape of the yacht. At last she saw moonlight glimmering down through the water. Switching to a flutter kick, she rose slowly, keeping a hand above her head for protection in case she collided with debris.

Her lungs ached. She was running out of air. At last her hand broke the water's surface. Immediately she stopped kicking and spread her arms to slow her ascent. She broke the surface with hardly a sound. She forced herself not to gasp for air, made herself breathe slowly through her nose until she was comfortable.

Still treading water, she turned in a circle. In one direction was the south riverbank; in the other was the yacht, a black silhouette against the city's night glow. She wished she could see Morgan. She waited, hoping he would dive off and join her.

Finally she rolled over onto her back and flutter-kicked beneath the surface, moving quietly toward shore. As she got farther from the yacht, she was able to see two men working on the mortar near the stern. One was bending over, probably adjusting its supports. Soon she saw a second man, holding a laptop, the screen's gray glow illuminating his face.

Her butt scraped something, then her right elbow banged a rock. She had reached land. Grass and palm trees were about ten yards away. She clambered up over the rocks and ran for cover.

84

CIA station chief Kari Timonen was sitting in Baghdaddy's bar in the U.S. Embassy compound. It was the CIA's fave watering hole. He was just setting down his gin and tonic when two red lights on opposite walls of the bar began flashing, accompanied by an obnoxious buzzer that cycled on and off in synch with the lights. Instantly he was on his feet and heading for the door. Everyone else was, too.

There were occasional rocket attacks, but the compound was built like a bunker, so nothing more than annoyance and inconvenience came from most of them.

Still, a warning of attack had to be taken seriously. As the alarm shrieked, and people held their hands over their ears, they did what they were supposed to do and exited the bar, heading for bombproof tunnels fifty feet belowground.

Hurrying with the crowd, he grabbed his cell to call HQ to find out what the fuck was going on. Before he could call out, it rang in his hand. He answered it.

It was Gloria Feit from Catapult. "Emergency, Timonen. Are the alarms ringing yet?"

"Just went off. What's up?"

"There's going to be a terrorist mortar strike on the embassy. It sounds as if it's some of those new mortars that blow through steel."

He cursed. "How soon?"

"Any minute."

"Do you know where the attack originates?"

"Yes, from a yacht in the Tigris about a mile south of you." She gave him precise coordinates, which he memorized. "Keep your head down." She hung up.

Continuing to move with the throng, he scrolled through his cell contacts until he found Karim Nagi. Nagi was the liaison to the Iraqi Air Force, which always kept three Apache helicopters and their crews on alert in the military section of Baghdad International. Nagi's unit should already have received an official alert detailing the attack; Timonen's call was a precautionary backup.

As soon as he heard Nagi's voice, he started talking: "Colonel, this is Kari Timonen. I've got a confirmed alert. There's a boat in the Tigris that's about to shell Fort Knock." *Fort Knock* was this month's code for the U.S. Embassy. He related the coordinates. "Questions?"

But the colonel had already ended the call.

In a central foyer area, Timonen slowed to study the controlled madness of hundreds of people moving at once and sometimes at cross purposes. Despite the embassy's best efforts, not everyone knew or remembered the entrances to the staircases that led down to the various security tunnels in each building. He found himself grabbing arms, turning people around, and acting as a traffic cop.

85

The celebration in the museum had quieted. Holding their buffet plates, people were listening to Prime Minister al-Lami speak about the accomplishments of his administration. He stood authoritatively behind the podium, a man of moderate height and girth. His muscular cheeks had their usual afternoon shadow. It was widely known he shaved three times a day, but it was not enough to keep the bristles under control. It was also said he refused to grow a beard because it was not modern, and he was a modern statesman, not some Arab just off a camel, a tent folded on his back, his beard filled with sand. This last sentiment about camels and sand offended voters both in the provinces and in the cities. His supporters claimed it was one of the ruinous lies that had been spread about him.

Still, he was a commanding figure on the two screens, and his oratory came through with the clarity of a Bose sound system. In fact, the video seemed unusually high quality, too, Judd noted. There was no evidence of anyone tending to the sound or video, which meant there was a control room somewhere. As he surveyed around, he began to have an idea.

But first Judd needed to find out who had called him. He went outdoors. The night was cool, inviting. When he caught up with Hilu, he
lowered his voice and said, "My phone vibrated. I'm going to check
my messages." He raised his voice: "Tell Mr. San Martino I'll join him
shortly."

"Certainly, sir." With a nod, Hilu resumed rolling Bosa across a spacious patio to a stone bench and table set under date palm trees.

Stepping back, Judd checked the display on his cell: *Missed Call.* He
checked for messages and found there was one. Glancing up, he saw the
Carnivore and Seymour had stopped at the bench.

Judd returned to the exhibit hall. As he skirted the party, he saw a
waiter knock on a door at the back of the room. There was a window in
the wall showing a man inside, wearing earphones. The door opened.
Judd moved closer and watched the waiter deliver a plate of food to the
man, who was sitting at a console, adjusting the controls—the audiovisual room.

When the waiter left, Judd grabbed the door, stuck his head inside
the room, and jabbed his thumb up in the air. "Good work!" he said in
Arabic. He noted the room was the size of a large closet, and the AV
system was computer-driven. *Perfect.*

The fellow pulled off one of his earphones and peered up question-
ingly at him.

"Good work!" Judd repeated.

Nodding, the technician smiled around a mouthful of food, adjusted
his earphones, and returned his focus to the controls.

Spotting a nearby door, Judd walked out into the night again. Traffic
was noisy here, but then the museum complex was on the bustling thor-
oughfare between the central train station and the financial districts.
Smartphone in hand, he stepped back into the shadow of an alcove
and tapped in his password.

Phone to ear, he heard Eva's voice: "Judd, I'm on a yacht in the Tigris. Al-Sabah's men are setting up big-time mortars on the deck to attack the U.S. Embassy. Looks like they'll start shooting soon. Don't
return my call."

Don't return her call? Horseshit. Judd tapped in the number, but there was no ringing on the other end, just dead silence. He tried again. Again, nothing. He hoped like hell nothing had happened to her.

He forced his thoughts away from Eva. Earlier, he had called Kari Timonen to warn him, but Timonen had blown him off. *What the hell.* He dialed Timonen's number again. This time he got a busy signal. He tried a second time with the same result. Frustrated, he decided to go back to Bash Badawi. Finding his number in his contacts list, Judd dialed overseas to Washington. Bash answered quickly.

"It's Judd Ryder. Just listen. I'm in Baghdad and the American embassy is about to be attacked by mortar."

"Whoa, Judd." Bash's voice was strong. "You need to talk to Gloria. She's tied up right now, but I'll make sure she phones you back right away."

The line went dead.

Controlling his frustration, Judd scanned this part of the museum grounds. When they had arrived, he had noted several security guards patrolling outside. All wore small arms on their hips. A few also carried carbines. Making certain his phone was still on vibrate, he slipped it inside his jacket and studied the classic buildings, the sandstone walls and turrets, the walkways. The complex spread across eleven city acres. There were two guards who seemed to have been assigned to patrol along this stretch.

As he timed the men, his phone finally vibrated.

"Judd Ryder, where exactly are you?" Gloria demanded.

"In Baghdad, the Iraq National Museum. There's going to be a mortar attack on our embassy here—"

"We know. I got a call from Eva Blake, and we've alerted everyone there. What are you and Eva doing in Baghdad?"

"It's too complicated to explain now. Where's Eva?"

"She was on a yacht in the Tigris. That's where the mortars are being launched. We've located the boat and turned the information over to the Iraqis. When she and I finished talking, she was going to swim for shore." Gloria tried to sound reassuring. "I doubt she's in danger."

"I hope you're right."

They said hurried good-byes.

Staying in the alcove's shadow, Judd resumed assessing the two sentries. One was about to pass him again. He was a middle-aged man with a calm demeanor, a solid man.

Judd ran from the building and rammed a fist into the sentry's solar plexus, right over his heart. The man inhaled sharply. The blow had made the man's heart skip a beat and shocked his cardiovascular system.

Before the man could recover, Judd pelted his kidneys then used both hands to slam his head sideways into the ground. It was over in seconds. Judd dragged the unconscious man back into the shadows and relieved him of his pistol.

Pressing back against the wall again, he waited for the second sentry.

86

The museum patio was rimmed by a lush bed of flowers, and the grounds were raked and swept, very different from the war zone of 2003 that the Carnivore remembered. Now that he had manipulated Seymour to where he wanted him, he felt himself adjust, leaving behind the persona of San Martino and his usual cover identity, Alex Bosa. With relief, he returned to himself: The Carnivore. Unique, arrogant in the ways of those who were usually right and able to enforce that right even when wrong. And angry. He had an old, deep anger that seethed just beneath his skin. He knew these things about himself, and he no longer made an effort to change them. For him, age was a respite from the demons of the past, when he had wanted nothing more than to be a hero.

The Carnivore focused. He had Seymour to deal with. With a dramatic sweep of his hand, he held out one of the glass cylinders that contained a cigar. "With pleasure, I present you with a gem from the New World."

Al-Sabah was sitting on a garden bench, and the Carnivore was in his wheelchair at a ninety-degree angle to him. At their knees was a low stone table.

Al-Sabah took the cylinder and regarded the cigar admiringly. Then he removed the wax, put the open end to his nose, and inhaled deeply. Taking it from its case, he smelled the cigar along its length. "Some art is permanent, and some art lives briefly, like ballet and music and an exceptional cigar. All are important to be savored in the moment."

"Yes. This is our moment." The Carnivore offered him a clipper.

Al-Sabah rolled the cigar next to his ear, listening to the fine tobacco, then he snipped the end. The Carnivore offered him a box of matches, and he lit the cigar. A look of deep pleasure crossed his face as he inhaled.

The Carnivore lit his own cigar. The aroma and taste thrilled him.

"I'm in your debt," al-Sabah said. "This is a remarkable smoke."

There was the sound of footsteps. They turned.

"I thought you might be hungry," Judd told them. "I brought food from the buffet."

Judd exchanged a quick look with the Carnivore then with Hilu. Hilu took two plates off the tray and set them on the table between the Carnivore and al-Sabah. The plates were piled with colorful arrays of cheeses, breads, and saucers of herb-infused olive oil.

"These are René's medications." Judd picked up the last item on the tray—a plate with a warming cover. He set the covered dish on the Carnivore's lap.

The Carnivore stared for a second then understood. Staying in the San Martino character, he laughed and clapped his hands with amusement. "Trying to render an old man's medication elegant is as futile as putting earrings on a mule."

The Carnivore was enjoying himself, not just the cigar, but that al-Sabah—Seymour—had not yet made him. He smiled at al-Sabah. "I have a friend who's received a message from an unknown source. He's asked me to determine whether you might know who the source is."

The Carnivore smoked. But as he watched Seymour's black eyes, he sensed a subtle change.

"And your friend is?" Seymour asked.

The Carnivore ignored the question. "He tells me the last time he saw you was more than a decade ago here, on these grounds, at the time of the invasion."

Seymour put his cigar in his mouth and inhaled. His good humor had disappeared. His broad bearded face was blank, his gaze cold. The Carnivore could feel menace radiate from him. At the same time, Seymour seemed to be trying to assess how much to reveal, how much immediate danger "San Martino" represented.

Seymour exhaled smoke. "What was the subject of this message?"

"The subject was an archaeological treasure—a cuneiform tablet, I'm told."

Seymour got to his feet. "I know of no message about any such object. Your friend is mistaken."

The Carnivore looked up. "Alas. My friend is certain he's right because, he tells me, you and he are the only ones left, and so it can't have come from him."

Seymour frowned. Understanding came into his eyes.

The Carnivore snatched up the dome from the plate on his lap, grabbed the 9-mm Browning, and aimed it at Seymour.

Seymour blinked slowly, hiding his surprise.

"Judd," the Carnivore said, "Seymour's bodyguard."

But Judd was already moving toward the door where the bodyguard stood. At the moment, the Carnivore's body shielded the gun from the bodyguard's view, but that would not last.

"Hilu," the Carnivore said, "you should take the bodyguard's weapon for yourself."

Hilu nodded and ran after Judd.

His gaze on the Carnivore's Beretta, Seymour took a step back and was ready to take another.

"Stop." When Seymour settled down, the Carnivore kept his voice neutral as he said, "Excuse me, you and *I* are the only ones left."

Suddenly Seymour threw back his head and laughed. Then he studied the Carnivore. A calculating look crossed his face. He gestured at the wheelchair. "Are you really crippled, or is this one of your tricks?"

———

Eva was exhausted. Dripping water, she ran into a palm grove and dropped behind a tree. She looked back at the yacht just in time to see a giant burst from the stern mortar. A blinding streak of light shot above the yacht, and a thunderous noise reverberated along the river.

On the northern horizon, a great fiery ball of light and smoke billowed up. The noise of the explosion sounded like a distant bomb. The mortar had launched a shell, and it had hit something big. Judging by what she could see of where it landed, it was one of the U.S. Embassy buildings. With a sick feeling, she watched a second mortar launch.

87

As he had done with the two outdoor sentries, Judd surprised Seymour's bodyguard, who was glancing occasionally over to where his boss was talking. The man had a strong, youthful face, but his half-closed eyes said he was bored.

Putting on a disarming smile, Judd walked up to him and slammed a fist into his solar plexus. As the man gasped, Judd chopped the side of his throat, interrupting the blood flow for a few vital seconds. He caught the unconscious man before he hit the ground and dragged his body behind a bush.

Hilu had been watching. "You are a scary dude, Judd. You go around building free elementary schools, and then you knock out people. What am I to think?"

"In this case, don't think." Judd handed him the guard's pistol.

A bright flash erupted in the sky to the south followed by the booming sound of a great explosion.

Hilu shook a fist at the cloud rising above the lights of the city. "The big attack has started!" he bellowed. "We've got to tell everyone the truth about al-Sabah and Tabrizi!" He ran to the museum door.

Judd sprinted and caught his arm. "Wait. You want to expose them, but let's do it in a way we'll be believed. Put your gun in your pocket. Follow me." Judd slid his Beretta inside his belt under his jacket.

Another shell exploded, shaking the night. They stepped inside the exhibit hall. People were running to the windows to peer out. Their faces were ashen. Tabrizi was speaking, his voice full and resounding, while his image was magnified on the screens high on either side of the room: "I've just been told that the U.S. Embassy is being shelled, and it's the Sunnis doing it. It's always the Sunnis trying to intimidate us, to frighten us so we won't vote and they can take us back to the days of Saddam. They'll do anything—kill anyone—to control the government again—"

Leading Hilu, Judd pushed through the crowd then paused at the banquet table, where he picked up a plate of sugared figs. He took off again, heading to the rear of the hall.

Tabrizi was still talking, and the crowd had turned back from the windows to listen: "The prime minister is well intentioned, but he can't control or stop the violence. The very fact that the Sunnis would shell the Americans so boldly shows how far they'll go to get what they want. In international law, attacking a foreign embassy is an act of war. Are the Sunnis daring the Americans to invade us again, or are they living in the past and creating violence that has no purpose in the present? If you vote for me, I'll protect our country from anyone who would hurt you!"

On the patio outside the museum, the Carnivore glanced to the side. A third bright flash erupted in the southern sky followed by the sound of another shelling. "Your mortars look to be on target, Seymour. Congratulations. You always did like to kill in large groups." The Carnivore rose easily from the wheelchair.

Seymour watched him. "Damn."

"Yes. Bad luck for you. I'm not crippled. In fact, you and I are going to take a walk. Turn around and put your hands behind your back. Keep them there so I can see them, and go down the steps and turn left."

Seymour did not move. "What do you want?"

"Not your life, at least not yet. Do what I tell you, or I'll reevaluate that."

Seymour hesitated then turned, clasped his hands behind him, and walked down stone steps and onto a stone path.

More flashes. More explosions.

When they were beyond the view of the patio, the Carnivore ordered, "Stop. Lean forward and raise your hands up high."

Seymour started to separate his hands.

The Carnivore corrected him: "Keep your hands clasped. Lean over more."

Seymour muttered something under his breath, but he did as he was told. He looked like a swimmer on the starting block, bent forward, arms back.

The Carnivore lifted the rear flap of Seymour's jacket, revealing a pistol. He took it then checked the rest of his body. Only the one weapon. "You can straighten up, but keep your hands where they are."

Seymour complied.

They resumed walking. Rounding the corner of an adjacent building, they entered one of the museum's narrow streets. Here they were completely out of sight of anyone in the exhibit hall or on the patio.

"You asked what I wanted," the Carnivore told him. "I want those records you're threatening to send to news outlets and blogs. I want *The Assassins' Catalog*."

In the palm grove on the river's southern shore, Eva watched in horror the burning balls of flame and smoke above the U.S. Embassy. Then she heard a new noise. It was a high-pitched chopping whine. Low on the horizon, three dark smudges grew larger and louder. Apache helicopters. Suddenly streaks of yellow-white light shot out from them. Heat-seeking missiles, she guessed. The heat from the mortars would be a magnet.

Before she could take a breath, the yacht burst like a boil, spurting up flames, pieces of wood, and ragged chunks of metal. Blazing debris fell from the sky, hitting the river and the bank and pelting the palm fronds over her head.

"Morgan!" she shouted. "Morgan!" She held herself tightly, knowing the awful truth—there was no way anyone could survive the inferno burning on the river.

In the museum, Judd opened the door to the audiovisual control room, where the tech was working at a broad console of flashing lights and digital readouts. He and Hilu stepped inside, Hilu closing the door behind them.

The AV man turned from peering out through the small window that overlooked the party. He lifted his earphones and glanced at the sugared figs.

Handing the plate to him, Judd said in Arabic, "We thought you might be hungry."

With a nod, the tech stuffed two figs into his mouth.

Judd took out the memory stick he had used in the afternoon to record Mahmoud, the bar owner who had died when his office was bombed. "We need you to broadcast this through your AV system."

Hilu made a sound of pleasure deep in his throat. "Oh, this is good, Judd. I like this very much."

But the technician shook his head. "I can't do it. You're not on the schedule."

With a sigh, Judd pulled out his Beretta. *"Play it."*

88

Along with others standing at the windows, Zahra had been watching the attack. After all the work, all the planning, she savored the bursts of fire, the billowing smoke. When the shelling stopped too soon, she suspected something had happened, perhaps the authorities had found and destroyed the yacht. That had always been a possibility.

She turned back into the crowded hall, listening and watching. People were talking to one another:

"Tabrizi is right," one said.

"The violence is worse now," agreed a second.

"The Sunnis have to be stopped. They're going to start another war!"

Someone prayed, *"Allah yustur min bachir."* I hope God protects me from whatever evil tomorrow brings.

She smiled to herself. Her husband's plans were going forward just as he had hoped. She wanted to congratulate him. Where was he? She checked the stage. The American ambassador was hurrying off down the steps, talking on his cell phone. The prime minister was barking orders at two assistants.

Tabrizi had jumped down to the floor and was reassuring frightened well-wishers. "All law derives from Allah. Remember Muhammad's armed struggle against his enemies, all of the blood and deaths. There are still enemies of Islam. Just as Allah gave Muhammad permission to fight, we also have permission to wage holy war against anyone who'd hurt Islam."

It was an interpretation of the Koran that both Tabrizi and her husband lived by, and no one could overrule them because there was no established Islamic hierarchy, no Muslim pope, no excommunication of heretics.

She continued to look for him. She had not seen him in quite a while. The loudspeakers came on again, and a larger-than-life version of one of her husband's employees—Mahmoud Issa—appeared on the two screens high on either side of the room. She was puzzled. Others were, too.

A man spoke from off camera: "Tell us why you want out."

Mahmoud's deep-set eyes were sorrowful as he said, "Because al-Sabah has gone too far. I began working for him when I was young and angry and wanted to help my country. . . ."

Zahra looked quickly around. People had stopped to stare up at the towering man on the video screens, who was saying terrible things about her husband: "What finally made up my mind is al-Sabah ordered one of my oldest friends to be executed just because he fell in love with a girl whose father works for the opposition—for the prime minister. . . ."

Zahra elbowed her way through the crowd. She had to stop whoever was broadcasting Mahmoud.

"It's not only al-Sabah," the voice went on, "but it's also his wife, Zahra, and Tariq Tabrizi. . . . And it's all for one goal—they're determined to join Iraq and Iran into one nation. They're calling it the Union of Shiite States. . . ."

People had been murmuring. Now they were shaking their heads, their voices alternately upset and disbelieving, angry and worried.

As she passed by, someone pointed her out: "That's her! That's al-Sabah's wife, Zahra!"

Behind her, Tabrizi was yelling something. She heard the words *hoax* and *my enemies.*

The door to the audiovisual room was closed. She turned the knob and pulled it open. Inside, three men peered around at her.

"Turn that thing off!" she demanded.

"No, Roza." The tall man shook his head. "It's playing until the end, and you know the end, don't you? I've heard so much about you, Roza Levinchev. And about Seymour, of course. I'm sorry about your daughter, Katia—"

Roza. Seymour. Katia. How did he know those names? Where was her husband? She was frightened for him. He might need her help. She had to find him. Shoving people aside, she pushed through the crowd to the patio doors.

Watching Roza's retreating back, Judd told Hilu, "I'm going to follow her." He was out the door and winding through the throngs just as his own voice sounded from the speakers: *"When is the attack? I need all the details."*

Judd remembered the painful moment vividly.

Taller than many in the hall, Judd spotted Zahra's blond head as she reached a patio door and looked back. He moved toward her.

"It's tonight," Mahmoud said. He jammed the stopper into the scotch decanter.

There was a tremendous roar. The cabinet beneath the decanter exploded. The movie ended. Zahra ran outdoors.

And Judd followed.

Kari Timonen emerged from the tunnel under the U.S. Embassy and trotted outdoors. The all-clear siren had sounded. Using his classified smartphone, he listened to the report that Iraqi choppers had blasted to smithereens the yacht that had been the launching pad for the shells.

Waiting for a preliminary report of injuries and damage, he walked around, inspecting. Brown smoke shrouded the buildings. Craters tore apart the manicured grounds. Palm trees were uprooted and splintered. Blast-resistant window glass was shattered, and chunks of concrete the size of large boulders littered the ground. Cars, trucks, and some of the outbuildings were covered in flames. The air reeked of oil fires.

Finally he got his first report—injuries, no deaths so far. There had been enough warning that people were able to get down to the safety tunnels. He did not like to think how bad it would have been had there not been an alert.

The rest of the report was that the compound's major systems—water, electricity, and sewage—appeared to be functioning. He heaved a sigh of relief. Looking around, he saw every major building was still standing, but then engineers had used advanced concrete structural designs to erect them. The U.S. Embassy in Baghdad was not called Fortress America for nothing.

The tension between the Carnivore and Seymour was electric where they stood on the stone walkway in the museum complex, the Carnivore aiming his weapon at Seymour's back.

"I'll tell you what *I* want." Seymour turned slowly, bringing his hands forward to where the Carnivore could see they were empty. "I want to be part of the new Iraqi national government. But the Padre, Eli Eichel, Morgan, Krot, and you could've exposed me. So to answer one of your questions—there's no *Assassins' Catalog*. All I needed was the threat of it, so all of you would be provoked into trying to win it. As for the cuneiform tablet, if it leads to a treasure, of course I want it. But you can have the tablet. It's yours. I'll give you my pieces. Just walk away and forget I'm still alive."

"Bullshit." *There was no damn* Assassins' Catalog? All of the risk and danger of this whole ruinous ride from Washington to Baghdad had been built on Seymour's stupid personal ambition. "I suppose you're going to tell me you're in training to be the next Mother Teresa, too. I know all about your campaign to put your pal Tabrizi in as prime minister. How many Iraqis do you think you've killed to get him there—a thousand, two thousand, more? And then there's your plan to make Iraq and Iran into one country. My guess is the cost of that in human life will be even higher. And finally, damn clever of you to keep Toma Asker alive and turn him into über-politician Tariq Tabrizi. How many of Saddam's billions did he give you?"

It was Seymour's turn to look irritated. "My payoff comes when *Tabrizi* gets elected prime minister."

"So you don't know where Saddam's money is either?"

"Of course not. All of the records are inside Tabrizi's head." Seymour hesitated, then he explained: "When I found out he was the lead financier on the hit list that Saddam gave Morgan, I arranged to have him for my target. I faked his death and had new identities made—"

At that moment, the Carnivore heard voices then footsteps coming from the far side of the building, about twenty yards ahead.

Seymour bellowed, "Guards, help!" and dived to his right, rolled twice, and came up sprinting toward an open door into a building on the Carnivore's left.

As the men aimed, the Carnivore fired twice in quick succession. They stumbled and fell back, and he dashed into the building through the door Seymour had used.

He was in the Assyrian Gallery, where he and his five fellow assassins had found the cuneiform tablet more than a decade earlier. Memories flashed through his mind. What irony that he was running through here again. At least this time, he had more than a flashlight. Low-wattage security lamps glowed every thirty feet or so, casting long shadows.

He listened. Someone was walking quietly near the other end of the gallery. *Seymour.* As he sped toward the corner, the sound stopped.

"Delighted you're here, Alex," Seymour called out. "We'll have a party."

The Carnivore still had Seymour's pistol. With his right hand, he inched it out past the corner. A shot slapped it back, which answered that question—Seymour had somehow concealed another weapon.

"That was stupid," Seymour told him. "You thought I wouldn't come prepared?"

The Carnivore turned to face the wall and took from his shirt pocket a small mirror and opened its arm. "Where'd you hide the gun, you prick?" he asked as he lifted the mirror to the ceiling and angled it around so he could see the intersecting corridor. In an instant he snapped the mirror back. He had gotten lucky: A pair of three-foot-high wood crates, each about five feet long, were stored directly around the corner, butt end to butt end. Seymour was behind the last one, head and shoulders in view, showing confidence as he trained a small pistol to where he expected the Carnivore to appear. The crates looked well constructed. If they were full, they would be too heavy, and his plan would fail. On the other hand, staying where he was was getting him nowhere.

"It's a sweet little gun. Mostly plastic," Seymour said. "A lot of small parts that I spread around to my pockets. When you patted me down, you didn't feel a weapon, because there wasn't one—yet." He laughed. "And you thought you were smart, you arrogant fucker."

But while Seymour talked, the Carnivore had dropped flat onto his back and slithered feet-first around the corner. There was a soft sound coming from where Seymour was hiding—he was getting ready to do something.

The Carnivore bent his knees and rammed his feet into the first crate with such force that it crashed forward, propelling the second crate ahead of it. He heard a grunt, which told him Seymour had been hit.

The Carnivore jumped to his feet, and Seymour stumbled into view, looking for a target. Running, the Carnivore fired a quick shot to his thigh. As Seymour staggered, the Carnivore smashed his shoulder into him, sending him sliding across the floor. Seymour grunted.

The Carnivore kicked away the plastic pistol and stood over him. "No time for sweet good-byes." He pointed his weapon down at the bridge of Seymour's nose.

Seymour stared up, his large body somehow diminished by the vastness of the gallery. His beard looked more white than gray. "You were always sentimental."

The Carnivore fired.

"Monster, monster!" Roza Levinchev came screaming in Russian around the corner, firing wildly.

A bullet grazed the Carnivore's side. More bullets slashed into the wood boxes and ricocheted off the floor tiles. He plunged behind a crate.

"Give me the gun, Roza!" Judd's voice was loud and commanding. "Dammit, are you insane? I'll shoot you if I have to!"

In the sudden quiet, high heels clicked on the hard floor. Warily, the Carnivore stood up, watching Judd shepherd an unarmed Roza toward him. In one hand, Judd held the gun he had taken from the museum guard, and in the other hand the one he must have taken from her.

Furious and grief-stricken, she was cursing the Carnivore in Russian. Her head was up, her chin high. Tears streaked her cheeks. She knotted her hands and shook them wordlessly at him.

"I didn't kill Katia," the Carnivore told her. "Morgan's the one who did it. His target was Krot, not her, if that's any help. Yes, I shot Seymour. What did you expect? He paid the price all of us pay when we fail in our business."

If there was such a thing as living fury, it was Roza. Her eyes blazed like blue fire. "Katia was my only child. I loved my husband. You're an animal!"

The Carnivore could handle her anger. What was giving him pause was her grief. "I lost my daughter, too," he found himself saying. "She's my only child. I'd give a lot to have her back." He studied her.

She stared silently at him. He saw despair in her eyes, then hopelessness.

"You want me to kill you," he realized. Then: "I don't do mercy killings. Get the hell out of here."

She frowned. She took a step toward him.

Judd ran in front of her again, blocking her advance. "Get *out*!" he bellowed in her face. "Leave while you can!"

She seemed to shake herself. As if awakened from a trance, she peered jerkily around and rushed back the way she had come.

The Carnivore walked to Seymour, fished through his pockets, and retrieved a small leather pouch. Pocketing it, he saw a side door farther along the gallery.

"Time for me to go." He jogged toward it.

Judd called, "Bosa."

His hand on the door latch, the Carnivore gazed back. The younger man's weathered face was not just exhausted but somber. Something more had happened.

"Have you heard from Eva?" the Carnivore asked.

"Yes. She made it." Judd walked toward him. "Morgan didn't."

The Carnivore sighed. Suddenly he felt old. Morgan and he had been together so long he had allowed himself to grow fond of the old man. Still, Morgan knew the risks. For a long moment, the Carnivore felt his own advancing years. "I'm getting close to when I'm going to have to retire," he admitted. "I need to train a successor. I want to pass on what I know. I've been waiting for the right person to come along. You're the right person, Judd. Think about it." He lifted two fingers and touched his forehead.

Judd hesitated.

"I'll be in contact." The Carnivore thrust open the door and disappeared into the darkness.

THE CARNIVORE

To say that assassination never solved anything is as inaccurate as saying crime never pays. Or that all assassins come to a bad end.

—*The Book of Assassins*, George Fetherling

89

Silver Spring, Maryland

It was three months later. April brought a gentle spring, with daffodils and tulips blooming around the old colonial house that Eva and Judd had bought. After some discussion, they had decided that since they were starting a fresh life, they needed new digs, too.

They relished their privacy, the long mornings over coffee, the dinners in front of their fireplace with glasses of wine. Their leisurely days and wonderfully sexy nights were a tonic. It had not been like this the first month after their return. They had been called in to give closed-door testimony to the Joint Intelligence Committee about the Iraq political situation and the events leading up to the shelling of the U.S. Embassy. Frequently they were also asked to brief government officials and contractors about Iraq, the Gulf, the Middle East, and Islam. They refused no one and did their best to be helpful. In return, Langley had been able to keep their involvement secret in the events and follow-up; it had helped that they had been in Iraq under their cover identities of Greg and Courtney Roman.

After Judd had left Hilu at the museum party in Baghdad, Hilu had announced through the loudspeakers that Tariq Tabrizi was a fraud, that he was really Toma Asker, the financial wizard who had hidden Saddam's missing fortune. The next day, the police arrived to take Tabrizi into custody for questioning. But Tabrizi was already gone.

It was said Tabrizi had had another identity prepared for just such an emergency. It was also said that during the night the prime minister had sent the secret police, and he was being held covertly in Abu Ghraib prison. The final rumor was that Saddam's family had snatched him. They believed the money was theirs, and they wanted all of it. Judd figured that if Seymour could not convince the financier to reveal where the billions were, no one else had much of a chance.

In all the drama of the shelling of the embassy and the revelations at the museum gala, the murder of Siraj al-Sabah had barely made the news. After all, in Baghdad, what was one more dead body?

"He's here!" Eva ran through the living room, her hair flying, a big smile on her face. Barefoot, her toenails painted shiny red, she was dressed comfortably in sweatpants and a tank top.

"I'm coming." He closed the novel he'd been enjoying—*Reel Stuff* by Don Bruns—and joined her at the front door.

Tucker Andersen was rolling his walker toward the house. Tucker was thinner than before he was shot, and his coordination was not great, but he had a glint in his eyes that told the world he was far from done. His wife, Karen, was at his side. She was a few years younger and a half head taller, athletic, with the loose sexy walk of a race horse. She was carrying Tucker's beat-up old brown cowhide briefcase.

Judd ran down the steps. "Good to see you both. Karen must have talked you into getting your hair cut, Tucker."

The gray fringe that usually brushed Tucker's collar was barely visible, just a few feathery strands showing beneath his Red Sox cap.

Tucker shot him a pained look. "Is that the way you greet a returning warrior?"

"Returning from where, the coffee shop?"

"What, you want a bagel? No, returning from Langley. I've brought loot—photos and news."

Karen interrupted: "Hello, Judd. Nice to see you."

He hugged her. Then to Tucker: "I'll help you up the steps."

Surprisingly, Tucker did not argue. He was in rehab but able to live at home. The prognosis was good that he would regain most of his abilities, but it would take time.

The four of them sat in the dining room around the table, drinking coffee and tea. Being with Tucker and Karen was warm and comfortable, Judd thought, the way a home was supposed to feel.

"Matt Kelley sends his regards," Tucker was saying. "He's impressed by what you both did, and he says I can hire you, Judd."

"I can see myself working for Scott Bridgeman," Judd said. "Yeah, a honeymoon for both of us."

"You're safe—Scott has quit," Tucker announced. "He's gone to work for his father-in-law in some kind of home furnishings business."

"Home furnishings?" Eva repeated.

"People need home furnishings," Tucker said, straight-faced. "He's a vice president."

"Oh, Lord." Karen laughed.

"You've got to give up the idea you can stay out of the game, Judd," Tucker said. "It's dangerous to ignore your innate nature."

Judd just stared at him. His insides were in turmoil. Tucker was right, it was his innate nature.

"Who's the head of Catapult now?" Eva asked.

"I am." Tucker sighed. "I can't exactly do fieldwork the way I am. The docs say another couple of months, and I should be able to sit behind a desk. It's better than looking for some pasture to die in."

Eva reached across the table and put her hand over his. "Good decision. I'm happy for you, Tucker. And for Catapult, too. What about me? Did Matt say you could hire me?"

Tucker nodded. "As a matter of fact, he did. But of course, it's back to the Farm for you, and expect some hazing. I'm sure you'll enjoy that."

"Right. Hazing. Can't wait." Still, Eva grinned. But then she checked with Judd.

He kept his expression blank.

"I'll talk to Judd and get back to you," she said.

Judd took a deep breath. For an uncomfortable moment, he wondered how brave he was. He had just had an experience with the Carnivore in which he had remembered how good it was to be able to do what needed to be done without the restraining hand of a boss or even the law. What did that make him? He did not want to be part of the bureaucracy of the intelligence community, and he did not want to go around murdering people for money . . . and yet he was tempted by the Carnivore's offer.

Tucker was talking to him. "If you change your mind, Judd, we'd like to have you on board. I have other news for you, too. A package was left on Catapult's doorstep last month, wrapped in plain brown paper, no return address. After the bomb squad discovered it wasn't ticking, we opened it and found all of the pieces of the cuneiform tablet."

"From the Carnivore," Eva said.

Tucker nodded. "We think so. Anonymous, mysterious, faintly sinister. Yes, I'd say it was from him, especially since he's the only one who had all of the pieces. There was an unsigned note, too, asking that the tablet be assembled, translated, and given to the Iraq National Museum."

"My God, the Carnivore is a philanthropist now," Eva said. "No wonder the donation is anonymous."

"What's in it for him?" Judd wondered.

"Same question I've been asking myself," Tucker agreed. "So far, I don't have an answer, but I do have a translation. And it's led to a treasure. But, as it turns out, it's a contemporary one. Saddam hired someone to make the tablet, and whoever it was was so good he or she fooled all of us into thinking it was thousands of years old. Here's the result."

Karen handed him his briefcase, and from it he took a half dozen eight-by-ten color photos and spread them on the table. They showed different angles of a model of what looked like an ancient city built of shimmering gold.

Eva inhaled. "Stunning."

"In 1982, Saddam decided he was going to re-create the ancient city of Babylon as it was in its heyday, some twenty-five hundred years ago." Tucker pointed to various pictures as he talked about two great palaces, broad boulevards, markets, homes, courtyards, government buildings, law courts, and the legendary Hanging Gardens.

"The Hanging Gardens was one of the seven wonders of the ancient world," Karen reminded them. "And Babylon was the capital of the Mesopotamian dynasties."

"The model shows the city Saddam was planning," Tucker explained. "For some reason, he'd decided he was heir to Nebuchadnezzar the Second, probably the greatest Babylonian king. He started his rebuilding program with the king's six-hundred-room palace, which he decided to put on top of archaeologically sensitive land that hadn't been excavated yet. To make matters worse, instead of faithfully reproducing the palace, he got entrepreneurial. The original bricks were inscribed with praises for Nebuchadnezzar, but Saddam ordered his workers to make new bricks inscribed with the words, 'In the era of Saddam Hussein, protector of Iraq, who rebuilt civilization and rebuilt Babylon.' In just a decade, the new bricks began to crack."

Eva shook her head. "Symbolic of Saddam himself. So the cuneiform tablet led to this model. Incredible."

"Between the gold, the artistry, and the craftsmanship—and of course the fact that the model is supposedly a historical re-creation—it's easily worth the twelve million dollars the assassins were told," Tucker said. "Saddam ordered the gold model buried in the desert near Babylon while he held on to the tablet until Babylon was rebuilt. Then he was going to use the tablet as a publicity stunt to bring in the tourists."

Eva sat back. "What's going to happen to the model now?"

Karen gathered up the photos. "It'll be displayed in the Iraq National Museum. They're delighted to have it. Just as Saddam planned—it'll be a huge draw."

They drank second cups of coffee and tea, and Eva served chocolate chip cookies she had baked that morning. Another hour passed in easy conversation. Then Tucker grew quiet, and it became obvious he was tiring. His face was drawn and his hands trembled.

"Time to go home," Karen announced.

Judd and Eva stood on their front porch and waved good-bye. Judd put his arms around her and they returned inside.

"I'm glad Tucker is staying in the business," Eva told him. "I think it'd kill him if he couldn't."

"And what will you do?"

"I'd like to go back to the Farm and finish my training. But we're a real couple now, and it's a big decision. We should make the big decisions together, don't you think?"

Uneasiness swept through him. It was one of the problems with Eva—she was less selfish than he was. "I think you should do it," he said firmly. "It'll make you happy."

"Being with you makes me happiest of all." She stepped back, assessing him. "What's going on inside that brain of yours, Judd? You look sad."

He grabbed her and pulled her close. He breathed into her hair, smelling how clean it was. If he decided to work with the Carnivore, everything would change for them. "Sometimes thinking is a bad idea," he decided. "Let's just enjoy our lives. You've made one big decision, but I don't have to make any yet. Maybe never."

A dusty Ford van was parked at the curb across the street and a half block back. It was an older model, indistinguishable from thousands of others in the metropolis. The lone occupant sat in the rear at a darkened window, aiming a directional mike and demodulator at the big picture window of the residence where Judd Ryder and Eva Blake lived.

Picking up his smartphone, he called his longtime boss, Alex Bosa. "She's going back to the CIA."

"What about Judd?"

"He seems to be staying out of the game."

"So far. He'll change his mind."